新世纪英语丛书
New Century English

东南大学外国语学院大学英语测试中心
主 编 程俊瑜
编 者 杨茂霞 刘 萍 曹育珍

CET-6

大学英语6级考试710分模拟测试

★听力原文在光盘中

含MP3光盘

新题型 NEW

含2008年6月试题

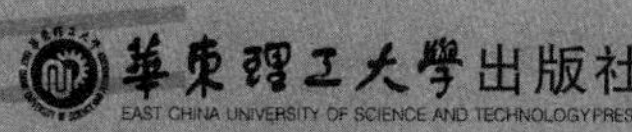

图书在版编目(CIP)数据

大学英语6级考试710分模拟测试:新题型(含MP3光盘)/程俊瑜主编.
—上海:华东理工大学出版社,2008.4(2008.8重印)
(新世纪英语丛书)
ISBN 978-7-5628-2274-5

Ⅰ.大... Ⅱ.程... Ⅲ.英语-高等学校-水平考试-习题
Ⅳ.H319.6

中国版本图书馆CIP数据核字(2008)第023518号

新世纪英语丛书
大学英语6级考试710分模拟测试(新题型)(含MP3光盘)

主　　编/程俊瑜
编　　者/杨茂霞　刘　萍　曹育珍
策划编辑/王耀峰
责任编辑/李清奇
责任校对/张　波
封面设计/大象设计　金　丹
出版发行/华东理工大学出版社
　　地　　址:上海市梅陇路130号,200237
　　电　　话:(021)64250306(营销部)
　　　　　　(021)64251904(编辑室)
　　传　　真:(021)64252707
　　网　　址:www.hdlgpress.com.cn
印　　刷/常熟华顺印刷有限公司
开　　本/787mm×1092mm　1/16
印　　张/16.25
字　　数/418千字
版　　次/2008年4月第1版
印　　次/2008年8月第2次
印　　数/6051-11070册
书　　号/ISBN 978-7-5628-2274-5/H·701
定　　价/29.00元(含MP3光盘)
(本书如有印装质量问题,请到出版社营销部调换。)

前言

大学英语四、六级考试是高校大学英语课程实行分级教学的一项重要配套措施。四级考试最早从 1987 年 9 月开始，二十多年来，大学英语四、六级考试规模越来越大，事实证明了大学英语四、六级考试是符合社会需要的，得到了社会的普遍认同，产生了良好的社会效益，也为我国大学英语教学质量的提高作出了巨大的贡献。

随着新的情况、新的形势、新的变化，《大学英语课程教学要求》（以下简称《课程要求》）已于 2004 年 1 月由国家教育部正式颁布实施。2005 年 2 月，教育部对四、六级考试的方案做了一些调整和改革。从 2005 年 6 月开始，记分体制进行改变，考试成绩改为分布在 290～710 分之间，具体是正态分，均值是 500 分，标准差是 70 分，成绩低可以到 290 分，高可以到 710 分，不设及格分数线，给每个学生报总分和各部分的单项分。

考试内容的改革从 2006 年 6 月考试开始试点，全面推行时间是 2007 年 1 月。改革后的试卷有以下几个部分：

试卷构成	测试内容		测试题型	比例
第一部分 听力理解	听力对话	短对话	多项选择	35%
		长对话	多项选择	
	听力短文	短文理解	多项选择	
		短文听写	复合式听写	
第二部分 阅读理解	仔细阅读理解	篇章阅读理解	多项选择	35%
		篇章词汇理解或短句问答	选词填空或短句回答	
	快速阅读理解		是非判断（多项选择）+ 句子填空或其他	
第三部分 完型填空 或改错	完型填空		多项选择	10%
	改错		错误辨认并改正	
第四部分 写作和翻译	写作		短文写作	20%
	翻译		中译英	

从上表可以看出，四、六级考试的重点是听力、阅读方面的测试，听力总体的百分比从原来的 20%提高到 35%，考核听力短对话、长对话、短文理解和短文听写。阅读部分也由原来的 40%调整为 35%，其中包括了仔细阅读和快速阅读，仔细阅读占 25%，快速阅读占 10%。第三部分是完型填空或者改错，占 10%。第四部分有两个题型：一是写作，此部分变动不大，有议论文、说明文等写作，占 15%；另外一个题型是翻译，为中译英，占 5%。从以上分析可以看出选择题型是考试中的主要题型，但适当增加了非选择性试题的比例。非选择性试题在听力当中有，在阅读当中

有。改错、翻译或者写作等都是非选择性题型，这个比例增加到了35％～45％。

为了使同学们认真学好大学英语并为顺利通过全新的大学英语六级考试提供一个高效度、高信度的复习自测系统，作为大学英语教学，特别是六级教学多年的研究者和实践者，通过研究改革内容和CET－6试点考试样卷，我们精心编写了这本《大学英语6级考试710分模拟测试(新题型)(含MP3光盘)》。本书内容体现了六级考试的命题规律，提炼了各种题型的考点和重点。全书共有十套模拟试题和四套最新全真试题，每套题后除参考答案外，还有全面准确的注释，结合试题讲解了解题方法和技巧，努力使同学们能举一反三，触类旁通。

在编写过程中，由于编者水平有限，错误和不足之处在所难免，敬请读者批评指正。

编者

目　录

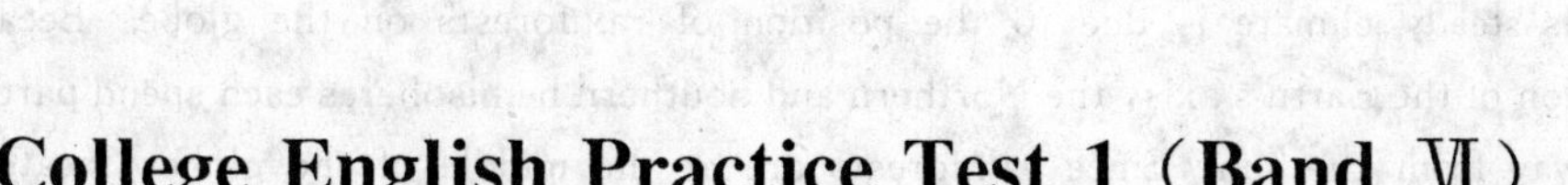

College English Practice Test 1 (Band Ⅵ)

Part Ⅰ Writing (30 minutes)

Directions: *For this part, you are allowed 30 minutes to write a short essay entitled* **Say No to Pirated Products**. *You should write at least* **150** *words following the outline given below.*

1. 目前盗版的现象比较严重;
2. 造成这种现象的原因及其危害;
3. 我们应该怎么做。

Useful words and expressions:

盗 版:piracy (*n.*)

盗版产品:pirated products

知识产权:intellectual property rights

侵犯版权:infringe sb.'s copyright; copyright infringement

Part Ⅱ Reading Comprehension (Skimming and Scanning) (15 minutes)

Directions: *In this part, you will have 15 minutes to go over the passage quickly and answer the questions on the* **Answer Sheet**.

For questions 1 - 4, mark

Y(for YES) *if the statement agrees with the information given in the passage;*

N(for NO) *if the statement contradicts the information given in the passage;*

NG(for NOT GIVEN) *if the information is not given in the passage.*

For questions 5 - 10, complete the sentences with the information given in the passage.

Rainforests

Tropical rainforests are the most diverse *ecosystem* (生态系统) on Earth, and also the oldest. Today, tropical rainforests cover only 6 percent of the Earth's ground surface, but they are home to over half of the planet's plant and animal species.

What Is a Rainforest?

Generally speaking, a rainforest is an environment that receives high rainfall and is dominated by tall trees. A wide range of ecosystems fall into this category, of course. But most of the time when people talk about rainforests, they mean the tropical rainforests located near the equator.

These forests receive between 160 and 400 inches of rain per year. The total annual rainfall is

spread pretty evenly throughout the year, and the temperature rarely dips below 60 degrees Fahrenheit.

This steady climate is due to the position of rainforests on the globe. Because of the orientation of the Earth's axis, the Northern and Southern hemispheres each spend part of the year tilted away from the sun. Since rainforests are at the middle of the globe, located near the equator, they are not especially affected by this change. They receive nearly the same amount of sunlight, and therefore heat, all year. Consequently, the weather in these regions remains fairly constant.

The consistently wet, warm weather and ample sunlight give plant life everything it needs to thrive. Trees have the resources to grow to tremendous heights. and they live for hundreds, even thousands, of years. These giants, which reach 60 to 150 ft in the air, form the basic structure of the rainforest. Their top branches spread wide in order to capture maximum sunlight. This creates a thick *canopy* (树冠) level at the top of the forest, with thinner greenery levels underneath. Some large trees grow so tall that they even tower over the canopy layer.

As you go lower, down into the rainforest, you find less and less greenery. The forest floor is made up of moss, fungi, and decaying plant matter that has fallen from the upper layers. The reason for this decrease in greenery is very simple: the overabundance of plants gathering sunlight at the top of the forest blocks most sunlight from reaching the bottom of the forest, making it difficult for robust plants to thrive.

The Forest for the Trees

The ample sunlight and extremely wet climate of many tropical areas encourage the growth of towering trees with wide canopies. This thick top layer of the rainforest dictates the lives of all other plants in the forest. New tree seedlings rarely survive to make it to the top unless some older trees die, creating a "hole" in the canopy. When this happens, all of the seedlings on the ground level compete intensely to reach the sunlight.

Many plant species reach the top of the forest by climbing the tall trees. It is much easier to ascend this way, because the plant doesn't have to form its own supporting structure.

Some plant species, called epiphytes, grow directly on the surface of the giant trees. These plants, which include a variety of orchids and ferns, make up much of the understory, the layer of the rainforest right below the canopy. Epiphytes are close enough to the top to receive adequate light, and the runoff from the canopy layer provides all the water and *nutrients*(养分) they need, which is important since they don't have access to the nutrients in the ground.

Stranglers and Buttresses

Some epiphytes eventually develop into stranglers. They grow long, thick roots that extend down the tree trunk into the ground. As they continue to grow, the roots form a sort of web structure all around the tree. At the same time, the strangler plant's branches extend upward, spreading out into the canopy. Eventually, the strangler may block so much light from above, and absorb such a high percentage of nutrients from the ground below, that the host tree dies.

Competition over nutrients is almost as intense as competition for light. The excessive rainfall rapidly dissolves nutrients in the soil, making it relatively infertile except at the top layers. For this reason, rainforest tree roots grow outward to cover a wider area, rather than downward to lower levels. This makes rainforest trees somewhat unstable, since they don't have very strong anchors in the ground. Some trees compensate for this by growing natural buttresses. These buttresses are basically tree trunks that extend out from the side of the tree and down to the ground, giving the tree additional support.

Rainforest trees are dependent on bacteria that are continually producing nutrients in the ground. Rainforest bacteria and trees have a very close, *symbiotic* (共生的) relationship. The trees provide the bacteria with food, in the form of fallen leaves and other material, and the bacteria break this material down into the nutrients that the trees need to survive.

One of the most remarkable things about rainforest plant life is its diversity. The temperate rainforests of the Pacific Northwest are mainly composed of a dozen or so tree species. A tropical rainforest, on the other hand, might have 300 distinct tree species.

All Creatures, Great and Small

Rainforests are home to the majority of animal species in the world. And a great number of species who now live in other environments, including humans, originally inhabited the rainforests. Researchers estimate that in a large rainforest area, there may be more than 10 million different animal species.

Most of these species have adapted for life in the upper levels of the rainforest, where food is most plentiful. Insects, which can easily climb or fly from tree to tree, make up the largest group (ants are the most abundant animal in the rainforest). Insect species have a highly symbiotic relationship with the plant life in a rainforest. The insects move from plant to plant, enjoying the wealth of food provided there. As they travel, the insects may pick up the plants' seeds, dropping them some distance away. This helps to disperse the population of the plant species over a larger area.

The numerous birds of the rainforest also play a major part in seed dispersal. When they eat fruit from a plant, the seeds pass through their digestive system. By the time they *excrete* (排泄) the seeds, the birds may have flown many miles away from the fruit-bearing tree.

There are also a large number of reptiles and mammals in the rainforest. Since the weather is so hot and humid during the day, most rainforest mammals are active only at night, dusk or dawn. The many rainforest bat species are especially well adapted for this lifestyle. Using their sonar, bats navigate easily through the mass of trees in the rainforest, feeding on insects and fruit.

While most rainforest species spend their lives in the trees, there is also a lot of life on the forest floor. Great apes, wild pigs, big cats and even elephants can all be found in rainforests. There are a number of people who live in the rainforests, as well. These tribes—which, up until recently, numbered in the thousands—are being forced out of the rainforests at an alarming rate because of deforestation.

Deforestation

In the past hundred years, humans have begun destroying rainforests at an alarming rate.

Today, roughly 1.5 acres of rainforest are destroyed every second. People are cutting down the rainforests in pursuit of three major resources:

- land for crops
- lumber for paper and other wood products
- land for livestock pastures

In the current economy, people obviously have a need for all of these resources. But almost all experts agree that, over time, we will suffer much more from the destruction of the rainforests than we will benefit.

The world's rainforests are an extremely valuable natural resource, to be sure, but not for their lumber or their land. They are the main cradle of life on Earth, and they hold millions of unique life forms that we have yet to discover. Destroying the rainforests is comparable to destroying an unknown planet—we have no idea what we're losing. If deforestation continues at its current rate, the world's tropical rainforests will be wiped out within 40 years.

1. Virtually all plant and animal species on Earth can be found in tropical rainforests.
2. There is not much change in the weather in the tropical rainforests all the year round.
3. The largest number of rainforests in the world are located on the African continent.
4. Below the canopy level of a tropical rainforest grows an overabundance of plants.
5. New tree seedlings will not survive to reach the canopy level unless ________.
6. Epiphytes, which form much of the understory of the rainforest, get all their water and nutrients from ________.
7. Stranglers are so called because they ________ by blocking the sunlight and competing for the nutrients.
8. Since rainforest bacteria and trees depend on each other for life, the relationship they form is termed ________.
9. Plant species are dispersed over a large area with the help of ________.
10. As we are still ignorant of millions of unique life forms in the rainforest, deforestation can be compared to the destruction of ________.

Part Ⅲ Listening Comprehension (35 minutes)

Section A

Directions: *In this section, you will hear 8 short conversations and 2 long conversations. At the end of each conversation, one or more questions will be asked about what was said. Both the conversation and the questions will be spoken only once. After each question there will be a pause. During the pause, you must read the four choices marked A), B), C) and D), and decide which is the best answer. Then mark the corresponding letter on* **Answer Sheet 2** *with a single line through the center.*

11. A) She isn't going to change her major.
    B) She plans to major in tax law.
    C) She studies in the same school as her brother.
    D) She isn't going to work in her brother's firm.
12. A) She will do her best if the job is worth doing.
    B) She prefers a life of continued exploration.
    C) She will stick to the job if the pay is good.
    D) She doesn't think much of job-hopping.
13. A) Stop thinking about the matter.
    B) Talk the drug user out of the habit.
    C) Be more friendly to his schoolmate.
    D) Keep his distance from drug addicts.
14. A) The son. B) The father.
    C) The mother. D) Aunt Louise.
15. A) Stay away for a couple of weeks.
    B) Check the locks every two weeks.
    C) Look after the Johnsons' house.
    D) Move to another place.
16. A) He didn't want to warm up for the game.
    B) He didn't want to be held up in traffic.
    C) He wanted to make sure they got tickets.
    D) He wanted to catch as many game birds as possible.
17. A) It will reduce government revenues.
    B) It will stimulate business activities.
    C) It will mainly benefit the wealthy.
    D) It will cut the stockholders' dividends.
18. A) The man should phone the hotel for directions.
    B) The man can ask the department store for help.
    C) She doesn't have the hotel's phone number.
    D) The hotel is just around the corner.

Questions 19 to 21 are based on the conversation you have just heard.

19. A) To interview a few job applicants.
    B) To fill a vacancy in the company.
    C) To advertise for a junior sales manager.
    D) To apply for a job in a major newspaper.
20. A) A hardworking ambitious young man.
    B) A young man good at managing his time.
    C) A college graduate with practical working experience.
    D) A young man with his own idea of what is important.
21. A) Not clearly specified. B) Not likely to be met.
    C) Reasonable enough. D) Apparently sexist.

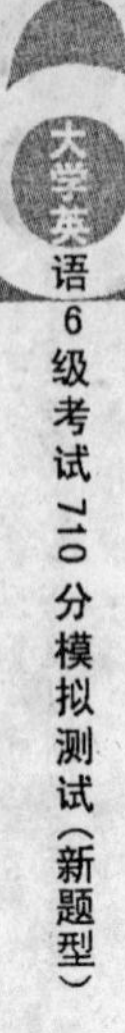

Questions 22 to 25 are based on the conversation you have just heard.

22. A) The latest developments of an armed rebellion in Karnak.
    B) The fall of Karnak's capital city into the hands of the rebel forces.
    C) The epidemic that has just broken out in the country of Karnak.
    D) The peace talks between the rebels and the government in Karnak.
23. A) The epidemic has been brought under control.
    B) There are signs of progress in the peace process.
    C) Great improvements are being made in its capital.
    D) There's little hope of bringing the conflict to an end.
24. A) Late in the morning.
    B) Early in the afternoon.
    C) Sometime before dawn.
    D) Shortly after sunrise.
25. A) Inadequate medical care.
    B) Continuing social unrest.
    C) Lack of food, water and shelter.
    D) Rapid spreading of the epidemic.

Section B

Directions: *In this section, you will hear 3 short passages. At the end of each passage, you will hear some questions. Both the passage and the questions will be spoken only once. After you hear a question, you must choose the best answer from the four choices marked A), B), C) and D). Then mark the corresponding letter on* **Answer Sheet 2** *with a single line through the center.*

Passage One

Questions 26 to 28 are based on the passage you have just heard.

26. A) One of the bridges between North and South London collapsed.
    B) The heart of London was flooded.
    C) An emergency exercise was conducted.
    D) A hundred people in the suburbs were drowned.
27. A) Fifty underground stations were made waterproof.
    B) A flood wall was built.
    C) An alarm system was set up.
    D) Rescue teams were formed.
28. A) Most Londoners were frightened.
    B) Most Londoners became rather confused.
    C) Most Londoners took Exercise Floodwall calmly.
    D) Most Londoners complained about the trouble caused by Exercise Floodwall.

Passage Two

Questions 29 to 31 are based on the passage you have just heard.

29. A) It limited their supply of food.
    B) It made their eggshells to fragile.
    C) It destroyed many of their nests.
    D) It killed man baby bald eagles.

30. A) They found ways to speed up the reproduction of bald eagles.
B) They developed new types of feed for baby bald eagles.
C) They explored new ways to hatch baby bald eagles.
D) They brought in bald eagles from Canada.
31. A) Pollution of the environment.
B) A new generation of pest killers.
C) Over-killing by hunters.
D) Destruction of their natural homes.

Passage Three

Questions 32 to 35 are based on the passage you have just heard.

32. A) Why people hold back their tears.
B) Why people cry.
C) How to restrain one's tears.
D) How tears are produced.
33. A) What chemicals tears are composed of.
B) Whether crying really helps us feel better.
C) Why some people tend to cry more often than others.
D) How tears help people cope with emotional problems.
34. A) Only one out of four girls cries less often than boys.
B) Of four boys, only one cries very often.
C) Girls cry four times as often as boys.
D) Only one out of four babies doesn't cry often.
35. A) Only humans respond to emotions by shedding tears.
B) Only humans shed tears to get rid of imitating stuff in their eyes.
C) Only human tears can resist invading bacteria.
D) Only human tears can discharge certain chemicals.

Section C

Directions: *In this section, you will hear a passage three times. When the passage is read for the first time, you should listen carefully for its general idea. When the passage is read for the second time, you are required to fill in the blanks numbered from 36 to 43 with the exact words you have just heard. For blanks numbered from 44 to 46 you are required to fill in the missing information. For these blanks, you can either use the exact words you have just heard or write down the main points in your own words. Finally, when the passage is read for the third time, you should check what you have written.*

He was a funny-looking man with a cheerful face, good-natured and a great talker. He was (36) ________ by his student, the great philosopher Plato, as "the best and most just and wisest man." Yet this same man was (37) ________ to death for his beliefs by a jury composed of the leading figures of the time in Athens.

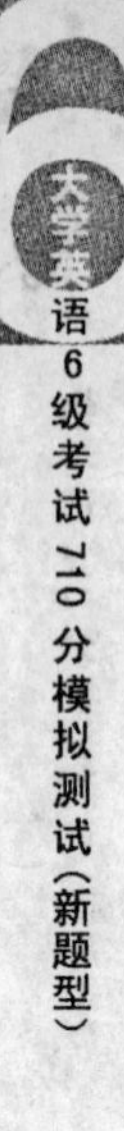

The man was the Greek philosopher Socrates, and he was put to death for not believing in the recognized gods and for (38) ________ young people. The second charge steamed from his (39) ________ with numerous young men who came to Athens from all over the (40) ________ world to study under him.

Socrates's method of teaching was to ask questions and, by (41) ________ not to know the answers, to (42) ________ his students into thinking for themselves. His teachings had (43) ________ influence on all the great Greek and Roman schools of philosophy. Yet for all his fame and influence. Socrates himself never wrote a word.

Socrates (44) ________________________________ in Athens. They wanted him silenced. Yet many were probably surprised that he accepted death so readily.

Socrates (45) ________________________________. But Socrates, as a firm believer in law, reasoned that it was proper to submit to the death sentence. (46) ________________________________.

Part Ⅳ Reading Comprehension(Reading in Depth) (25 minutes)

Section A

Directions: *In this section, there is a short passage with 5 questions or incomplete statements. Read the passage carefully. Then answer the questions or complete the statements in the fewest possible words on* ***the Answer Sheet.***

Questions 47 to 51 are based on the following passage.

America is a country that now sits atop the cherished myth that work provides rewards, that working people can support their families. It's a myth that has become so divorced from reality that it might as well begin with the words "Once upon a time". Today 1.6 million New Yorkers suffer from "food insecurity", which is a fancy way of saying they don't have enough to eat. Some are the people who come in at night and clean the skyscrapers that glitter along the river. Some pour coffee and take care of the aged parents of the people who live in those buildings. The American Dream for the well-to-do grows from the bowed backs of the working poor, who too often have to choose between groceries and rent.

In a new book called "The Betrayal of Work", Beth Shulman says that even in the booming 1990s one out of every four American workers made less than $8.70 an hour, an income equal to the government's poverty level for a family of four. Many, if not most, of these workers had no health care, sick pay or retirement provisions.

We ease our consciences, Shulman writes, by describing these people as "low skilled", as though they're not important or intelligent enough to deserve more. But low-skilled workers today are better educated than ever before, and they constitute the *linchpin* (关键) of American industry. When politicians *crow* (得意洋洋地说) that happy days are here again because jobs are on the rise, it's these jobs they're really talking about. Five of the 10 occupations expected to grow big in the next decade are in the lowest-paying job groups. And before we sit back and decide that's just the way it is, it's instructive to consider the rest of the world. While the bottom 10 percent of American workers earn just 37 percent of our average wage, their counterparts in other industrialized countries earn upwards of 60 percent. And those are countries that provide health care and child care, which eases the economic pinch considerably.

Almost 40 years ago, when Lyndon Johnson declared war on poverty, a family with a car and a house in the suburbs felt prosperous. Today that same family may well feel poor, overwhelmed by credit card debt, a second mortgage and the cost of the stuff that has become the backbone of American life. When the middle class feels poor, the poor have little chance for change, or even recognition.

47. By saying "it might as well begin with the words 'Once upon a time'" (Line 3, Para. 1), the author suggests that the American myth is ________.
48. What is the American Dream of the well-to-do built upon?
49. Some Americans try to make themselves feel less guilty by attributing the poverty of the working people to ________.
50. We learn from the passage that the difference in pay between the lowest paid and the average worker in America is ________ than that in other industrialized countries.
51. According to the author, how would an American family with a car and a house in the suburbs probably feel about themselves today?

Section B

Directions: *There are 2 passages in this section. Each passage is followed by some questions or unfinished statements. For each of them there are four choices marked A), B), C) and D). You should decide on the best choice and mark the corresponding letter on* ***the Answer Sheet*** *with a single line through the center.*

Passage One

Questions 52 to 56 are based on the following passage.

As a wise man once said, we are all ultimately alone. But an increasing number of Europeans are choosing to be so at an ever earlier age. This isn't the stuff of gloomy philosophical contemplations, but a fact of Europe's new economic landscape, embraced by sociologists, real-estate developers and ad executives alike. The shift away from family life to solo lifestyle, observes a French sociologist, is part of the "irresistible momentum of individualism" over the last century. The communications revolution, the shift from a business culture of stability to one of mobility and the mass entry of women into the workforce have greatly wreaked *havoc on*(扰乱) Europeans' private lives.

Europe's new economic climate has largely fostered the trend toward independence. The current generation of home-aloners came of age during Europe's shift from social democracy to the sharper, more individualistic climate of American-style capitalism. Raised in an era of privatization

and increased consumer choice, today's *tech-savvy*(精通技术的) workers have embraced a free market in love as well as economics. Modern Europeans are rich enough to afford to live alone, and temperamentally independent enough to want to do so.

Once upon a time, people who lived alone tended to be those on either side of marriage—twenty something professionals or widowed senior citizens. While pensioners, particularly elderly women, make up a large proportion of those living alone, the newest crop of singles are high earners in their 30s and 40s who increasingly view living alone as a lifestyle choice. Living alone was conceived to be negative—dark and cold, while being together suggested warmth and light. But then came along the idea of singles. They were young, beautiful, strong! Now, young people want to live alone.

The booming economy means people are working harder than ever. And that doesn't leave much room for relationships. Pimpi Arroyo, a 35-year-old composer who lives alone in a house in Paris, says he hasn't got time to get lonely because he has too much work. "I have deadlines which would make life with someone else fairly difficult. "Only an ideal woman would make him change his lifestyle, he says. Kaufmann, author of a recent book called "The Single Woman and Prince Charming," thinks this fierce new individualism means that people expect more and more of mates, so relationships don't last long—if they start at all. Eppendorf, a blond Berliner with a deep tan, teaches grade school in the mornings. In the afternoon she sunbathes or sleeps, resting up for going dancing. Just shy of 50, she says she'd never have wanted to do what her mother did—give up a career to raise a family. Instead, "I've always done what I wanted to do: live a self-determined life."

52. More and more young Europeans remain single because? ________.
    A) they are driven by an overwhelming sense of individualism
    B) they have entered the workforce at a much earlier age
    C) they have embraced a business culture of stability
    D) they are pessimistic about their economic future
53. What is said about European society in the passage?
    A) It has fostered the trend towards small families.
    B) It is getting closer to American style capitalism.
    C) It has limited consumer choice despite a free market.
    D) It is being threatened by irresistible privatization.
54. According to Paragraph 3, the newest group of singles are ________.
    A) warm and light hearted
    B) on either side of marriage
    C) negative and gloomy
    D) healthy and wealthy
55. The author quotes Eppendorf to show that ________.
    A) some modern women prefer a life of individual freedom
    B) the family is no longer the basic unit of society in present-day Europe
    C) some professional people have too much work to do to feel lonely
    D) most Europeans conceive living a single life as unacceptable

56. What is the author's purpose in writing the passage?

A) To review the impact of women becoming high earners.

B) To contemplate the philosophy underlying individualism.

C) To examine the trend of young people living alone.

D) To stress the rebuilding of personal relationships.

Passage Two

Questions 57 to 61 are based on the following passage.

Supporters of the biotech industry have accused an American scientist of misconduct after she testified to the New Zealand government that a genetically modified(GM) bacterium could cause serious damage if released.

The New Zealand Life Sciences Network, an association of pro-GM scientists and organizations, says the view expressed by Elaine Ingham, a soil biologist at Oregon State University in Corvallis, was exaggerated and irresponsible. It has asked her university to discipline her.

But Ingham stands by her comments and says the complaints are an attempt to silence her. "They're trying to cause trouble with my university and get me fired," Ingham told New Scientist.

The controversy began on 1 February, when Ingham testified before New Zealand's Royal Commission on Genetic Modification, which will determine how to regulate GM organisms. Ingham claimed that a GM version of a common soil bacterium could spread and destroy plants if released into the wild. Other researchers had previously modified the bacterium to produce alcohol from organic waste. But Ingham says that when she put it in soil with wheat plants, all of the plants died within a week.

"We would lose *terrestrial*(陆生的)plants... this is an organism that is potentially deadly to the continued survival of human beings," she told the commission. She added that the U. S. Environmental Protection Agency (EPA) canceled its approval for field tests using the organism once she had told them about her research in 1999.

But last week the New Zealand Life Sciences Network accused Ingham of "presenting inaccurate, careless and exaggerated information" and "generating speculative *doomsday scenarios*(世界末日的局面)that are not scientifically supportable". They say that her study doesn't even show that the bacteria would survive in the wild, much less kill massive numbers of plants. What's more, the network says that contrary to Ingham's claims, the EPA was never asked to consider the organism for field trials.

The EPA has not commented on the dispute. But an e-mail to the network from Janet Anderson, director of the EPA's *bio-pesticides*(生物杀虫剂)division, says "there is no record of a review and/or clearance to field test".

Ingham says EPA officials had told her that the organism was approved for field tests, but says she has few details. It's also not clear whether the organism, first engineered by a German institute for biotechnology, is still in use.

Whether Ingham is right or wrong, her supporters say opponents are trying unfairly to silence her.

"I think her concerns should be taken seriously. She shouldn't be harassed in this way," says Ann Clarke, a plant biologist at the University of Guelph in Canada who also testified before the commission. "It's an attempt to silence the opposition."

57. The passage centers on the controversy ________.
   A) between American and New Zealand biologists over genetic modification
   B) as to whether the study of genetic modification should be continued
   C) over the possible adverse effect of a GM bacterium on plants
   D) about whether Elaine Ingham should be fired by her university
58. Ingham insists that her testimony is based on ________.
   A) evidence provided by the EPA of the United States
   B) the results of an experiment she conducted herself
   C) evidence from her collaborative research with German biologists
   D) the results of extensive field tests in Corvallis, Oregon
59. According to Janet Anderson, the EPA ________.
   A) has canceled its approval for field tests of the GM organism
   B) hasn't reviewed the findings of Ingham's research
   C) has approved field tests using the GM organism
   D) hasn't given permission to field test the GM organism
60. According to Ann Clarke, the New Zealand Life Sciences Network ________.
   A) should gather evidence to discredit Ingham's claims
   B) should require that the research by their biologists be regulated
   C) shouldn't demand that Ingham be disciplined for voicing her views
   D) shouldn't appease the opposition in such a quiet way
61. Which of the following statements about Ingham is TRUE?
   A) Her testimony hasn't been supported by the EPA.
   B) Her credibility as a scientist hasn't been undermined.
   C) She is firmly supported by her university.
   D) She has made great contributions to the study of GM bacteria.

Part Ⅴ Error Correction (15 minutes)

Directions: *This part consists of a short passage. In this passage, there are altogether 10 mistakes, one in each numbered line. You may have to change a word, add a word or delete a word. Mark out the mistakes and put the corrections in the blanks provided. If you change a word, cross it and write the correct word in the corresponding blank. If you add a word, put an insertion mark (∧) in the right place and write the missing word in the blank. If you delete a word, cross it out and put a slash (/) in the blank.*

The Seattle Times company is one newspaper firm that has recognized the need for change and done something about it. In the

newspaper industry, papers must reflect the diversity of the communities
to which they provide information. It must reflect that diversity with their 62. ______
news coverage or risk losing their readers' interest and their advertisers'
support. Operating within Seattle, which has 20 percents racial 63. ______
minorities, the paper has put into place policies and procedures for hiring
and maintain a diverse workforce. The underlying reason for the change is 64. ______
that for information to be fair, appropriate, and subjective, it should be 65. ______
reported by the same kind of population that reads it.

A diversity committee composed of reporters, editors, and
photographers meets regularly to value the Seattle Times' content and to 66. ______
educate the rest of the newsroom staff about diversity issues. In an 67. ______
addition, the paper instituted a content *audit* (审查) that evaluates the
frequency and manner of representation of woman and people of color in 68. ______
photographs. Early audits showed that minorities were pictured far too
infrequently and were pictured with a disproportionate number of negative
articles. The audit has resulted from improvement in the frequency of 69. ______
majority representation and their portrayal in neutral or positive 70. ______
situations. And, with a result, the Seattle Times has improved as a 71. ______
newspaper. The diversity training and content audits helped the Seattle
Times Company to win the Personnel Journal Optimas Award for
excellence in managing change.

Part Ⅵ Translation (5 minutes)

Directions: *Complete the following sentences on Answer Sheet 2 by translating into English the Chinese given in brackets.*

72. It was essential that ______________________ (我们在月底前签订合同).
73. To our delight, she ______________________ (进大学一个月就适应了校园生活).
74. The new government was accused ______________________ (未实现其降低失业率的承诺).
75. The workmen think ______________________ (遵守安全规则很重要).
76. The customer complained that no sooner ______________________ (他刚试着使用这台机器，它就不运转了).

参考答案(1)

Part Ⅰ Sample Writing

Say No to Pirated Products

Nowadays, the problem of piracy has become more and more serious. Books, tapes, VCDs and others high-tech products have been pirated. For instance, when a new product comes onto

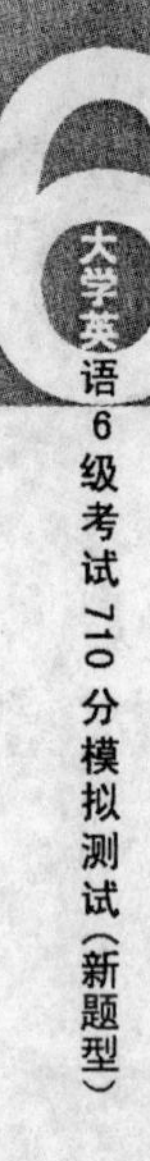

market, most probably, its pirated counterpart will soon put on its appearance in the market, too.

Piracy has caused a great loss to legitimate producers, inventors and writers in many ways. To start with, the pirated products often cost much less than the genuine ones so that they enjoy a better trading position in spite of their relatively poor quality. The genuine products, on the contrary, sell poorly. What's worse, pirated books sometimes do great harm to the authors' reputation due to some misprints. In the long run, pirated products may have a negative impact on customers. Those legitimate producers' creativity and enthusiasm may be deeply hurt by the fact that some customers are more interested in the pirated products for the sake of small gains.

In my opinion, it's high time that everyone started the battle against piracy. First, customers should develop their consciousness to resist the pirated products. Second, the government should take effective measures to put an end to piracy. Finally, laws must be strictly enforced to completely ban piracy. Only in this way can we wipe the pirated products out of our life.

Part Ⅱ Reading Comprehension (Skimming and Scanning)

1. N 2. Y 3. NG 4. N
5. some older trees die
6. the canopy layer
7. kill the host tree
8. symbiotic
9. insects and birds/insects/birds/animals
10. an unknown planet

Part Ⅲ Listening Comprehension

Section A

11—15 DBDCA 16—20 CCACA 21—25 BADCC

Section B

26—30 CBCBD 31—35 DBDCA

Section C

36. described 37. condemned 38. corrupting 39. association
40. civilized 41. pretending 42. press 43. unsurpassed
44. encouraged new ideas and free thinking in the young, and this was frightening to the conservatives
45. had the right to ask for a less severe penalty, and he probably could have persuaded the jury to change the verdict
46. So he calmly accepted his fate and drank a cup of poison in the presence of his grief-stricken friends and students

Part Ⅳ Reading Comprehension (Reading in Depth)

Section A

47. divorced from reality/unrealistic
48. The backbreaking labor of the working poor. /The bowed backs of the working poor.

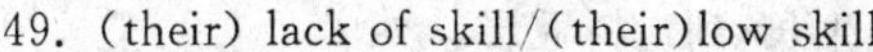
49. (their) lack of skill/(their)low skill

50. much greater

51. Poor.

Section B

52—56　ABDAC　57—61　CBDCA

Part Ⅴ　Error Correction

62. It →They
63. percents→percent
64. maintain→maintaining
65. subjective→objective
66. value→evaluate
67. 删除 an
68. woman→women
69. from→in
70. majority→minority
71. with→as

Part Ⅵ　Translation

72. we sign the contract before the end of the month
73. adapted (herself) to campus life a month after entering college
74. of failure to fulfill its promise to reduce the unemployment rate
75. it very important to comply with/follow the safety regulations
76. had he tried to use the machine than it stopped working

试题解答(1)

Part Ⅱ　Reading Comprehension (Skimming and Scanning)

1. [N] 第一段第二句"Today, tropical rainforests cover only 6 percent of the Earth's ground surface,but they are home to over half of the planet's plant and animal species"中提到，热带雨林占全球面积的6%,却拥有超过地球一半以上的动植物种类。这句话表明,不是所有动植物物种都能在热带雨林中找到,比如很多海洋生物就不能在热带雨林中找到。
2. [Y] 根据"What Is a Rainforest?"部分第三段中的"Since rainforests are at the middle of the globe, located near the equator, they are not especially affected by this change. They receive nearly the same amount of sunlight,and therefore heat, all year. Consequently, the weather in these regions remains fairly constant",此说法是正确的。
3. [NG] 文中并未提及哪里拥有最多、最大的热带雨林,只讲到热带雨林通常在赤道附近,常年炎热、降水充分、物种丰富。
4. [N] 由"What Is a Rainforest?"部分最后一段中的两句话"As you go lower, down into the rainforest, you find less and less greenery."和"The overabundance of plants gathering sunlight at the top of the forest blocks most sunlight from reaching the bottom of the forest,making it difficult for robust plants to thrive."可见,由于浓密的树冠层挡住了大部分阳光,地面的植被并不茂盛。所以,题中说法是错误的。
5. "The Forest for the Trees"部分第一段中的"New tree seedlings rarely survive to make it to the top unless some older trees die, creating a "hole" in the canopy."因此,答案是"some older

trees die"。只有老树死亡后,新的树苗才能成活,向上生长,到达树冠层。

6. "The Forest for the Trees"部分最后一段中提到"Epiphytes are close enough to the top to receive adequate light, and the runoff from the canopy layer provides all the water and nutrients they need, which is important since they don't have access to the nutrients in the ground."可见为附生植物提供水和养分的是树冠层。故正确答案为"the canopy layer"。

7. 由"Strangler and Buttresses"部分的第一段最后一句"Eventually, the strangler may block so much light from above, and absorb such a high percentage of nutrients from the ground below, that the host tree dies."可见附生植物最终导致宿主树木死亡。故答案为"kill the host tree"。

8. 由"Strangler and Buttresses"部分的第三段中的"Rainforest bacteria and trees have a very close, symbiotic relationship. The trees provide the bacteria with food, in the form of fallen leaves and other material, and the bacteria break this material down into the nutrients that the trees need to survive."可知树木为细菌提供食物,细菌则分解这些东西,反过来为树木提供养分。它们之间是密切的共生关系。故答案为"symbiotic"。

9. 由"All Creatures, Great and Small"部分第二段"As they travel, the insects may pick up the plants' seeds, dropping them some distance away."和第三段"This helps to disperse the population of the plant species over a larger area. By the time they excrete the seeds, the birds may have flown many miles away from the fruit-bearing tree."可见昆虫和鸟类都能帮助植物传播种子。雨林中生活的大量动物其实也帮助植物传播种子。所以,答案可以是"insects and birds/insects/birds/animals"。

10. 由"Deforestation"部分的最后一段"Destroying the rainforests is comparable to destroying an unknown planet—we have no idea what we're losing."可知正确答案为"an unknown planet"。

Part Ⅲ Listening Comprehension(听力原文在光盘中)

Part Ⅳ Reading Comprehension (Reading in Depth)

Section A

47. 文章一开始作者讲到美国人一直相信这样一个神话:只要工作就有回报,工作的人完全可以养家。但紧接着作者说"It's a myth that has become so divorced from reality that it might as well begin with the words 'Once upon a time.'"(这个神话和现实有如此大的差距以至于我们在这么说之前得加上"很久很久以前……"。)所以本题可以填写原文中的原词"divorced from reality"。这样要填写的句子的意思就符合原文了,作者说"我们最好在前面加上很久很久以前",暗示美国神话已经脱离了现实。基于对这部分意思的理解,也可以填写"unrealistic",表示这一神话般的说法是不现实的。

48. 第一段最后一句"The American Dream for the well-to-do grows from the bowed backs of the working poor, who too often have to choose between groceries and rent."中的 grows from 和问题中的 is built upon 是一个意思。因此,本题可以用"The bowed backs of the working poor."来回答,也可以基于理解,回答成"The backbreaking labor of the working labor."。

49. 第三段第一句"We ease our consciences, Shulman writes, by describing these people as 'low skilled,' as though they're not important or intelligent enough to deserve more."中的"ease our consciences"就是"减轻负疚感"的意思。因此只要回答归咎于劳动者"技能低下"就可以了。原文用的是形容词"low skilled",题目中在介词 to 后用名词。因此答案可以是"(their)

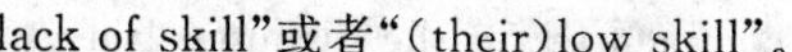

lack of skill"或者"(their)low skill"。

50. 第三段倒数第二句,"While the bottom 10 percent of American workers earn just 37 percent of our average wage, their counterparts in other industrialized countries earn upwards of 60 percent."中提到美国工资最低的10%的劳动者的收入占美国人均收入的37%,而在其他工业国家,这类劳动者的收入达到这些国家平均收入的60%。由此可见,美国劳动者的最低收入和人均收入的差距要比其他工业国家的大很多。因此,正确答案为"much greater"。
51. 文章最后一段说"Almost 40 years ago, when Lyndon Johnson declared war on poverty, a family with a car and a house in the suburbs felt prosperous. Today that same family may well feel poor..."。可见正确答案是"Poor"。

Section B

52. [A] 因果推断题。由第一段前两句"Europeans are choosing to be so at an ever earlier age... The shift away from family life to solo lifestyle... is part of the 'irresistible momentum of individualism'"可知欧洲年轻人选择单身是个人主义使然,他们向往自由、向往个性因而选择 single。
53. [B] 根据文中第二段开头"Europe... trend toward independence... shift from social democracy to the sharper, more individualistic climate of American-style capitalism."可以判断应该选择B项。
54. [D] 细节推断题。根据第三段中"the newest crop of singles are high earners in their 30s and 40s who increasingly view living alone as a lifestyle choice... They were young, beautiful, strong! Now, young people want to live alone.",可以推断 the newest group of singles are high earners and strong,即 healthy and wealthy。
55. [A] 例证题。根据文章最后部分"Eppendorf... teaches grade school in the mornings. In the afternoon she sunbathes or sleeps, resting up for going dancing... she says she'd never...—give up a career to raise a family. Instead. 'I've always done what I wanted to do: live a self-determined life.'"。可以推断现代的女性更喜欢个人的、独立的生活。
56. [C]写作目的题。认真阅读文章前两句,就可以看出作者的 keynote:"... we are all ultimately alone. But an increasing number... are choosing to be so at an ever earlier age",第三段再次提到"the newest crop of singles are high earners in their 30s and 40s who increasingly view living alone as a lifestyle choice. ... came along the idea of singles. They were young, beautiful, strong! Now, young people want to live alone"。因此,正确答案为C项。
57. [C] 主旨题。第一段提及"Supporters of the biotech industry have accused an American scientist of misconduct ... genetically modified(GM) bacterium could cause serious damage if released",即一位美国科学家认为 GM 细菌一旦释放即可能造成严重损害;而支持 GM(pro-GM)的则认为对方发言"exaggerated and irresponsible"。第四段直接指出"The controversy began...",由此可以推断本文主要讲述双方针对 GM 细菌是否会造成严重损害,各执一词。
58. [B] 细节推断题。根据文章第四段末"Ingham says that when she put it in soil with wheat plants, all of the plants died within a week."以及第五段后半部分"She added that ... canceled its approval for field tests... once she had told them about her research in 1999."可推断是 Ingham 自己做试验来印证她的观点。

59. [D] 细节判断题。根据第七段"The EPA has not commented on the dispute. But... Janet Anderson, director of the EPA... says 'there is no record of a review and/or clearance to field test'."由此可以看出EPA没有field test的记录,也没有审核、消除field test的记录,意思是与该争论划清界限,表示并没有授权进行GM field test,也没有参与。

60. [C] 推断题。根据第十段"'I think her concerns should be taken seriously. She shouldn't be harassed in this way,' says Ann Clarke... 'It's an attempt to silence the opposition.'", Ann Clarke认为Ingham的担忧应该被慎重对待,反对她的人不应该通过起诉来骚扰她,反对者这么做是想让她对此事保持沉默。由此推断,Ann Clarke认为Ingham的观点应该被重视(先甭管对否),通过试验或其他方式来论证,而不是通过法律强制手段让她对此事保持沉默。

61. [A] 细节判断题。由第59题的详细解释可以看出EPA并不支持Ingham的观点,这一点显而易见。至于Ingham对GM细菌研究有多大贡献,Ingham的学校对此事持什么态度都没有提及,由此排除B、C、D三项。

Part Ⅴ　Error Correction

62. It→They。通过上下文可以明白,在报业内,报纸在新闻报道面上应该反映社会的多样性。此处不是仅指一家报纸,而是泛指多家报纸,因此此处"it"其实应为上文中的"papers",所以应为复数"They"。

63. percents→percent。此处为常规语法的考查。percent在与具体数字的百分比连接时,不必更改为复数,而是单数形式。

64. maintain→maintaining。此处考查前后文的一致性。在前文的介词"for"之后,hiring为分词形式,因此对称位置的动词maintain也应该为分词形式。

65. subjective→objective。此处考查对上下文的理解。根据上下文,本句的句意为"此变化的潜在的原因是若要信息能够公正、妥当并客观地被报道,那新闻就应该由与读者群相同的种族新闻人来报道",而subjective表示"主观性的",不符合上下文语境,应改为其反义词objective,意为"客观的"。

66. value→evaluate。此处考查词性的使用。根据上下文语意,该句含义为"由记者、编辑和摄影师组成的多元化委员会定期举行会议来评估西雅图时报的内容",value作为动词时,其含义为"估价,计算……的价格",而只有evaluate才能表达"评估"的含义。

67. 删除an:此题考查常规用法。in addition表示"此外,另外",使用时中间无需加an。

68. woman→women。此处与后文的people of color(有色人种)一样,都是以复数形式来泛指这一类群的人,因此woman应改为复数形式women。

69. from→in。此处考查词组的使用。result from表示"因……而引起",而result in表示"导致,造成"。本句的上下文语意为"早期的审查表明少数人群的报道频率过低而且被描述成负面文章,且这些文章的数量极其失衡。审查使得少数人群提高了报道频率并改善了他们在中性和正面报道情况下的形象"。因此,result from不符合句意。

70. majority→minority。本题考查对上下文一致性的理解。前后文甚至是通篇短文都在关注的是报业对少数人群的报道,所以此处根据对上下文的领会,也应保持统一。

71. with→as。固定用法,词组as a result,表示"结果"。

Part Ⅵ　Translation

72. [答案]:we sign the contract before the end of the month

[注释]:本句的翻译难点在短语"签订合同(sign the contract)"上。

73. [答案]:adapted (herself) to campus life a month after entering college

[注释]:本句考查的翻译语言点为"适应",即 adapt to,类似的表达如 get accustomed to 也是正确的。但在校园生活一词的翻译上,可能出现的错误译法是 university life。

74. [答案]:of failure to fulfill its promise to reduce the unemployment rate

[注释]:此句考查的语言点有多个。首先必须与主干谓语动词 accused 保持词组使用的准确性,即 accuse...of 词组的搭配使用。其次,在介词 of 后必须接名词性的介词宾语,"无法实现"既可以翻译成 failure to fulfill 也可以相应翻译成 failing to fulfill。最后,句子中"失业率"的准确译文应为 unemployment rate。

75. [答案]:it very important to comply with/follow the safety regulations

[注释]:本句翻译中要注意 it 作为形式宾语的用法。其次,"遵守"的译文可以是正式语体中的 comply with,也可以是常规词 follow。"安全规则"既可以翻译为 safety regulations 也可以是 safety rules。

76. [答案]:had he tried to use the machine than it stopped working

[注释]:本句翻译的关键是句型"no sooner... than...",表示"刚……就",同时在 no sooner 紧接的从句中应使用倒装。由于抱怨的内容发生在抱怨之前,因此 no sooner 从句中谓语动词必须为过去分词形式。

College English Practice Test 2（Band Ⅵ）

Part Ⅰ Writing (30 minutes)

Directions: *In this section you are required to write a composition on the topic* **"Reduce Waste on Campus"**. *You should write at least* **150** *words and base your composition on the outline given in Chinese below.*

1. 目前有些校园内浪费现象严重；
2. 浪费的危害；
3. 从我做起，杜绝浪费。

Part Ⅱ Reading Comprehension (Skimming and Scanning) (15 minutes)

Directions:（略）

Some Notes on Gender-Neutral Language

General

The practice of assigning masculine gender to neutral terms comes from the fact that every language reflects the prejudices of the society in which it evolved, and English evolved through most of its history in a male-centered, patriarchal society. Like any other language, however, English is always changing. One only has to read aloud sentences from the 19th century books assigned for this class to sense the shifts that have occurred in the last 150 years. When readers pick up something to read, they expect different conventions depending on the time in which the material was written. As writers in 1995, we need to be not only aware of the conventions that our readers may expect, but also conscious of the responses our words may elicit. In addition, we need to know how the shifting nature of language can make certain words awkward or misleading.

"Man"

Man once was a truly generic word referring to all humans, but has gradually narrowed in meaning to become a word that refers to adult male human beings. Anglo-Saxons used the word to refer to all people. One example of this occurs when an Anglo-Saxon writer refers to a seventh-century English princess as "a wonderful man". Man paralleled the Latin word homo, "a member of the human species," not vir, "an adult male of the species." The Old English word for adult male was waepman and the old English word for adult woman was wifman. In the course of time, wifman evolved into the word "woman." "Man" eventually ceased to be used to refer to individual women and replaced waepman as a specific term distinguishing an adult male from an adult female. But man continued to be used in generalizations about both sexes.

By the 18th century, the modern, narrow sense of man was firmly established as the predominant one. When Edmund Burke, writing of the French Revolution, used men in the old, inclusive way, he took pains to spell out his meaning: "Such a deplorable havoc is made in the minds of men (both sexes) in France..." Thomas Jefferson did not make the same distinction in declaring that "all men are created equal" and "governments are instituted among men, deriving their just powers from the consent of the governed." In a time when women, having no vote, could neither give nor withhold consent, Jefferson had to be using the word men in its principal sense of "males," and it probably never occurred to him that anyone would think otherwise. Looking at modern dictionaries indicate that the definition that links "man" with males is the predominant one. Studies of college students and school children indicate that even when the broad definitions of "man" and "men" are taught, they tend to conjure up images of male people only. We would never use the sentence "A girl grows up to be a man," because we assume the narrower definition of the word man.

The Pronoun Problem

The first grammars of modern English were written in the 16th and 17th centuries. They were mainly intended to help boys from upper class families prepare for the study of Latin, a language most scholars considered superior to English. The male authors of these earliest English grammars wrote for male readers in an age when few women were literate. The masculine-gender *pronouns*(代词) did not reflect a belief that masculine pronouns could refer to both sexes. The grammars of this period contain no indication that masculine pronouns were sex-inclusive when used in general references. Instead these pronouns reflected the reality of male cultural dominance and the male-centered world view that resulted.

"He" started to be used as a generic pronoun by grammarians who were trying to change a long-established tradition of using "they" as a singular pronoun. In 1850 an Act of Parliament gave official *sanction*(批准) to the recently invented concept of the "generic" he. In the language used in acts of Parliament, the new law said, "words importing the masculine gender shall be deemed and taken to include females." Although similar language in contracts and other legal documents subsequently helped reinforce this grammatical edict in all English-speaking countries, it was often conveniently ignored. In 1879, for example, a move to admit female physicians to the all-male Massachusetts Medical Society was effectively blocked on the grounds that the society's by-laws describing membership used the pronoun he.

Just as "man" is not truly generic in the 1990s, "he" is not a true generic pronoun. Studies have confirmed that most people understand "he" to refer to men only. Sentences like "A doctor is a busy person; he must be able to balance a million obligations at once" imply that all doctors are men. As a result of the fact that "he" is read by many as a masculine pronoun, many people, especially women, have come to feel that the generic pronouns excludes women. This means that more and more people find the use of such a pronoun problematic.

Solving the Pronoun Problem

They as a Singular—Most people, when writing and speaking informally, rely on singular they as a matter of course: "If you love someone, set them free" (Sting). If you pay attention to your own speech, you'll probably catch yourself using the same construction yourself. "It's enough to drive anyone out of their senses" (George Bernard Shaw). "I shouldn't like to punish anyone, even if they'd done me wrong" (George Eliot). Some people are annoyed by the incorrect grammar that this solution necessitates, but this construction is used more and more frequently.

He or She—Despite the charge of clumsiness, double-pronoun constructions have made a comeback: "To be black in this country is simply too pervasive an experience for any writer to omit from her or his work," wrote Samuel R. Delany. Overuse of this solution can be awkward, however.

Pluralizing—A writer can often recast material in the plural. For instance, instead of "As he advances in his program, the medical student has increasing opportunities for clinical work," try "As they advance in their program, medical students have increasing opportunities for clinical work."

Eliminating Pronouns—Avoid having to use pronouns at all; instead of "a first grader can feed and dress himself," you could write, "a first grader can eat and get dressed without assistance."

Further Alternatives—he/she or s/he, using one instead of he, or using a new generic pronoun (thon, co, E, tey, hesh, hir).

1. "Man" could be used to refer to female human being in the past.
2. In "all men are created equal" in *Declaration of Independence* by Thomas Jefferson, the word "men" refer to both males and females whether they have vote right or not.
3. In 1879, Massachusetts Medical Society refused to admit more than ten female physicians because the society's by-laws describing membership used the pronoun he.
4. The first grammars of modern English were written in order to help boys from the upper class prepare for the study of Latin.
5. "Man" paralleled the Latin word "homo" which means ________.
6. Studies show that even when students are taught the broad definition of "man" and "men", they think of ________.
7. Grammarians started to use "he" as a generic pronoun because they were trying to change a tradition of using "they" as ________.
8. When most people read the word "he", they would understand it to refer to ________.
9. Although some people are annoyed by ________ of singular they, this construction is used more and more frequently to solve the pronoun problem.
10. Another way of solving the pronoun problem is to use ________ instead of the singular.

Part Ⅲ　　Listening Comprehension　　(35 minutes)

Section A

Directions:(略)

11. A) The play was the first he'd seen. B) The play wasn't too bad.
C) He hasn't seen the play yet. D) He wants to see the play again.

12. A) It will be finished on time.
B) It is only open during the day.
C) Something has happened to the building.
D) The workers are about to complete it.

13. A) He lost a button at work.
B) He doesn't know where he put the calculator.
C) He thinks he broke something the woman lent him.
D) He's not sure how to solve the math problem.

14. A) The old houses should be turned into stores.
B) The city needs even more modern modernization.
C) This shopping center is quite old.
D) New shopping centers are very common.

15. A) Whether the woman knows how to type.
B) Why the woman is in a hurry.
C) How much typing the woman needs done.
D) Whether the woman has a typewriter.

16. A) He goes along with the woman's suggestion.
B) He can't decide whether to go or not.
C) He will go to the concert alone.
D) He thinks the performance will be very good.

17. A) It involved a few lunches. B) There were free lunches.
C) There were three lunches. D) There are more than free lunches.

18. A) 13. B) 17. C) 30. D) 15.

Questions 19 to 22 are based on the conversation you have just heard.

19. A) He has got a bad cold.
B) He has caught whooping cough.
C) He has a fever and a bad appetite.
D) He has been coughing for several days.

20. A) Because he is only a 3-year-old child.
B) Because others' cough may be contagious to him.
C) Because he also has a fever.
D) Because he cries all the time.

21. A) Because he is too young to catch that.
B) Because he has not been exposed to that.
C) Because his sister hasn't caught that.
D) Because he has been immunized recently.

22. A) Give the child lot of fluid to drink.
B) Let him have a hot bath before bedtime.
C) Keep an eye on the cough.

D) Send him to the clinic if he has a fever.

Questions 23 to 25 are based on the conversation you have just heard.

23. A) Boss and employee. B) Teacher and student.
    C) Interviewer and candidate. D) Colleagues.
24. A) A human resources manager. B) A computer programmer.
    C) A graduate. D) A teacher.
25. A) Team spirit. B) Competition.
    C) Coordination. D) Problem-solving.

Section B

Directions:(略)

Passage One

Questions 26 to 28 are based on the passage you have just heard.

26. A) Your first impression on the interviewer.
    B) Your job skill qualifications and background.
    C) Your communication skills.
    D) Your attitude.
27. A) To have an intimate talk with you.
    B) To know you as a person.
    C) To confirm your qualifications.
    D) To know more about your family background.
28. A) The interview usually last about half an hour.
    B) Your appearance and your communication skills count approximately the same during the interview.
    C) You are requested to submit all your background information during the interview.
    D) Employers compare your information with that of other applicants before the interview.

Passage Two

Questions 29 to 31 are based on the passage you have just heard.

29. A) Around 1930. B) Around 1940.
    C) Around 1950. D) Around 1960.
30. A) There is not enough financial support from the government.
    B) There are more retirees taking money out of the system, and not enough additional workers to support them.
    C) More and more people refuse to pay their income taxes.
    D) The economic growth has been slowed down.
31. A) Fewer retirees will be entitled to receive Social Security.
    B) Payroll taxes may be increased.
    C) Younger workers can save some of their payroll taxes in a personal account.

D) Beneficiaries will receive less money from the Social Security.

Passage Three

Questions 32 to 35 are based on the passage you have just heard.

32. A) The strength of its shipbuilding industry.
    B) The physical features of the river itself.
    C) The abundance of fruit, vegetables, and livestock.
    D) The similarity of climate to that in Europe.
33. A) There are no rapids or waterfalls.
    B) There is a constant, strong wind.
    C) Navigation is rather difficult.
    D) Frequent storms cause problems for riverboats.
34. A) Big waves pose a threat to commercial navigation.
    B) The river current never flows faster ten miles per hour.
    C) The river reverses its flow several times a day.
    D) High tides can create sudden and unexpected rapids.
35. A) To allow several sails to be rigged.
    B) To add to the beauty of the basic design.
    C) To catch winds coming from over the hills.
    D) To allow the sails to be raised more quickly.

Section C

Directions: (略)

Today I would like to talk about the early days of movie making in the late nineteenth and early (36) ________ centuries. Before the (37) ________ films of D. W. Griffith, film makers were limited by several (38) ________ questions of the era. According to one, the camera was always fixed at a viewpoint (39) ________ to that of the spectator in the theatre, a position now known as the long shot. It was another convention that the (40) ________ of the camera never changed in the middle of a (41) ________. In last week's films, we saw how Griffith ignored both these limiting (42) ________ and brought the camera closer to the actor.

This shot, now known as a full shot, was considered (43) ________ at the time. For Love of Gold, was the name of the film in which the first use of the full shot. After progressing from a long shot to the full shot, the next logical step for Griffith was to bring in the camera still closer, in what is now called the close-up. (44) ____ ____, as for example, in Edqaed Asport's The Great Train Robbery, which was made in 1903.

But not until 1908 in Griffith's movie (45) ____ ____. In the scene from After Many Years that we are about to see, pay special attention to the close-up of Annie Lee's worried face as she awaits her husband's return. In 1908, this close-up shocked everyone in

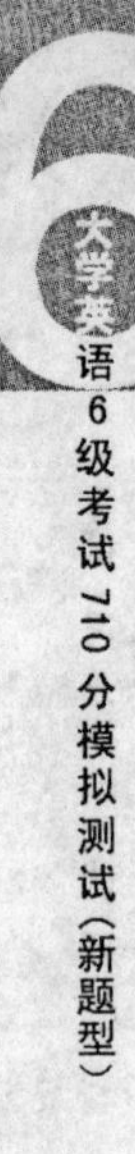

the Biogress Studio. But Griffith had no time for argument. He had another surprise even more radical to offer. Immediately following close-up of Annie, he inserted a picture of the object of her thought—her husband cast sway on a desert aisle. (46) ________________________________
________________________________.

Part Ⅳ Reading Comprehension(Reading in Depth) (25 minutes)

Section A

Directions:(略)

Questions 47 to 51 are based on the following passage.

Women who apply for jobs in middle or senior management have a higher success rate than men, according to an employment survey. But of course far fewer of them apply for these positions. The study, by *recruitment*(征召新成员) consultants NB Selection, shows that while one in six men who appear on interview shortlist get jobs, the figure rises to one in four for women.

Reasons for higher success rates among women are difficult to isolate. One explanation suggested is that if a woman candidate manages to get on a shortlist, then she has probably already proved herself to be an exceptional candidate. Dr. Marx said that when women apply for positions they tend to be better qualified than their male counterparts but are more selective and conservative in their job search. Women tend to research thoroughly before applying for positions or attending interviews. Men, on the other hand, seem to rely on their ability to sell themselves and to convince employers that any shortcomings they have will not prevent them from doing a good job.

Managerial and executive progress made by women is confirmed by the annual survey of boards of directors carried out by Korn International. This year the survey shows a doubling of the number of women serving as non-executive directors compared with the previous year. However, progress remains painfully slow and there were still only 18 posts filled by women out of a total of 354 non-executive positions surveyed.

In Europe a recent feature of corporate life in the recession has been the de-layering of management structures. Hilary Sears said that this has halted progress for women in as much as de-layering has taken place either where women are working or in layers they aspire to. Sears also noted a positive trend from the recession, which has been the growing number of women who have started up on their own.

In business as a whole, there are a number of factors encouraging the prospect of greater equality in the workforce. Demographic trends suggest that the number of women going into employment is steadily increasing. In addition a far greater number of women are now passing through higher education, making them better qualified to move into management positions. Organizations such as the European Women's Management Development Network provide a range of opportunities for women to enhance their skills and contacts.

However, Ariane Antal, director of the International Institute for Organization Change for Archamps in France, said that there is only anecdotal evidence of changes in recruitment patterns.

And she said: "It's still so hard for women to even get on to shortlists—there are so many hurdles and barriers." She agreed that there have been some positive signs but said: "Until there is a belief among employers, until they value the difference, nothing will change."

47. From the passage, we can see that males applicants ________ female applicants for top posts.
48. Women are more ________ than men when they apply for positions or attending interviews.
49. What aspect of company structuring has disadvantaged women in getting management positions?
50. According to Sears, the number of female-run business is ________.
51. Which group of people should change their attitude to recruitment so as to have a greater equality in the workforce?

Section B

Directions:(略)

Passage One

Questions 52 to 56 are based on the following passage.

The radical transformation of the Soviet society had a profound impact on women's lives. Marxists had traditionally believed that both capitalism and the middle-class husbands exploited women. The Russian Revolution of 1917 immediately proclaimed complete equality of rights for women. In the 1920s divorce and abortion were made easily available, and women were urged to work outside the home and liberate themselves sexually. After Stalin came to power, sexual and familial liberation was played down, and the most lasting changes for women involved work and education.

These changes were truly revolutionary. Young women were constantly told that they had to be equal to men, that they could and should do everything men could do. Peasant women in Russia had long experienced the equality of backbreaking physical labor in the countryside, and they continued to enjoy that equality on collective farms. With the advent of the five-year-plans, millions of women also began to toil in factories and in heavy construction, building dams, roads and steel mills in summer heat and winter frost. Most of the opportunities open to men through education were also open to women. Determined women pursued their studies and entered the ranks of the better-paid specialists in industry and science. Medicine practically became a woman's profession. By 1950, 75 percent of doctors in the Soviet Union were women.

Thus Stalinist society gave women great opportunities but demanded great sacrifices as well. The vast majority of women simply had to work outside the home. Wages were so low that it was almost impossible for a family or couple to live only on the husband's earnings. Moreover, the full-time working woman had a heavy burden of household tasks in her off hours, for most Soviet men in the 1930s still considered the home and the children the woman's responsibility. Men continued to **monopolize** the best jobs. Finally, rapid change and economic hardship led to many broken families, creating further physical, emotional, and mental strains for women. In any event, the

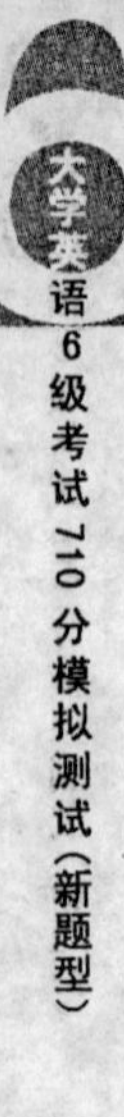

often-neglected human resource of women was mobilized in Stalinist society.

52. The main idea of this passage is that women in Stalinist society ________.
   A) had economic opportunities that had never been available before
   B) had difficulty balancing their work and family responsibilities
   C) had new opportunities but also many hardships
   D) moved quickly into the highest levels of government
53. In the last paragraph, "monopolize" probably means ________.
   A) hold　　B) earn　　C) leave　　D) pay
54. The author's main purpose in writing this passage is to ________.
   A) compare different systems of government
   B) tell stories about women in Soviet Union
   C) amuse the reader
   D) provide information
55. The author's tone in this passage can best be described as ________.
   A) disapproving　　B) emotional
   C) objective　　D) sympathetic
56. We can conclude that the economic and social status of women in Stalinist society ________.
   A) had been improved
   B) was worse than before
   C) had not changed much
   D) was better than that in capitalistic countries

Passage Two

Questions 57 to 61 are based on the following passage.

The General Electric Company, often criticized for the complexity of its structure and the resulting opacity of its numbers, said yesterday that it would break GE Capital, by far its largest business, into four businesses. The reorganization effectively eliminates the job of Denis J. Nayden, 48, the chairman of GE Capital. Each of the new units will have its own chief, who will report directly to Jeffrey R. Immelt, G. E.'s chairman. "The reason for doing this is simple. I want more direct contact with the financial services teams," Mr. Immelt said.

The new businesses are GE Commercial Finance, GE Insurance, GE Consumer Finance and GE Equipment Management. Some support functions within GE Capital, including risk management and treasury, will now report to Dennis Dammerman, 57, a G. E. vice chairman who preceded Mr. Nayden as GE Capital's chief. Mr. Nayden will remain at G. E. as an adviser for now, but is expected to leave shortly to start a financial services firm.

Mr. Dammerman insisted that the reorganization had nothing to do with the increasing clamor from investors, regulators and the news media for greater transparency in accounting and for chief executives to take more responsibility for businesses. Analysts seem to believe him. "This is just what it appears to be, a managerial reorganization which gives leaders more direct access to the office of the chairman," said Martin A. Sankey, a G. E. analyst.

The executives leading the new units will also sit on G. E. 's corporate executive council, a committee made up of the company's top 25 executives, which meets periodically and discusses various strategic and management issues.

GE Capital, the company's largest nit, provided $55 billion of G. E. 's $124 billion in revenue last year and $5. 6 billion of its $19. 7 billion in pretax profits. The rest of G. E. had been divided into 11 other businesses, many of them—lighting and appliances are examples-much smaller than the new GE Capital units, yet each run by someone who reports directly to the chairman. Mr. Dammermn said that Mr. Immelt began talking about breaking GE Capital into more manageable pieces as soon as he took over as chief executive last September. "Jeff didn't like the extra layer between him and the GE Capital businesses,"

G. E. has tried to make GE Capital less mysterious to the outside world. Although GE Capital was officially one unit, it had begun to report quarterly results in five product-related segments—a number that will be reduced to four with the new organization. And analysts say GE Capital's management has been more accessible than it was in past years, and that Mr. Immelt and other G. E. corporate executives have been willing to discuss GE Capital in more depth.

57. After the reorganization, GE will have altogether ________.
   A) six businesses　　B) sixteen businesses
   C) four businesses　　D) fifteen businesses
58. Which of the following statements is NOT true of Dennis Dammerman?
   A) He is now a GE's vice chairman.
   B) He is expected to leave GE to start a new financial services firm.
   C) He was once the chairman of GE Capital.
   D) He regards the reorganization of GE as an initiative of its own.
59. All the following statements are False of Denis Nayden EXCEPT that ________.
   A) the reorganization makes him lose his position as a chairman
   B) he will remain for some time at GE as an analyst
   C) he is currently GE's chairman
   D) he is expected to start a new GE financial firm in the near future
60. The reorganization will enable GE's chief executive to ________.
   A) quiet down the unrest in the world
   B) work in a more friendly business environment
   C) have more direct contact with GE's financial services teams
   D) appear less mysterious to the outside world
61. The General Electric Capital ________.
   A) is divided into five product-related segments now
   B) provided more than 1/3 of GE's revenue last year
   C) is going to be broken into more businesses
   D) now has smaller units than all other businesses in GE

Part Ⅴ Cloze (15 minutes)

Directions: *There are 20 blanks in the following passage. For each blank there are four choices marked A), B), C) and D) on the right side of the paper. You should choose the ONE that best fits into the passage. Then mark the corresponding letter on Answer Sheet 2 with a single line through the center.*

We all know that a magician does not really depend on "magic" to perform his trick, __62__ on his ability to act at great speed. __63__, this does not prevent us from enjoying watching a magician __64__ rabbits from a hat. __65__ the greatest magician of all time was Harry Houdini who died in 1926. Houdini mastered the art of __66__. He could free himself from the tightest knots or the most complicated locks in seconds. __67__ no one really knows __68__ he did this, there is no doubt __69__ he had made a close study of every type of lock ever __70__. He liked to carry a small steel needle-like tool strapped to his leg and he used this in __71__ of a key. Houdini once asked the Chicago police to lock him in prison. They __72__ him in chains and locked him up, but he freed himself __73__ an instant. The police __74__ him of having used a tool and locked him up again. This time he wore no clothes and there were chains around his neck, waist, wrists, and legs; but he again escaped in a few minutes. Houdini had probably hidden his "needle" in a waxlike __75__ and dropped it on the floor in the passage. __76__ he went past, he stepped on it so that it stuck to the bottom of his foot. His most famous escape, however, was __77__ astonishing. He was heavily chained __78__ and enclosed in an empty wooden chest, the lid of __79__ was nailed down. The __80__ was dropped into the sea in New York harbor. In one minute Houdini had swum to the surface. When the chest was __81__, it was opened and the chains was found inside.

62. A) but B) then C) and D) however
63. A) Generally B) However C) Possibly D) Likewise
64. A) to produce B) who produces C) produce D) how to produce
65. A) Out of question B) Though C) Probably D) Undoubted
66. A) escaping B) locking C) opening D) dropping
67. A) Surprisingly B) Obviously C) Perhaps D) Although
68. A) when B) where C) how D) what
69. A) if B) whether C) as to D) that
70. A) invented B) invent C) being invented D) inventing
71. A) use B) place C) view D) absence
72. A) involved B) closed C) connected D) bound
73. A) at B) by C) in D) for
74. A) rid B) charged C) accused D) deprived
75. A) candle B) mud C) something D) substance
76. A) As B) Usually C) Maybe D) Then
77. A) overall B) all but C) no longer D) altogether

78. A) up B) down C) around D) in
79. A) it B) which C) that D) him
80. A) chest B) body C) lid D) chain
81. A) brought up B) sunk C) broken apart D) snapped

Part Ⅵ Translation (5 minutes)

Directions:

82. It is well-known that ______________(退休工人有资格享受免费的医疗).
83. Because his health is getting worse, ______________(他不得不克制自己以免饮酒过度).
84. Mike has never done anything against law, ______________(即使像打碎邻居家的窗户这样的小过错也都没有犯过).
85. The truth in question is that success in life depends chiefly on sustained efforts ______________(这种努力来源于对所选职业的一种深厚的兴趣).
86. But ability and patience do not account for all scientific discoveries which ______________(常常与创造性的想象力紧密相关).

参考答案(2)

Part Ⅰ Sample Writing

Reduce Waste on Campus

As is known to all, waste on campus has become a more and more serious problem. We can easily see many students dump a lot of food in the garbage can. Some students spend thousands of *yuan* buying fashionable clothes and so on.

The negative effects of waste can be shown in the following aspects. In the first place, it makes some students dependent on their parents for money, which is harmful to their development. If they don't learn to support themselves, they will be "useless people" when they graduate. In the second place, it is not easy for our parents to arrange for our schooling. Last but not the least important, there is no denying the fact that our country is still poor. There are many people who cannot go to university and many poor people still need our help.

As far as I am concerned, I should set a good example to reduce waste on campus. First of all, I will refrain from wasting anything, from food to stationery. What's more, I'm determined to call on more schoolmates to fight against waste. Only through these measures can we hope to reduce waste on campus.

Part Ⅱ Reading Comprehension (Skimming and Scanning)

1. Y 2. N 3. NG 4. Y

5. a member of the human species
6. male people only
7. a singular pronoun
8. men only
9. the incorrect grammar
10. the plural

Part Ⅲ　Listening Comprehension

Section A

11—15　BDCDC　16—20　ABBDB　21—25　DDCBA

Section B

26—30　DBCAB　31—35　CBACC

Section C

36. twentieth　37. pioneering　38. misguided　39. corresponding
40. position　41. scene　42. conventions　43. revolutionary
44. The close-up had been used before though only rarely and merely as a visual stunt
45. called After Many Years was the dramatic potential of the close-up exploited
46. This cutting from one scene to another without finishing either of them brought a torrent of criticism on the experiments

Part Ⅳ　Reading Comprehension (Reading in Depth)

Section A

47. exceed/are more than
48. well-prepared/better qualified
49. De-layering.
50. increasing/on the increase
51. The employers. /Employers.

Section B

52—56　CADCA　57—61　DBACB

Part Ⅴ　Cloze

62—66　ABCCA　67—71　DCDAB
72—76　DCCDA　77—81　DABAA

Part Ⅵ　Translation

82. retired workers are entitled to free medical care
83. he has to restrain himself from drinking too excessively
84. even for such a minor offense as breaking a window of his neighbor
85. springing out of a deep interest in one's chosen occupation

86. often have much to do with creative imagination

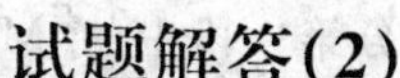

试题解答(2)

Part Ⅱ Reading Comprehension (Skimming and Scanning)

1. [Y] 根据"'Man'"部分第一段"Man once was a truly generic word referring to all humans, but has gradually narrowed in meaning to become a word that refers to adult male human beings. Anglo-Saxons used the word to refer to all people. One example of this occurs when an Anglo-Saxon writer refers to a seventh-century English princess as 'a wonderful man.'"可见,"man"这个词最初是泛指所有人的,到了17世纪还有作家把公主描述成"a wonderful man."。故此句判断为YES。
2. [N] 由"'Man'"部分第二段中的"By the 18th century, the modern, narrow sense of man was firmly established as the predominant one... Jefferson had to be using the word men in its principal sense of "males," and it probably never occurred to him that anyone would think otherwise."可知到了18世纪"man"这个词已经狭义指男性了。接着作者举了两个例子。第二个例子是杰斐逊的《独立宣言》。由于当时女性没有选举权,杰斐逊所用的"man"是专指男性的。故此句判断为NO。
3. [NG] 由"The Pronoun Problem"部分第二段最后一句"In 1879, for example, a move to admit female physicians to the all-male Massachusetts Medical Society was effectively blocked on the grounds that the society's by-laws describing membership used the pronoun he."可知拒绝女医生加入协会的原因是该协会的细则在描述其成员时用的是代词"he"。因此,原文只是说明了拒绝接纳女成员的原因,并没有提及多少人被拒之门外。故信息不充分。此句判断为NOT GIVEN。
4. [Y] 根据"The Pronoun Problem"部分第一段第一、二句"The first grammars of modern English were written in the 16th and 17th centuries. They were mainly intended to help boys from upper class families prepare for the study of Latin, a language most scholars considered superior to English."可知现代英语的语法最初写于16、17世纪,是为了上流社会家庭的男孩子学习拉丁语而写的。故此句判断为YES。
5. 由"'Man'"部分第一段第三句"Man paralleled the Latin word homo, 'a member of the human species,' not vir, 'an adult male of the species.'"。可知此题正确答案为"a member of the human species"。
6. 由"'Man'"部分第二段倒数第二句"Studies of college students and school children indicate that even when the broad definitions of 'man' and 'men' are taught, they tend to conjure up images of male people only."可见即使教学生了解了这两个词的广义含义是指泛指人,他们仍然还是只想到男性。故本题正确答案为"male people only"。
7. 由"The Pronoun Problem"部分第二段第一句"'He' started to be used as a generic pronoun by grammarians who were trying to change a long-established tradition of using 'they' as a singular pronoun."可知语法学家用"he"来作泛指代词是试图改变用"they"来作单数代词的传统。故此题正确答案为"a singular pronoun"。
8. 由"The Pronoun Problem"部分第三段第二句"Studies have confirmed that most people

understand 'he' to refer to men only."可见人们看到代词"he"想到的只是男性。故此题答案为"men only"。

9. 由"Solving the Pronoun Problem"部分第一段中的"Most people, when writing and speaking informally, rely on singular they as a matter of course... Some people are annoyed by the incorrect grammar that this solution necessitates, but this construction is used more and more frequently."可见人们经常把"they"用作单数代词来解决代词的性别歧视问题。尽管有人认为这种用法不合语法,但它的使用频率越来越高。故本题的正确答案是"the incorrect grammar"。

10. 由"Solving the Pronoun Problem"部分第三段中的"Pluralizing—A writer can often recast material in the plural. For instance, instead of 'As he advances in his program, the medical student has increasing opportunities for clinical work,' try 'As they advance in their program, medical students have increasing opportunities for clinical work.'"可见避免代词的性别歧视的另一个方法是用复数替代单数。故此句正确答案为"the plural"。

Part Ⅲ　Listening Comprehension(听力原文在光盘中)

Part Ⅳ　Reading Comprehension (Reading in Depth)

Section A

47. 第一段第一句说女性在应聘中、高管理职位的时候成功率比男性高。紧接着作者又补充了"But of course far fewer of them apply for these positions.",可见应聘中、高管理职位的女性要比男性少。这也是她们成功率高的原因之一。因此,应该填写的答案是"超过"的意思,可以填"cxceed"或者"are more than"。

48. 第二段在分析女性管理职位申请者成功率高的时候,提及"Women tend to research thoroughly before applying for positions or attending interviews.",可见在应聘或者面试前,女性会做充分而彻底的调研,以对公司和工作有所了解,使自己成为"exceptional candidate",因此女性比男性准备更充分。所以我们可以概括为"well-prepared"。另外,从第二段第三句"Dr. Marx said that when women apply for positions they tend to be **better qualified than** their male counterparts but are more selective and conservative in their job search."可见女性考虑周到、准备充分使自己更为合格。因此,我们也可以填写"better qualified"。

49. 第四段第一句说欧洲最近经济不景气,公司出现管理结构等级减少的特点。"de-layering"的意思和"layering"相反,是指公司在经济萧条的时候,精减原有的管理机构,使等级变少,人员减少。作者接着补充了"... this has halted progress for women in as much as de-layering has taken place either where women are working or in layers they aspire to."可见管理机构的精简使女性获得管理职位的希望变小了。因此,答案为"De-layering."。

50. 根据第四段最后一句"Sears also noted a positive trend from the recession, which has been the growing number of women who have started up on their own."可知 Sears 还注意到在萧条时期的一个积极的趋势:越来越多的女性自己开办企业。因此,正确答案是"increasing"或者含义相似的表达。

51. 由文章最后一句"Until there is a belief among employers, until they value the difference, nothing will change."可见要改变态度的是雇主们。因此,答案为"The employers. / Employers."。

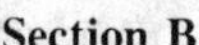

Section B

52. [C] 主旨题。文章第一段作者提出话题,苏联的根本性社会变革对女性的生活产生了深刻的影响。第二段作者描述了这些变化:女性获得了参与各种工作和受教育的同等机会,甚至进入了一些专业领域。第三段作者指出,女性在获得机会的同时也不得不付出巨大的代价。因此,纵观全文,作者既写到了变革带给女性的机会,也提到了她们面对的困难。故正确答案为C项。

53. [A] 词义推断题。第三段作者陈述了变革后女性面对的各种困境。女性参与工作导致工资水平下降。这又反过来迫使她们不得不出去工作,补充丈夫的收入来养家,但女性还得同时兼顾家庭。除此之外,在工作方面,男性继续垄断了好的工作机会。因此,这里和"monopolize"意思最为接近的是"hold",故答案为A项。

54. [D] 写作目的题。结合第一题主旨题可以看出作者写作此文不是为了娱乐读者(选项C),也不是在讲故事(选项B),更没有比较不同的政府体制(选项A),作者只陈述了苏联社会变革对女性的生活产生了深刻的影响,是属于提供信息,故答案为D项

55. [C] 文章基调(作者态度)题。作者既陈述了变革给女性带来的机会,也写到她们由此不得不做出的牺牲。因此,作者客观地提供信息,文章基调是客观的。故正确答案为C项。

56. [A] 推断题。文章第二段指出变革赋予女性和男性平等的权利。她们可以从事同样的工作,接受相同的教育,通过努力同样进入专业领域。尽管第三段提到她们由此也不得不付出很大的代价,但我们可以推断,和过去相比,女性的经济和社会地位还是有所提高的。故正确答案为A项。

57. [D] 文章第五段提到"the rest of G. E. had been divided into 11 other businesses",也就是除GE Capital之外共有11家公司。文章第一段指出GE Capital将被分成4家公司。因此,调整结构以后,GE共有15家公司。答案为D项。

58. [B] 第二段第二句指出Dennis Dammerman是GE的副总裁,曾在Nayden之前做过GE Capital的主席。因此,选项A和C都排除。第三段中,Dammerman否认GE的结构调整和外界的压力有关,因此选项D说结构调整是GE自己的主动性举措符合原文意思,可排除。而第二段的最后一句中明确陈述即将离开GE的是Nayden,故答案为B项。

59. [A] 根据文章第一段中的"The reorganization effectively eliminates the job of Denis J. Nayden, 48, the chairman of GE Capital."可知正确答案为A项。

60. [C] 第三段的最后一句"This is just what it appears to be, a managerial reorganization which gives leaders more direct access to the office of the chairman"指出了结构调整的目的是以主席为首的GE高层可以和GE Capital的管理者更直接有效地沟通。文章最后一段提到调整结果时再次出现了这一信息,即"And analysts say GE Capital's management has been more accessible than it was in past years",因此,答案为C项。

61. [B] 此题是关于GE Capital的细节信息题。文章第五段第一句"GE Capital, the company's largest nit, provided $55 billion of G. E.'s $124 billion in revenue last year and $5.6 billion of its $19.7 billion in pretax profits."提到去年GE Capital收入550亿美金占GE总收入1240亿的三分之一多。因此,正确答案为B项。

Part Ⅴ Cloze

62. 此题考点为not...but的句型搭配,表示"不是……而是",符合句意,因此答案为A项。

63. 根据上下文结构与句意,此处需要一个关联性的状语,而且根据句意需要一个表示转折意义的副词,故B项 However 为正确答案。Generally 意为"广泛地,普遍地,总的来说",可作评述性状语;Possibly 意为"可能地",也可作为评述性状语和一般修饰性状语;Likewise 意为"同样地,照样地",在句子中可作关联性的状语,但不是转折意义的。
64. 此题涉及某些感官动词,如:see, hear, watch, feel 等词后接宾语的用法。这些动词后可接复杂宾语结构,即 see, hear, watch, feel+sb. + do 或 see, hear, watch, feel+sb. +doing,因此正确答案为C项。
65. 通过上下文可知,此空需要一个副词,因此可以排除选项B和选项D。Out of the question 意为"不可能",不符合上下文语意。Probably 意为"很有可能地",用在此处表示作者比较肯定的猜测,故正确答案为C项。
66. 根据上下文可知,魔术家擅长"逃脱",他可以轻易地开锁,从被锁处脱逃。因此,正确答案为A项。
67. 通过阅读上下文可知此处需要一个引导让步状语从句的连词,只有选项D符合。
68. 本题考查考生对关联词程度的掌握。根据句意,此处应填入表示方式的关系词表示"如何",因此C项 how 符合句意,为正确答案。
69. 本题的同位语从句应用 that 引导,故正确答案为D项。
70. 本题考查过去分词的用法。过去分词 invented 为后置定语修饰前面的名词,表示以前发明的各种锁,因此,可排除选项B和选项D。选项C则表示过去分词的进行时,根据"... every type of lock ever",可排除。因此,正确答案为A项。
71. in place of 为固定搭配,表示"代替……位置",符合句意,故选B项。
72. bound 是 bind 的过去式,意为"捆绑"。其他三词意义不符,故正确答案为D项。
73. in an instant 是固定搭配,意为"立刻,马上",故正确答案为C项。
74. 四个选项中动词 charge 一般不与 of 搭配使用。rid...of 意为"除掉",不符句意。dcprive... of 意为"剥夺……",不符句意。C项 accuse 和 of 搭配意为"指控……"符合句意,故选C项。
75. mud 和 something 是不可数名词,不符句型结构;像 candle 是不合逻辑的;因此,只有D项 substance(物质)正确。
76. 通过阅读本句可断定此空需要一个从属连词引导时间状语,四个选项中只有A项 as 正确。
77. overall 是形容词,不能修饰形容词;all but 意为"几乎,差不多",不符句意;no longer 不符句意。只有 altogether(总体来说)符合上下文语意,故为正确答案。
78. 根据上下文意思,此句意为"他被铁链紧紧缚住并关进了一只空木箱"。在四个选项中,A项 chain sb./sth. up 表示"用链子等物束缚住某人或某物",符合句意,其他选项均不能与 chain 搭配,故选A项。
79. 只有 which 能用于介词后引导定语从句,故选B项。
80. 根据句意可知,此处就是上文中所指的 chest,故选A项。
81. 通过阅读上下文可知,Houdini 被装进木桶扔进了海里,但他很快就逃了出来,当木桶被捞上来时,人们发现木桶被打开了,捆在木桶外的铁链子却被放到了桶里面,由此可知此题应选A项 brought up,意为"把……弄上来"。

Part Ⅵ Translation

82. [答案]:retired workers are entitled to free medical care
[注释]:此句的翻译主要在于 be entitled to 句型的使用,表示"有资格,有权"。

83. [答案]:he has to restrain himself from drinking too excessively

[注释]:此句的翻译有两个难点,第一是“克制”,应使用 restrain... from 句型。第二个是“过度”,可用副词 excessively 来表达这一含义。

84. [答案]:even for such a minor offense as breaking a window of his neighbor

[注释]:此句的翻译首先要注意的是“such... as...”这个结构的使用。此外,“小过错”的翻译也许会出现像 small mistake 这样的错误译法。

85. [答案]:springing out of a deep interest in one's chosen occupation

[注释]:“来源于”的翻译是此句的一个难点。此外,除了使用现在分词来修饰中心词 efforts 之外,也可以使用定语从句来修饰 efforts。

86. [答案]:often have much to do with creative imagination

[注释]:本句关键在于“与……紧密相关”的翻译,可以简洁地翻译成 has much to do with。

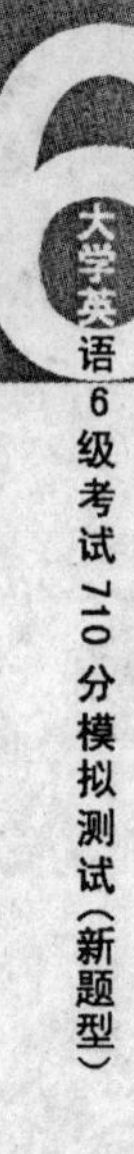

College English Practice Test 3 (Band Ⅵ)

Part Ⅰ Writing (30 minutes)

Directions: *For this part, you are allowed 30 minutes to write a composition on the topic **"Problems about Reducing Students' Heavy Burden"**. You should write at least **150** words, and base your composition on the outline (given in Chinese) below.*

1. 目前学生负担过重的现状；
2. 导致学生负担过重的原因；
3. 减轻学生负担过重的措施。

Part Ⅱ Reading Comprehension (Skimming and Scanning) (15 minutes)

Directions:（略）

Soichiro Honda

The founder of Honda, Soichiro Honda was a mechanical engineer with a passion for motorcycle and automobile racing. Honda started his company in 1946 by building motorized bicycles with small, war-surplus engines. Honda would grow to become the world's leading manufacturer of motorcycles and later one of the leading automakers. Following its founder's lead, Honda has always been a leader in technology, especially in the area of engine development.

Soichiro Honda was described as a *maverick*(特立独行的人) in a nation of conformists. He made it a point to wear loud suits and wildly colored shirts. An inventor by nature who often joined the work on the floors of his factories and research laboratories, Honda developed engines that transformed the motorcycle into a worldwide means of transportation.

Born in 1906, Honda grew up in the town of Tenryu, Japan. The eldest son of a blacksmith who repaired bicycles, the young Soichiro had only an elementary school education when, in his teens, he left home to seek his fortune in Tokyo. An auto repair company hired him in 1922, but for a year he was forced to serve as a baby-sitter for the auto shop's owner and his wife. While employed at the auto shop, however, Honda built his own racing car using an old aircraft engine and handmade parts and participated in racing. His racing career was short lived, however. He suffered serious injuries in a 1936 crash.

By 1937, Honda had recovered from his injuries. He established his own company, manufacturing piston rings, but he found that he lacked a basic knowledge of casting. To obtain it, he enrolled in a technical high school, applying theories as he learned them in the classrooms to his own factory. But he did not bother to take examinations at the school. Informed that he would not be graduated, Honda commented that a diploma was "worth less than a movie theater ticket. A ticket guarantees that you can get into the theater. But a diploma doesn't guarantee that you can make a living."

Honda's burgeoning company mass-produced metal propellers during WW Ⅱ, replacing wooden ones. Allied bombing and an earthquake destroyed most of his factory and he sold what was left to Toyota in 1945.

In 1946, he established the Honda Technical Research Institute to motorize bicycles with small, war-surplus engines. These bikes became very popular in Japan. The institute soon began making engines. Renamed Honda Motor in 1948, the company began manufacturing motorcycles. Business executive Takeo Fujisawa was hired to manage the company while Honda focused on engineering.

In 1951, Honda brought out the Dream Type E motorcycle, which proved an immediate success thanks to Honda's innovative overhead valve design. The smaller F-type cub (1952) accounted for 70% of Japan's motorcycle production by the end of that year. A public offering and support from Mitsubishi Bank allowed Honda to expand and begin exporting. The versatile C100 Super Cub, released in 1958, became an international bestseller.

In 1959, the American Honda Motor was founded and soon began using the slogan, "You meet the nicest people on a Honda," to offset the stereotype of motorcyclists during that period. Though the small bikes were dismissed by the dominant American and British manufacturers of the time, the inexpensive imports brought new riders into motorcycling and changed the industry forever in the United States.

Ever the racing enthusiast, Honda began entering his company's motorcycles in domestic Japanese races during the 1950s. In the mid-1950s, Honda declared that his company would someday win world championship events—a declaration that seemed unrealistic at the time.

In June 1959, the Honda racing team brought their first motorbike to compete in the Isle of Man Tourist Trophy race, then the world's most popular motorcycle race. This was the first entry by a Japanese team. With riders Naomi Taniguchi, who finished sixth, Teisuke Tanaka, who finished eighth, and Kiyoshi Kawashima, who would later succeed Soichiro as Honda Motor president, as team manager, Honda won the manufacturer's prize.

However, they were not pleased with their performance. Kawashima remembers: "We were clobbered. Our horsepower was less than half that of the winner."

Learning from this experience, Soichiro and his team worked even harder to make rapid progress in their motorsports activities. Two years after their first failure, they were the sensation at the TT by capturing the first five places in both the 125cc and 250cc classes. The upstart Japanese had outclassed all their rivals. As a result of the team's stellar performance, the Honda name became well known worldwide, and its export volume rose dramatically. Soichiro seemed to have foreseen the future of Japan, which, twenty years later, was to become one of the world's leading economies.

Honda would become the most successful manufacturer in all of motorcycle racing. Honda has since won hundreds of national and world championships in all forms of motorcycle

competition.

While Honda oversaw a worldwide company by the early-1970s (Honda entered the automobile market in 1967), he never shied away from getting his hands greasy. Sol Sanders, author of a Honda biography, said Honda appeared "almost daily" at the research lab where development work was being done. Even as president of the company, "he worked as one of the researchers," Sanders quoted a Honda engineer as saying. "Whenever we encountered a problem, he studied it along with us."

In 1973, Honda, at 67, retired on the 25th anniversary of Honda's founding. He declared his conviction that Honda should remain a youthful company. "Honda has always moved ahead of the times, and I attribute its success to the fact that the firm possesses dreams and youthfulness," Honda said at the time.

Unlike most chief executive officers in Japan, who step down to become chairmen of their firms, Honda retained only the title of "supreme adviser". In retirement, Honda devoted himself to public service and frequent travel abroad. He received the Order of the Sacred Treasure, first class, the highest honor bestowed by Japan's emperor. He also received the American auto industry's highest award when he was admitted to the Automotive Hall of Fame in 1989. Honda was awarded the AMA's highest honor, the Dud Perkins Award, in 1971.

Honda died on August 5, 1991 from liver failure at 84. His wife, Sachi, and three children survived him.

1. Soichiro Honda was a man who preferred to wear plain clothes.
2. When enrolled in a technical high school to obtain basic knowledge of casting, Soichiro Honda finally got the diploma after attending the examinations.
3. Like most chief executive officers in Japan, Soichiro Honda stepped down to become chairmen of Honda after his retirement.
4. Even as the president of a worldwide company, Soichiro Honda would work at the research lab with the employees.
5. Following its founder's lead, Honda has always been a leader in technology, especially in the area of ________.
6. After WW Ⅱ, Honda mounted ________ on bicycles and these motorized bicycles sold rapidly in Japan.
7. A public offering and support from ________ allowed Honda to expand his business and begin to invade the international market.
8. In 1959, the American Honda Motor used the slogan, "________" to change the negative image of motorcyclists in America.
9. In 1959 with their first motorbike Honda racing team participate in ________ race, which was the most popular motorcycle race at that time.
10. According to Honda, ________ are the major factors that led to the success of Honda company.

Part Ⅲ　Listening Comprehension　(35 minutes)

Section A

Directions:(略)

11. A) The class thought the demonstration was too complex.
    B) Too many students showed up.
    C) The professor didn't show up.
    D) The professor cancelled it.
12. A) Many guests didn't give a performance at the party.
    B) Many guests didn't show their faces. They are masks.
    C) The party wasn't held, because many guests didn't come.
    D) The party was held last night, but many guests didn't come.
13. A) She prefers the stadium.
    B) She agrees with the man.
    C) The light isn't bright enough.
    D) The dining hall isn't large enough.
14. A) Four contestants failed to win prizes.　B) The man ate during the show.
    C) The woman missed the show.　D) Five contestants won cars.
15. A) Riding a horse.　B) Shooting a movie.
    C) Playing a game.　D) Taking a photo.
16. A) She's going away for a while.
    B) She did well on the test.
    C) She worked hard and earned a lot of money.
    D) She's didn't have to work hard for the exam.
17. A) Susan is a fast worker.
    B) Susan did Jack's homework.
    C) Susan didn't do the homework on her own.
    D) Susan has not finished her homework.
18. A) He read the cabinet report.　B) He read the newspaper.
    C) He listened to a radio report.　D) He's secretary telephoned him.

Questions 19 to 22 are based on the conversation you have just heard.

19. A) He wants to finish his term paper that day.
    B) He has seen the film before.
    C) He has another appointment.
    D) He wants to go to the cinema with Yamada.
20. A) The rules are too hard to follow.
    B) The guests should give some presents to the hosts.
    C) Only tea is served at the tea ceremonies.

D) The food is not as important as the atmosphere in tea ceremonies.

21. A) Taking off his shoes. B) Washing his hands in a pool.
    C) Washing his hands in a stone basin. D) Bowing to the hosts.
22. A) In bamboo chairs. B) On bamboo mats.
    C) On the floor. D) On knees.

Questions 23 to 25 are based on the conversation you have just heard.

23. A) She had her vacation there. B) She took a diving course there.
    C) She was there on a field trip. D) She visited a marine exhibition.
24. A) She spent most of her time under the sea.
    B) She spent most of her time lying in the sun.
    C) She spent most of her time looking for sunken treasure.
    D) She spent most of her time taking photographs of the sea.
25. A) Planktons are too small to be seen.
    B) Most planktons have transparent tissues.
    C) Most planktons are practically invisible to predators.
    D) Planktons are fascinating organisms.

Section B

Directions:（略）

Passage One

Questions 26 to 28 are based on the passage you have just heard.

26. A) Because a headman had no legal authority.
    B) Because people didn't own land.
    C) Because there were no strict laws against homicide.
    D) Because there were limited resources.
27. A) A man who had a dispute with the man whose wife was stolen.
    B) A man who borrowed goods from the man whose wife was stolen.
    C) A man who wanted to be superior to the man whose wife was stolen.
    D) A man who was attracted by the beauty of a particular woman.
28. A) The lack of a real form of government structure.
    B) The creativeness of Eskimos.
    C) The excitement of a legal system with strict laws.
    D) The strong judicial powers of a headman.

Passage Two

Questions 29 to 31 are based on the passage you have just heard.

29. A) 1788. B) 1840. C) 1842. D) 1850.
30. A) European immigrants flooded into the city.
    B) More and more rushed there for gold.

C) It became a resting place for US soldiers.

D) The Darling Harbor redevelopment project boosted the expansion.

31. A) 7 years. B) 9 years.

C) 12 years. D) 16 years.

Passage Three

Questions 32 to 35 are based on the passage you have just heard.

32. A) They can easily learn quite long poems by heart.

B) They can remember long story by heart.

C) They can remember almost everything they have read.

D) They can remember things they have only read once.

33. A) Because they are too small to understand the rules.

B) Because they are absent-minded.

C) Because they have so little time for it.

D) Because they are not interested in it.

34. A) A camera. B) A film. C) Photo. D) Picture.

35. A) Time. B) Memory. C) Habit. D) Text-book.

Section C

Directions:(略)

Smoking means something different to various cultures. In (36) ________, many people smoke. In the winter, it is often (37) ________ to breathe in the cafes because of the tobacco (38) ________ in the air. In Romania, smoking is an (39) ________ social habit. Women, (40) ________, do not smoke on the street. The brand of (41) ________ a person smokes shows his/her (42) ________, especially if it is a foreign (43) ________.

In Latin American cultures, smoking is very common. (44) ____.

In parts of Asia, tobacco is used in wedding ceremonies and in religious offerings. It is also used in many kinds of occasions. In Cambodia, (45) ____. In Vietnam, people are often smoking at business meetings and in coffee houses. Most of the women in Cambodia and Vietnam tend not to smoke. But when they enter a friend's home, they may be given a tobacco leaf to chew on. During the war, Vietnamese soldiers would smoke to pass the time while waiting to go into battle. (46) ____.

Smoking was a comforting thing to do. In both Vietnam and Cambodia, people who were not smokers before the war, started to smoke during the war and became addicted.

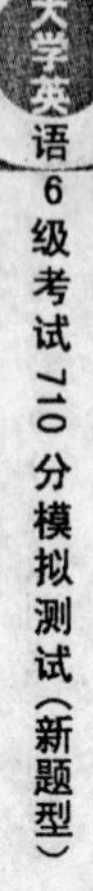

Part Ⅳ Reading Comprehension (Reading in Depth) (25 minutes)

Section A

Directions: (略)

Questions 47 to 51 are based on the following passage.

The discovery that language can be a barrier to communication is quickly made by all who travel, study, govern or sell. Whether the activity is tourism, research, government, policing, business or data dissemination, the lack of a common language can severely impede progress or can halt it altogether.

Although communication problems of this kind must happen thousands of times each day, very few become public knowledge. Publicity comes only when a failure to communicate has major consequences, such as strikes, lost orders, legal problems or fatal accidents—even, at times, war. One reported instance of communication failure took place in 1970, when several Americans ate a species of poisonous mushroom. No remedy was known, and two of the people died within days. A radio report of the case was heard by a chemist who knew of a treatment that had been successfully used in 1959 and published in 1963. Why had the American doctors not heard of it seven years later? Presumably because the report of the treatment had been published only in journals written in European languages other than English.

Several comparable cases have been reported. But isolated examples do not give an impression of the size of the problem—something that can come only from studies of the use or avoidance of foreign-language materials and contacts in different communicative situations. In the English-speaking scientific world, for example, surveys of books and documents consulted in libraries and other information agencies have shown that very little foreign-language material is ever consulted. Library requests in the field of science and technology showed that only 13 percent were for foreign language periodicals.

The language barrier presents itself in stark form to firms who wish to market their products in other countries. British industry, in particular, has in recent decades often been criticized for its linguistic insularity—for its assumption that foreign buyers will be happy to communicate in English, and that awareness of other languages is not therefore a priority. In the 1960s, over two-thirds of British firms dealing with non-English-speaking customers were using English for outgoing correspondence; many had their sales literature only in English; and as many as 40 percent employed no-one able to communicate in the customer's languages. A similar problem was identified in other English-speaking countries, notably the USA, Australia and New Zealand. And non-English speaking countries were by no means exempt—although the widespread use of English as an alternative language made them less open to the charge of insularity.

The criticism and publicity given to this problem since the 1960s seems to have greatly improved the situation. Industrial training schemes have promoted an increase in linguistic and cultural awareness. Many firms now have their own translation services. Some firms run part-time language courses in the languages of the countries with which they are most involved; some produce their own technical glossaries, to ensure consistency when material is being translated. It is now much more readily appreciated that marketing efforts can be delayed, damaged or disrupted by a failure to take account of the linguistic needs of the customer.

47. Language problems may come to the attention of the public when they have ________ such as fatal accidents or social problems.
48. What can we infer about American doctors from the case of the poisonous mushrooms?
49. Evidence of the extent of the language barrier can be gained from ________ of materials used by scientists such as books and periodicals.
50. An example of British linguistic insularity is the use of English for materials such as ________.
51. What ways have been used by the British companies to solve the problem of language barrier since the 1960s?

Section B

Directions:(略)

Passage One

Questions 52 to 56 are based on the following passage.

On the last shopping day before Christmas, stores across the United States were busy but not jam-packed as shoppers scrambled for last-minute gifts, even though some refused to admit it. At Boston's Copley Mall, a small crowd gathered outside the main entrance of luxury department store Neiman Marcus, but no one waiting for the store to open would admit to being a last-minute shopper. "I'm really here to use a gift certificate and get something for myself and maybe someone else with what's left over," said Matt Doran, who lives in Boston and had been waiting since 8:30 a. m. for the store's 10 a. m. opening. Ilya Polykoff, who moved to Boston from Russia, said he was waiting "because I had the day off and I wanted to get some perfume." But he insisted that he was really shopping early because for him Christmas comes in January. The Orthodox Christmas will be celebrated on Jan. 7.

"There are lots of men out there today," said Karen McDonald, a spokes-woman for mall operator Taubman Centers, after returning from the Lakeside Mall in Sterling Heights, Michigan. "There is panic out there but people seem to be in good spirits," she said, adding that most shopping traffic peaked around midday. According to the International Council of Shopping Centers, December 24 was the sixth busiest holiday shopping day in 1997, while 44 percent of holiday sales were recorded in the December15 to December 24 period. Ed Nally, manager of the Swatch Store known mostly for its brightly colored plastic watches, described the atmosphere as **festive** rather than crazed. He did say, however, that Dec. 21 was the turning point date, after which shoppers started. "The closer to Christmas, the crazier they get," Nally said. "They become more agitated, less patient." He said red-hot items this year were phones, beepers and the new digital swatch watch that costs $70 and came onto the market a week before Christmas.

52. The best title for this passage is ________.
    A) Last-Minute Christmas Shoppers Fill U. S. Stores
    B) Digital Watches Are the Red-hot Items This Year
    C) The Excuse of the Last-Minute Shoppers
    D) Christmas, the Best Shopping Season
53. From the passage we can infer that people would not admit to be a last-minute shopper because ________.
    A) they wanted to use a gift certificate
    B) Christmas would be celebrated on Jan. 7th
    C) they did not want gifts recipients to know that they bought them gifts on the last day
    D) they bought gifts during the shopping season lasting from December 15th to December 24th
54. Which of the following statement is true?
    A) Most customers came to the mall early in the morning.
    B) Shop assistants were most busy at noon.
    C) There were more shoppers in the mall from 7:00 to 9:00 p. m.
    D) Less people went shopping around midday.
55. Which of the following statement is NOT true?
    A) More people went shopping on Dec. 20th than on Dec. 22nd according to Ed Nally.
    B) On Dec. 24th, people were crowded outside Boston's Copley Mall, but they were happy.
    C) Dec. 24th was the sixth busiest holiday shopping day in 1997.
    D) One can buy brightly colored plastic watches in Swatch Store.
56. The word "festive" in paragraph 2 can not be understood as ________.
    A) cheery B) fetish C) joyous D) merry

Passage Two

Questions 57 to 61 are based on the following passage.

A few years ago, Ann and Walter Taylor thought it might be time to move out of their New York City apartment to the suburbs. They had one young son and another child on the way. But after months of looking, they became discouraged and decided to buy an old townhouse right in the middle of Brooklyn, which is a part of New York City. To their delight, they discovered that they weren't the only young couple to have made such a decision. In fact, the entire area in Brooklyn had been settled by young families. And as a result, the neighborhood, which had been declining for years, was now being restored.

Brooklyn isn't the only city in the United States to experience this kind of renewal. So are Philadelphia and St. Louis. And Charleston, South Carolina, has so successfully rebuilt its old central area that it now ranks as one of America's most charming cities. The restoration of the old port city of Savannah, Georgia, is also living proof that downtown areas do not need to die. But encouraging as these developments may be, they are among the few bright spots in a mass of difficulties that today's cities face. Indeed, their woes are so many that it is fair to ask whether or not the inner city, the core of most urban areas will manage to survive at all.

In the 1940s, urban Americans began a mass move to the suburbs in search of fresh air,

elbowroom, and privacy. Suburbs began to sprawl out across the countryside. Since most of those making the move were middle-class, they took with them the tax money the cities needed to maintain the neighborhoods in which they had lived. The people left in the cities were often those who were too old or too poor to move. Thus, many cities began to fall into disrepair. Crime began to soar, and public transportation was neglected. (In the past sixty years San Francisco is the only city in the United States to have completed a new mass transit system.) Meanwhile, housing construction costs continued to rise higher and higher. Middle-class housing was allowed to decay, and little new housing was constructed.

Eventually, many downtown areas existed for business only. During the day they would be filled with people working in offices, and at night they would be deserted. Given these circumstances, some business executives began asking, "Why bother with going downtown at all? Why not move the offices to the suburbs so that we can live and work in the same area?" Gradually, some of the larger companies began moving out of the cites, with the result that urban centers declined even further and the suburbs expanded still more. This movement of businesses to the suburbs is not confined to the United States. Businesses have also been moving to the suburbs in Stockholm, Sweden, in Bonn, Germany, and in Brussels, Belgium, as well.

But it may well be that this movement to the suburbs has reached its peak. Some people may be tired of spending long hours commuting, and they may have begun to miss the advantages of culture and companionship provided by city life. Perhaps the decision made by the Taylors is a sign that people will return to the cities and begin to restore them. It begins to look as if suburban sprawl may not have been the answer to man's need to create an ideal environment in which to live and work.

57. The author of the passage suggests that ________.
    A) moving to suburbs is not the answer to an ideal environment
    B) cities are likely to be replaced by the suburbs
    C) downtown areas are too crowded to live
    D) American people move a lot in history
58. The word "elbowroom" in Paragraph 3 most probably means "________".
    A) private space　　B) room to move freely
    C) peaceful places　　D) confined room
59. Which of the following statements is true?
    A) There are just old and poor people left in the cities.
    B) The movement to the suburbs begins to decline.
    C) Downtown areas must die in the future.
    D) Suburbs are sure to replace cities.
60. Why have businesses been moving to suburbs?
    A) Because the environment is pleasant in the suburbs.
    B) Because the suburbs have developed rapidly.
    C) Because rich people have moved to suburbs.
    D) Because many people work in cites and live in suburbs.

61. Many cities began to fall into disrepair in the 1940s because ________.
A) housing construction costs continued to rise
B) housing was allowed to decay
C) many people moved out of the cities
D) only old and poor people were left in the cities

Part Ⅴ Error Correction (15 minutes)

Directions:(略)

In the past, women tended to assume that they would be overtaken
by men in the race to the top. And, today's young women are far less 62. ________
philosophical about their status and are more aggressive in their 63. ________
resentment in being treated as in some way inferior than men. On the 64. ________
other hand, since lack of drive is one of the criticisms leveled with 65. ________
women, perhaps this aggression is a positive advantage. Some young
women, though, find it very difficult to come to term with the feeling that 66. ________
characteristics of authority which are acceptable in men are often not
acceptable in women. A reason often advanced for women fail to reach the 67. ________
top is their desire for balance between work and a life outside work.
Employers know this and tend, when a woman with young children
applies for promotion, treat the fact that she has young children as an 68. ________
important factor and, giving the choice, are more likely to give promotion 69. ________
to a man than to her.

What about women whose children are almost grown up? Well, the
writers of the study recommend a far much more positive approach to 70. ________
women who want to return to their careers before their children are off 71. ________
their hands.

Part Ⅵ Translation (5 minutes)

Directions:

72. Due to big floods in the south, ________________________
(中央政府不得不动用储备以渡过粮食危机).

73. Although my boss is very positive, ________________________
(我确信这项所谓的明智的决定,与预期相反,会带来严重的后果).

74. To their great astonishment, ________________________
(在调查中,他们发现了种种形式的腐败并揭露了许多贪污的官吏).

75. As the chief accountant, ________________________(玛丽的两难处境在于是把真相告诉老板还是让他蒙在鼓里而辜负他的信任).

76. We have every reason to believe Jason for ________________________
________(他是一位有经验的老师,知道如何将学生的最佳状态发挥出来).

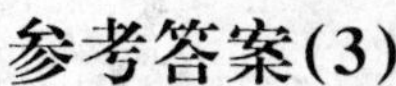

参考答案(3)

Part Ⅰ Sample Writing

Problems about Reducing Students' Heavy Burden

Nowadays, students' heavy burden makes them so nervous that it does harm to their health. It is not difficult to find out too many problems appearing in our society: some students give up studying, even kill themselves. Some other students go to kill their parents or their teachers because they can't bear any more.

The factors that lead to students' heavy burden are the following three: firstly, it is because of educational system. Such system forces students to learn too much complex but useless information. Secondly, schools only quest for higher rate of entering schools. In order to get higher rate, schools try their best to do more training so that students can't have their spare time. Thirdly, parents have good wishes. Parents do not want their children to fail in the future competition. They have no other way but to send their children to attend more training.

It becomes urgent to reduce students' heavy burden now. In my own opinion, it is important to change the educational system into high quality education system, to reduce the content of the training, to change the way of evaluating education quality, to change parents and society's attitude towards talents. All these are the basic ways that help reduce students' heavy burden.

Part Ⅱ Reading Comprehension (Skimming and Scanning)

1. N　　2. N　　3. N　　4. Y
5. engine development
6. small, war-surplus engines
7. Mitsubishi Bank
8. You meet the nicest people on a Honda.
9. the Isle of Man Tourist Trophy
10. dreams and youthfulness

Part Ⅲ Listening Comprehension

Section A

11—15 DDBCD　　16—20 BCBCD　　21—25 CBCAA

Section B

26—30 DCACA　　31—35 DACAB

Section C

36. France　　37. difficult　　38. smoke　　39. acceptable
40. however　　41. cigarette　　42. wealth　　43. brand
44. Some men think that smoking makes them looks more manly. As in other cultures, smoking is a way to socialize and belong
45. the bride lights her husband's cigarette to show her devotion to him

46. Cambodian men smoked when they took a break from working in the fields, to ease their hunger and to keep mosquitoes away

Part Ⅳ Reading Comprehension (Reading in Depth)

Section A

47. major consequences
48. They probably only read reports written in English.
49. surveys/ studies
50. sales literature/ outgoing correspondence
51. Industrial training schemes, translation services, part-time language courses and technical glossaries.

Section B

52—56 ACBAB 57—61 ABBDC

Part Ⅴ Error Correction

62. And → However/But
63. in → at
64. than → to
65. with → against
66. term → terms
67. fail →failing 或在 fail 之前插入 who
68. 在 treat 之前插入 to
69. giving → given
70. 删除 far 或 much
71. before → after

Part Ⅵ Translation

72. the central government had to draw on its reserves so as to pull through the food crisis
73. I'm convinced that, contrary to expectations, the so-called informed decision will bring grave consequences
74. in the course of their investigation, they discovered various forms of political corruption and exposed a number of corrupted officials
75. Mary's dilemma was whether to tell her boss the truth or to betray his trust by keeping him in the dark
76. he is an experienced teacher and knows how to bring out the best in his students

试题解答(3)

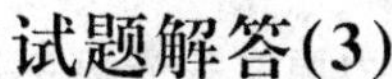

Part Ⅱ Reading Comprehension (Skimming and Scanning)

1. [N] 由第二段第一、二句"Soichiro Honda was described as a maverick in a nation of conformists. He made it a point to wear loud suits and wildly colored shirts."可知在强调顺从和一致的国度里,本田是个特立独行的人。他坚持穿花哨的西装,异常艳丽的衬衫。故本题判断为NO。
2. [N] 由第四段中后半部分"To obtain it, he enrolled in a technical high school, ... But he did not bother to take examinations at the school. Informed that he would not be graduated, Honda commented that a diploma was 'worth less than a movie theater ticket. A ticket guarantees that you can get into the theater. But a diploma doesn't guarantee that you can make a living'"。可见他不屑为了获得文凭而参加考试。故此题判断为NO。
3. [N] 由第十六段中的:"Unlike most chief executive officers in Japan, who step down to become chairmen of their firms, Honda retained only the title of 'supreme adviser'"判断此题为NO。
4. [Y] 由第十四段"While Honda oversaw a worldwide company by the early-1970s (Honda entered the automobile market in 1967), he never shied away from getting his hands greasy. ... Even as president of the company, 'he worked as one of the researchers,' Sanders quoted a Honda engineer as saying. 'Whenever we encountered a problem, he studied it along with us.'"可见本田从不摆架子,喜欢和职员一起在实验室解决技术问题。故此题判断为YES。
5. 由第一段最后一句"Following its founder's lead, Honda has always been a leader in technology, especially in the area of engine development."可见本田在引擎技术方面一直领先。故正确答案为"engine development"。
6. 由第六段第一、二句"In 1946, he established the Honda Technical Research Institute to motorize bicycles with small, war-surplus engines. These bikes became very popular in Japan."可本见田把战争剩下的小引擎装在自行车上。这种有了动力的自行车在日本很受欢迎。故本题答案为"small, war-surplus engines"。
7. 由第七段第三句"A public offering and support from Mitsubishi Bank allowed Honda to expand and begin exporting."可见三菱银行的支持使本田得以扩大发展并进军国际市场,开始出口。故本题答案为"Mitsubishi Bank"。
8. 由第八段第一句"In 1959, the American Honda Motor was founded and soon began using the slogan, 'You meet the nicest people on a Honda,' to offset the stereotype of motorcyclists during that period."可见本田公司用这样的一个口号去改变美国人对摩托车手的消极看法。故本题答案为"You meet the nicest people on a Honda."。
9. 由第十段第一句"In June 1959, the Honda racing team brought their first motorbike to compete in the Isle of Man Tourist Trophy race, then the world's most popular motorcycle race."可见本题正确答案为"the Isle of Man Tourist Trophy"。
10. 由第十五段第二句"'Honda has always moved ahead of the times, and I attribute its success to the fact that the firm possesses dreams and youthfulness,' Honda said at the time."可见本

田认为是梦想和朝气使本田公司一直领先于时代。故本题答案为"dreams and youthfulness"

Part Ⅲ Listening Comprehension(听力原文在光盘中)

Part Ⅳ Reading Comprehension (Reading in Depth)

Section A

47. 第二段第二句"Publicity comes only when a failure to communicate has major consequences, such as strikes, lost orders, legal problems or fatal accidents—even, at times, war."中的"Publicity"就是题目中的"come to the attention of the public",由此可见,当语言障碍导致"重大后果(major consequences)",如罢工等等社会问题或者致命的事故时,才会引起关注。因此,答案为"major consequences"。
48. 毒蘑菇事件是作者在第二段关于语言问题导致致命事故所举的例子。第二段最后一句作者讲道"Presumably because the report of the treatment had been published only in journals written in European languages other than English.",由此我们可以推断美国医生大概很少读用英语以外的语言所写的报道或论著。故答案为"They probably only read reports written in English"。
49. 第三段第二句"But isolated examples do not give an impression of the size of the problem—something that can come only from studies of the use or avoidance of foreign-language materials and contacts in different communicative situations."中的"size of the problem"就是指问题的严重程度,即题目中的"extent of the language barrier"。可见"研究"外语材料的使用情况可以帮助了解语言障碍问题的程度。由此,答案可以是"studies"。第三段第三句"In the English-speaking scientific world, for example, surveys of books and documents consulted in libraries and other information agencies have shown that very little forcign-language material is ever consulted."指出调查信息机构中书和文件的查阅情况可以知道对外语材料的查阅很少。可见"调查"这些材料的查阅情况可以获得证据。由此,答案也可以是"surveys"。
50. 由第四段第三句"In the 1960s, over two-thirds of British firms dealing with non-English-speaking customers were using English for outgoing correspondence; many had their sales literature only in English"可见他们用英语来写往来函件和产品说明、销售宣传这样的一些材料。由于题目只要求写出一个例子,所以答案可以是"sales literature"或者"outgoing correspondence"。
51. 文章最后一段提到了20世纪60年代以来英国的各家公司用于解决语言障碍问题的四种方法:"Industrial training schemes have promoted an increase in linguistic and cultural awareness. Many firms now have their own translation services. Some firms run part-time language courses in the languages of the countries with which they are most involved; some produce their own technical glossaries, to ensure consistency when material is being translated.",因此,答案为"Industrial training schemes, translation services, part-time language courses and technical glossaries."。

Section B

52. [A] 主旨题。第一段开始便提到,尽管是圣诞节前最后一天,人们却拒绝承认是 last-minute

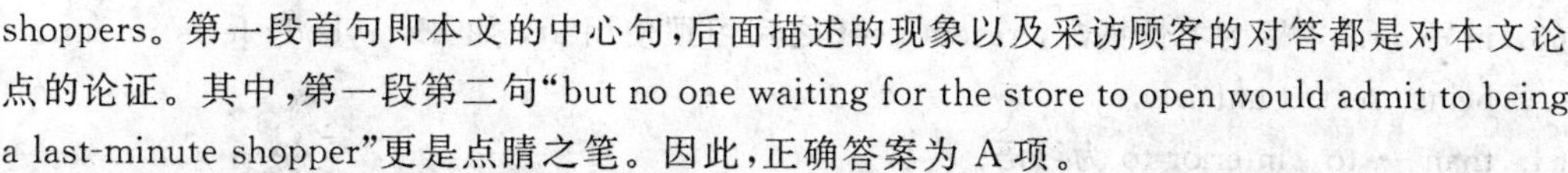

shoppers。第一段首句即本文的中心句,后面描述的现象以及采访顾客的对答都是对本文论点的论证。其中,第一段第二句"but no one waiting for the store to open would admit to being a last-minute shopper"更是点睛之笔。因此,正确答案为A项。

53. [C] 因果推断题。人们拒绝承认是last-minute shoppers是因为担心收到礼物的人认为该礼物是最后一刻才购买的,难免会让人失望。选项C文中并没有提及,但是按人之常情以及排除法可以断定正确答案为C项。其中,选项A是被采访的人不愿意承认的托词,选项B只是对来自俄罗斯的Polykoff说是如此。

54. [B] 细节判断题。由第二段第二句"most shopping traffic peaked around midday"可以判断选项A、选项C、选项D选项错误。因此,正确答案为B项。

55. [A] 细节判断题。第一段开篇提及"the last shopping day before Christmas",第二段第二句提及"people seem to be in good spirits",因此选项B是对的。第二段第三句"December 24 was the sixth busiest holiday shopping day in 1997",由此可以判断选项C也是正确的。文中最后谈及"brightly colored plastic watches in Swatch Store",由此断定选项D正确。因此,正确答案为A项。

56. [B] 词义推断题。圣诞节前的商店气氛"the atmosphere as festive",而不是crazed(疯狂的),可以推断出festive大约是"快乐的,节日的"的意思。文前还提到"people seem to be in good spirits",由此可以判断festive的意义相当于cheery, joyous, happy, merry。因此,正确答案为B项。

57. [A] 推断题。作者提到,过去人们大量移居郊区使得城市建设一度破落,商业区迁至郊区进一步加剧了城市的没落。但人们最终厌倦了每天在城市和郊区之间数小时的往返,开始怀念城市的文化生活,最终重新搬回城市。文章最后得出结论:向郊区迁移并不能为我们创建一个理想的工作和生活环境。因此,答案为A项。

58. [B] 词义推断题。结合上下文可以看出人们迁往郊区是为了改善工作和生活环境。第三段中提到的新鲜空气、个人的私密性和"elbowroom"都是城市没有而郊区拥有的。与郊区相比,城市的活动空间相对狭小,由此可以推断"elbowroom"是指自由活动的空间。因此,正确答案为B项。

59. [B] 细节题。第三段中提到"The people left in the cities were often those who were too old or too poor to move."但选项A说留下的只有(just)老人和穷人,太过于绝对,因而排除。由第二段第四句可知选项C错误。最后一段提到泰勒夫妇的决定表明人们最终将回到城市,重新建设城市,因此郊区不可能替代城市,故选项D也错误。因此,正确答案为B项。

60. [D] 细节题。第四段提到人们白天进城工作,晚上离城回家。因此有人提出"Why bother with going downtown at all? Why not move the offices to the suburbs so that we can live and work in the same area?"不如把商业也迁至郊区,省得人们两地奔波。故正确答案为D项。

61. [C] 细节题。从第三段第三、四、五句可知纳税人迁离城市使城市没有足够的资金去维护和建设,因而破败失修。因此正确答案为C项。

Part Ⅴ Error Correction

62. And → However/But。本文第一句话陈述了女性过去对于高层职位的态度,但第二句话话锋一转,一直到本文结束,作者摆出了当代女性对高层职位的态度"today's young women are far less philosophical about their statues and..."，这表明女性的态度发生了转变,因此使用表示转折的关联词才符合上下文语境。

63. in → at。本题为习惯搭配。resentment 之后习惯使用 at，如：Everybody feels resentment at being treated unfairly.
64. than → to。inferior to 为习语。
65. with → against。level against sb. 意指"对某人提出的批评/控告"，与上下文意义吻合。
66. term → terms。习语 come to terms (with) 意为"达成协议，妥协"，如，They came to terms after long bargaining. 他们经过长时间的讨价还价之后达成了协议。
67. fail →failing 或在 fail 之前插入 who。现在分词短语或定语从句修饰 women。
68. 在 treat 之前插入 to。与谓语动词 tend 构成不定式，后接宾语 treat the fact that she has young children as an important factor。
69. giving → given。根据上下文 given 此处有 granting or assuming that one has，表示"假定，倘若"，如：Given good health，I hope to finish the work this year. 假如身体健康，我希望今年完成这工作。
70. 删除 far 或 more。只需要其中之一修饰 more positive 即可。
71. before → after。根据上下文，其逻辑关系应为表达"当她们的孩子成年后"。

Part Ⅵ Translation

72. [答案]：the central government had to draw on its reserves so as to pull through the food crisis
[注释]：此句关键在于"动用"和"渡过"两个谓语动词的翻译。"动用"应使用词组 draw on 来表示；而"渡过"则应该使用 pull through 来表示。
73. [答案]：I'm convinced that，contrary to expectations，the so-called informed decision will bring grave consequences
[注释]：此句的翻译关键之一是 I'm convinced that... 句型。此外"明智的决定"既可以翻译为 informed decision 也可以翻译为 wise decision。"严重的后果"中"严重"既可以用 grave 来表达，也可以用 severe 或 serious 表示。
74. [答案]：in the course of their investigation，they discovered various forms of political corruption and exposed a number of corrupted officials
[注释]：本句是并列句，句子结构简单。此句的翻译主要在于两个谓语动词"发现"和"揭露"，可译为 discover 和 expose。
75. [答案]：Mary's dilemma was whether to tell her boss the truth or to betray his trust by keeping him in the dark
[注释]：本句第一是考查"两难处境"的翻译，应为 dilemma；其次是 whether to... or to... 句型的使用；再次，是"蒙在鼓里"的翻译，为固定表达，keep sb. in the dark。
76. [答案]：he is an experienced teacher and knows how to bring out the best in his students
[注释]：本句翻译的重点在于"将……最佳状态发挥出来"，也就是句型 bring out the best in...。

College English Practice Test 4 (Band Ⅵ)

Part Ⅰ Writing (30 minutes)

Directions: *In this part, you are allowed 30 minutes to write a short essay entitled* ***An Eye-witness Account of a Traffic Accident****. You should write at least* ***150*** *words following the outline given below.*

1. 车祸发生的时间及地点;
2. 你所见到的车祸情况;
3. 你对车祸原因的分析。

Part Ⅱ Reading Comprehension (Skimming and Scanning) (15 minutes)

Directions: (略)

A Brief History of Clock

Clocks

At best, historians know that 5,000-6,000 years ago, great civilizations in the Middle East and North Africa started to examine forms of clock-making instead of working with only the monthly and annual calendar. Little is known on exactly how these forms worked or indeed the actual deconstruction of the time, but it has been suggested that the intention was to maximize time available to achieve more as the size of the population grew. Perhaps such future periods of time were intended to benefit the community by allotting specific lengths of time to tasks. Was this the beginning of the working week?

Sun Clocks

With the disappearance of any ancient civilization, such as the Sumerian culture, knowledge is also lost. Whilst we can only hypothesize on the reasons of why the equivalent to the modern wristwatch was never completed, we know that the ancient Egyptians were next to layout a system of dividing the day into parts, similar to hours.

"Obelisks" (tall four-sided tapered monuments) were carefully constructed and even purposefully geographically located around 3500 BC. A shadow was cast as the Sun moved across the sky by the obelisk, which it appears was then marked out in sections, allowing people to clearly see the two halves of the day. Some of the sections have also been found to indicate the

"year"s longest and shortest days, which it is thought were developments added later to allow identification of other important time subdivisions.

Another ancient Egyptian "shadow clock" or "sundial" has been discovered to have been in use around 1500 BC, which allowed the measuring of the passage of "hours". The sections were divided into ten parts, with two "twilight hours" indicated, occurring in the morning and the evening. For it to work successfully then at midday or noon, the device had to be turned 180 degrees to measure the afternoon hours.

Water Clocks

"Water clocks" were among the earliest time keeping devices that didn't use the observation of the celestial bodies to calculate the passage of time. The ancient Greeks, it is believed, began using water clocks around 325 BC. Most of these clocks were used to determine the hours of the night, but may have also been used during daylight. An inherent problem with the water clock was that they were not totally accurate, as the system of measurement was based on the flow of water either into, or out of, a container which had markers around the sides. Another very similar form was that of a bowl that sank during a period as it was filled of water from a regulated flow. It is known that water clocks were common across the Middle East, and that these were still being used in North Africa during the early part of the twentieth-century.

Mechanical Clocks

In 1656, "Christian Huygens" (Dutch scientist), made the first "*Pendulum*(钟摆) clock", with a mechanism using a "natural" period of *oscillation*(振幅). "Galileo Galilei" is credited, in most historical books, for inventing the pendulum as early as 1582, but his design was not built before his death. Huygens' clock, when built, had an error of "less than only one minute a day". This was a massive leap in the development of maintaining accuracy, as this had previously never been achieved. Later refinements to the pendulum clock reduced this margin of error to "less than 10 seconds a day".

The mechanical clock continued to develop until they achieved an accuracy of "a hundredth-of-a-second a day", when the pendulum clock became the accepted standard in most astronomical observatories.

Quartz Clocks

The running of a "Quartz clock" is based on the piezoelectric property of the quartz crystal. When an electric field is applied to a quartz crystal, it actually changes the shape of the crystal itself. If you then squeeze it or bend it, an electric field is generated. When placed in an appropriate electronic circuit, this interaction between the mechanical stress and the electrical field causes the crystal to vibrate, generating a constant electric signal which can then be used for example on an electronic clock display. The first wrist-watches that appeared in mass production used "LED", "Light Emitting Diode" displays. By the 1970's these were to be replaced by a "LCD", "Liquid Crystal Display".

Quartz clocks continue to dominate the market because of the accuracy and reliability of the

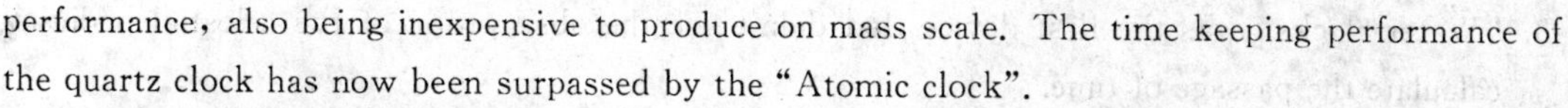

performance, also being inexpensive to produce on mass scale. The time keeping performance of the quartz clock has now been surpassed by the "Atomic clock".

Atomic Clocks

Scientists discovered some time ago that atoms and molecules have "resonances" and that each chemical element and compound absorbs and emits "electromagnetic radiation" within its own characteristic "frequencies". This we are told is highly accurate even over "Time and Space".

The development of radar and the subsequent experimentation with high frequency radio communications during the 1930s and 1940s created a vast amount of knowledge regarding "electromagnetic waves", also known as "microwaves", which interact with the atoms. The development of atomic clocks focused firstly on microwave resonances in the chemical Ammonia and its molecules. In 1957, "NIST", the "National Institute of Standards and Technology", completed a series of tests using a "Cesium Atomic Beam" device, followed by a second program of experiments by NIST in order to have something for comparison when working at the atomic level. By 1960, as the outcome of the programs, "Cesium Time Standards" were incorporated as the official time keeping system at NIST.

The "Natural frequency" recognized currently is the measurement of time, used by all scientists, defines the period of "one second" as exactly "9,192,631,770 Oscillations" or "9,192,631,770 Cycles of the Cesium Atom's Resonant Frequency". From the "Macrocosm", or "Planetary Alignment", to the "Microcosm", or "Atomic Frequency", the cesium now maintains accuracy with a degree of error to about "one-millionth of a second per year".

Much of modern life has come to depend on such precise measurements of time. The day is long past when we could get by with a *timepiece*(钟) accurate to the nearest quarter hour. Transportation, financial markets, communication, manufacturing, electric power and many other technologies have become dependent on super-accurate clocks. Scientific research and the demands of modern technology continue to drive our search for ever more accuracy. The next generation of Cesium Time Standards is presently under development at NIST's "Boulder Laboratory" and other laboratories around the world.

Something to Remember

The only thing that should be remembered during all this technological development is that we should never lose the ability to tell the time approximately by natural means and the powers of deduction without requiring *crutches*(拐杖) to lean on.

Our concept of TIME and using it together with TECHNOLOGY still has room for radical re-assessment in terms of man's evolutionary thinking regarding our view of the past, our onward journey into the future and our concept of time in relationship to universe.

1. It is suggested that 5,000-6,000 years ago people in the Middle East and North Africa started to allot specific lengths of time to tasks.
2. Ancient Egyptian "shadow clock" or "sundial" discovered around 1500 BC, could measure passage of "hours" automatically and continuously.

3. "Water clocks" was the first device that didn't use the observation of the celestial bodies to calculate the passage of time.
4. Galileo Galilei built the first "pendulum clock" as early as 1656.
5. Water clocks were mostly used to determine ________.
6. Huygens' clock, a mechanical one, had an error of "less than only one minute a day", which was a massive leap in the development of ________.
7. Since Quartz clocks are both inexpensive to produce in mass scale and ________ in performance, they continue to dominate the market.
8. Scientific research and the ________ continue to drive our search for ever more accuracy in time.
9. Of all the clocks introduced in the passage, the one with the most accuracy is ________.
10. No matter how advanced the technology of measuring time will be we should never lose the ability to tell the time approximately by ________.

Part Ⅲ Listening Comprehension (35 minutes)

Section A

Directions:(略)

11. A) The transportation far the trip is free.
    B) The class didn't enjoy going on the field trip.
    C) Some people may not go on the trip.
    D) All of the class members have paid the fee.
12. A) Take a lot of money.
    B) Go to a different restaurant.
    C) Don't invite John.
    D) Wear different clothes.
13. A) They didn't have a good talk.
    B) They decided to go by plane.
    C) They weren't able to take a walk.
    D) They talked about geology.
14. A) She doesn't need an umbrella.
    B) She left her umbrella in the car.
    C) She can hold her umbrella over the man's head.
    D) She's the only one who doesn't have an umbrella.
15. A) He would send a postcard if he went away.
    B) He would be able to take a vacation.
    C) He had already gone back to work.
    D) He didn't want to go to Florida.
16. A) The man wants to move to San Francisco, but the woman doesn't agree.
    B) The man thinks it's too cold to move to San Francisco.
    C) The woman agrees with the man's idea.
    D) The woman doesn't want to move because the children will have no fun.
17. A) To go to the movies.
    B) To go out for lunch.

C) To look in the newspaper. D) To ask for information.

18. A) Study in a quiet place.
 B) Improve her grades gradually.
 C) Change the conditions of her dorm.
 D) Avoid distractions while studying in her dorm.

Questions 19 to 22 are based on the conversation you have just heard.

19. A) At an accommodation office. B) At a swimming school.
 C) At a summer school. D) At Oxford.
20. A) The whole summer. B) Twenty-three hours.
 C) Twelve days. D) Three weeks.
21. A) 3 July. B) 20 July.
 C) 24 July. D) 10 August.
22. A) A dormitory at school.
 B) Living with a British family.
 C) Sharing a house with other students.
 D) Staying in a small inn with bed and breakfast.

Questions 23 to 25 are based on the conversation you have just heard.

23. A) She bought a new car. B) She was injured in an accident.
 C) She went out with David. D) She had a little accident.
24. A) She got engaged. B) She had a party.
 C) She got married. D) She was hurt.
25. A) Because church wedding is romantic. B) Because Diana is a catholic.
 C) Because her parents ask her to do so. D) Because David likes church wedding.

Section B

Directions:(略)

Passage One

Questions 26 to 28 are based on the passage you have just heard.

26. A) $600,000. B) $4,000,000.
 C) $5,000,000. D) $5,000,000,000.
27. A) Because he was famous for his view to keep the Union by force.
 B) Because he was famous for his anti-slavery views.
 C) Because he was famous for his democratic views.
 D) Because he was famous for his view to develop economy.
28. A) The Battle in South Carolina. B) The Battle in northern Pennsylvania.
 C) The Battle in Gettysburg. D) The Battle in North Carolina.

Passage Two

Questions 29 to 31 are based on the passage you have just heard.

29. A) From the place where the agreement was signed.
    B) From the people who signed the agreement.
    C) From the significance it tried to find in the international finance system.
    D) None of the above.
30. A) To lower their exchange rates.
    B) To regulate their exchange rates.
    C) To raise their regulated rates.
    D) To make no change of their rates.
31. A) Some developed countries.
    B) Countries that wanted to borrow money.
    C) All the member countries.
    D) The World Bank.

Passage Three

Questions 32 to 35 are based on the passage you have just heard.

32. A) A driver's license. B) A passport.
    C) An international credit card. D) A deposit.
33. A) Turning right at a red light.
    B) Driving in freeways without a local driver's license.
    C) Passing a school bus that is letting off children.
    D) All of the above.
34. A) The size of the country.
    B) Large areas of virgin forest.
    C) The rich natural resources of the land.
    D) Wild animals and plants.
35. A) Because nearly 1,000 million acres of land was burned off.
    B) Because natural resources are being used up.
    C) Because animals and plants are in danger of extinction.
    D) Because natural beauty of the land would be ruined.

Section C

Directions:(略)

The International Olympic Committee chose a doctor from Belgium as its (36) ________. Jacques Rogge will serve at least eight years. He replaced Juan Antonio Samaranch of Spain who served as president for (37) ________ years.

Doctor Rogge received support from more than half the (38) ________ in a second vote during a meeting in Moscow. He has worked for many years with the International Olympic Committee. He is fifty-nine years old.

Observers called the (39) ________ of Doctor Rogge a move to reform the worldwide sports organization. The new president says he will place great importance on preventing Olympic competitors from using (40) ________ drugs. Experts say his long record of (41) ________ may help the Olympics recover from charges of (42) ________ actions.

The (43) ________ are linked to the winter games of 2002. Ten Olympic Committee members reportedly accepted gifts and large amounts of money to choose Salt Lake City to hold the events. (44) ____. Earlier this week, a federal judge dismissed four of fifteen charges against two men who led Salt Lake City's campaign to get the Olympics. The judge also postponed their trial.

(45) ____. Jacques Rogge is a champion sailor who competed in three Olympic sailing events, the last in 1976. He has been a member of the International Olympic Committee for ten years. Doctor Rogge had a major responsibility for plans for the 2000 Olympics in Sydney, Australia. (46) ____.

Part Ⅳ Reading Comprehension(Reading in Depth) (25 minutes)

Section A

Directions:(略)

Questions 47 to 51 are based on the following passage.

One of London Zoo's recent advertisements caused me some irritation, so patently did it distort reality. Headlined "Without zoos you might as well tell these animals to get stuffed", it was bordered with illustrations of several endangered species and went on to extol the myth that without zoos like London Zoo these animals "will almost certainly disappear forever". With the zoo world's rather mediocre record on conservation, one might be forgiven for being slightly skeptical about such an advertisement.

Zoos were originally created as places of entertainment, and their suggested involvement with conservation didn't seriously arise until about 30 years ago, when the Zoological Society of London held the first formal international meeting on the subject. Eight years later, a series of world conferences took place, entitled "The Breeding of the Endangered Species", and from this point onwards conservation became the zoo community's buzzword. This commitment has now been clearly defined in *The World Zoo Conservation Strategy* (WZCS, 1993), which does seem to be based on an unrealistic optimism about the nature of the zoo industry.

The WZCS estimates that there are about 10,000 zoos in the world, of which around 1,000 represent a core of quality collections capable of participating in coordinated conservation programs. This is probably the document's first failing, as I believe that 10,000 is a serious underestimate of the total number of places masquerading as zoological establishments.

The second flaw in the reasoning of the WZCS document is the naïve faith it place in its 1,000 core zoos. One would assume that the caliber of these institutions would have been carefully examined, but it appears that the criterion for inclusion on this select list might merely be that the

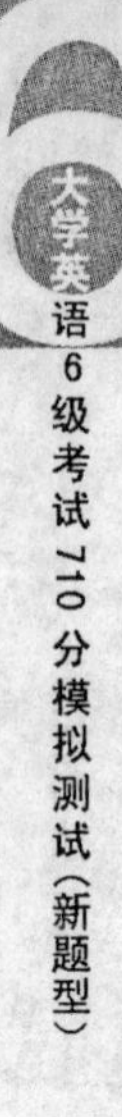

zoo is a member of a zoo federation or association. This might be a good starting point, working on the premise that members must meet certain standards, but again the facts don't support the theory.

Even assuming that the 1,000 core zoos of the WZCS are all of a high standard, what might be the potential for conservation? Colin Tudge, author of *Last Animals at the Zoo* argues that if the world's zoos worked together in cooperative breeding programs they could save around 2,000 species of endangered land vertebrates. This seems an extremely optimistic proposition from a man who must be aware of the failings and weaknesses of the zoo industry. Moreover, where are the facts to support such optimism?

Today approximately 16 species might be said to have been "saved" by captive breeding programs, although a number of these can hardly be looked upon as resounding successes. Beyond that, about a further 20 species are being seriously considered for zoo conservation programs. Given that the international conference at London Zoo was held 30 years ago, this is pretty slow progress, and a long way off Tudge's target of 2,000.

47. Zoos made an insignificant contribution to conservation up until ________ years ago.
48. According to the writer, one of WZCS's failings is it ________ the number of zoos in the world.
49. In accordance with WZCS, what kind of zoos can participate in the international coordinated conservation programs?
50. The writer doubts the value of the WZCS document partly because of its failure to examine the ________ of the "core zoos".
51. What word best describes the writer's response to Colin Tudge's prediction on captive breeding programs?

Section B

Directions:(略)

Passage One

Questions 52 to 56 are based on the following passage.

U. S. college students are increasingly burdened with credit card debt, according to a study released Tuesday, and the consequences can be serious—ranging from higher drop-out rates to future employment problems and even suicide.

Based on hundreds of face-to-face interviews and surveys with students, sociologist Robert Manning of Georgetown University concluded both the number with credit card debt and their indebtedness had been "systematically underreported" in previous studies—which failed to reflect the "survival strategies" many used to cope with their debts. These included the use of federal student loans to pay off credit cards, effectively shifting the debt, appeals to parents for loans, cutting back on course work to increase time at paid jobs, or even dropping out altogether to work full time. "Official drop-out rates include growing numbers of students who are unable to cope with the stress of their debts and/or part time jobs for servicing their credit cards," the study said.

Even then, debts can haunt students. "Student credit card debts are increasingly scrutinized during the recruitment process and may be an important factor in evaluating prospective employee," it noted. And the stress can also manifest in far more tragic ways. Janne O'Donnell's 22-year-old son, a junior at the University of Oklahoma, committed O'Donnell and Manning agreed students should bear some responsibility for reckless use of credit, but said credit card companies also had to be held accountable for making it so easy for them to get into debt. Manning said one of the most disturbing aspects of the student credit card issue was "the seduction of college and university administrators by the credit card industry." Card issuers were sponsoring school programs, funding activities and even entering into business partnerships with schools involving college-branded "affinity" cards, he said. "As a result, rather than protecting the economic and educational interests of their students, college administrators are playing an active and often disingenuous role in promoting the prominence of credit cards in collegiate life."

52. Which is NOT one of the strategies American students may use to deal with their credit card debt?
    A) Use federal student loans.
    B) Seek part-time jobs to get money.
    C) Promote the prominence of credit cards.
    D) Ask parents to help them pay the debt.
53. Which may NOT be the consequence of students' credit card debt?
    A) High drop-out rates.
    B) Enter into business partnerships with schools.
    C) Commit suicide.
    D) Future employment problems.
54. Who should be least criticized for negative consequences of students' credit card debt according to the passage?
    A) Parents.
    B) Students themselves.
    C) College and university administrators.
    D) Credit card issuers.
55. The main idea of this passage is ________.
    A) negative consequences of students' using credit card
    B) college administrators are playing their proper roles in promoting credit cards
    C) card issuers or college administrators promoted credit card
    D) reasons for high drop-out rates in universities
56. We can infer from the passage that ________.
    A) students should not have part-time jobs
    B) credit cards should not be used
    C) if there is no credit card, college students may not commit suicide

D) college students should learn to wisely manage their personal finances

Passage Two

Questions 57 to 61 are based on the following passage.

The estimates of the numbers of home-schooled children vary widely. The U. S. Department of Education estimates there are 250,000 to 350,000 home-schooled children in the country. Home school advocates put the number much higher—at about a million.

Home school advocates take a harsh attitude toward home schoolers, perceiving their actions as the ultimate slap in the face for public education and a damaging move for the children. Home schoolers harbor few kind words for public schools, charging shortcomings that range from lack of religious perspective in the curriculum to a herdlike approach to teaching children.

Yet, as public school officials realize they stand little to gain by remaining hostile to the home school population, and as home schoolers realize they can reap benefits from public schools, these hard lines seem to be softening a bit.

Public schools and home schoolers have moved closer to tolerance and, in some cases even cooperation. Says John Marshall, an education official, " we are becoming relatively tolerant of home schoolers. The idea is, let's give the kids access to public school so they'll see it's not as terrible as they've been told, and they'll want to come back. " Perhaps, but don't count on it, say home school advocates.

Home schoolers oppose the system because they have strong convictions that their approach to education—whether fueled by religious enthusiasm or the individual child's interest and natural pace—is the best. "The bulk of home schoolers just want to be left alone." Says Enge Cannon, associate director of the National Center For Home Education. She says home schoolers choose that path for a variety of reasons, but religion plays a role 85 percent of the time.

. Professor Van Galen breaks home schoolers into two groups. Some home schoolers want their children to learn not only traditional subject matter but also "strict religious doctrine and a conservative political and social perspective". Not incidentally, they also want their children to learn—both intellectually and emotionally—that the family is the most important institution in society." Other home schoolers contend "not so much that the schools teach heresy, but that schools teach whatever they teach inappropriately." Van Galen writes. "These parents are highly independent and strive to take responsibility for their own lives within a society that they define as bureaucratic and inefficient.

57. Which of the following statements is true?
    A) Home schoolers engage private teachers to provide additional education for their children.
    B) Home schoolers don't go to school but are educated at home by their parents.
    C) Home schoolers educate their children at home instead of sending them to school.
    D) Home schoolers advocate combining public education with home schooling.
58. Public schools are softening their position on home schooling because ________.
    A) they want to show their tolerance for different teaching systems
    B) there isn't much they can do to change the present situation

C) public schools have so many problems that they cannot offer proper education for all children

D) home schooling provides a new variety of education for children

59. Most home schoolers' opposition to public education stems from their ________.

A) concern with the cost involved

B) worry about the inefficiency of public schools

C) devotion to religion

D) respect fro the interests of individuals

60. From the passage we know that home school advocates think that ________.

A) home schooling is superior and therefore they will not easily give in

B) their increased cooperation with public school will bring about the improvement of public education

C) things in public schools are not so bad as has often been said

D) their tolerance of public education will attract more kids to public schools

61. It can be concluded from Van Galen's research that some home schoolers believe that ________.

A) teachers in public schools are not as responsible as they should be

B) public schools take up a herdlike approach to teaching children

C) public schools are the source of bureaucracy and inefficiency in modern society

D) public schools cannot provide education that is good enough for their children

Part Ⅴ Cloze

Directions:(略)

Every profession or trade, every art, and every science has its technical vocabulary, the function of __62__ is partly to __63__ things or processes with no names in ordinary English, and partly to secure greater exactness in terminology. __64__, they save time, for it is much more __65__, to name a process than to describe it. Thousands of these technical terms are very __66__ included in every large dictionary, yet, as a whole, they are rather __67__ the outskirts of the English language than actually within its borders.

Different occupations, however, differ __68__ in their special vocabularies. It __69__ largely of native words, or of borrowed words that have __70__ themselves into the very fiber of our language. __71__, though highly technical in many details, these vocabularies are more familiar in sound, and more generally __72__, than most other technical terms. __73__ every vocation still possesses a large __74__ of technical terms that remain essentially foreign, even __75__ educated people. And the proportion has been much __76__ in the last fifty years. Most of the newly __77__ terms are __78__ to special discussion, and seldom get into general literature or conversation. Yet no profession is nowadays, as all professions once __79__, a close federation. What is called "popular science" makes everybody __80__ with modern view and recent discoveries. Any important experiment , __81__ made in a remote or provincial laboratory, is at once reported in the newspaper, and everybody is soon talking about it. Thus our common speech is always taking up new technical terms and making them commonplace.

	A	B	C	D
62.	A) which	B) what	C) who	D) whom
63.	A) describe	B) talk about	C) designate	D) indicate
64.	A) Consequently	B) In contrast	C) However	D) Besides
65.	A) economical	B) economic	C) thrift	D) economized
66.	A) properly	B) possibly	C) probably	D) potentially
67.	A) in	B) on	C) at	D) beyond
68.	A) largely	B) widely	C) generally	D) extensively
69.	A) constitutes	B) comprises	C) composes	D) consists
70.	A) worked	B) made	C) taken	D) brought
71.	A) However	B) Because	C) Hence	D) In addition
72.	A) understood	B) considered	C) known	D) thought
73.	A) Therefore	B) Yet	C) In contrast	D) So
74.	A) series	B) body	C) set	D) range
75.	A) for	B) as	C) to	D) among
76.	A) decreased	B) diminished	C) increasing	D) increased
77.	A) made	B) coined	C) produced	D) formed
78.	A) related	B) addressing	C) confined	D) connected
79.	A) is	B) are	C) was	D) were
80.	A) associated	B) known	C) acquainted	D) connected
81.	A) though	B) when	C) as	D) since

Part Ⅵ Translation (5 minutes)

Directions:(略)

82. We are always advised that ______________________________(从书本汲取知识的最有效办法是在页边空白处做有见地的笔记).

83. In this information age, ______________________________(人们的流动性比任何时候都大,这也许就是为什么移动电话十分普及的原因).

84. We are told that ______________________________(老师在评价一篇文章并打分时,可能是根据总体印象而不是根据仔细的分析).

85. It is common sense that ______________________________(几乎每个孩子都曾梦想去太空旅游,体会一下在失重环境下生活的样子).

86. The journalist got promoted ______________________________(因为他设法抓住了一个机会,独家采访了总统并上了头条).

参考答案(4)

Part Ⅰ Sample Writing

An Eye-witness Account of a Traffic Accident

Yesterday afternoon, I happened to witness a terrible traffic accident on my way home from school. It was 5:30 p. m., I was riding my favorite Giant back home. When I got to the last crossing on the Golden Lion Street, the red light was on. So I applied the brakes, along with a long queue of vehicles waiting to pass.

Just at that moment, a heavy-load truck with earth roared forward at my side and bumped against a private Accord of Honda traveling eastbound. As a result, the windshield of the lorry was broken into pieces and its driver got fatally wounded on the head on the steering wheel. The driver of the Accord and his girlfriend, the only passenger in the car, only got minor injuries, but his car lost its rear axel and two wheels and was totally dead.

As for the cause of the accident, I think the driver of the lorry should be held responsible: the light was red then; he should have stopped and waited. It was he who had broken the traffic regulations. In addition, the bad weather was part of the cause. It was drizzling then, and the road was quite slippery. Finally, drunk driving was probably an important factor. As the police discovered on the spot, there was a heavy alcoholic smell on the dead body of the lorry driver.

Part Ⅱ Reading Comprehension (Skimming and Scanning)

1. Y 2. N 3. NG 4. N
5. the hours of the night
6. maintaining accuracy
7. accurate and reliable
8. demands of modern technology
9. the atomic clock
10. natural means

Part Ⅲ Listening Comprehension

Section A

11—15 CDAAB 16—20 CCADD 21—25 CBDAB

Section B

26—30 DBCAB 31—35 CBCAD

Section C

36. president 37. twenty-one 38. delegates 39. election
40. banned 41. honesty 42. illegal 43. accusations
44. The American government charged five people in connection with these gifts
45. The new president has been active in the Olympics since he was a young man
46. Those games were highly successful

Part Ⅳ Reading Comprehension (Reading in Depth)

Section A

47. 30
48. underestimates
49. Any zoo that is a member of a zoo federation or association.
50. caliber/ criterion/ standard
51. Disbelieving. / Skeptical. / Doubtful.

Section B

52—56 CBAAD 57—61 CBCAD

Part Ⅴ Cloze

62—66 ACDAA 67—71 BBDAC 72—76 ABBCD 77—81 BCDCA

Part Ⅵ Translation

82. one of the most effective means of absorbing knowledge from a book is to make intelligent notes in the margins
83. people are more mobile than ever before and perhaps this is why mobile phones have become so popular
84. a teacher may evaluate and grade an essay on the basis of his general impression rather than on a detailed analysis
85. virtually every child has dreamed of traveling in space and experiencing what it would be like to live in a gravity-free environment
86. because he managed to get an exclusive interview with the president and published as the front page headline

试题解答(4)

Part Ⅱ Reading Comprehension (Skimming and Scanning)

1. [Y] 由"Clocks"部分第一、二句"At best, historians know that 5,000-6,000 years ago, great civilizations in the Middle East and North Africa started to examine forms of clock-making instead of working with only the monthly and annual calendar... but it has been suggested that the intention was to maximize time available to achieve more as the size of the population grew."可见中东和北非的一些民族在五六千年前就开始研制钟表了。由于人口的增长,研制计时的钟表可以最大化地利用可用的时间来完成更多的工作。故可以判断"他们开始分配特定的时间段用于工作"是正确的。因此,答案为 YES。
2. [N] 由"Sun Clocks"部分最后一段"Another ancient Egyptian 'shadow clock' or 'sundial' has been discovered to have been in use around 1500 BC, which allowed the measuring of the passage of 'hours'... For it to work successfully then at midday or noon, the device had to be

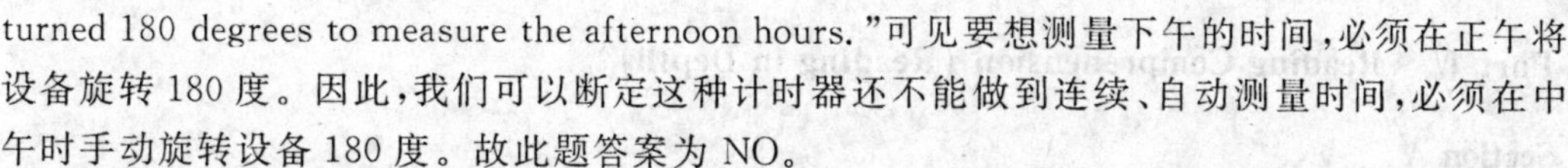

turned 180 degrees to measure the afternoon hours."可见要想测量下午的时间,必须在正午将设备旋转180度。因此,我们可以断定这种计时器还不能做到连续、自动测量时间,必须在中午时手动旋转设备180度。故此题答案为NO。

3. [NG] 由"Water Clocks"部分第一句"'Water clocks' were among the earliest time keeping devices that didn't use the observation of the celestial bodies to calculate the passage of time."可见水钟是不靠观察天体来测量时间的最早的设备之一。但文章并没有进一步提供信息说它是否是第一个这样的计时设备。因此信息不充分,本题判断为NOT GIVEN。
4. [N] 由"Mechanical Clocks"部分第一段"In 1656, 'Christian Huygens' (Dutch scientist), made the first 'Pendulumclock'... 'Galileo Galilei' is credited, in most historical books, for inventing the pendulum as early as 1582, but his design was not built before his death."可以看出,大多数历史教科书认为Galileo Galilei是第一位早在1582年就设计出摆钟的人,但直到他去世也没有制作出摆钟。第一个摆钟是荷兰科学家Christian Huygens制作出来的。故此句答案为NO。
5. 由"Water Clocks"部分第三句"Most of these clocks were used to determine the hours of the night, but may have also been used during daylight."可见水钟主要用于夜间计时。故本题答案为"the hours of the night"。
6. 由"Mechanical Clocks"部分第三、四句"Huygens' clock, when built, had an error of 'less than only one minute a day.' This was a massive leap in the development of maintaining accuracy, as this had previously never been achieved."可见这个钟的误差每天不到一分钟。这在计时准确性的发展史上,是巨大的飞跃。因此,本题的正确答案是"maintaining accuracy"。
7. 由"Quartz Clocks"部分第二段第一句"Quartz clocks continue to dominate the market because of the accuracy and reliability of the performance, also being inexpensive to produce on mass scale."可见由于其准确和稳定,也由于其成本低,适于大规模生产,石英钟将继续占有市场的主导地位。故此题正确答案为"accurate and reliable"。
8. 由"Atomic Clocks"部分第四段第三、四句"Transportation, financial markets, communication, manufacturing, electric power and many other technologies have become dependent on super-accurate clocks. Scientific research and the demands of modern technology continue to drive our search for ever more accuracy."可见是科学研究和现代技术的要求驱使我们不断探寻日益精确的计时方法。故本题答案为"demands of modern technology"。
9. 由"Atomic Clocks"部分第三段最后一句"From the 'Macrocosm', or 'Planetary Alignment', to the 'Microcosm', or 'Atomic Frequency', the cesium now maintains accuracy with a degree of error to about 'one-millionth of a second per year'."可见随着技术的发展,原子钟已经可以达到一年误差大约一百万分之一秒。比起前面的钟表不知道精确了多少倍。故本题答案为"the atomic clock"。
10. 由"Something to Remember"部分第一段"The only thing that should be remembered during all this technological development is that we should never lose the ability to tell the time approximately by natural means and the powers of deduction without requiring crutches to lean on."可见无论计时技术如何发展,我们不能失去通过自然手段判定大概时间的基本能力。故本题答案为"natural means"。

Part Ⅲ Listening Comprehension(听力原文在光盘中)

Part Ⅳ Reading Comprehension (Reading in Depth)

Section A

47. 由第二段第一句"Zoos were originally created as places of entertainment, and their suggested involvement with conservation didn't seriously arise until about 30 years ago..."可知正确答案为"30"。

48. 从第三段第二句"This is probably the document's first failing, as I believe that 10,000 is a serious underestimate of the total number of places masquerading as zoological establishments."中可以看出,作者认为文件的第一个缺点是大大低估了全世界动物园的数目。明目繁多但实质是动物园的机构远远多于一万这个数目。可见此处要填的词是意为"低估"的动词。因此,正确答案为"underestimates"。

49. 第四段作者谈到选择参与保护项目的核心动物园的标准时提到"One would assume that the caliber of these institutions would have been carefully examined, but it appears that the criterion for inclusion on this select list might merely be that the zoo is a member of a zoo federation or association.",实际上列入候选的唯一标准可能是:该动物园是动物园联盟或者动物园协会的成员。故该题可以答为"Any zoo that is a member of a zoo federation or association."。

50. 由第四段第二句和第三句"One would assume that the caliber of these institutions would have been carefully examined, but it appears that the criterion for inclusion on this select list might merely be that the zoo is a member of a zoo federation or association. This might be a good starting point, working on the premise that members must meet certain standards, but again the facts don't support the theory."可见人们都以为参与保护项目的动物园应该按照标准(caliber)严格筛选,但没想到例如候选的唯一标准(criterion)可能只是该动物园是动物园协会或者联盟的成员。如果这些协会的成员达到一定的标准(standards)也就罢了,但事实并非如此。两句话中"标准"三次出现。可见作者认为WZCS的第二个缺点是在挑选参与保护项目的动物园时,没有严格的标准。因此,此题要填的词为文中所出现的"caliber/ criterion/ standard"中的任何一个。

51. 文章第五段作者提到:Colin Tudge预测全球合作的喂养保护项目可以保护大约2 000种濒临灭绝的陆地脊椎动物。随后,在第六段中作者讲到30年以来只有16种物种可以说是被圈养保护项目所拯救了。这离Tudge所说的2 000种物种得到保护的目标还差得很远。稍加推测可知,作者对Tudge预测的目标是不信任的、怀疑的。因此,答案可以是"Disbelieving. / Skeptical. / Doubtful."。

Section B

52. [C] 细节甄别题。文中第二段提及"These included the use of federal student loans to pay off credit cards, effectively shifting the debt, appeals to parents for loans, cutting back on course work to increase time at paid jobs, or even dropping out altogether to work full time.",因此,正确答案为C项。选项C是college administrators从事的活动,不是美国学生。

53. [B] 细节甄别题。文中开篇提到"the consequences can be serious—ranging from higher drop-out rates to future employment problems and even suicide",最后一段谈到"Card issuers were sponsoring school programs, funding activities and even entering into business partnerships

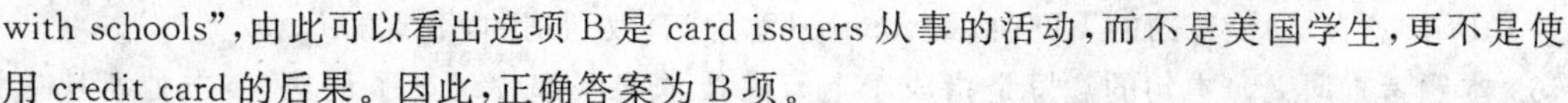

with schools”,由此可以看出选项B是card issuers从事的活动,而不是美国学生,更不是使用credit card的后果。因此,正确答案为B项。

54. [A] 细节题。文末倒数第二句、第三句中提到了“students, card companies, university administrators”都应该为信用卡负面影响负责。因此,正确答案为A项。

55. [A] 主旨题。本文首句即提到“U. S. college students are increasingly burdened with credit card debt”,第二段主旨是“growing numbers of students who are unable to cope with the stress of their debts and/or part time jobs for servicing their credit cards”。第三段讲“debts can haunt students”,最后一段主要讲述“who should answer for the negative consequences”。因此,正确答案为A项。

56. [D] 推断题。文章主要讲述学生使用信用卡的负面影响,但也不能千篇一律断然否定使用信用卡,因而选项B不对。不使用信用卡也不能保证美国学生不自杀,故选项C不对。美国学生有part-time工作,是司空见惯也不能因为信用卡的负面影响而取消,故排除选项A。采用逐个排除法,可以确定正确答案为D项。

57. [C] 细节题。通过阅读文章可知“home schoolers”和“public schools”是相对立的。前者是指那些让孩子在家里接受教育的社会群体。故答案为C项。

58. [B] 细节题。从文章第三段可知,由于公立学校的官员们意识到,和提倡让孩子在家接受教育的社会群体一直保持敌对态度是无益处的,因此双方的矛盾有了一定的缓和。故答案为B项。

59. [C] 细节题。第五段最后一句作者提到:home schoolers之所以坚持自己的教育方法主要是因为宗教原因,因此答案为C项。

60. [A] 细节推断题。从文章最后两段可知,home schoolers认为他们的教育方法是最好的,并希望自己的这种生活方式、教育方法不受打扰。故答案为A项。

61. [D] 推断题。从文章最后一段可知,home schoolers希望自己的孩子不仅要学习传统课程,而且要学习严格的宗教知识。从这一角度来说,他们认为家是最好的教育场所。而另一些home schoolers则认为学校的教育方法是不恰当。他们倒不十分在意学校的教学内容。因此答案为D项。

Part Ⅴ Cloze

62. 本题考查关系代词。A项which作关系代词时,意指“那些,那个”,指物,而此句先行词为technical vocabulary,因此A项为正确答案。B项what作关系代词时,意指“所……事物(或人)”,C项who和D项whom都是指人的关系代词,不合句意。

63. 本题考查词义。根据上下文可知,此处单词要与things or processes搭配,C项designate意为“标明,表示”,用在一起,说明专业词汇的作用是表示事物和过程,因此为正确答案。A项describe意为“描述”,根据后文,我们知道专业词汇不具备这样的作用,命名是比描述更简单的过程,所以排除。B项talk about意为“讨论,谈论”;D项indicate意为“指出”,更加不符合上下文的语意。

64. 本题考查句子之间的逻辑关系。上文中提到了专业词汇的作用,下文则说明专业词汇还能节省时间,显然是对上文的补充,D项besides表示补充关系故正确;选项A consequently表示因果关系;B项in contrast表示对比关系;C项however表示转折关系。

65. 本题考查词义。分析句意可知,空白处所填单词的意思应为“经济的,实惠的”,A项economical意为“经济的,实惠的”,故正确。B项economic意为“经济上的,经济学的”;C项

thrift 意为“勤俭节约的”;D 项 economized 意为“有效利用的,节省的”。

66. 本题考查词义。本句的意思是指成千上万的技术词汇都收录进了词典,空白处所填单词为副词修饰这个句子,A 项 properly 意为“恰当地”,符合上下文语意,故正确。B 项 possibly 意为“可能地”;C 项 probably 意为“大概,或许”;D 项 potentially 意为“潜在地”。

67. 本题考查固定搭配。on the outskirts 构成固定搭配,指“在郊区, 在……边缘上”,在句中是指专业词汇还处在英语的边缘上,因此正确答案为 B 项。

68. 本题考查词义。分析句中空白处可知所填单词为副词,修饰动词 differ(不同,不一致),A 项 largely 意为“主要地,很大程度上地”;B 项 widely 意为“广泛地,相差很大地”;C 项 generally 意为“一般地,普通地”;D 项 extensively 意为“广泛地,广阔地”,其中 widely 经常与 differ 搭配,并符合题意,故选 B 项。

69. 本题考查词义。根据上下文本句的意思是专业词汇主要包括本族词和外来词,A 项 constitutes 意为“组成……”,不合句意;B 项 comprises 意为“包含,由……组成”,为及物动词;C 项 composes 意为“组成,作曲”,经常用于 be composed of 句型,不符合本句的结构要求;D 项 consists 意为“包括”,用于 consist of 句型,符合句子要求,为正确答案。

70. 本题考查固定搭配。本句中 work oneself into... 意为“进入”,句中表示外来词进入了我们的语言结构,故选 A 项。

71. 本题考查句子之间的逻辑关系。上文中提到了专业词汇主要由本族词和那些进入我们语言结构的外来词构成,下文则说这些词在声音上更为熟悉,显然上下文之间构成了因果关系,上文是因,下文是果,A 项 However 表示转折关系;B 项 Because 表示原因;C 项 Hence 表示结果;D 项 In addition 表示补充关系,因此正确答案为 C 项。

72. 本题考查词义。本句是个比较句,是比较本族词和那些进入我们语言结构的外来词构成的专业词汇,A 项 understood 意为“理解”,说这些词汇更好地为人们所理解,符合句意;B 项 considered 意为“考虑”;C 项 known 意为“被人所知的”;D 项 thought 意为“思考”,都不太准确,因此正确答案为 A 项。

73. 本题考查句子之间的逻辑关系。上下文提到专业词汇主要由本族词和那些进入我们语言结构的外来词构成,下文则说各行业还有很多不为人们所熟知的词汇,显然上下文之间是转折关系,A 项 Therefore 表示因果关系;B 项 Yet 表示转折关系;C 项 In contrast 表示对比关系;D 项 So 表示因果关系,因此正确答案为 B 项。

74. 本题考查词义。本句意为每个行业都还有很多词汇不被人们所知,分析句子可知空白处所填单词应为量词,A 项 series 意为“系列”;B 项 body 作量词意为“大量”;C 项 set 意为“一套,一副”;D 项 range 意为“范围,行列”,只有 B 项最为恰当,为正确答案。

75. 固定搭配题。句中 be(remain) foreign to 构成固定搭配,意为“与……无关,不为……所知”,句中意思是每个行业都还有很多词汇甚至不被受过教育的人所知,因此正确答案为 C 项。

76. 本句中 proportion(比例)是指不为人们所知的词汇的比例,本句所说的是这个比例在过去的 50 年以来发生的变化,A 项 decreased 意为“减少”,显然不合题意与常识;B 项 diminished 意为“减少,变小”,也不正确;C 项 increasing 意为“增加,提高”,但-ing 形式不符合句子结构;因此,D 项 increased 为正确答案。

77. 本题考查词义。空白处所填单词修饰 terms(术语),A 项 made 意为“制造”,说术语是制造出来的不合适;B 项 coined 意为“造字,造词”,符合句意;C 项 produced 意为“生产”;D 项 formed 意为“形成”,都不符合句意,因此正确答案为 B 项。

78. 本题考查词义。A 项 related 意为“有关系的”;B 项 addressing 意为“从事于,忙于,写姓名地

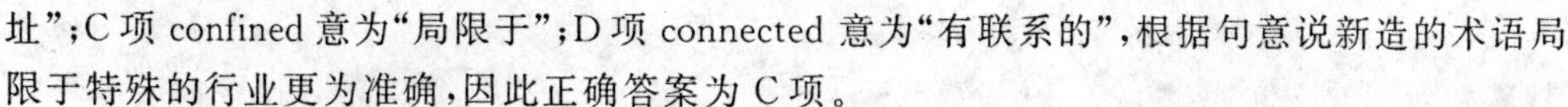

址”;C 项 confined 意为“局限于”;D 项 connected 意为“有联系的”,根据句意说新造的术语局限于特殊的行业更为准确,因此正确答案为 C 项。

79. 语法知识题。本句中 once 意为“曾经”,因此要用过去时,而主语为复数,所以正确选项为 D 项。

80. 本题考查固定搭配。句中 be acquainted with 构成固定搭配,意为“熟悉……”,句中意思为大众科学使每个人都熟悉现代的观点和最新发现。A 项 associated 和 D 项 connected 也能与 with 构成搭配,意思分别是“与……有关联”,“与……联系在一起”,都不合句意,因此正确答案为 C 项。

81. 本句表达的意思是任何科学实验,即便是在很远的实验室完成的,都能被人们尽快熟知,A 项 though 引导让步状语从句,符合句意;B 项 when 引导时间状语从句,C 项 as 意为“像”,D 项 since 表示原因,都不符合句意,因此正确答案为 A 项。

Part Ⅵ Translation

82. [答案]:one of the most effective means of absorbing knowledge from a book is to make intelligent notes in the margins

[注释]:本句的翻译关键在于“汲取”、“空白处”和“做笔记”。知识的“汲取”或“吸收”应使用 absorb;“空白处”固定表达为 margin,虽然 margin 也有“边际”的含义;“做笔记”则为 make notes。

83. [答案]:people are more mobile than ever before and perhaps this is why mobile phones have become so popular

[注释]:本句翻译不难。首先是“比任何时候”的翻译使用句型“... than ever before”。其次,“流动,移动”翻译为 mobile。

84. [答案]:a teacher may evaluate and grade an essay on the basis of his general impression rather than on a detailed analysis

[注释]:本句的翻译首先要做到就是“是……而不是……”应使用句型“rather... than”。其次,“根据”翻译为 on the basis of,当然也可以使用 by 这一类词;此外,“总体印象”应翻译为 general impression。

85. [答案]:virtually every child has dreamed of traveling in space and experiencing what it would be like to live in a gravity-free environment

[注释]:首先“梦想”的翻译使用词组 dream of ;本句的一个难点是“失重”——gravity-free 的翻译。

86. [答案]:because he managed to get an exclusive interview with the president and published as the front page headline

[注释]:本句翻译的难点是“独家采访”和“头条”。“独家”即表示排除其他,因此翻译为 exclusive;“头条”则应译为 front page headline。

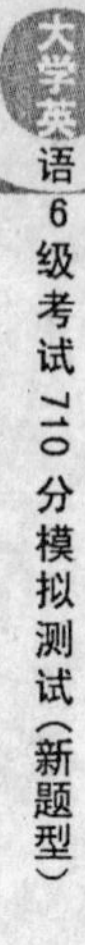

College English Practice Test 5 (Band Ⅵ)

Part Ⅰ Writing (30 minutes)

Directions: *For this part, you are allowed 30 minutes to write a letter to ask for some information about an international conference held in your city. You should write at least* **150** *words following the outline given below.*

有一个会议在你所在的城市召开,你想去参加。给会议的组织者写一封信。说一下你想参加的原因,并简单介绍一下自己。并请他提供一些会议的相关信息。

Part Ⅱ Reading Comprehension (Skimming and Scanning) (15 minutes)

Directions:(略)

It's Never Too Late to Start Exercise

Researchers Find Great Rewards When Mild Exercise Programs Are Started Late In Life.

May 13, 2003—You know the benefits of exercise programs. And if you've been inactive, you may have also felt them—with sore muscles and bruised motivation to continue. But a new study in women shows that the old adage is true—it's never too late to start when it comes to exercise programs. So now what can you do to jump on the exercise *bandwagon*(乐队花车)? WebMD got exercise tips from the experts.

"There certainly seems to be something here to suggest that women can start exercising later in life and still reap the rewards," lead researcher and CDC epidemiologist Edward W. Gregg, PhD, tells WebMD. His findings are published in the May 14 issue of The Journal of the American Medical Association.

Researchers tracked 9,500 women for 12 years, starting when they were at least age 66. In that time, they found that those who went from doing little or nothing to walking just a mile a day *slashed*(减少) their risk of death from all causes and from cancer by nearly half. Their risk of heart disease also fell by more than a third. In fact, they enjoyed nearly as much protection as women who were physically active before the study began and remained so.

During the study, he and his colleagues surveyed the women on their exercise levels at the start of the trial and again up to six years later. Years later, the researchers tracked their rates of death and disease.

The new information we found is that older women who went from being *sedentary*(少活动的) or walking about two miles a week to "walking eight miles a week between the two visits had

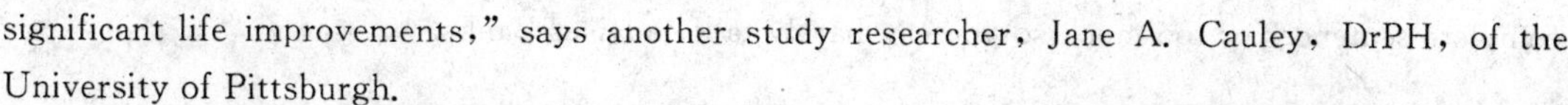

significant life improvements," says another study researcher, Jane A. Cauley, DrPH, of the University of Pittsburgh.

"We're talking about women with an average age of 77 at the second visit," she tells WebMD. "And we're talking about their engaging in very mild exercise—and not running marathons."

But if the only *workout*(运动) you've been getting lately involves the TV remote, here's how to avoid those walks around the block from making your body feel as if it just tackled Boston Marathon's infamous "Heartbreak Hill".

Get a checkup before a workout.

A visit to your doctor is wise for anyone beginning an exercise program, but it's crucial for the elderly or others who have been inactive because of health problems. In addition to the obvious—checking your heart and lungs—your doctor can help determine if your *regimen*(养生法) needs to consider other medical conditions, and the drugs you take for them.

"People can sometimes control conditions such as diabetes and high blood pressure with weight loss and exercise so they don't need to continue their medications," says William A. Banks, MD, professor of geriatrics at Saint Louis University School of Medicine. It's important to let your doctor know about your new exercise program in case your medication doses need to be changed.

"A doctor can also help facilitate the best type of exercise if you have a disability or impairment. For instance, many of my patients have bad knees, so I tell them that if they start running or even walking, they're going to have problems that will likely impact their ability to continue," he tells WebMD. "So I try to steer them to another activity, such as swimming, which is especially good for people with joint problems or *obesity*(肥胖)."

Start slow.

Once you get the green light, the key to avoiding fatigue and muscle pain is to pull out of the gate very slowly. "You hear so much about the importance of getting 30 minutes of exercise a day, but those recommendations should not be viewed as goals if you've been sedentary—even if you're healthy," Banks says. "Initially, you should actually shoot below your comfort level.

"Too often, people—especially those who are older—overdo it in the beginning and hurt themselves to the point where they need two weeks to recover. It's better to walk for a few minutes a day, every day, than do 10 minutes your first day and then not be able to walk for the rest of the week."

Go more often.

Of course, those few minutes of your exercise program can be done several times a day. First, try to do some activity for a few minutes several times a day. Then slowly increase the time spent in each session. But don't worry about going faster until you've exercised regularly for at least one month. A key to intensity: Ideally, you want to be *aerobic*(需要氧气的) enough so you can utter a few words or syllables in each sentence, but not so little that you're speaking in

complete sentences or too much so you can barely talk, advises Banks.

Don't go solo.

Although there is no evidence that people are fitter when they exercise with others, they are more likely to stick to an exercise program, or anything else, with the buddy system. "We're always better in the company of others," says Banks.

Another benefit to group activities: Organized exercise programs, like those available for low or no cost at the YMCA or local hospitals, often include professional guidance—especially useful for those with conditions such as obesity, diabetes, and arthritis. "There are exercise therapists or physiologists who can expertly guide you to the proper way to increase your endurance and intensity without risking injury or fatigue," says Gregg.

Do what you enjoy.

While Gregg's study and others have focused on walking because it's among the easiest and most popular forms of exercise, you should pick an activity you like, so you continue it. It could be gardening, swimming, tennis, or the old favorite, walking. "If you absolutely hate exercise, like me, I recommend exercise machines," says Banks. "Since I hate to exercise, I run on a *treadmill*(踏车) while watching TV. I'm especially fond of working out while watching the cartoon Pinky and the Brain."

1. It is suggested that women should not do exercises if they are over sixty.
2. According to Edward W. Gregg, it's never too late for women to start exercise.
3. All the 9,500 women who participated in the research would have little exercises or would only walk just a mile a day before the research.
4. Another benefit of group activities is that professional guidance in the group can help cure obesity, diabetes, and arthritis.
5. Since exercises may control conditions such as diabetes and high blood pressure, some old people don't need to ________ if they begin an exercise program.
6. As is suggested by William A. Banks, ________ is especially good for people with joint problems or obesity.
7. For those who just start to exercise, the best way to avoid fatigue and muscle pain is to ________.
8. For the exerciser, a simple method in checking the intensity of the exercise is to see that whether one can ________ while having the exercise.
9. In organized exercise programs, exercise therapists or physiologists can expertly guide an exerciser to the proper way to increase his or her ________ without risking injury or fatigue.
10. It is recommended that the exerciser should pick up an activity he/she likes so that he/she may ________.

Part Ⅲ Listening Comprehension (35 minutes)

Section A

Directions:(略)

11. A) The woman thinks Joseph will remarry.
    B) Joseph will not remarry in fear that he might feel disappointed again.
    C) Joseph doesn't want to remarry because he hates being cheated.
    D) Joseph doesn't like the woman.
12. A) The man and the woman are going to get married.
    B) The woman wants to invite many people to the wedding ceremony.
    C) The woman wants the man to agree with her idea.
    D) The man doesn't want to invite many people to their wedding ceremony.
13. A) The man didn't see eye to eye with Professor Clark.
    B) The man caught the most important point of the topic.
    C) The man's presentation had a right purpose.
    D) The man was right to give the presentation.
14. A) The woman shouldn't believe everything Dave tells her.
    B) The woman shouldn't let Dave get the best of her.
    C) Dave is not serious with the woman.
    D) Dave is always true to his words.
15. A) Everyone in the town misses Lora.
    B) Everyone in the town expects Lora to come back.
    C) Everyone in the town respects Lora.
    D) Everyone in the town wants to see Lora.
16. A) Hurry to the conference. B) Skip the conference.
    C) Take the subway. D) Take a bus.
17. A) He is confident. B) He is worried.
    C) He is bored. D) He is angry.
18. A) He used to be a workman himself.
    B) He likes to do repairs and make things himself.
    C) He is professional builder.
    D) He paid workmen to decorate the house.

Questions 19 to 22 are based on the conversation you have just heard.

19. A) To help students prepare to enter American Universities.
    B) To teach students how to use English at work.
    C) To provide work opportunities for graduating students.
    D) To help students learn to communicate with others in their daily lives.
20. A) Business English. B) US Culture.

C) TOEFL. D) Computer.

21. A) $2,030. B) $2,300. C) $2,013. D) $23,000.

22. A) Call the English Language Center to apply.
 B) Fill in the application form on the website.
 C) Send an email to the English Language Center.
 D) Visit the English Language Center personally.

Questions 23 to 25 are based on the conversation you have just heard.

23. A) Teacher and student. B) Manager and guest.
 C) Receptionist and guest. D) Friends.

24. A) One week. B) Two weeks.
 C) Three days. D) Seventeen days.

25. A) Call room service. B) Come to the reception desk.
 C) Both A) and B). D) Go to the canteen.

Section B

Directions:(略)

Passage One

Questions 26 to 28 are based on the passage you have just heard.

26. A) Nicotine. B) Ashes. C) Smoke. D) Tar.

27. A) To keep selling people by producing cigarettes with less tar.
 B) To persuade people to give up smoking entirely.
 C) To reduce the risk to people's health.
 D) To let people know the risk to people's health.

28. A) Smoking. B) Smokers.
 C) Why Do People Smoke? D) The Tar.

Passage Two

Questions 29 to 31 are based on the passage you have just heard.

29. A) Musical films. B) The Western movie.
 C) Science fiction films. D) The gangster movie.

30. A) Because he can protect people's ideals.
 B) Because he can straighten out any trouble.
 C) Because he is brave and smart.
 D) Because he is highly independent.

31. A) The cherished individualism.
 B) The role of individuals in society.
 C) The loner hero fighting evil forces.
 D) The ideals of independence and freedom.

Passage Three

Questions 32 to 35 are based on the passage you have just heard.

32. A) It has an intense gravity.
    B) It can change space and time in basic ways.
    C) Nothing can escape from it.
    D) It has been predicted by theory but never confirmed.
33. A) About 700 million light-years from Sun.
    B) About 700 million light-years from Earth.
    C) About 700 million light-years from the black hole.
    D) About 700 million light-years from a galaxy.
34. A) Gases have been heated to a temperature of multimillion-degree.
    B) Gases have been drawn to the black hole at a very high speed.
    C) Gases have been tearing apart by the black hole.
    D) Gases have been sucked by the black hole.
35. A) It may exist in the neighborhood of big stars.
    B) It may exist in the neighborhood of a galaxy.
    C) It may exist at the center of X-rays.
    D) It may exist at the center of a galaxy.

Section C

Directions:(略)

The World Trade Organization was established in 1995. It (36) ________ out of the General Agreement on Tariffs and Trade or GATT. GATT was created in 1948 after the end of World War Ⅱ. It led to a series of international trade negotiations, which (37) ________ a world trading system. The WTO supervises and makes (38) ________ to that system.

The WTO organizes trade negotiations and settles trade (39) ________. It supervises trade agreements reached by member nations. It also provides developing countries with technical assistance and training programs in trade (40) ________. And, it cooperates with other international organizations.

The top decision-making group of the WTO is the Ministerial Conference. It (41) ________ at least once every two years in different cities around the world. WTO members reach agreements by debate and (42) ________. WTO agreements then go to the governments of each country for (43) ________ or rejection.

(44) ____. GATT was designed to lower import taxes and remove other barriers to trade in goods. However, (45) ____. This industry includes banks, communications companies, hotels and transport businesses. The WTO also supervises an agreement on what is called intellectual property. (46) ____.

Part Ⅳ Reading Comprehension(Reading in Depth) (25 minutes)

Section A

Directions:(略)

Questions 47 to 51 are based on the following passage.

Of 2,000 commercial beekeepers in the United States about half migrate. Migratory beekeeping is nothing new. The ancient Egyptians moved clay hives, probably on rafts, down the Nile to follow the bloom and nectar flow as it moved toward Cairo. In the 1880s North American beekeepers experimented with the same idea, moving bees on barges along the Mississippi lighter, wooden hives kept falling into the water. Other keepers tried the railroad and horse drawn wagons, but that didn't prove practical. Not until the 1920s when cars and trucks became affordable and roads improved, did migratory beekeeping begin to catch on.

For the Californian beekeeper, the pollination season begins in February. At this time, the beehives are in particular demand by farmers who have almond groves; they need two hives an acre. For the three-week long bloom, beekeepers can hire out their hives for $32 each.

By early March it is time to move the bees. It can take up to seven nights to pack the 4,000 or so hives that a beekeeper may own. These are not moved in the middle of the day because too many of the bees would end up homeless. But at night, the hives are stacked onto wooden pallets, back-to-back in sets of four, and lifted onto a truck. It is not necessary to wear gloves or a beekeeper's veil because the hives are not being opened and the bees should remain relatively quiet. Just in case some are still lively, bees can be pacified with a few puffs of smoke blown into each hive's narrow entrance.

In their new location, the beekeeper will pay the farmer to allow his bees to feed in such places as orange groves. The honey produced here is fragrant and sweet and can be sold by the beekeepers. To encourage the bees to produce as much honey as possible during this period, the beekeepers open the hives and stack extra boxes called supers on top. These temporary hive extensions contain frames of empty comb for the bees to fill with honey. In the brood chamber below, the bees will stash honey to eat later. To prevent the queen from crawling up to the top and laying eggs, a screen can be inserted between the brood chamber and the supers.

Three weeks later the honey can be gathered. Foul smelling chemicals are often used to irritate the bees and drive them down into the hive's bottom boxes, leaving the honey-filled supers more or less bee free. These can then be pulled off the hive. They are heavy with honey and may weigh up to 90 pounds each. The supers are then taken to a warehouse where the extracting process takes place.

After this, approximately a quarter of the hives weakened by disease, mites or an ageing or dead queen, will have to be replaced. To create new colonies, a healthy double hive, teeming with bees, can be separated into two boxes. One half will hold the queen and a young, already mated queen can be put in the other half, to make two hives from one. By the time the flowers bloom, the new queens will be laying eggs, filling each hive with young worker bees. The beekeeper's

family will then migrate with them to their summer location.

47. First attempts at migratory beekeeping in America were ________.
48. In March, beekeepers prepare for migration at night when the hives are ________ and the bees are generally tranquil.
49. They transport their hives to orange groves where farmers ________ beekeepers for placing them on their land.
50. Where do the bees keep honey for themselves to eat later?
51. To create new colonies, what will beekeepers do with the hives in good condition?

Section B

Directions:(略)

Passage One

Questions 52 to 56 are based on the following passage.

That particularly humorless boss or dour neighbor may not have a personality defect—but a different brain structure, research published Wednesday suggests. Scientists in Canada say they have found how brain damage can affect a person's sense of humor, adding to evidence that humor may be hard-wired into the brain.

A team at the University of Toronto and the Baycrest Center for Geriatric Care in Toronto found that people with damage to the right frontal lobe of their brains do not really "get" ironic jokes the way they should. Instead, they prefer slapstick humor. "We always thought of humor as an intangible part of our personality," Prathiba Shammi of the University of Toronto, a psychologist who worked on the study, said in a statement. "Now we know humor can be tested and scientifically scrutinized."

Shammi compared the responses of 42 volunteers aged 18 to 70 to written and verbal jokes and cartoons. Half the group had a brain injury caused by stroke, tumor or surgical removal. People with damage to the right anterior frontal lobe were the least able to appreciate jokes and cartoons, Shammi reported in the journal Brain. Instead, they showed a preference for silly slapstick humor. Shammi gave an example of one of her jokes and the responses.

A teen-ager is being interviewed for a summer job. "You'll get $50 a week to start off," says his boss. "Then after a month you'll get a raise to $75 a week." Volunteers were offered three possible punch lines:

a. "I'd like to take the job. When can I start?"

b. "That's great! I'll come back in a month."

c. "Hey boss, your nose is too big for your face!"

52. According to the passage a humorless person ________.

A) has a personality defect　　B) may have a different brain structure

C) has been injured in the brain　　D) does not understand any joke

53. Traditionally people believe that humor ________.
   A) can be tested and scientifically scrutinized
   B) has something to do with a person's brain
   C) cannot be found in brain-damaged people
   D) is an intangible part of a person's personality
54. Which of the following statement is true?
   A) 42 volunteers were tested with both written and verbal jokes.
   B) Only people with damage to the right anterior frontal lobe could not appreciate jokes.
   C) Humorless people prefer silly slapstick humor.
   D) The author had a humorless boss and a dour neighbor.
55. Which of the following statements about the volunteers in the experiment is NOT true?
   A) The oldest volunteer was seventy years old.
   B) They are tested with jokes both in written and spoken form.
   C) The majority of the volunteers suffered from brain damage.
   D) Comparatively people suffered from right anterior frontal lobe damage was most humorless.
56. Look at the joke in the last part of the passage. We can infer that most people with damage to the right anterior frontal lobe ________.
   A) did not understand the joke
   B) would choose answer c
   C) would choose answer b
   D) would choose answer a

Passage Two

Questions 57 to 61 are based on the following passage.

Film is a medium that might have been especially made for America, a vast country which, by the beginning of the twentieth century, had a large immigrant population, many of whom could hardly speak English. These people would have had little use for the theatre, even if they lived within easy distance of one, or for most of the books they could buy because they did not have enough English. But the movies—the silent movies—these they could all understand, so what America had more than any European country was a huge captive audience, a large proportion of them pretty well uneducated. And what these people wanted were simple stories in which, irrespective of the fact they couldn't understand the captions, the action told all.

In feeding the growing demand for screen entertainment, America was greatly helped by the First World War. Between 1914 and 1918 the making of films was not exactly high on the list of any European country's priorities. Films continued to be made but not to the same extent as before, and to fill the gap in foreign imports, America had to increase its own production. By the end of the decade, with Hollywood now firmly established as the center of the industry, America was well on its way to monopolizing the world market.

But if by the beginning of the 1920s America was the world leader in film production, it was not then nor has it been since—in the lead when it comes to developing film as an art form. Hollywood film is not interested in art; it is interested in money and the two rarely go together. To Hollywood film is, and really always has been, an industry. There is nothing about this attitude that should make us look down on it. The maker of decent, serviceable and mass-produced furniture is not to be looked down on because he isn't Chippendale. You might wish he were, but that is another matter. So Hollywood quickly recognized film as an entertainment medium with a unique ability to put people onto seats and money in the pockets of producers, distributors and cinema managers and, mostly, left **it** to others to develop its potential as an art form.

Generally speaking, the efforts to extend the boundaries of film—to show that it could do more than car chases, romance and clowning—were being made elsewhere. In the 1920s in Germany, for example, expressionism was an artistic movement which used film as a medium. Expressionism is described in the *Oxford Companion to Film* as "a movement whose main aim was to show in images man's inner world and in particular the emotions of fear, hatred, love and anxiety". These days, most serious and sometimes not so serious—films attempt to do something like that as a matter of course.

57. The large immigrant population in America prefer film to other entertainment media Because ________.
    A) the films, especially silent films, were usually easy to understand
    B) they could not afford to buy books or magazines
    C) they did not have theatres close enough to their homes
    D) the film captions were simple enough for them to understand
58. What made the American film industry develop during the First World War?
    A) The drastic drop in imports.
    B) The poor quality of European films.
    C) The growing demand for war films.
    D) The rapid growth of population.
59. What can we learn about the American film industry around 1920?
    A) Art films produced in American were better than those made elsewhere.
    B) The Americans played a leading role in developing film as an art form.
    C) Americans looked down upon their own films.
    D) More films were made in America than anywhere else.
60. What does "it" in the last sentence of Paragraph 3 refer to?
    A) To develop the potential of a movie as the an art form.
    B) An entertainment medium in Hollywood.
    C) Movie industry of America.
    D) Money for the producer, distributor and cinema managers.
61. What do we learn about expressionism?
    A) Its objective was to depict romance and car chases.
    B) Its aim was to display man's various types of emotions.
    C) It was developed in America in the 1920s.
    D) Its motivation was to show man's varied facial expressions.

Part Ⅴ Error Correction (15 minutes)

Directions:（略）

At the first sight the planet Mars does not appear very welcoming to 62. ______
any kind of life. It has very little oxygen and water, the temperature at
night is below -50 degrees and winds of 100 miles per hour cause severe
dusty storms. However, the surface of the planet seems to show that 63. ______
water flowed across at some time in the past, and it is believed that there 64. ______
is enough ice at the poles to cover the planet with water if it melts. 65. ______
Although there is no life on Mars, some scientists think that there may
have some form of life a long time ago. At that time, the planet had active 66. ______
volcanoes; the atmosphere was thinner and warmer; and there was water. 67. ______
In fact, in some ways Mars may have been different to earth, where life 68. ______
exists.

Some people believe that Mars could support life in the future if the
right conditions were produced. The first step would be to warm the
planet used certain gases which trap the sun's heat in the planet's 69. ______
atmosphere. By warmth, water and carbon dioxide, simple plants could 70. ______
begin to grow. These plants could slowly make Mars habitable. It is
established that the whole process might spend between 100,000 and 200,000 71. ______
years. In the meantime, people could begin to live on the planet in special
closed environments. They would provide a lot of useful information about
conditions on Mars and the problems connected with living there.

Part Ⅵ Translation (5 minutes)

Directions:（略）

72. In fact, ____ (有人说通过强制执行严格的规范可以使人们得到改造，这种说法是没有根据的).

73. It is common sense that ____ (医生往往为自己能够医治好病人罕见的疾病而自豪).

74. According to recent research, ____ (退休的人如果找不到什么事情可做，常会意志消沉).

75. To prepare us for the debate, ____ (教练经常要我们注意与自己论点相悖的观点).

76. For any country, ____ (如打算为它的年青一代提供一个可靠的未来，就应该把环保放在优先地位).

参考答案(5)

Part Ⅰ Sample Writing

November 12，2007

Dear Professor Huang，

I write for information regarding the forthcoming International Education Conference to be held at your prestigious university.

I am a first-year student from Nanjing University majoring in Education，and have a particular interest in the teaching of work place skills and employer's perceptions of new graduates.

I plan to attend the conference and would like information about the contributory speakers，the content of their talks，and their research interests. Besides，if you could please also send the details of how to get to your university it would make my arrangements much easier.

In addition，if you could let me have details of the accommodation that is available I would be more than grateful.

I look forward to receiving the information and meeting you in person.

Sincerely yours，

Frank

Part Ⅱ Reading Comprehension (Skimming and Scanning)

1. N　2. Y　3. N　4. NG

5. continue their medications
6. swimming
7. pull out of the gate very slowly/start slow
8. utter a few words or syllables in each sentence
9. endurance and intensity
10. continue it

Part Ⅲ Listening Comprehension

Section A

11—15　BDBAB　16—20　DABCA　21—25　ABCBC

Section B

26—30　DBCAD　31—35　BDBAD

Section C

36. developed　37. established　38. improvements　39. disputes
40. issues　41. meets　42. compromise　43. approval
44. At first the trade agreements among the countries dealt mainly with goods
45. WTO members later agreed on trade rules for the service industry
46. That agreement provides rules to protect trade and investment in ideas and creative activities

Part Ⅳ Reading Comprehension (Reading in Depth)

Section A

47. unsuccessful
48. full
49. charge
50. In the brood chambers. /In the bottom of the hives.
51. They will be separated/split into two boxes.

Section B

52—56 BDACB 57—61 AADAB

Part Ⅴ Error Correction

62. 删除 first 之前的 the
63. dusty → dust
64. 在 across 之后加 it
65. melts → melted
66. 在 have 之后加 been
67. thinner → thicker
68. different → similar
69. used → using
70. By → With
71. spend → take

Part Ⅵ Translation

72. it is groundless to hold that people can be changed by having strict rules imposed on them
73. a doctor often prides himself on the ability to cure his patient of a rare disease
74. retired people are often depressed if they can't find something to do
75. the coach wanted us to be always aware of the arguments that are quite the reverse of ours
76. environmental protection should be given priority if it plans to provide a secure future for the younger generation

试题解答(5)

Part Ⅱ Reading Comprehension (Skimming and Scanning)

1. [N] 文章第一段第三句"But a new study in women shows that the old adage is true—it's never too late to start when it comes to exercise programs."指出，一份新的女性调查显示，那句老话仍然实用：对于锻炼从来都不晚。意思就是说年纪大了，要想锻炼仍然是可以的，并不是建议老年女性不锻炼。至于60岁以上女性不能锻炼这一说法更不正确，随后还提及被调查的女性有9 500人之多，从她们66岁开始一直追踪调查到77岁，前后12年时间。故此句判断为NO。

2. [Y] 由文章第二段第一句"'There certainly seems to be something here to suggest that women can start exercising later in life and still reap the rewards,' lead researcher and CDC epidemiologist Edward W. Gregg, PhD, tells WebMD."可见女性即使在人生晚年才开始锻炼,仍然能够收到回报,因此晚一些开始锻炼是亡羊补牢为时未晚。故此句判断为 YES。
3. [N] 文章第三段中的"Researchers tracked 9,500 women for 12 years, starting when they were at least age 66. In that time, they found that those who went from doing little or nothing to walking just a mile a day slashed(减少) their risk of death from all causes and from cancer by nearly half. Their risk of heart disease also fell by more than a third. In fact, they enjoyed nearly as much protection as women who were physically active before the study began and remained so."讲到研究者们对 9 500 名女性进行了 12 年的跟踪调查,结果发现对那些原来很少运动或者每天只走一英里的老年女性来说,增加运动后她们死亡的风险降低了一半,患心脏病的风险也降低了三分之一以上。最后作者讲到,实际上和那些在研究开始之前就积极运动(physically active)并在研究中一直保持运动(remained so)的女性相比,后来才开始运动的女性得到的好处是一样多的。由此可见,参与实验的老年女性中有很少运动的,也有一直积极运动的。故此句判断为 NO。
4. [NG] 由"Don't go solo."部分第二段"Another benefit to group activities: Organized exercise programs, like those available for low or no cost at the YMCA or local hospitals, often include professional guidance—especially useful for those with conditions such as obesity, diabetes, and arthritis. 'There are exercise therapists or physiologists who can expertly guide you to the proper way to increase your endurance and intensity without risking injury or fatigue,' says Gregg. 可以看出集体运动中常常会有专业指导,对肥胖、糖尿病以及关节炎患者会很有帮助,但并没有讲他们能够治疗这些症状。故此句判断为 NOT GIVEN。
5. "Get a checkup before a workout."部分第一段中说明老年人在开始锻炼之前要去拜访医生,做个检查。第二段作者讲到原因:"People can sometimes control conditions such as diabetes and high blood pressure with weight loss and exercise so they don't need to continue their medications...",即锻炼和减肥可以改善糖尿病和高血压的情况,病人的服药治疗也要进行相应的调整。故此题正确答案为"continue their medications"。
6. "Get a checkup before a workout."部分第三段最后一句说"So I try to steer them to another activity, such as swimming, which is especially good for people with joint problems or obesity."。此段紧接着第二段继续陈述 William A. Banks 的观点。他认为开始锻炼之前去看医生的另外一个好处是医生可以就病人的情况建议进行何种类型的锻炼。比如对关节病患和肥胖病患来说,游泳是比较好的。故此题正确答案为"swimming"。
7. "Start slow."部分第一句"Once you get the green light, the key to avoiding fatigue and muscle pain is to pull out of the gate very slowly."说明一旦得到医生的允许开始锻炼,避免疲劳和肌肉酸痛的关键是慢慢开始。故本题答案可以是"pull out of the gate very slowly/ start slow"或者也可以用本部分的标题"start slow"。
8. 由"Go more often."部分的最后一句"A key to intensity: Ideally, you want to be aerobic enough so you can utter a few words or syllables in each sentence, but not so little that you're speaking in complete sentences or too much so you can barely talk, advises Banks."指出理想的运动强度是运动时能一句话说出几个单词或音节。如果运动强度太低,能说完整的句子,或者运动过度,几乎说不出话来,都不太合适。可见,正确答案是"utter a few words or syllables

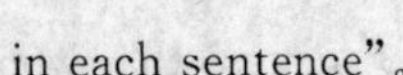

in each sentence"。

9. "Don't go solo."部分第二段最后一句:"There are exercise therapists or physiologists who can expertly guide you to the proper way to increase your endurance and intensity without risking injury or fatigue..."可见,专家可以引导锻炼者提高运动中的持久力和强度。故正确答案为"endurance and intensity"。

10. 由"Do what you enjoy."部分第一句:"... you should pick an activity you like, so you continue it."可见,选择自己喜欢的运动有助于坚持此项运动。故正确答案为"continue it"。

Part Ⅲ Listening Comprehension(听力原文在光盘中)

Part Ⅳ Reading Comprehension (Reading in Depth)

Section A

47. 文章第一段讲到迁徙式养蜂的历史时作者提到"In the 1880s North American beekeepers experimented with the same idea, moving bees on barges along the Mississippi lighter, wooden hives kept falling into the water. Other keepers tried the railroad and horse drawn wagons, but that didn't prove practical.",可见19世纪80年代美国人就开始尝试迁徙式养蜂。但用驳船运输蜂箱不成功;用火车或马车则不实际。因此,早期的尝试都是不成功的。答案可以概括为"unsuccessful"。

48. 由第三段第二、三句"These are not moved in the middle of the day because too many of the bees would end up homeless. But at night, the hives are stacked onto wooden pallets, back-to-back in sets of four, and lifted onto a truck."可见晚上运送蜂箱是因为白天蜜蜂飞出去采蜜,如果蜂箱被运走,蜜蜂就无法回到蜂箱中了(end up homeless)。稍加推测可知,晚上蜜蜂都回巢了,蜂箱是满的。因此,答案是"full"或者其他含义相近的表达。

49. 从第四段可知从橘林中采的蜜香甜可口,可以出售。所以养蜂人是要向农场主付费的。"In their new location, the beekeeper will pay the farmer to allow his bees to feed in such places as orange groves."这一句中"beekeeper"是主语,宾语是"the farmer",动词用"pay"。题目中主语和宾语位置互换了,因此动词要变成"向……收费"。故正确答案为"charge"。

50. 第四段倒数第二句"In the brood chamber below, the bees will stash honey to eat later."中的"stash"就是"keep"的意思。因此,答案为"In the brood chambers."。此段讲到蜂箱的结构分成三个部分,最上边是为了让蜜蜂多采蜜而增加的"临时扩展部分",被称为"supers";最下面就是蜜蜂自己储藏蜂蜜的地方,"brood chambers";为了防止蜂后爬上来产卵,中间加了一层隔板,"screen"。因此,"brood chambers"位于蜂箱的最下层。故答案也可以是"In the bottom of the hives."。

51. 由文章最后一段第二句"To create new colonies, a healthy double hive, teeming with bees, can be separated into two boxes."可知养蜂人是把状况良好的双层蜂箱分成两个蜂箱。因此,正确答案为"They will be separated/ split into two boxes."。

Section B

52. [B] 细节判断题。由第一段开篇的"humorless boss or dour neighbor may not have a personality defect—but a different brain structure"可见本题答案为B项。由第三段"People with damage to the right anterior frontal lobe were the least able to appreciate jokes and

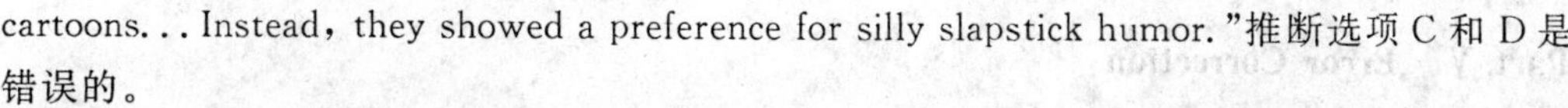

cartoons... Instead, they showed a preference for silly slapstick humor."推断选项C和D是错误的。

53. [D] 细节题。由第二段中的"We always thought of humor as an intangible part of our personality"可以判断出正确答案是D项。由第二段最后一句"Now we know humor can be tested and scientifically scrutinized"可以排除选项A。

54. [A] 细节判断题。由第三段开头的"responses of 42 volunteers aged 18 to 70 to written and verbal jokes and cartoons"可判断正确答案为A项。由第三段中的"People with damage to the right anterior frontal lobe were the least able to appreciate jokes and cartoons... Instead, they showed a preference for silly slapstick humor"可以断定选项B和C是错误的。

55. [C] 细节推断题。由第三段第一句"Shammi compared the responses of 42 volunteers aged 18 to 70 to written and verbal jokes and cartoons."可见参与实验的志愿者是介于18到70岁之间。Shammi分析他们对书面的(written)和口头的(verbal)笑话和动画做出的回应。选项A和B都符合原文,可以排除。由第三段第二句"Half the group had a brain injury caused by stroke, tumor or surgical removal."可见,半数的志愿者是由于中风、肿瘤或者手术而脑部受损。half和majority并不一致。因此,正确答案为C项。

56. [B] 逻辑推断题。原文中的选项A不存在任何幽默,只是现实中最常见的、正常的回应。原文中B选项的回应是幽默的:"既然现在周薪是50美金,一个月后是75美金,那我一个月后再来好了。"而原文中的选项C则是较为粗俗的玩笑。由最后一段的"People with damage to the right anterior frontal lobe were the least able to appreciate jokes and cartoons... Instead, they showed a preference for silly slapstick humor."可推断正确答案是B项,他们会选择开粗俗的玩笑。

57. [A] 因果推断题。文章开头即提及"America... had a large immigrant population, many of whom could hardly speak English" 和"the silent movies—these they could all understand"。而根据第一段末尾"irrespective of the fact they couldn't understand the captions",可以排除选项D,也就是说美国初期移民们爱看无声电影,因为无声电影易懂,不用管能否看懂字幕。因此,正确答案为A项。

58. [A] 细节甄别题。由第二段的"Films continued to be made..., and to fill the gap in foreign imports"可知美国一战期间电影继续发展(尽管没有先前的发展速度),以此来弥补从欧洲进口电影数量的减少。故正确答案为A项。

59. [D] 推断题。细读第三段,文中提及"America was the world leader in film production, it was not then nor has it been since—in the lead when it comes to developing film as an art form",这句话耐人寻味,意思是说:尽管上世纪20年代美国在电影制造业领先,但这决不表示当时美国电影在艺术形式上领先(暗示数量、制造工艺可能领先,但对艺术的领悟和把捏并非领先)。因而选项A和B错误,选项C是一个普通的、正常的美国人绝对不会做的,因而属于常识性错误。故正确答案为D项。

60. [A] 词义推断题。从上下文可以推断出代词it指示American movie industry。且it文后有"to develop its potential as an art form",因此,正确答案为A项。

61. [B] 细节题。文末直接给出了"expressionism"的定义"a movement whose main aim was to show in images man's inner world and in particular the emotions of fear, hatred, love and anxiety"。毫无疑义,正确答案为B项。

Part Ⅴ Error Correction

62. 删除 first 之前的 the。一般说来，作为定语的序数词之前要加定冠词，但在某些词组中，序数词前面不加定冠词，at first sight 就是其中一例。
63. dusty → dust。在没有同根形容词的情况下，很多名词都可以用作定语，作用和形容词差不多，试比较：food industry 和 chemical industry，cotton production 和 agricultural production。如果有同根形容词，还是用形容词作定语较好，有时两者都可以用作定语，但意义上有些差别，例如：gold reserve（黄金储备），golden sunshine（金色的阳光）；rain drops（雨点）；rainy season（雨季）；color film（彩色影片）。此处 dust storm 意为"尘暴"，指基本成分是 dust，而不是"似粉状的"。
64. 在 across 之后加 it。介词 across 之后需要宾语，指代 the surface。
65. melts → melted。根据常识以及我们现在掌握的科技知识，我们并不确定火星两极的冰有没有融化，本文只是作了一个假设而已。
66. 在 have 之后加 been。此处为 there be 结构，根据时间状语 a long time ago，作者在对过去可能曾经有过生命形式的一种推测。
67. thinner → thicker。根据上下文意义，如果大气层中的空气稀薄，就不可能有生命存在，而且稀薄的空气就不可能暖和。
68. different → similar。根据上下文意义以及介词 to 判断。
69. used → using。现在分词作方式状语。
70. By →With。with 表示"具备"的含义。
71. spend → take。spend 的主语即该动作的发出者往往是有生命的人或动物，the whole process 不属于该范畴，所以不合适。take 则常常可由无生命的东西作主语。

Part Ⅵ Translation

72. [答案]：it is groundless to hold that people can be changed by having strict rules imposed on them

    [注释]：首先，本句的翻译应使用"it is ＋*adj.* ＋that＋从句"的句型。其次，本句的一个难点是"强制执行"的翻译，大多数的考生可能会想不到使用 impose on 词组。
73. [答案]：a doctor often prides himself on the ability to cure his patient of a rare disease

    [注释]：本句考查的是两个词组的使用，其一为 pride on，表示"以……为豪"；其二为 cure of，表示"治愈"。
74. [答案]：retired people are often depressed if they can't find something to do

    [注释]：本句主要考查"意志消沉"的翻译，也就是 be depressed。
75. [答案]：the coach wanted us to be always aware of the arguments that are quite the reverse of ours

    [注释]：本句主要是考查"相悖"的翻译，应使用 reverse。
76. [答案]：environmental protection should be given priority if it plans to provide a secure future for the younger generation

    [注释]：本句主要是考查"优先地位"的翻译，即 give priority to 词组。

College English Practice Test 6 (Band Ⅵ)

Part Ⅰ Writing (30 minutes)

Directions: *For this part, you are allowed 30 minutes to write a short essay entitled* ***On Graduate Mania****. You should write at least* ***150*** *words following the outline given below.*

1. 目前很多人报考研究生;
2. 你认为此现象的原因是什么;
3. 你的看法。

Part Ⅱ Reading Comprehension (Skimming and Scanning) (15 minutes)

Directions:(略)

Preparing for Weight Loss Surgery

For those who consider weight loss surgery, they are at the end of their ropes. Traditional methods of diet and exercise have had no effect, and this procedure is a last resort. But by no means is the leap from thinking about weight loss surgery to the operating table a short one.

"People need to be aware, in great detail, of the risk and benefits of weight loss surgery so they understand what it is all about," says Harvey J. Sugerman, president of the American Society for Bariatric Surgery. "The procedure is not without risk, and there is a great deal of anxiety that comes with it, so it takes considerable preparation."

From checking on insurance coverage to psychological exams to support groups, preparing for this life-changing procedure takes time, physical and mental readiness, and most of all, commitment.

First Steps

"From the time a person first thinks about having weight loss surgery, to the time they make the commitment to have it done is typically about two years," says James Kolenich, a bariatric surgeon at the University of Pennsylvania Medical Center, Horizon. "Most people don't rush into this, they talk to family and friends, they talk to the hospital, they go home and they think about it more; it's usually a very thoughtful approach."

More than 60 million obese people are living in the U. S., according to the American Obesity Association (AOA), and about 9 million are severely obese. Weight loss surgery, also called bariatric surgery, can be successful when diet and exercise have failed, and a person's health is on

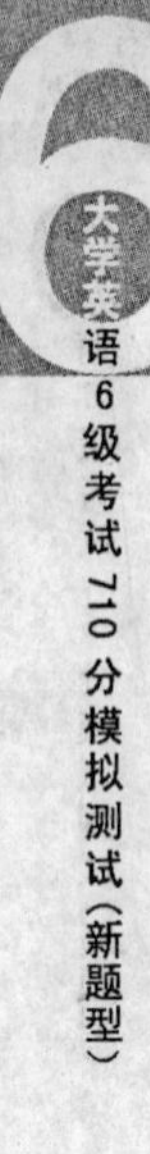

the line. Overweight is the second leading cause of preventable death, after smoking, in the U. S., according to the AOA.

"The first thing a person should do is contact his insurance company to learn if he is covered for the surgery, and he should contact his primary care doctor to find out if there is documentation of his struggle with obesity," says Kolenich. "Many insurance companies want to know that a primary care doctor has tried to help the patient lose weight with psychological counseling, diet, and an exercise plan for five years, and for many patients, this is a big road block."

While there are other options, such as personally financing the procedure, they are costly: The National Institute of Diabetes and Digestive and Kidney Diseases web site states that this procedure can run from $20,000 to $35,000.

With such a hefty price tag on weight loss surgery, it pays to ensure that your doctor documents your battle with obesity early on, to open up options down the road. When you've crossed all your t's and dotted all your i's in the insurance category, it is time to find a hospital or center, and a surgeon, which are first-rate.

Finding a Bariatric Surgeon

"When you're looking for a surgeon, ask if he or she is board-certified by the American Board of Surgery," says Kolenich. "Is he a member of the American Society of Bariatric Surgeons? What is the mortality rate of the surgeon, the morbidity rate, the success rate?"

Clearly, the surgeon you find should be well experienced in the area of weight loss surgery.

"Make sure the surgeon you choose is an experienced and qualified bariatric surgeon," says Daniel Herron, chief of bariatric surgery at Mt. Sinai Hospital in New York. "It's clear that the more experienced the surgeon, the lower the risk of mortality. Ideally, you would prefer to find a surgeon who has performed at least 100 of these procedures."

What you are looking for doesn't stop with numbers and statistics—you will also need a support system. Look for a center or hospital that offers educational seminars to those who are just beginning the process so you can learn more about the actual procedure, the benefits, and the risks. Also look for support groups, that can be utilized pre- and post-operatively.

Preparing for Weight Loss Surgery

"The single most important factor is that they have to realize the surgery is not a cure for obesity," says Herron. "It's a very powerful tool used in the fight against obesity. It needs to be considered as part of a process, and a lifelong commitment to follow up with physicians, a regular exercise program, and healthy eating. If a person doesn't understand that this is a lifelong commitment, that it's not a quick fix, then he or she is not a good candidate."

From a physical standpoint, the preparation for weight loss surgery involves meeting with doctors—a lot of them.

A person also needs to meet with a nutritionist, to begin to better understand the elements of healthy eating, and how eating habits need to change before and after the surgery. "By getting into a proper nutritional mindset before surgery, such as learning to eat smaller portions, eating slowly, paying closer attention to the nutritional make-up of meals, a person is better adapted for

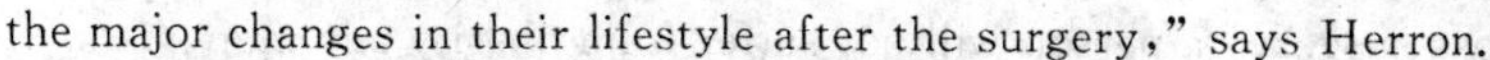

the major changes in their lifestyle after the surgery," says Herron.

Understanding the Risks

Understanding the possible outcomes of weight loss surgery, including the risks, is an important part of preparing for the procedure. "Education is a tremendously important part of the preoperative process," says Herron. "There is no question that there are major risks associated with the operation. However, those risks can be minimized by having a thorough preoperative workup so there aren't surprises during the procedure, and by making sure the surgeon is experienced and qualified."

Nonetheless, dealing with the emotional toll of this procedure can be difficult, especially when considering the possibility of death. "There have been good studies looking at the risk of dying after weight loss surgery, showing that although there is a risk of death with surgery, the overall survival rate is improved with surgery compared to not having the surgery at all, and living with obesity," says Herron.

It helps that most centers and hospitals and insurance companies, require psychological evaluations prior to the allowing the procedure—which benefits both patient and doctor. "You have to fill your mind with as much optimism and positive thinking as possible," says Joe De Simone, PhD, a psychiatrist in private practice in N. Y., who works with patients preparing for weight loss surgery. "Basically, the preparation is to become more conscious of what you are thinking and feeling, and start preparing yourself to think of food and your life in a different way. This is a courageous step for people to take, and it's not just about weight changing—it's about life changing."

Post-Op Expectations

While weight loss surgery does have a major impact on a person's life, it requires, like any surgical procedure, some recovery time. "The recovery period is quite variable," says Herron. "I have some patients who take a week off and are back full time, and others who take three to four weeks to recover. While it's certainly physically possible to be back to 90% of capacity after a week, most people take longer to adjust to the new lifestyle."

New techniques have also helped to lessen recovery time. Today, the procedure can be performed minimally invasively via small incisions. In a few centers around the country it can even be done on an outpatient basis.

Patients also need to remember weight loss surgery is not a cure. "It's not a magic bullet, but is an amazingly powerful weight-loss tool," says Herron. "A person will find they will lose about a pound per day for the first month or so. Then they'll lose between 50%-75% of their excess body weight typically during the first 12 months after surgery." What follows is dedication to a healthy diet and exercise regimen, continual follow-up with doctors to monitor progress, and commitment to a new life.

1. Weight loss surgery is one of the traditional ways of losing weight.
2. Many people have weight loss surgery possibly because overweight may give rise to death.

3. After having the weight loss surgery, a person will not suffer from obesity any more.
4. A person also might be required to quit smoking to improve the outcome of the operation.
5. It is advisable that a patient have his/her operation covered by the insurance company because weight loss surgery is usually ________.
6. A person who thinks about having weight loss surgery should find ________ bariatric surgeon.
7. Eating smaller portions, eating slowly, paying attention to the nutritional ________ of meals are examples of healthy eating habits.
8. During the preparing procedure, one important part is to help the candidates understand the possible outcomes and ________.
9. According to Herron, after having the surgery, the recovery time ________ from person to person.
10. With the development of ________, the recovery period may become shorter and shorter.

Part Ⅲ Listening Comprehension (35 minutes)

Section A

Directions:（略）

11. A) Husband and wife. B) Doctor and patient.
    C) Teacher and student. D) Doctor and nurse.
12. A) To do whatever the committee asks of him.
    B) To make decisions in agreement with the committee.
    C) To run the committee according to his own ideas.
    D) To elect the committee chairman himself.
13. A) At 8:45. B) At 8:15. C) At 8:05. D) At 8:35.
14. A) The man would understand if he had Frank's job.
    B) Frank could help him get a job on an airplane.
    C) Waiting on tables is an enjoyable job.
    D) She is tired of waiting for him there.
15. A) It's not important how he dances. B) It's too crowded to dance anyway.
    C) If he's careful, no one will notice. D) No one knows the steps to the dance.
16. A) They'd better hurry because they have no time to lose.
    B) They needn't hurry because they still have time.
    C) They will not be late because it is easy to get there.
    D) They should take the easiest way in order not to be late.
17. A) Meet his client. B) Prepare the dinner.
    C) Work at his office. D) Fix his car.
18. A) The man deserved the award.
    B) The woman helped the man succeed.
    C) The man is thankful to the woman for her assistance.

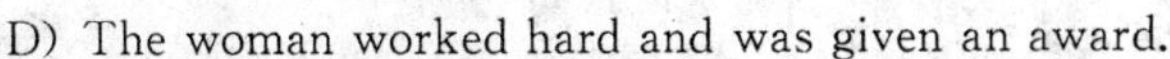

D) The woman worked hard and was given an award.

Questions 19 to 22 are based on the conversation you have just heard.

19. A) The size is very small.
    B) Professors do the presentation in lecture classes.
    C) Students can't ask questions.
    D) Students should be very active in lecture classes.
20. A) A lot of preparation is needed. B) The size is very big.
    C) Professors are always absent. D) Students sit around a big table.
21. A) It is smaller.
    B) The classroom atmosphere is warmer.
    C) Students can't ask questions.
    D) Students don't need to stand up when the class begins.
22. A) More than 100 students. B) About 50 students.
    C) About 200 students. D) 8 to 10 students.

Questions 23 to 25 are based on the conversation you have just heard.

23. A) They are friends. B) They are counselor and client.
    C) They are teacher and student. D) They are colleagues.
24. A) There are some interesting items on the grocery list.
    B) There are some mistakes in the list.
    C) It is actually his notes.
    D) She's never seen a grocery list before.
25. A) The list appears on the man's desk.
    B) The man says he has to buy some things.
    C) The man has made some mistakes in the list.
    D) The handwriting is identical to the man's.

Section B

Directions:(略)

Passage One

Questions 26 to 28 are based on the passage you have just heard.

26. A) She felt doubtful. B) She felt satisfied.
    C) She felt delighted. D) She felt surprised.
27. A) She was asked to call the chairman's wife.
    B) She was asked to make a copy of English final exam.
    C) She was asked to go to the chairman's wife's office.
    D) She was asked to retake the final exam.
28. A) Because she was a black girl.
    B) Because she got the highest average in the class.
    C) Because she wanted to hit the chairman's wife.

D) Because she refused to retake the exam.

Passage Two

Questions 29 to 31 are based on the passage you have just heard.

29. A) He trained as an electronics engineer.
    B) He trained as a mechanical engineer.
    C) He trained as a communication engineer.
    D) He trained as a nuclear engineer.
30. A) Fishing and hunting.
    B) He began to show great interest in natural beauty.
    C) Nuclear science.
    D) Amateur radio.
31. A) An old friend of his. B) His elder brother.
    C) His younger brother. D) His younger son.

Passage Three

Questions 32 to 35 are based on the passage you have just heard.

32. A) To adopt a three-year policy.
    B) To provide subsidies.
    C) To create more job opportunities.
    D) To adopt a system of unemployment insurance.
33. A) 1,530,000. B) 930,000. C) 600,000. D) 105,800,000.
34. A) Eastern. B) Southern. C) Northern. D) Western.
35. A) Because the industrial development has been unbalanced.
    B) Because college enrolment has been expanded.
    C) Because they are not adaptable.
    D) Because they can not meet market demands.

Section C

Directions:(略)

Unemployment is a deeply (36) __________ sensitive political issue for Chancellor Gerhard Schroeder. Back in 1998 he was (37) __________ for his first term on a promise that the jobless count would be brought down to (38) __________.

He (39) __________ on that and now the official unemployment figure is above five million, the first time since the great depression of the 1930s, which brought the Nazis to power. And to make matters (40) __________, the official figures may greatly (41) __________ the real extent of the problem. Once those on government training schemes and the like are (42) __________, the actual number of people looking for work could be as high as (43) __________.

The German economy has yet to fully recover from the boom and bust that followed reunification a decade ago. (44) ____

____, where work has shifted to new manufacturing centers such as China.

But, despite the latest unemployment figures, there are some recent signs of economic improvement in what is still by far Europe's largest economy. (45) ____. Meanwhile businesses are more optimistic than they were a couple of years ago. Welfare benefits have been reduced. Companies have been re-organized to cut costs.

(46) ____. The German economy is growing again: though slowly, and it is seen as one of the more robust in the European Union.

Part Ⅳ Reading Comprehension(Reading in Depth) (25 minutes)

Section A

Directions:(略)

Questions 47 to 51 are based on the following passage.

The concept of health holds different meanings for different people and groups. These meaning of health have also changed over time. This change is no more evident than in western society today, when notions of health and health promotion are being challenged and expanded in new ways.

For much of recent western history, health has been viewed in the physical sense only. That is, good health has been connected to the smooth mechanical operation of the body, while ill health has been attributed to a breakdown in this machine. Health in this sense has been defined as the absence of disease or illness and is seen in medical terms. According to this view, creating health for people means providing medical care to treat or prevent disease and illness. During this period, there was an emphasis on providing clean water, improved sanitation and housing.

In the late 1940s the World Health Organization challenged this physically and medically oriented view of health. They stated that "health is a complete state of physical, mental and social well-being and is not merely the absence of disease" (WHO, 1946). Health and the person were seen more holistically and not just in physical terms.

The 1970s was a time of focusing on the prevention of disease and illness by emphasizing the importance of the lifestyles and behavior of the individual. Specific behaviors which were seen to increase risk of disease, such as smoking, lack of fitness and unhealthy eating habits, were targeted. Creating health meant providing not only medical health care, but health promotion programs and policies which would help people maintain healthy behaviors and lifestyles. While this individualistic healthy lifestyles approach to health worked for some (the wealthy members of society), people experiencing poverty, unemployment, underemployment or little control over the conditions of their daily lives benefited little from it. This was largely because both the healthy lifestyles approach and the medical approach to health ignored the social and environmental conditions affecting the health of people.

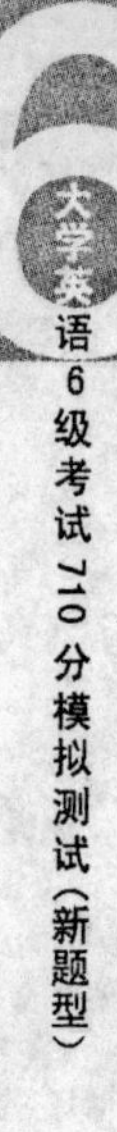

During the 1980s and 1990s there has been a growing swing away from seeing lifestyle risks as the root cause of poor health. While lifestyles factors still remain important, health is being viewed also in terms of the social, economic and environmental contexts in which people live. This broad approach to health is called the socio-ecological view of health. It was endorsed at the first International Conference of Health Promotion held in 1986, Ottawa. People from 38 countries attended the meeting and reached an agreement about the creation of health. It is clear from their agreement that the creation of health is about much more than encouraging healthy individual behaviors and lifestyles and providing appropriate medical care. It must include addressing issues as poverty, pollution, urbanization, natural resource depletion, social alienation and poor working conditions. The social, economical and environmental contexts which contribute to the creation of health do not operate separately or independently of each other. Rather, they are interacting and interdependent, and it is the complex interrelationships between them which determine the conditions that promote them.

47. In which year did the World Health Organization define health in terms of mental, physical and social wellbeing?
48. ________ benefited most from the healthy lifestyles approach to health.
49. The approach to health during the 1970s included the introduction of health ______ programs.
50. What are the three broad areas which relate the people's health according to the socio-ecological view of health?
51. According to the agreement reached at the first International Conference of Health Promotion, the ________ between social, economical and environmental contexts determine the conditions that promote health.

Section B

Directions:（略）

Passage One

Questions 52 to 56 are based on the following passage.

In the first year or so of Web business, most of the action has revolved around efforts to tap the consumer market. More recently, as the Web proved to be more than a fashion, companies have started to buy and sell products and services with one another. Such business-to-business sales make sense because businesspeople typically know what product they're looking for.

However, many companies still hesitate to use the Web because of doubts about its reliability. "Businesses need to feel they can trust the pathway between them and the supplier," says senior analyst Blane Erwin of Forrester Research. Some companies are limiting the risk by conducting online transactions only with established business partners.

Another major shift in the model for Internet commerce concerns the technology available for marketing. Until recently, Internet marketing activities have focused on strategies to "pull" customers into sites. In the past year, however, software companies have developed tools that allow companies to "push" information directly out to customers, transmitting marketing messages directly to targeted customers. Most notably, the Pointcast Network uses a screen saver to deliver a continually updated stream of news and advertisements to subscribers' computer monitors. Subscribers can customize the information they want to receive and proceed directly to a company's Web site. Companies such as Virtual Vineyards are already starting to use similar technologies to push messages to customers about special sales, product offering, or other events. But push technology has earned the contempt of many Web users. Inline culture thinks highly of the notion that the information flowing onto the screen comes there by specific request. Once commercial promotion begins to fill the screen uninvited, the distinction between the Web and television fades.

But it is hardly inevitable that companies on the Web will need to resort to push strategies to make money. The examples of Virtual Vineyards, Amazon. com, and other pioneers show that a Web site selling the right kind of products with the right mix of interactivity, hospitality, and security will attract online customers. And the cost of computing power continues to fall, which is a good sign for any enterprise setting up shop in silicon. People looking back 5 or 10 years from now may well wonder why so few companies took the online plunge.

52. We learn from the beginning of the text that Web businesses ________.
   A) has been striving to expand its market
   B) intended to follow a fanciful fashion
   C) tried but in vain to control the market
   D) has been booming for one year or so

53. Speaking of the online technology available for marketing, the author implies that ________.
   A) the technology is popular with many Web users
   B) businesses have faith in the reliability of online transactions
   C) there is a radical change in strategy
   D) it is accessible limitedly to established partners

54. In view of Net purists, ________.
   A) there should be no marketing messages in online culture
   B) money making should be given priority to on the Web
   C) the Web should be able to function as the television set
   D) there should be no online commercial information without requests

55. We learn from the last paragraph that ________.
   A) pushing information on the Web is essential to Internet commerce
   B) interactivity, hospitality and security are important to marketing
   C) leading companies began to take the online plunge decades ago
   D) setting up shops in silicon is independent of the cost of computing power

56. The purpose of the author in writing the text is to ________.
   A) urge active participation in online business
   B) elaborate on various marketing strategies
   C) compare Web business with traditional commerce
   D) illustrate the transition from the push to pull strategy

Passage Two

Questions 57 to 61 are based on the following passage.

Telecommunications is just one of the means by which people communicate and, as such, we need to look at telecommunications and any other communications technologies within the wider context of human communication activity. Early findings show that many people are uneasy and even fearful of information technology by avoiding it or by using it in minimal ways.

To obtain this type of data we have spent time with individuals, watching how they communicate where they get confused, what they don't understand and the many mistakes they make. You can do this type of research yourself in an informal way. Just watch someone at the desk next to you trying to use a phone or trying to fill in a form. What you will quickly notice about people on the phone is that they use very few of the buttons available on the keypad, and they get quite anxious if they have to use any buttons outside their normal ones. Most will not use the instruction book, and those that do will not necessarily have a rewarding experience. Watch someone fill out a form—a good meaty one such as an application form or a tax form—and you will see a similar pattern of distressed behavior.

The simple fact we can all observe from how people use these ordinary instruments of everyday communication is how messy, uncertain and confusing the experience can be. Now multiply these individual close encounters of the communicative kind to take account of the full range you may experience in a single day, from getting up in the morning until you go to bed at night and the world takes on a slightly different appearance.

Even watching television which for many provides an antidote to the daily confusion is itself fraught with a kind of low level confusion. For example, if you ring people up five minutes after the evening news has finished and ask them what the news was about, many cannot remember, and those who do remember get some of it wrong.

One of the reasons why this obvious confusion gone unnoticed is because "communication" is a word we associate with success, and therefore we expect the process to work effectively most of the time. To suggest otherwise is to challenge one of our society's most deeply held beliefs.

57. How do scientists know many people are uneasy about information technology?
    A) By asking people to answer questions orally.
    B) By asking people to fill in various question forms.
    C) By making people use instruments of everyday communication.
    D) By watching people using information technology.
58. Which of the following about reading the instruction book is TRUE?
    A) Those who read it benefit a great deal.
    B) Generally, it is poorly written.
    C) Generally, it is too long to read.
    D) Most people do not refer themselves to it.
59. The writer includes the example of watching TV in Paragraph 4 for the purpose of ________.
    A) illustrating that watching TV itself is a source of low-level confusion

B) recommending that watching TV is an antidote to removing confusion

C) indicating that TV viewers cannot remember all its programs

D) supporting the view that all people poor and rich, enjoy watching TV

60. What does the last paragraph want to indicate?

A) The kinds of confusion gone unnoticed.

B) What makes some confusion go unnoticed.

C) The contents of confusion gone unnoticed.

D) The people with some confusion gone unnoticed.

61. What conclusion about new technology can you obtain from this passage?

A) It takes time to get familiar with new technology.

B) New technology is developing rapidly.

C) Not everybody likes new technology.

D) People take a positive attitude toward new technology.

Part Ⅴ Cloze (15 minutes)

Directions:(略)

Painting, the execution of forms and shapes on a surface by means of pigment, has been continuously practiced by humans for some 20,000 years. Together with other activities __62__ ritualistic in origin but have come to be designated as artistic(such as music or dance), painting was one of the earliest ways in which man __63__ to express his own personality and his __64__ understanding of an existence beyond the material world. __65__ music and dance, however, examples of early forms of painting have survived to the present day. The modern eye can derive aesthetic as well as antiquarian satisfaction __66__ the 15,000-year-old-cave murals of Lascaux—some examples __67__ to the considerable powers of draftsmanship of these early artists. And painting, unlike other arts, exhibits universal qualities that __68__ for viewers of all nations and civilizations to understand and appreciate.

The major __69__ examples of early painting anywhere in the world are found in Western Europe and the Soviet Union. But some 5,000 years ago, the areas in which important paintings were executed __70__ to the eastern Mediterranean Sea and neighboring regions. __71__ Western shared a European cultural tradition the Middle East and Mediterranean Basin and, later, the countries of the New World.

Western painting is in general distinguished by its concentration __72__ the representation of the human __73__, whether in the heroic context of antiquity or the religious context of the early Christian and medieval world. The Renaissance __74__ this tradition through a __75__ examination of the natural world and an investigation of balance, harmony, and perspectives in the visible world, linking painting __76__ the developing sciences of anatomy and optics. The first real __77__ from figurative painting came with the growth of landscape painting in the 17th and 18th centuries. The landscape and figurative traditions developed together in the 19th century in an atmosphere that was increasingly __78__ "painterly" qualities of the __79__ of light and color and the expressive qualities of paint handling. In the 20th century these interests __80__ to the

development of a third major tradition in Western painting, abstract painting, which sought to __81__ and express the true nature of paint and painting through action and form.

62. A) may have been B) that may have
C) may have D) that may have been
63. A) seek B) sought C) seek for D) sought for
64. A) emerging B) emergency C) merging D) merger
65. A) As B) Unlike C) Like D) Since
66. A) from B) to C) into D) for
67. A) ratify B) testify C) certify D) gratify
68. A) make easy B) make it easy C) make hard D) make it hard
69. A) extinct B) extent C) extant D) exterior
70. A) had shifted B) have shifted C) shifting D) shifted
71. A) Nevertheless B) Moreover C) However D) Therefore
72. A) to B) in C) on D) for
73. A) figure B) shape C) shadow D) form
74. A) extracted B) extended C) extorted D) extruded
75. A) closing B) close C) closed D) closure
76. A) on B) for C) in D) to
77. A) break B) breakage C) breakdown D) breaking
78. A) concerned with B) concerning C) concerning with D) concerned for
79. A) reaction B) action C) interaction D) relation
80. A) distributed B) attributed C) contributed D) construed
81. A) discover B) uncover C) recover D) cover

Part Ⅵ Translation (5 minutes)

Directions:(略)

82. ________________________________(令我们宽慰的是,观众对我们的演出十分欣赏). Most of them were college students.

83. Even if you're best in class, ________________________________(要保持成绩也得常常温习功课才行).

84. ________________________________(她被这突如其来的打击吓得讲不出话来) for several minutes.

85. In general, ________________________________(通过增加供给或减少需求可以降低物价).

86. As far as I know, ________________________________(他们相互感情上疏远已有一段时间了).

参考答案(6)

Part Ⅰ Sample Writing

On Graduate Mania

In recent years, people who would like to go to graduate school became more and more. For one thing, thousands of enterprising young men sit for National Graduate Entrance Exam each year. For example, 50 thousand candidates took part in the National Graduate Entrance Exam last year. For another, not only the undergraduates but also the work employees try their best to be postgraduates.

There are several reasons which lead to this phenomenon. To begin with, it is because of employment pressure that large numbers of people enroll in the National Graduate Entrance Exam. Owing to enhancement of educational standard, a bachelor's degree is no longer evaluated as a sufficient qualification to ensure a decent job. Secondly, some people, though have been employed for several years, find their knowledge inadequate to meet the demand of this ever-changing world. Finally, many people only follow the suit with no specific purpose.

In my opinion, we have to think carefully before we decide to apply for graduate school. Can graduate school offer me what I want to learn? Do I need practical work experience or theoretical knowledge? Before we make the choice these questions need to be answered.

Part Ⅱ Reading Comprehension (Skimming and Scanning)

1. N　2. Y　3. N　4. NG
5. costly/expensive
6. an experienced and qualified/a well experienced
7. make-up
8. the risks of weight loss surgery
9. varies
10. technology/new techniques

Part Ⅲ Listening Comprehension

Section A

11—15 BCDAA　16—20 BADBA　21—25 BDCCD

Section B

26—30 ADAAD　31—35 CDCDB

Section C

36. sensitive　37. elected　38. 3,500,000　39. failed
40. worse　41. understate　42. included　43. 9,000,000
44. German firms with their high wage and social costs have struggled in an increasingly globalized world economy
45. Consumers are spending more in the shops, a sign they're more confident about the future

46. It's been a painful process but economists say it's beginning to produce results.

Part Ⅳ Reading Comprehension (Reading in Depth)

Section A

47. 1946
48. The wealthy members of society. /The wealthy.
49. promotion/awareness
50. Social, economic and environmental contexts. /Society, economy and environment.
51. interrelationships

Section B

52—56 ACDBA 57—61 DDABD

Part Ⅴ Cloze

62—66 DBABA 67—71 BBCDD 72—76 CABBD 77—81 AACCB

Part Ⅵ Translation

82. Much to our relief, our performance was fully appreciated by the audience
83. in order to maintain your grades you must review your lessons often
84. She was so scared by the unexpected blow that she could not speak a word
85. prices may be brought down by increasing supply or decreasing demand
86. they have been emotionally detached from each other for quite some time

试题解答(6)

Part Ⅱ Reading Comprehension (Skimming and Scanning)

1. [N] 由文章第一、二句"For those who consider weight loss surgery, they are at the end of their ropes. Traditional methods of diet and exercise have had no effect, and this procedure is a last resort."可知当传统的节食和运动等瘦身方式都没有效果时,人们才不得已选择"减肥手术",可见"手术"并非传统的瘦身方法。故判断为 NO。
2. [Y] 由"First Steps"部分第二段最后一句"Overweight is the second leading cause of preventable death, after smoking, in the U. S., according to the AOA."和"Understanding the Risks"部分第二段第二句"'There have been good studies looking at the risk of dying after weight loss surgery, showing that although there is a risk of death with surgery, the overall survival rate is improved with surgery compared to not having the surgery at all, and living with obesity,' says Herron."可见体重超重会导致死亡。因此人们在传统的减肥方法无效的时候选择手术。故此题判断为 YES。
3. [N] 由"Preparing for Weight Loss Surgery"部分第一段第一、二句"'The single most important factor is that they have to realize the surgery is not a cure for obesity,' says Herron. 'It's a very powerful tool used in the fight against obesity. It needs to be considered as part of

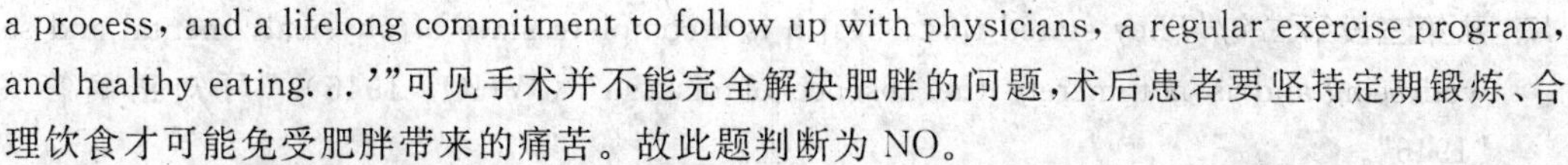

a process, and a lifelong commitment to follow up with physicians, a regular exercise program, and healthy eating...'"可见手术并不能完全解决肥胖的问题,术后患者要坚持定期锻炼、合理饮食才可能免受肥胖带来的痛苦。故此题判断为NO。

4. [NG] 文章中没有提到要求患者手术前戒烟的问题。故判断为NOT GIVEN。
5. 由"First Steps"部分第四段"While there are other options, such as personally financing the procedure, they are costly: The National Institute of Diabetes and Digestive and Kidney Diseases web site states that this procedure can run from $20,000 to $35,000."和第五段第一句"With such a hefty price tag on weight loss surgery, it pays to ensure that your doctor documents your battle with obesity early on, to open up options down the road."可见减肥手术费用高昂,接受手术的病人最好出具医生的证明,从而让保险公司支付手术费用。故此题答案为"costly/expensive"。
6. 由"Finding a Bariatric Surgeon"部分第二段"Clearly, the surgeon you find should be well experienced in the area of weight loss surgery."和第三段"'Make sure the surgeon you choose is an experienced and qualified bariatric surgeon,' says Daniel Herron, chief of bariatric surgery at Mt. Sinai Hospital in New York."可见要选择合格的、有经验的外科医生。故正确答案为"an experienced and qualified/a well experienced"。
7. 由"Preparing for Weight Loss Surgery"部分第二段,"A person also needs to meet with a nutritionist, to begin to better understand the elements of healthy eating, and how eating habits need to change before and after the surgery. 'By getting into a proper nutritional mindset before surgery, such as learning to eat smaller portions, eating slowly, paying closer attention to the nutritional make-up of meals, a person is better adapted for the major changes in their lifestyle after the surgery,' says Herron."可见少量进食、细嚼慢咽、注重食物的营养构成都是良好的饮食习惯。故正确答案为"make-up"。
8. 由"Understanding the Risks"部分第一段第一句"Understanding the possible outcomes of weight loss surgery, including the risks, is an important part of preparing for the procedure."可见,准备过程中,很重要的一个环节是帮助患者了解手术可能带来的后果和风险。故正确答案为"the risks of weight loss surgery"。
9. 由"Post-Op Expectations"部分第一段第二、三句"'The recovery period is quite variable,' says Herron. 'I have some patients who take a week off and are back full time, and others who take three to four weeks to recover...'"可见,病人康复时间长短不一样。有的需要一周即可、有的则需要三到四周时间。句中需要填写动词。因此,只要把原文中的"variable"改成相应的动词"varies"就可以了。
10. 由"Post-Op Expectations"部分第二段第一、二句话"New techniques have also helped to lessen recovery time. Today, the procedure can be performed minimally invasively via small incisions."可见新的手术技巧可以缩小手术创口,从而缩短康复时间。因此,可以推断随着技术的发展,康复时间会日渐缩短。故正确答案为"technology/new techniques"。

Part Ⅲ Listening Comprehension(听力原文在光盘中)

Part Ⅳ Reading Comprehension (Reading in Depth)

Section A

47. 从第三段第二句"They stated that 'health is a complete state of physical, mental and social well-being and is not merely the absence of disease' (WHO, 1946)."可知正确答案是"1946"。

48. 文中第四段讲到20世纪70年代,人们强调生活方式和行为对健康的影响。但对富有阶层这种方法是有效果的,而失业的、贫困的人从中受益很小。由第四段第四句"While this individualistic healthy lifestyles approach to health worked for some (the wealthy members of society), people experiencing poverty, unemployment, underemployment or little control over the conditions of their daily lives benefited little from it."可见受益最多的是富有阶层。因此,正确答案是:"The wealthy members of society"或者表达为"The wealthy"。

49. 第四段第三句讲到促进健康不仅要提供医疗服务,还要引入帮助人们了解和保持健康的行为和生活方式的健康增进计划和政策(Creating health meant providing not only medical health care, but health promotion programs and policies which would help people maintain healthy behaviors and lifestyles.),因此可见此处要填写的答案是"promotion"。当然根据理解,要引入的是帮助人们了解和保持健康生活方式的项目或计划,所以此处也可以填写"awareness"。

50. 从最后一段第二、三句"While lifestyles factors still remain important, health is being viewed also in terms of the social, economic and environmental contexts in which people live. This broad approach to health is called the socio-ecological view of health."可知,影响人们健康的是:"Social, economic and environmental contexts."。还可以直接用名词来表示这三个领域"Society, economy and environment."。

51. 从文章最后两句"The social, economical and environmental contexts which contribute to the creation of health do not operate separately or independently of each other. Rather, they are interacting and interdependent, and it is the complex interrelationships between them which determine the conditions that promote them."可以看出社会、经济和环境三个因素在增进健康方面是相互作用的,不是彼此独立的。正是三者的相互作用、相辅相成的复杂"相互关系"(interrelationships)决定健康改善情况。因此正确答案为"interrelationships"。

Section B

52. [A] 细节题。由第一段第一句"In the first year or so of Web business, most of the action has revolved around efforts to tap the consumer market."可知在网络商业第一年左右的时期里,大多数的努力都是围绕着打开市场而展开的。因此正确答案为A项。

53. [C] 细节推断题。第三段第一句"Another major shift in the model for Internet commerce concerns the technology available for marketing."可知网络商业的另一个重大的改变是关于市场营销的可用技术。接着作者讲到一直以来网络市场的营销活动都以如何把顾客"拉"到网站中为中心。而最近几年,软件公司已经开发出工具让公司直接把信息"推"到目标客户面前。由此可见,市场营销技术在策略上发生了根本性的变化。故答案为C项。

54. [D] 细节推断题。由第三段倒数第二和第三句"Inline culture thinks highly of the notion that the information flowing onto the screen comes there by specific request. Once commercial promotion begins to fill the screen uninvited, the distinction between the Web and television fades."可知原来网络文化所认同的是电脑屏幕上的信息都是人们所查询的。否则一旦商业广告不请自来,充斥屏幕,网络和电视就没有差别了。所以可以看出网络纯粹主义者认为商

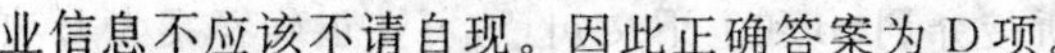

业信息不应该不请自现。因此正确答案为D项。

55. [B] 细节题。由最后一段第二句可知网络销售获得成功的一些公司都使用了恰当的产品,加上适当的互动、热情和安全,由此来吸引顾客的。因此,正确答案为B项。

56. [B] 写作目的题。纵观全文,作者首先讲到最初进行网络商业的公司努力去开拓市场,然后讲了网络营销策略的变化,以及取得成绩的公司的成功之道。文章最后两句作者提到网络营销成本不断下降,对想建立网络商业的公司是个好现象。人们现在回顾过去,也许会想五年前或者十年前致力于网络商业的公司怎么会这么少。可见作者以为网络商业在不断发展,拓展市场的方法也日渐成熟,加入这一领域的公司必将越来越多。文章有劝告人们参与网络商业之意。因此,正确答案为A项。由于作者没有详细阐释多种营销策略,排除选项B没有着重比较传统商业和网络商业,排除选项C。选项D中提到的两种营销策略的变化顺序颠倒,可排除。

57. [D] 细节题。文章第二段提到"To obtain this type of data we have spent time with individuals, watching how they communicate where they get confused, what they don't understand and the many mistakes they make."只要观察他们就可以获得数据。作者接着举例:"Just watch someone at the desk next to you trying to use a phone or trying to fill in a form."可以观察他们如何使用电话,如何填写表格。因此,选项D通过观察人们如何使用信息技术了解人们对信息技术的态度是正确答案。

58. [D] 细节题。由第二段倒数第二句"Most will not use the instruction book, and those that do will not necessarily have a rewarding experience."可知大多数人都不看说明书,那些看说明书的人也不一定能得到有益的帮助。因此正确答案为D项。

59. [A] 细节题。由第四段段首主题句"Even watching television which for many provides an antidote to the daily confusion is itself fraught with a kind of low level confusion."可知哪怕是看电视被很多人看作是消除日常信息混乱的方法,其本身也充斥着一种程度较低的信息混乱。紧接着作者以看电视新闻为例,指出人们看电视也不能获得准确全面的信息。可见,此例是为了阐释段首主题句的。因此正确答案为A项。

60. [B] 细节推断题。最后一段作者指出这种明显的信息混乱没有引起人们注意的原因是人们总把"communication"和成功联系在一起。人们总是期待这个过程是成功的,否则就是挑战人们所深信不疑的信念。可见最后一段是在分析原因,正确答案为B项。

61. [D] 推断题。最后一段作者提到人们总是把新技术(例如 communication)和成功相联系。人们期待这个过程成功,对此深信不疑。由此可见,尽管有混乱和迷惑,人们对新技术的态度是积极的、客观的。故正确答案为D项。

Part Ⅴ Cloze

62. 根据上下文,此处为定语从句,而空格后为形容词,需填一个系动词,因此正确答案为D项。

63. seek 为及物动词,不需接介词 for,与 look for 词组不同。所填动词要与上下文时态保持一致,应使用过去式,故正确答案为B项。

64. 本题考查词义辨析。A项 emerging 意为"出现",B项 emergency 意为"紧急",C项 merging 意为"合并",D项 merger 意为"合并",为名词。根据上下文,正确答案为A项。

65. 根据上下文,此处表示绘画与舞蹈、音乐不一样,下一句有转折词 however,因此正确答案为B项。

66. 本题考查固定搭配。derive... from... 意为"从……得到……",因此正确答案为A项。

67. 本题考查词义辨析。A项 ratify 意为"批准",B项 testify 意为"证明",C项 certify 意为"出证

明",D 项 gratify 意为"使满意",从后面所接介词 to 和上下文句意,可知正确答案为 B 项。

68. 从上下文我们得知,绘画不像其他艺术,容易被不同时代和地区的人所理解,这正是它与众不同之处,因此正确答案为 B 项。

69. 本题考查词义辨析。A 项 extent 意为"灭绝的",B 项 extent 意为"范围",C 项 extant 意为"尚存的",D 项 exterior 意为"外部的",根据上下文此处的意思是"尚存的早期的画主要是在西欧和苏联发现的",因此正确答案为 C 项。

70. 本题考查时态。阐述一个发生在过去的事实,用一般过去式,故正确答案为 D 项。

71. 根据上下文,此处与上文有一个因果关系,由于地区的转移,才有下面产生的结果,故正确答案为 D 项。

72. 本题考查固定搭配。concentration 与介词 on 搭配,表示集中精力,故正确答案为 C 项。

73. 本题考查词义辨析。A 项 figure 意为"画像",B 项 shape 意为"形状",C 项 shadow 意为"阴影",D 项 form 意为"形式",根据上下文选项 A 符合句意。

74. 本题考查词义辨析。A 项 extracted 意为"提取",B 项 extended 意为"延伸",C 项 extorted 意为"敲诈",D 项 extruded 意为"挤压出",根据上下文,选项 B 符合句意。

75. 本题考查词义辨析。A 项 closing 意为"结束的",B 项 close 意为"近的,仔细的",C 项 closed 意为"关闭",D 项 closure 意为"结束",故正确答案为 B 项。

76. 本题考查固定搭配。link... to... 意为"把……和……连起来",故正确答案为 D 项。

77. 本题考查词义辨析。A 项 break 意为"分裂",B 项 breakage 意为"破损",C 项 breakdown 意为"损坏",D 项 breaking 意为"断开", A 项符合上下文句意。

78. 本题考查固定搭配。be connected with 意为"与……有关",故正确答案为 A 项。

79. 本题考查词义辨析。A 项 reaction 意为"反应",B 项 action 意为"动作",C 项 interaction 意为"相互作用",D 项 relation 意为"关系" ,其中 C 项符合句意。

80. 本题考查词义辨析。A 项 distributed 意为"分配",B 项 attributed 意为"把……归因为……",C 项 contributed 意为"造成",D 项 construed 意为"解释",C 项符合上下文意思。

81. 本题考查词义辨析。A 项 discover 意为"发现",B 项 uncover 意为"揭露",C 项 recover 意为"恢复",D 项 cover 意为"覆盖",其中 B 项符合上下文句意。

Part Ⅵ Translation

82. [答案]:Much to our relief, our performance was fully appreciated by the audience

[注释]:本句首先是考查 much to our relief 的使用,意为"令人宽慰的是";其次,是谓语动词"欣赏"的翻译,可用 be appreciated。

83. [答案]:in order to maintain your grades you must review your lessons often

[注释]:本句考查的就是 maintain 作为"保持"的含义和 review lessons 表示"温习功课"的含义的使用。

84. [答案]:She was so scared by the unexpected blow that she could not speak a word

[注释]:本句首先考查的是 so... that... 句型的使用;本句的另一个难点是"突如其来的打击"的翻译,可用 unexpected blow。

85. [答案]:prices may be brought down by increasing supply or decreasing demand

[注释]:本句的重点就是"降低"的翻译。

86. [答案]:they have been emotionally detached from each other for quite some time

[注释]:本句考查 be detached from 词组的使用,意为"疏远"。

College English Practice Test 7 (Band Ⅵ)

Part Ⅰ　　Writing　　(30 minutes)

Directions: *For this part, you are allowed 30 minutes to write a Campaign Speech. You should write at least **150** words following the outline given below.*

1. 你认为自己具备了什么条件(能力、性格、爱好等)可以胜任学生会主席的工作。
2. 如果当选,你将为本校同学做些什么。

Part Ⅱ　　Reading Comprehension (Skimming and Scanning)　　(15 minutes)

Directions: *In this part, you will have 15 minutes to go over the passage quickly and answer the questions **on the Answer Sheet**. For questions 1—7, choose the best answer from the four choices marked A), B), C) and D). For questions 8—10, complete the sentences with the information given in the passage.*

Bird Brains

Cracking Walnuts

The scene: a traffic light crossing on a university campus in Japan. Carrion crows and humans line up patiently, waiting for the traffic to halt. When the lights change, the birds hop in front of the cars and place walnuts, which they picked from the adjoining trees, on the road. After the lights turn green again, the birds fly away and vehicles drive over the nuts, cracking them open. Finally, when it's time to cross again, the crows join the pedestrians and pick up their meal.

Biologists already knew the corvine family—it includes crows, ravens, rooks, magpies and jackdaws—to be among the smartest of all birds. But this remarkable piece of behavior would seem to be a particularly acute demonstration of bird intelligence. Researchers believe they probably noticed cars driving over nuts fallen from a walnut tree overhanging a road. The crows already knew about dropping clams from a height on the seashore to break them open, but found this did not work for walnuts because of their soft green outer shell.

Other birds do this, although not with quite the same precision. In the Dardia Mountains of Greece, eagles can be seen carrying tortoises up to a great height and dropping them on to rocks below.

Do Birds Have Intelligence?

Scientists have argued for decades over whether wild creatures, including birds, show genuine intelligence. Some still consider the human mind to be unique, with animals capable of only the simplest mental processes. But a new generation of scientists believes that creatures, including birds, can solve problems by insight and even learn by example, as human children do. Birds can even talk in a meaningful way.

Good Memory

Some birds show quite astonishing powers of recall. A type of North American crow may have the animal world's keenest memory. It collects up to 30,000 pine seeds over three weeks in November, and then carefully buries them for safe keeping across over an area of 200 square miles. Over the next eight months, it succeeds in retrieving over 90 percent of them, even when they are covered in feet of snow.

Making and Using Tools

On the Pacific island of New Caledonia, the crows demonstrate a tool-making, and tool using capability comparable to Paleolithic man's. Dr Gavin Hunt, a New Zealand biologist, spent three years observing the birds. He found that they used two different forms of hooked "tool" to pull grubs from deep within tree trunks. Other birds and some primates have been seen to use objects to forage. But what is unusual here is that the crows also make their own tools. Using their beaks as scissors and snippers, they fashion hooks from twigs, and make barbed, serrated rakes or combs from stiff leathery leaves. And they don't throw the tools away after one use— they carry them from one foraging place to another.

Scientists are still debating what this behavior means. Man's use of tools is considered a prime indication of his intelligence. Is this a skill acquired by chance? Did the crows acquire tool making skills by trial and error rather than planning? Or, in its ability to adapt and exploit an enormous range of resources and habitats, is the crow closer to humans than any other creature?

Dr Hunt said this of his research: "There are many intriguing questions that remain to be answered about crows' tool behavior. Most important would be whether or not they mostly learn or genetically inherit the know-how to make and use tools. Without knowing that it is difficult to say anything about their intelligence, although one could guess that these crows have the capability to be as clever as crows in general."

The woodpecker finch is another consummate toolmaker. It will snap off a twig, trim it to size and use it to pry insects out of bark. In captivity, a cactus finch learnt how to do this by watching the woodpecker finch from its cage. The teacher helped the pupil by passing a ready-made spine across for the cactus finch to use.

Communication Ability

Another sign of intelligence, thought to be absent in most non-human animals, is the ability to engage in complex, meaningful communication. The work of Professor Irene Pepperberg of the

University of Arizona, Tucson, has now shown the general perception of parrots as mindless mimics to be incorrect.

The captive African grey parrot Alex is one of a number of parrots now believed to have the intelligence and emotional make-up of a 3 to 4 year old child. Under the tutelage of Professor Pepperberg, he acquired a vocabulary of over 100 words. He could say the words for colors and shapes and, apparently, use them meaningfully. He has learned the labels for more than 35 different objects; he knows when to use "no," and phrases such as "come here," "I want X," and "Wanna go Y."

A bird's ability to understand, or speak, another bird's language can be very valuable. New Zealand saddlebacks occupy the same territory for years. They have distinct song "dialects" passed on through the generations. New territory vacancies are hard to find, so young males are always on the look-out for new widows into whose territory they can move. While they wander around the forest, they learn the different dialect songs, just as we might learn a language or develop a regional dialect. As soon as a territory-owning male dies, a new young male may move in to take over within 10 minutes. He will immediately start singing the dialect of the territory he is in.

Possessing Abstract Concepts

Intelligence—if this is what scientists agree these birds possess—is not limited to the birds we always thought of as "bright." In recent experiments at Cardiff University in Britain, a pigeon identified subtle differences between abstract designs that even art students did not notice. It could even tell that a Picasso was not the same as a Monet. The experiment seems to show that pigeons can hold concepts, or ideas, in their heads. The visual concept for the pigeon is Picasso's painting style.

Social Necessity Makes Birds Smart.

Scientists believe it is not physical need that drives creatures to become smarter, but social necessity. The complexities of living together require a higher level of intelligence. Corvids and parrots, along with dolphins, chimps, and humans are all highly social—and smart—animals.

Some ravens certainly apply their intelligence for the good of the flock. In North America, they contact other ravens to tell them the location of a *carcass*(动物尸体). Ravens are specialized feeders on the carcasses of large mammals such as moose during the harsh winter months of North America. The birds roost together at night on a tree, arriving noisily from all directions shortly before sunset. The next morning, all the birds leave the roost as highly *synchronized*(同步地) groups at dawn, giving a few noisy caws, followed by honking. They may all be flying off in the direction taken by a bird, which had discovered a carcass the previous day. This bird leads the others to his food store, apparently sharing his finding with the rest of the flock.

Ravens share information about their findings of food carcasses because dead animals are *patchily*(散落地) distributed and hard to find. Many eyes have a better chance of finding a carcass, and once one has been located, the information is *pooled*(共享的). Although the carcass now has to be shared between more individuals, the heavy snowfall and risk of mammal *scavengers*(食腐动物) taking the food mean that a single bird or a small group could not eat it all alone

anyway.

Intelligence Inheritance

The level of intelligence among birds may vary. But no living bird is truly stupid. Each generation of birds that leaves the protection of its parents to become independent has the inborn genetic information that will help it to survive in the outside world and the skills that it has learned from its parents. They would never have met the challenge of evolution without some degree of native cunning. It's just that some have much more than others.

1. The example of the Japanese carrion crows at the beginning of the passage is a demonstration of the ________.
   A) kindness of people
   B) harmonious living conditions
   C) ecological stability
   D) bird intelligence
2. ________ believe(s) that birds as well as some other non-human animals show intelligence.
   A) Biologists
   B) A new generation of scientists
   C) Researchers of the University of Arizona
   D) Only Dr Hunt and his colleagues
3. A type of North American crow can ________ most of the pine seeds it buried even they are in deep snow.
   A) eat up
   B) retrieve
   C) crack
   D) lose
4. The writer compares the ability of the crows on the Pacific island of New Caledonia in making and using tools with that of ________.
   A) Paleolithic man
   B) North American crow
   C) the woodpecker finch
   D) carrion crows
5. People generally regard parrots' speaking human language as ________.
   A) meaningful communication
   B) conveyance of feelings
   C) mindless mimics
   D) ridiculous noises
6. A New Zealand saddleback learns the language of another saddleback in order to ________.
   A) share information about food with it
   B) beat it in the competition for a spouse
   C) use the dialect to control the territory it just moves into
   D) show that it has the ability to acquire different dialects
7. It is ________ that drives birds to become intelligent.
   A) society necessity
   B) physical need
   C) genetic information
   D) psychological request
8. Some birds, such as ________, may hold ideas in their heads.
9. Some ravens in North America apply their intelligence for the good of the flock by ________ the others to his food store.
10. Birds genetically inherit skills and abilities to meet the ________.

Part Ⅲ　　Listening Comprehension　　(35 minutes)

Section A

Directions:(略)

11. A) The train seldom arrives on time.
    B) The schedule has been misprinted.
    C) The speakers arrived at the station late.
    D) The company has trouble printing a schedule.
12. A) She wants to borrow the man's student ID card.
    B) The tickets are less expensive than she expected.
    C) She won't be able to get any discount for the ticket.
    D) The performance turned out to be disappointing.
13. A) The organization of a conference.
    B) The cost of renting a conference room.
    C) The decoration of the conference room.
    D) The job of cleaning up the dining room.
14. A) The man will go in for business fight after high school.
    B) The woman is not happy with the man's decision.
    C) The man wants to be a business manager.
    D) The woman is working in a kindergarten.
15. A) The woman doesn't like jam.
    B) The woman forgot where she had left the jar.
    C) The man had an accident.
    D) The man broke the jar.
16. A) Opinions about the book are varied.
    B) The man thinks the book is excellent.
    C) You shouldn't believe everything you read.
    D) The woman wonders which newspaper the man is reading.
17. A) It's quite normal.　　B) It's too high.
    C) It's cheap indeed.　　D) It could be cheaper.
18. A) The admission of a patient.　　B) Diagnosis of an illness.
    C) The old man's serious condition.　　D) Sending for a doctor.

Questions 19 to 22 are based on the conversation you have just heard.

19. A) At a party.　　B) At school.
    C) At a friend's house.　　D) In the classroom.
20. A) Sharon.　　B) Susan.
    C) Sherry.　　D) Ben.
21. A) Marketing.　　B) International Business.
    C) Accounting.　　D) Education.

22. A) Yes. B) No.
    C) Hard to say. D) Not mentioned.

Questions 23 to 25 are based on the conversation you have just heard.

23. A) It is in the center of Yunnan Province.
    B) It is in the center of Kunming.
    C) It is in the northwest to Ningliang Yi autonomous County.
    D) It is in the northwest of Yunnan Province.
24. A) Its waterfalls and scenery. B) Its culture and scenery.
    C) Its autonomy and culture. D) Its natural wonders.
25. A) Six hours. B) Eighteen hours.
    C) Sixteen hours. D) Eight hours.

Section B

Directions:(略)

Passage One

Questions 26 to 28 are based on the passage you have just heard.

26. A) Within 1 year. B) Within 2 years.
    C) Within 3 years. D) Within 4 years.
27. A) About one third. B) About two thirds.
    C) Less than half. D) More than half.
28. A) To prepare disabled people for later life.
    B) To provide equal opportunities for disabled people.
    C) To analyze the success of disabled people.
    D) To measure the success of federal laws and programs.

Passage Two

Questions 29 to 31 are based on the passage you have just heard.

29. A) By greeting each other very politely.
    B) By exchanging their views on public affairs.
    C) By displaying their feelings and emotions.
    D) By asking each other some personal questions.
30. A) Refrain from showing his feelings. B) Argue fiercely.
    C) Express his opinion frankly. D) Yell loudly.
31. A) Getting rich quickly. B) Respecting individual rights.
    C) Distinguishing oneself. D) Doing credit to one's community.

Passage Three

Questions 32 to 35 are based on the passage you have just heard.

32. A) Watching sports on TV. B) Watching election returns.

C) Late snacks. D) Sleeping.

33. A) Defeat. B) Indifference.

C) Acceptance. D) Violation.

34. A) The Third Kingdom. B) The Weimar Republic.

C) The French Commune. D) Switzerland.

35. A) Hitler. B) De Gaulle.

C) Churchill. D) Hindenburg.

Section C

Directions:(略)

I asked successful people what the secret of their success was. I (36) ________ an early discussion with a vice president of a large oil company. "Oh, I just keep a To Do List," he said. I passed over that quickly, little (37) ________ the importance of what he said.

I was in another city the next day and I had lunch with a businessman who (38) ________ owned the town. He was chairman of the gas and light company, president of five (39) ________ companies, and had his hand in a dozen other (40) ________. I asked him how he (41) ________ to get everything done. "Oh, that's easy," he said. "I keep a To Do List." The first thing in the morning, he told me, he would come in and list what he wanted to (42) ________ that day. He would (43) ________ the items in priority.

During the day (44) ____. In the evening he would check to see how many of the items he had written down still remained undone and then give himself a score. (45) ____.

Again and again in the years since, when I have talked to successful people, the To Do List has come up. I have found that one difference between people at the top of the ladder and people at the bottom is that (46) ____.

Part Ⅳ Reading Comprehension(Reading in Depth) (25 minutes)

Section A

Directions:(略)

Questions 47 to 51 are based on the following passage.

One of the most eminent of psychologists, Clark Hull, claimed that the essence of reasoning lies in the putting together of two "behavior segments" in some novel way, never actually performed before, so as to reach a goal.

Two followers of Clark Hull, Howard and Tracey Kendler, devised a test for children that was explicitly based on Hulll's principles. The children were given the task of learning to operate a machine so as to get a toy. In order to succeed they had to go through a two-stage sequence. The children were trained on each stage separately. The stages consisted merely of pressing the correct

one of two buttons to get a marble; and of inserting the marble into a small hole to release the toy. The Kendlers found that the children could learn the separate bits readily enough. But they did not for the most part "integrate". They did not press the button to get the marble and then proceed without further help to use the marble to get the toy. So the Kendlers concluded that they were incapable of deductive reasoning.

The mystery at first appears to deepen when we learn, from anther psychologist, Michael Cole and his colleagues, that adults in an African culture apparently cannot do the Kendlers' task either. But it lessens, on the other hand, when we learn that a task was devised which was strictly analogous to the Kendlers' one but much easier for the African males to handle. Instead of the button-pressing machine, Cole used a locked box and two differently colored match-boxes, one of which contained a key that would open the box. Notice that there are still two behavior segments—"open the right match-box to get the key" and "use the key to open the box"—so the task seems formally to be the same. But psychologically it is quite different. Now the subject is dealing not with a strange machine but with familiar meaningful objects; and it is clear to him what he is meant to do. It then turns out that the difficulty of "integration" is greatly reduced.

Recent work by Simon Hewson is of great interest here for it shows that, for young children, too, the difficulty lies not in the inferential processes which the task demands, but in certain perplexing features of the apparatus and the procedure. Hewson made two crucial changes. First, he replaced the button-pressing mechanism in the side panels by drawers in these panels which the children could open and shut. This took away the mystery from the first stage of training. Then he helped the child to understand that there was no "magic" about the specific marble. The two modifications together produced a jump in success rates from 30% to 90% for five-year-olds and from 35% to 72.5% for four-year-olds. For three-year-olds, for reasons that are still in need of clarification, no improvement—rather a slight drop in performance—resulted from the change.

We may conclude, then, that children experience very real difficulty when faced with the Kendler apparatus; but this difficulty cannot be taken as proof that they are incapable of deductive reasoning.

47. Why did the Kendlers conduct the test described in the second paragraph?
48. The Kendlers trained their subjects separately in the two stages of their experiment, but not in how to ________ the two actions.
49. Michael Cole and his colleagues demonstrated that adult performance on deductive reasoning tasks depends on ________.
50. Who devised an experiment that investigated deductive reasoning without the use of any marbles?
51. ________ is cited as having demonstrated that earlier experiments into children's ability to reason deductively may have led to the wrong conclusion.

Section B

Directions：（略）

Passage One

Questions 52 to 56 are based on the following passage.

Much of the language used to describe monetary policy, such as "steering the economy to a soft landing" or "a touch on the brakes", makes it sound like a precise science. Nothing could be further from the truth. The link between interest rates and inflation is uncertain. And there are long, variable lags before policy changes have any effect on the economy.

Given all these disadvantages, central bankers seem to have had much to boast of about late. Average inflation in the big seven industrial economies fell to a mere 2.3% last year, close to its lowest level in 30 years, before rising slightly to 2.5% this July. This is a long way below the double-digit rates which many countries experienced in the 1970s and early 1980s.

It is also less than most forecasters had predicted. In late 1994 the panel of economists which *The Economist* polls each month said that America's inflation rate would average 3.5% in 1995. In fact, it fell to 2.6% in August, and is expected to average only about 3% for the year as a whole. In Britain and Japan inflation is running half a percentage below the rate predicted at the end of the last year. This is no flash in the pan; over the past couple of years, inflation has been consistently lower than expected in Britain and America.

Economists have been particularly surprised by favorable inflation figures in Britain and the United States, since conventional measures suggest that both economies, esp. America's, have little productive slack. America's capacity utilization, for example, hit historically high levels earlier this year, and its jobless rate has fallen below most

Why has inflation proved so wild? The most thrilling explanation is, unfortunately, a little defective. Some economists argue that powerful structural changes in the world have up-ended the old economic models that were based upon the historical link between growth and inflation.

52. According to the passage, making monetary policy changes ________.
    A) is comparable to driving a car
    B) is similar to carrying out scientific work
    C) will not influence the economy immediately
    D) will have an immediate impact on the inflation rate
53. From the passage we learn that ________.
    A) there is a clear relationship between inflation and interest rates
    B) the economy always follows particular trends
    C) the current economic problems are entirely predictable
    D) the present economic situation is better than expected
54. The passage suggests that ________.
    A) the previous economic models are still applicable

B) an extremely low jobless rate will lead to inflation

C) a high unemployment rate will result from inflation

D) interest rates have an immediate effect on the economy

55. By saying "This is no flash in the pan" (Paragraph 3, Line 6), the author implies that ________.

A) the low inflation rate will continue
B) the inflation rate will rise again
C) inflation will disappear entirely
D) there is no inflation at present

56. How does the author feel about the present situation?

A) Tolerant.
B) Indifferent.
C) Disappointed.
D) Surprised.

Passage Two

Questions 57 to 61 are based on the following passage.

If you live in a city in North America or Europe, you have probably never thought much about water. Whenever you need some, you turn on the tap and there it is. Millions of people in other parts of the world are not so lucky. They have trouble getting enough clean water for their basic needs. This situation may soon become common all around the world, scientists believe. In fact, they say that the lack of clean water may be one of the biggest issues in the twenty-first century.

The reasons for this are clear. On the one hand, people are using more water than ever before. Over the last fifty years, the population of the world has more than doubled. On the other hand, many sources of surface water—such as rivers, lakes, and streams—are too polluted and unhealthy for use as drinking water.

This has forced more and more people to drill wells so they can get water form underground. There are enormous amounts of water deep underground in lakes called aquifers. Until recently, scientists believed this underground water was safe from pollution. Then, in the 1980s, people in the United States began to find chemicals in their well water, and scientists took a closer look at what was happening. Weldon Spring, Missouri, for example, was the site of a bomb factory during World War Ⅱ. The factory was destroyed after the war, but poisonous chemicals remained on the ground. Very slowly, these chemicals dripped down through the ground and into the aquifer. Once they did, however, the water form that aquifer was no longer drinkable.

It probably never will be drinkable again. Underground water is not renewed regularly by the rain, like lake or river water. Thus, if a harmful chemical gets into an aquifer, it will stay there for a very long time. Furthermore, it is nearly impossible to remove all the water in an aquifer and clean out the pollutants.

Industrial sites like Weldon Spring are one cause of underground water pollution. There are thousands of such sites in the United States alone, and many others around the world. Underground water pollution is also caused by modern farming methods, which require the use of large amounts of chemicals in the fields. And finally, yet another important cause of underground water pollution is waste. That includes solid waste thrown away in dumps and landfills, and also untreated human and animal waste.

The situation is indeed very serious. Fortunately, there are many aquifers and they are very large. Only a small number have been seriously damaged so far. But if the world does not want to go thirsty in the near future, further pollution must be prevented. Around the world, governments must make real changes in industry, agriculture, and waste disposal.

57. This passage is mainly about ________.
    A) pollution problems in general
    B) people in North America or Europe are living happier than those in other parts
    C) people drilling wells to check chemicals in well water
    D) underground water pollution
58. In the first paragraph scientists express the idea that ________.
    A) clean water is no longer available for people in Europe
    B) there will always be enough water for everyone
    C) the water problem will soon be resolved in the twenty-first century
    D) many more people may soon be without clean water
59. One reason for water shortage is that ________.
    A) people in Europe don't turn off their taps
    B) people drill too many wells and pollute them
    C) the population has been continuously rising
    D) there is not much underground water
60. In Weldon Spring, people found ________.
    A) chemicals in well water
    B) many sources of surface water
    C) more aquifers than other places
    D) chemicals in the bomb factory
61. We can infer from this passage that industry, farming, and waste are ________.
    A) polluting all aquifers in the United States
    B) minor sources of underground water pollution
    C) causing problems in bomb factories
    D) the three main sources of underground water pollution

Part Ⅴ Error Correction (15 minutes)

Directions:(略)

Eye behavior, involving varieties of eye-contact, can give subtle messages which people pick up in their daily life. Warm looks or cold stares tell more than words can. Meeting or failing to meet another person's eye produce a particular effect. When two Americans look 62. ________
searchingly at each other's eye, emotions are heightened and the 63. ________
relationship becomes closer. However, Americans are careful about where 64. ________
and when to meet other's eye. In our normal conversation, each eye-contact lasts only a few seconds before one or both individuals look away, because the longer meeting of the eyes is rare, and after it happens, can 65. ________
generate a special kind of human-to-human awareness. For instance, by

simply using his eyes, a man can make a woman aware of him comfortably or uncomfortably; a long and steady gaze from a policeman or judge intimidates accused. In the U. S. proper street behavior requires a nice balance of attention and inattention. You are supposed to look at a passer-by just enough to show that you are being aware of his presence. If you look too little, you appear haughty; too much, inquisitive. Much eye behavior is such subtle that our reaction to it is largely instinctive. Besides, the codes of eye behavior vary dramatically from one culture to other. In the Middle east, it is impolite to look at other person all the time during a conversation; in England, the polite listener fixes the speaker with an inattentive stare and blinks eyes occasionally as a sign of interest and attention. In America, eye behavior functions as a kind of conversational traffic signal control the talking pace and time, and to indicate a change of topic. If you can understand this vital mechanism of interpersonal relations, the basic American idiom is there.

66. ________
67. ________
68. ________
69. ________
70. ________
71. ________

Part Ⅵ　　Translation　　(5 minutes)

Directions:(略)

72. ________________(这一丑闻对于正在力争赢得大选的工党来说无疑是一件尴尬的事). The negative effect could bring about terrible decrease in the votes.

73. ________________(不论他们如何努力,老一辈人往往发现要阻挡青年人发生变化是困难的) in a modern society.

74. We hold this belief firmly ________________(什么都不能阻挡中国人民实现现代化的决心).

75. It is protected by law that ________________(连续工作6个月后,雇员就可以享受带薪的假期和病假).

76. ________________(这位律师试图说服陪审团他的当事人是无辜的). But he failed due to the lack of evidence.

参考答案(7)

Part Ⅰ　Sample Writing

Good evening, ladies and gentlemen:

Thank you for coming to this election campaign today. With the trust and complete support of my team, I am delighted to announce that I am running for chairman of the Student Union.

As a diligent man with pleasant personality, I have been always considered to be a good team member. Meanwhile, as a big fan of sports I fully realize the importance of teamwork and advocate the spirit of being quicker and stronger. I possess strong determination to take firm steps toward achieving the objectives of my team. In addition, my working experience with the Student Union in the past two years will be extremely helpful to my future work here if I get elected.

A sign of a really strong organization is that it can change its leadership without hindering its progress and without damaging its values. If I am elected, I believe I have the capability to lead the Union to advance in the right direction. I will cooperate well with my fellow members of the Union and take innovative measures, including establishing a student-information center, forming a teacher-student-friendship association, to make the Union a true assistance to students' study and life here as well as a bridge of communication between teachers and students.

Thank you very much.

Part Ⅱ Reading Comprehension (Skimming and Scanning)

1. D 2. B 3. B 4. A 5. C 6. C 7. A

8. pigeons

9. leading/guiding/directing

10. challenge of evolution

Part Ⅲ Listening Comprehension

Section A

11—15 ACBCD 16—20 ACABA 21—25 ABDBB

Section B

26—30 BCDDA 31—35 CBCBA

Section C

36. recall 37. suspecting 38. practically 39. manufacturing

40. enterprises 41. managed 42. accomplish 43. arrange

44. he would cross off items and add others as they occurred to him

45. His goal manages to cross off every single item

46. those at the top use a To Do List every day to make better use of their time; those at the bottom don't

Part Ⅳ Reading Comprehension (Reading in Depth)

Section A

47. To test whether children are capable of deductive reasoning.

48. integrate/put together

49. features of the apparatus and procedure

50. Michael Cole and his colleagues.

51. Simon Hewson

Section B

52—56 CDBAD 57—61 DDCAD

Part Ⅴ Error Correction

62. produce → produces
63. at → into
64. where → how
65. after →when 或 if
66. 在 accuse 之前加 the
67. 删除 being
68. such →so
69. other → another
70. inattentive → attentive
71. 在 control 之前加 to

Part Ⅵ Translation

72. The scandal will undoubtedly be an embarrassment to the Labour Party which is trying hard to win the election
73. No matter how hard they try, the older generation often find it difficult to hold back changes among the young
74. nothing can stand in the way of the Chinese people in their resolve to modernize their country
75. after working for 6 months on end, employees are entitled to paid holidays and sick leaves
76. The lawyer tried to convince the jury of his client's innocence

试题解答(7)

Part Ⅱ Reading Comprehension (Skimming and Scanning)

1. [D] 由"Cracking Walnuts"部分第二段第二句 "But this remarkable piece of behavior would seem to be a particularly acute demonstration of bird intelligence. "可见乌鸦借助交通工具轧碎核桃的行为是鸟类具有智慧的例证。故本题正确答案为D项。
2. [B] 由"Do Birds Have Intelligence?"部分第三句"But a new generation of scientists believes that creatures, including birds, can solve problems by insight and even learn by example, as human children do. "可见新一代的科学家们认为鸟类和其他动物也具有智慧。因此本题正确答案为B项。
3. [B] "Good Memory"部分讲到有些鸟类拥有非凡的记忆力。作者以某类北美乌鸦为例。在每年11月份,该乌鸦将近三万粒松子储藏在广达两百平方英里的范围内。在随后的八个月里,它能够找回90%的松子,无论它们是否被厚厚的白雪覆盖。根据原文"Over the next eight months, it succeeds in retrieving over 90 percent of them, even when they are covered in feet of snow. "可知本题正确答案为B项。
4. [A] 由"Making and Using Tools"部分第一段第一句 "On the Pacific island of New Caledonia, the crows demonstrate a tool-making, and tool using capability comparable to Paleolithic man's. "可知新喀里多尼亚岛上的这种乌鸦所展示的制造和使用工具的能力可以和旧石器时

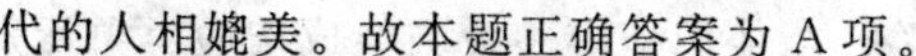

代的人相媲美。故本题正确答案为A项。

5. [C] 根据“Communication Ability”部分第一段最后一句“The work of Professor Irene Pepperberg of the University of Arizona, Tucson, has now shown the general perception of parrots as mindless mimics to be incorrect.”可知教授的工作证明了把鹦鹉说话当作愚蠢学舌的普遍看法是错误的。由此可以推断,人们一般认为鹦鹉说话是愚蠢的学舌。故本题正确答案为C项。

6. [C] 由“Communication Ability”部分第三段中的“While they wander around the forest, they learn the different dialect songs... As soon as a territory-owning male dies, a new young male may move in to take over within 10 minutes. He will immediately start singing the dialect of the territory he is in.”可知年轻的雄鸟学习不同的“方言”并不是为了和该领地的鸟交流关于食物的信息,而是为了在该领地的雄鸟死去后可以占据该领地,用“方言”统领其他鸟。因此本题的正确答案为C项。

7. [A] 由“Social Necessity Makes Birds Smart”部分第一句“Scientists believe it is not physical need that drives creatures to become smarter, but social necessity.”可知是社会需求并非生理需求使生物变得更有智慧。故本题正确答案为A项。

8. “Possessing Abstract Concepts”部分最后两句作者说:“The experiment seems to show that pigeons can hold concepts, or ideas, in their heads. The visual concept for the pigeon is Picasso's painting style.”作者举鸽子为例,讲到有些鸟类具有抽象概念。故本题答案为“pigeons”。

9. 根据“Social Necessity Makes Birds Smart”部分第二段“Some ravens certainly apply their intelligence for the good of the flock... This bird leads the others to his food store, apparently sharing his finding with the rest of the flock.”可知北美的这些乌鸦引导同伴到自己发现食物的地方,让大家一起分享食物。故此题答案可以填写“leading/ guiding/ directing”。

10. 根据“Intelligence Inheritance”部分倒数第二句“They would never have met the challenge of evolution without some degree of native cunning.”可见鸟类是通过基因遗传获得能力和智慧应对进化过程中的挑战。故本题答案为“challenge of evolution”。

Part Ⅲ Listening Comprehension(听力原文在光盘中)

Part Ⅳ Reading Comprehension (Reading in Depth)

Section A

47. 从第二段的最后一句“So the Kendlers concluded that they were incapable of deductive reasoning.”和全文的最后一句“... but this difficulty cannot be taken as proof that they are incapable of deductive reasoning.”可以推断,三组实验都是根据文章开头所提到的心理学家Clark Hull的理论,来验证实验对象是否有推理能力的。Kendler夫妇的实验对象是儿童。故可以回答为“To test whether children are capable of deductive reasoning.”。

48. 结合第二段倒数第三句“But they did not for the most part ‘integrate’.”和文章第一段“... the essence of reasoning lies in the putting together of two ‘behavior segments’ in some novel way, never actually performed before, so as to reach a goal.”,可见如果实验对象能把两个“行为”“结合”起来去达到一个目的,就是具备了推理能力。所以培训实验对象的时候显然不会教他们如何去“结合”两个步骤。故正确答案为“integrate”或者也可以是“put together”。

49. 文章第三段描述了 Michael Cole 和同事们的实验。当他们把实验设施换成实验对象所熟悉的东西时,他们的表现有所改善。可见影响实验结果的是实验设施的特点。到文章的第四段,作者对此做了总结:"Recent work by Simon Hewson is of great interest here for it shows that, for young children, too, the difficulty lies not in the inferential processes which the task demands, but in certain perplexing features of the apparatus and the procedure.",作者明确指出无论实验对象是成人还是儿童,影响他们表现的是实验设施和过程的特点。因此,正确答案为"features of the apparatus and procedure"。

50. 文章第二段描述 Kendler 夫妇的实验时作者提到:"The stages consisted merely of pressing the correct one of two buttons to get a marble; and of inserting the marble into a small hole to release the toy."。第四段描述 Simon Hewson 的实验时提到:"Then he helped the child to understand that there was no "magic" about the specific marble.",由此可见只有 Michael Cole 和他同事的实验没有用弹珠了。故正确答案是"Michael Cole and his colleagues."。

51. 第四段描述了 Simon Hewson 在前面两个研究者的实验的基础上改良了实验设施,对儿童进行了实验。结果证明五岁和四岁儿童的表现有大幅度提高。由此也证明,前面认为孩子不具备推理能力的实验结论是错误的。因此,本题的正确答案是"Simon Hewson"。

Section B

52. [C] 细节推断题。文中第一段末提出"The link between interest rates and inflation is uncertain. And there are long, variable lags before policy changes have any effect on the economy.",由此可以判断选项 C 为正确答案。

53. [D] 推断题。从文中第二段、第三段举例可以看出,我们的经济 inflation rate 总比预测的要低、要好。因而正确答案为 D 项。

54. [B] 意义推断题。第一段末谈到"And there are long, variable lags before policy changes have any effect on the economy",由此排除选项 D。最后一段说"since conventional measures suggest that both economies, esp. America's, have little productive slack",意思就是讲过去传统的方法对某些经济预测不管用了,由此可以看出选项 A 不对。再看文末"both economies, esp. America's, have little productive slack. America's capacity utilization, for example, hit historically high levels earlier this year, and its jobless rate has fallen below most",美国经济通胀率低,生产萧条状况少,生产能力极大发挥,失业率降到最高水平以下。由此可以反向推断:失业率高,经济通胀率就会低;失业率低,经济通胀率就会高。因而正确答案为 B 项。

55. [A] 意义推断题。先看其上下文"3.5% in 1995. In fact, it fell to 2.6% in August, and is expected to average only about 3% for the year as a whole. In Britain and Japan inflation is running half a percentage below the rate predicted at the end of the last year. This is no flash in the pan; over the past couple of years, inflation has been consistently lower than expected in Britain and America",文前、文后都讲经济通胀率低于预期,由此我们可以判断"This is no flash in the pan",也就意味着低经济通胀仍将继续(整个经济不会出现高通胀这样的情况)。

56. [D] 写作态度题。最后一段,作者首先提到经济学家们感到 surprised,随即作者便问"Why has inflation proved so wild?"笔者最后惊呼"powerful structural changes in the world have up-ended the old economic models that were based upon the historical link between growth and inflation",突然发现已经不能根据经济增长和经济通胀之间传统的联系来预测经济发展

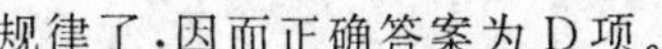

规律了，因而正确答案为D项。

57. [D] 主旨题。第一段后半部分引出主旨"They have trouble getting enough clean water for their basic needs. This situation may soon become common all around the world, ... lack of clean water may be one of the biggest issues in the twenty-first century."。第二段谈及 clean water 变少的两个主要原因，第三段告诉读者既然可饮用水减少，人们就拼命掘井。然而井水也被污染。第四段说一旦地下水被污染，就不是短时间内可以恢复的。第五段阐述地下水污染的三个主要原因(化学物质、农业和废物)。最后一段再次重申地下水问题的重要性并呼吁全球政府采取措施。因此，正确答案为D项。

58. [D] 细节推断题。请看上下文"They have trouble getting enough clean water for their basic needs. This situation may soon become common all around the world, ... lack of clean water may be one of the biggest issues in the twenty-first century"，由此可推断将有越来越多的人喝不上、用不上干净的水，故正确答案D项。

59. [C] 细节选择题。第二段讲干净的水减少的原因"On the one hand, people are using more water than ever before... population of the world has more than doubled... On the other hand, many sources of surface water...—are too polluted and unhealthy for use as drinking water."，即一方面人均用水量比以前增加，人口翻番；另一方面地表水污染严重，不适合饮用。因此正确答案为C项。

60. [A] 细节题。第三段中的"people in the United States began to find chemicals in their well water, ... Weldon Spring, ..., for example..."说明美国科学家发现 Weldon Spring 这些地方的井水里有化学物质。因此正确答案为A项。

61. [D] 推断题。倒数第二段"Industrial sites... are one cause of underground water pollution... Underground water pollution is also caused by modern farming methods, which require the use of large amounts of chemicals in the fields. And finally, yet another important cause of underground water pollution is waste"中清楚地说明了地下水污染的三大原因，即化学物质、农业化肥和废弃物。因此正确答案为D项。

Part Ⅴ Error Correction

62. produce → produces。两个主语 meeting 和 failing to meet another person's eye 用 or 连接，谓语动词通常和最邻近的主语一致。

63. at → into。表示方式的状语 searchingly 暗示这里应该是表示"注视"的词组 look into，而不是一般的"看"——look at。

64. where → how。根据上下文应为 eye contact 的方式方法问题。

65. after →when 或 if。应为条件或假设状语从句，而不是时间状语从句。

66. 在 accuse 之前加 the。形容词或过去分词前加定冠词，表示这一类人，此处 the accused 表示"被告"。

67. 删除 being。本文谈的是一般情形，不需要用进行时。

68. such →so。注意 so 和 such 在用法上的差异：so＋adj./adv.＋that；such＋n.＋that。

69. other → another。如果是三者以上，常用句法结构为 one...another。

70. inattentive → attentive。根据英国文化，礼貌的做法是交谈过程中，倾听对方说话时应该用专注的眼神注视说话的人，以示对所谈话题的兴趣和关注。

71. 在 control 之前加 to。不定式 to control the talking pace and time 和 to indicate a change of

topic一起作 conversational traffic signal 的定语。

Part Ⅵ Translation

72. [答案]:The scandal will undoubtedly be an embarrassment to the Labour Party which is trying hard to win the election

[注释]:本句主要考查"尴尬"的翻译,即 embarrassment。

73. [答案]:No matter how hard they try, the older generation often find it difficult to hold back changes among the young

[注释]:本句考查"阻拦"的翻译,也就是 hold back changes 的使用。

74. [答案]:nothing can stand in the way of the Chinese people in their resolve to modernize their country

[注释]:本句首先考查的也是"阻挡"的翻译,即 stand in one's way; 其次是"决心"的翻译,即 resolve。

75. [答案]:after working for 6 months on end, employees are entitled to paid holidays and sick leaves

[注释]:本句第一个难点是"连续"的翻译,可使用词组 on end; 其次,是"享受"的翻译,即 be entitled to。

76. [答案]:The lawyer tried to convince the jury of his client's innocence

[注释]:本句考查的是"说服"的翻译,也就是词组 convince ... of... 的使用。

College English Practice Test 8 (Band Ⅵ)

Part Ⅰ Writing (30 minutes)

Directions: *For this part, you are allowed 30 minutes to write a report to describe the information in the bar chart below. It shows the different modes of transport used to travel to and from work in one city, in 1950, 1970, 1990. You should write at least* ***150*** *words.*

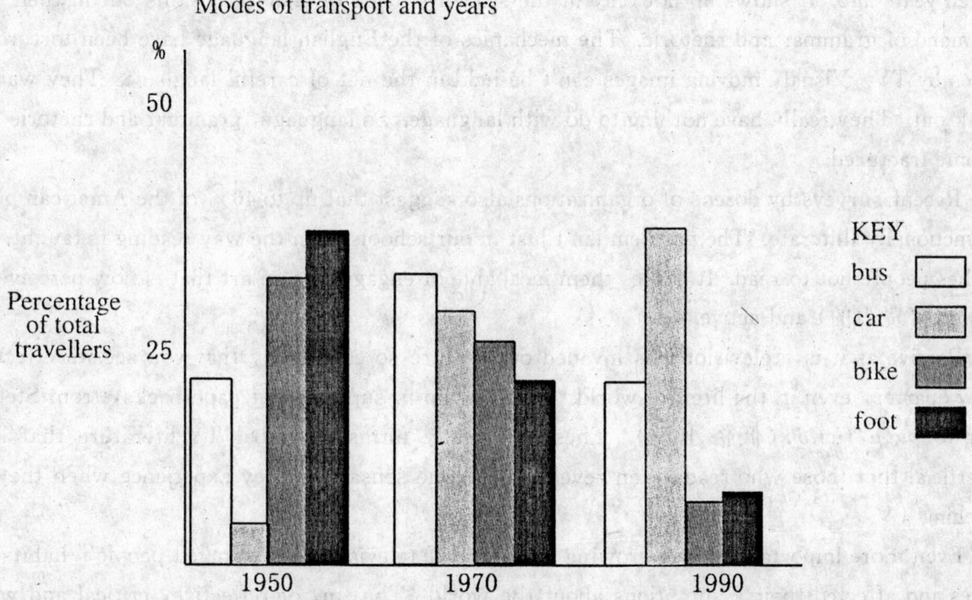

Part Ⅱ Reading Comprehension (Skimming and Scanning) (15 minutes)

Directions: (略)

Television: The Cyclops That Eats Books

What is destroying America today is not the liberal breed of politicians, or the International Monetary Fund bankers, misguided educational elite, or the World Council of Churches. These are largely symptoms of a greater disorder. But if there is any single institution to blame, it is television.

Television, in fact, has greater power over the lives of most Americans than any educational system or government or church. Children particularly are easily influenced. They are fascinated, *hypnotized*(着迷的) and tranquilized by TV. It is often the center of their world. Even when the

set is turned off, they continue to tell stories about what they've seen on it. No wonder, then, that when they grow up they are not prepared for the frontline of life; they simply have no mental defenses to confront the reality of the world.

The Truth About TV

One of the most disturbing truths about TV is that it eats books. Once out of school, nearly 60% of all adult Americans have never read a single book, and most of the rest read only one book a year. Alvin Kernan, author of The Death of Literature, says that reading books "is ceasing to be the primary way of knowing something in our society." He also points out that bachelor's degrees in English literature have declined by 33% in the last twenty years. American libraries, he adds, are in crisis, with few patrons to support them.

Thousands of teachers at the elementary, secondary and college levels can testify that their students' writing exhibits a tendency towards *superficiality*(肤浅) that wasn't seen, say, ten or fifteen years ago. It shows up not only in the students' lack of analytical skills but in their poor command of grammar and rhetoric. The mechanics of the English language have been tortured to pieces by TV. Visual, moving images can't be held in the net of careful language. They want to break out. They really have nothing to do with language. So language, grammar and rhetoric have become fractured.

Recent surveys by dozens of organizations also suggest that up to 40% of the American public is functionally illiterate. The problem isn't just in our schools or in the way reading is taught. TV teaches people not to read. It makes them incapable of engaging in an art that is now perceived as *strenuous*(费力的) and active.

Passive as it is, television has invaded our culture so completely that you see its effects in every quarter, even in the literary world. It shows up in supermarket paperbacks, from Stephen King to *pulp fiction*(低俗小说). These are really forms of verbal TV-literature that is so superficial that those who read it can revel in the same sensations they experience when they are watching TV.

Even more importantly, the growing influence of television has changed people's habits and values and affected their assumptions about the world. The sort of reflective, critical and value-laden thinking encouraged by books has been rendered out of date.

The Cyclops

In this context, we would do well to recall the *Cyclops*(独眼巨人)—the race of one-eyed giants in Greek myth. The following is Hamilton's description of the encounter between the adventurer Odysseus and Polyphemus, a Cyclops.

As Odysseus was on his way home, he and his crew found Polyphemus' cave. They stayed in it as a shelter and waited for the owner to come back. At last he came, hideous and huge, tall as a great mountain crag. Driving his flock before him he entered and closed the cave's mouth with a ponderous slab of stone. Then looking around he caught sight of the strangers. He roared out and stretched out his mighty arms and in each great hand seized one of the men and dashed his brains out on the ground. Slowly he feasted off them to the last shred, and then, satisfied, stretched himself out across the cavern and slept. He was safe from attack. None but he could roll back the huge stone before the door, and if the horrified men had been able to summon courage and strength enough to kill him they would have been imprisoned there forever.

What I find particularly appropriate about this myth as it applies today is that first, the Cyclops imprisons these men in darkness, and that, second, he beats their brains out before he devours them. It doesn't take much imagination to apply this to the effects of TV on us and our children.

TV's Effect on Learning

Quite literally, TV affects the way people think. In Four Arguments for the Elimination of Television (1978), Jerry Mander quotes from the Emery Report that when we watch television "our usual processes of thinking and *discernment*(识别能力) are semi-functional at best." The study also argues that while television appears to have the potential to provide useful information to viewers, the technology of television and the inherent nature of the viewing experience actually inhibit learning as we usually think of it.

When we watch TV we think we are looking at a picture, or an image of something, but what we are actually seeing is thousands of dots of light blinking on and off in a *strobe*(屏闪) effect that is calculated to happen rapidly enough to keep us from recognizing the phenomenon. More than a decade ago, Mander and others pointed to instances of "TV *epilepsy*(癫痫症)," in which those watching this strobe effect overextended their capacities, and the New England Journal of Medicine recently honored this affliction with a medical classification: video game epilepsy.

Shadows on the Screen

Television also teaches that people aren't quite real; they are images or little beings who move in a medium no thicker than a sliver of glass. Unfortunately, the tendency is to start thinking of them in the way children think when they see too many cartoons: that people are merely objects that can be destroyed. Or that can fall over a cliff and be smashed to pieces and pick themselves up again. This violence of cartoons has no basis in reality. Actual people aren't images but substantial, physical, corporeal beings with souls. And, of course, the violence on television leads to violence.

TV: Eating Out Our Substance

TV eats books. It eats academic skills. It eats positive character traits. It even eats family relationships. How many families do you know that spend the dinner hour in front of the TV, seldom communicating with one another? How many have a television on while they have breakfast or prepare for work or school?

And what about school? I've heard college professors say of their students, "Well, you have to entertain them." One I know recommends using TV and film clips instead of lecturing, "throwing in a commercial every ten minutes or so to keep them awake." A teacher should teach. But TV eats the principles of people who are supposed to be responsible, transforming them into passive servants of the Cyclops.

TV eats our substance. What we see, hear, touch, smell, feel and understand about the world has been processed for us. TV teaches that all life-styles and all values are equal, and that there is no clearly defined right and wrong.

Muggeridge concluded: "There is a danger in translating life into an image, and that is what television is doing. In doing it, it is *falsifying*(窜改) life. Far from the camera's being an accurate recorder of what is going on, it is the exact opposite. It cannot convey reality, nor does it even want to."

1. Television doesn't help build up mental defenses for people to ________.
   A) deal with violence
   B) face a sharp competition
   C) compete with rivals
   D) confront the reality of the world
2. Television is ________ the English language.
   A) destroying
   B) diffusing
   C) purifying
   D) standardizing
3. Television has ________ on people's character.
   A) a positive effect
   B) a negative effect
   C) no effect
   D) a beneficial effect
4. One of the most disturbing truths about TV is that it makes reading books cease to be ________ in our society.
   A) the most popular recreation
   B) the only method of acquiring literacy
   C) the primary way of getting information
   D) the financial resources
5. Television has invaded our culture so completely that that it even has effect on ________.
   A) the literary world
   B) foreign countries
   C) the highly-educated people
   D) those who don't watch TV at all
6. Television is compared to the Cyclops because ________.
   A) it deprives us of our thinking ability before destroying us
   B) it is also enormous in size
   C) it is as cruel as the one-eyed giant
   D) both TV and the Cyclops do harm to our children
7. In translating life into an image, television is ________ life.
   A) recording
   B) imitating
   C) creating
   D) falsifying
8. When we watch TV, our ________ are semi-functional at best.
9. When children see too many cartoons they may regard people as ________ instead of substantial, physical, corporeal beings with souls.
10. It is stated in the conclusion that by translating life into ________, television is falsifying life.

Part Ⅲ Listening Comprehension (35 minutes)

Section A

Directions:(略)

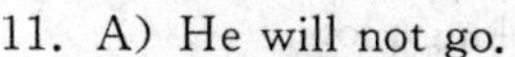

11. A) He will not go.
    B) He would like to go.
    C) He hasn't made up his mind.
    D) He doesn't think fishing is interesting.
12. A) Sailing a boat. B) Catching a worm.
    C) Fishing. D) Hanging clothes.
13. A) She leaves the office by 3:00 or 4:00 in the afternoon.
    B) She sends her employees for frequent medical check.
    C) She pays her employees by check.
    D) She inspects her employees' work several times a day.
14. A) She doesn't know whether the film is good or not.
    B) The film is hard to understand.
    C) She saw the film from beginning to end.
    D) She saw only the last part of the film.
15. A) At the doctor's office. B) At the hospital.
    C) At the drugstore. D) At the department store.
16. A) Tom is very rich now. B) Tom is a very important person.
    C) Tom has become very bad guy. D) Tom is arrogant to his old friends.
17. A) She doesn't like a heart-to-heart talk with Sally.
    B) She thinks the topic is too serious for her.
    C) She thinks the news is too hard for Sally.
    D) She dares not to tell Sally the bad news.
18. A) Mary called to tell them she couldn't come to the dinner party.
    B) Mary didn't originally want to come to the dinner party.
    C) The couple is unhappy because Mary changed her mind.
    D) The woman doesn't believe the Mary really changed her mind.

Questions 19 to 22 are based on the conversation you have just heard.

19. A) Movies play an important role in persuading young people not to smoke.
    B) Movies fail to reflect social reality and need improvement in this respect.
    C) Movies are in many ways competing with TV to gain young viewers.
    D) Movies partly contribute to the increasing number of young smokers.
20. A) They insert advertisements when the movies are near the most appealing part.
    B) They give actors free lifetime supply of cigarettes and ask them to smoke in the movies.
    C) They promote their products by giving cigarettes as gifts to the viewers before the movies start.
    D) They sponsor the moviemakers on the condition that the actors use their products.
21. A) Because the smoking actors in the movies have good-looking bodies.
    B) Because the movies show that smoking is necessary for social activities.
    C) Because the movies convey that smoking enhances the image of a man.
    D) Because the actors tell the audience that smoking causes no harm.

22. A) They agree that the moviemakers should select nonsmoking actors.
    B) They agree that viewers are entitled to reject the movies with smoking plots.
    C) They agree that a law should be made to reduce smoking in movies.
    D) They agree that the actors and the moviemakers should not take bribes.

Questions 23 to 25 are based on the conversation you have just heard.

23. A) They are talking about a job interview.
    B) They are talking about a phone interview.
    C) They are talking about a TV interview.
    D) They are talking about an Internet interview.
24. A) The employer and the time is not set.
    B) The job hunter and the time is not set.
    C) The employer and the time is set.
    D) The job hunter and the time is set.
25. A) A copy of your resume. B) Information about the employer.
    C) Information about the company. D) All of the above.

Section B

Directions:（略）

Passage One

Questions 26 to 28 are based on the passage you have just heard.

26. A) They should not be too strict with the children.
    B) They should limit their demands on some children.
    C) They should demand more of their children.
    D) They should demand more of the bright children.
27. A) To do comprehensive exercises. B) To read simple sentences.
    C) To copy out from the textbooks. D) To do all of the above.
28. A) She assigned people to do this report.
    B) She made investigations in the 700 schools.
    C) She supported the report.
    D) She wrote this report.

Passage Two

Questions 29 to 31 are based on the passage you have just heard.

29. A) Listening. B) Speaking. C) Reading. D) Writing.
30. A) They cannot express themselves in class.
    B) They cannot understand English properly.
    C) They cannot think critically.
    D) They cannot get used to the new life style.
31. A) For international-based test. B) For intelligent-based test.

C) For internet-based test. D) For information-based test.

Passage Three

Questions 32 to 35 are based on the passage you have just heard.

32. A) Seasoned foods. B) Salads.
    C) Sea fish. D) Sweets.
33. A) "Would you order now or later"?
    B) "Do you like to have your tea now or later"?
    C) "Would you like to settle the bill now or after you finish your meal"?
    D) "Do you want coffee with your meal or after it"?
34. A) To take whatever drink being served.
    B) To ask for the drink you like best.
    C) To have soft drinks rather than alcoholic drinks.
    D) To make sure that the hostess will give you a choice of drinks.
35. A) Poultry. B) Meat. C) Bread. D) Fish.

Section C

Directions:(略)

Japanese electronics firm Hitachi has produced its first human-like robot, called Emiew, to (36)________ Honda's Asimo and Sony's Qrio robots.

Two wheel-based Emiews, Pal and Chum, introduced themselves to reporters at a press (37) ________ in Japan.

Explaining why Hitachi's Emiew used wheels instead of feet, Toshihiko Horiuchi, from Hitachi's Mechanical Engineering Research (38) ________, said: "We (39) ________ to create a robot that could live and co-exist with people. We want to make the robots (40) ________ for people. If the robots moved slower than people, users would be (41) ________."

Emiew—Excellent Mobility and Interactive Existence as Workmate—can move at (42) ________ on its "wheel feet". With sensors on the head, waist, and near the wheels, Pal and Chum (43) ________ demonstrated how they could react to commands. Hitachi said Pal and Chum, (44) ____.

Honda's Asimo was "born" five years ago. Since then, Honda and Sony's Qrio (45) ____. Sony's Qrio has been the fastest robot on two legs until last year. But its record was beaten by Asimo. It is capable of 3km/h, which is almost four times as fast as Qrio. (46) ____.

Part Ⅳ Reading Comprehension(Reading in Depth) (25 minutes)

Section A

Directions:(略)

Questions 47 to 51 are based on the following passage.

There are now over 700 million motor vehicles in the world—and the number is rising by more than 40 million each year. The average distance driven by car users is growing too—from 8 km a day per person in Western Europe in 1965 to 25 km a day in 1995. This dependence on motor vehicles has given rise to major problems, including environmental pollution, depletion of oil resources, traffic congestion and safety.

While emissions from new cars are far less harmful than they used to be, city streets and motorways are becoming more crowed than ever, often with older trucks, buses and taxis, which emit excessive levels of smoke and fumes. This concentration of vehicles makes air quality in urban areas unpleasant and sometimes dangerous to breathe.

In Europe most cities are still designed for the old modes of transport. Adaptation to the motor car has involved adding ring roads, one-way systems and parking lots. In the United Sates, more land is assigned to car use than to housing. Urban sprawl means that life without a car is next to impossible. Mass use of motor vehicles has also killed or injured millions of people. Other social effects have been blamed on the car such as alienation and aggressive human behavior.

A 1993 study by the European Federation for Transport and Environment found that car transport is seven times as costly as rail travel in terms of the external social costs it entails such as congestion, accidents, pollution, loss of cropland and natural habitats, depletion of oil resources and so on. Yet cars easily surpass trains or buses as a flexible and convenient mode of personal transport. It is unrealistic to expect people to give up private cars in favor of mass transit.

Technical solutions can reduce the pollution problem and increase the fuel efficiency of engines. But fuel consumption and exhaust emissions depend on which cars are preferred by customers and how they are driven. Many people buy larger cars than they need for daily purposes or waste fuel by driving aggressively. Besides, global car use is increasing at a faster rate than the improvement in emission and fuel efficiency which technology is now making possible.

One solution that has been put forward is the long-term solution of designing cities and neighborhoods so that car journeys are not necessary—all essential services being located within walking distance or easily accessible by public transport. Not only would this save energy and cut carbon dioxide emissions, it would also enhance the quality of community life, putting the emphasis on people instead of cars. Good local government is already bringing this about in some places. But few democratic communities are blessed with the vision—and the capital—to make such profound changes in modern lifestyles. A more likely scenario seems to be a combination of mass transit systems for travel into and around cities, with small low emission cars for urban use and larger hybrid or lean burn cars for use elsewhere.

47. From the third paragraph we can see that motor vehicles have a great ________ on city development.
48. What are the relative merits of cars?
49. People's ________ of car and attitude to driving is a factor in the pollution problem brought by motor vehicles.
50. What is the long-term solution for the motor vehicle problems?
51. According to the writer, a more ________ solution to the car problems is to combine mass transportation system with cars of low emission and low fuel consumption.

Section B

Directions:(略)

Passage One

Questions 52 to 56 are based on the following passage.

In recent years, railroads have been combining with each year, merging into supersystems, causing heightened concerns about monopoly. As recently as 1995, the top four railroads accounted for under 70% of the total ton-miles moved by rails. Next year, after a series of mergers is completed, just four railroads will control well over 90% of all the freight moved by major rail carriers.

Supporters of the new supersystems argue that these mergers will allow for substantial cost reductions and better coordinated service. Any threat of monopoly, they argue, is removed by fierce competition from trucks. But many shippers complain that for heavy bulk commodities traveling long distances, trucking is too costly and the railroads

The vast consolidation within the rail industry means that most shippers are served by only one rail company. Railroads typically charge such "captive" shippers 20 to 30 percent more than they do when another railroad is competing for the business. Shippers who feel that they are being overcharged have the right to appeal to the federal government's Surface Transportation Board for rate belief, but the process is expensive, time consuming, and will work only in truly extreme cases.

Railroads justify rate discrimination against captive shippers on the grounds that in the long run it reduces everyone's cost. If railroads charged all customers the same average rate, they argue, shippers who have the option of switching to trucks or other forms of transportation would do so, leaving remaining customers to shoulder the cost of keeping up the line. It's a theory to which many economists subscribe, but in practice it often leaves railroads in the position of determining which companies will flourish and which will fail. "Do we really want railroads to be the **arbiters** of who wins and who loses in the marketplace?" asks Martin Bercovici, a Washington lawyer who frequently represents shippers.

Many captive shippers also worry they will soon be hit with a round of huge rate increases. The railroad industry as a whole, despite its brightening fortunes, still does not earn enough to cover the cost of the capital it must invest to keep up with its surging traffic. Yet railroads

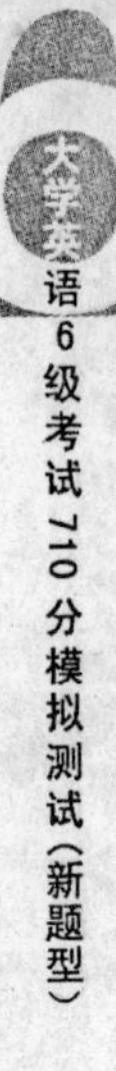

continue to borrow billions to acquire one another, with Wall Street cheering them on. Consider the $10.2 billion bid by Norfolk Southern and CSX to acquire Conrail this year. Conrail's net railway operating income in 1996 was just $427 million, less than half of the carrying cost of the transaction. Who's going to pay for the rest of the bill? Many captive shippers fear that they will, as Norfolk Southern and CSX increase their grip on the market.

52. According to those who support mergers, railway monopoly is unlikely because ________.
  A) cost reduction is based on competition
  B) services call for cross-trade coordination
  C) outside competitors will continue to exist
  D) shippers will have the railway by the throat

53. What is many captive shippers' attitude towards the consolidation in the railway industry?
  A) Indifferent.   B) Supportive.
  C) Indignant.   D) Worried.

54. It can be inferred from Paragraph 3 that ________.
  A) shippers will be charged less without a rival railroad
  B) all shippers are served by only one rail company
  C) overcharged shippers are unlikely to appeal for rate relief
  D) a government board ensures fair play in railway business

55. The word "arbiters" (Paragraph 4) most probably refers to those ________.
  A) who work as coordination   B) who function as judges
  C) who supervises transactions   D) who determine the price

56. According to the passage, the rate increase in the rail industry is caused by ________.
  A) the continuing acquisition   B) the growing traffic
  C) the cheering Wall street   D) the shrinking market

Passage Two

Questions 57 to 61 are based on the following passage.

Many objects in daily use have clearly been influenced by science. However, their form and function, their dimensions and appearance, were determined by technologists, designers, inventors, and engineers using nonscientific modes of thought. Many features and qualities of the objects that a technologist thinks about cannot be reduced to unambiguous verbal descriptions; they are dealt with in the mind by a visual, nonverbal process, pyramids, cathedrals, and rockets exist not because of geometry or *thermos-dynamics*(热动力学), because they were first the picture in the minds of those.

The creative shaping process of a technologist's mind can be seen in nearly every artifact that exists. For example, in designing a diesel engine, a technologist might express individual ways of nonverbal thinking on the machine by continually using an intuitive sense of rightness and fitness. What would be the shape of the combustion chamber? Where should the valves be placed? Would it have a long or short piston? Such questions have a range of answers that are supplied by experience, by physical requirement, by limitations of available space, and not in the least by a sense of form. Some decisions, such as wall thickness and pin diameter, may depend on scientific calculations, but the nonscientific component design remains primary.

Design courses, then should be an essential element of engineering curricula. Nonverbal thinking, a central mechanism in engineering design, involves perceptions, which is the special technique of the artists, not the scientist. Because perceptive processes are not assumed to need "hard thinking", nonverbal thought is sometimes seen as a primitive stage in the development of cognitive processes and inferior to verbal mathematical thought.

If courses in design, which in a strongly analytical engineering curriculum provide the background required for practical problem-solving, are not provided, we can expect to encounter silly but costly errors occurring in advanced engineering systems. For example, early modes of high-speed railroad cars loaded with sophisticated controls were unable to operate in a snowstorm because the fan sucked snow into the electrical system. Absurd random failures that plague automatic control systems are a reflection of the chaos that results when design is assumed to be primarily a problem in mathematics.

57. In the passage, what is the writer primarily concerned with?
   A) Identifying the kinds of thinking that are used by technologists.
   B) Stressing the importance of scientific thinking in engineering design.
   C) Proposing a new role for nonscientific thinking in engineering.
   D) Contrasting the goals of engineers with those of technologists.
58. Which of the following is NOT mentioned as an example of nonverbal thinking in Paragraphs 1 and 2?
   A) Building cathedrals. B) Creating rockets.
   C) Designing diesel engines. D) Making automobiles.
59. It can be inferred that the writer thinks engineering curricula are ________.
   A) strengthened when they include courses in design
   B) weakened by the courses designed to develop mathematical skills
   C) weak because they include some non-scientific components
   D) strong despite the absence of nonscientific modes of thinking
60. Why is the example of diesel engine used in the passage?
   A) To challenge the argument that errors in engineering design are unavoidable.
   B) To support the idea that engineering design involves more than a sense of form.
   C) To criticize the view that mathematics is a necessary part of the study of design.
   D) To questions the idea that design courses form a part of engineering curricula.
61. What contributes to random failures in automatic control systems?
   A) Using too many inexperienced engineers in the field.
   B) Relying too heavily on the role of mathematics in design.
   C) Attaching too much importance to nonverbal thinking in Engineering.
   D) Depending very little on verbal mathematical thought.

Part Ⅴ Cloze (15 minutes)

Directions:(略)

What's your earliest childhood memory? Can you remember learning to walk? Or talk? The first time you __62__ thunder or watched a television program? Adults seldom __63__ events much earlier than the year or so before entering school, just as children younger than three or four __64__ retain any specific, personal experiences. A variety of explanations have been __65__ by psychologists for this "*Childhood amnesia*"(儿童失忆症). One argues that the hippocampus, the region of the brain which is responsible for forming memories, does not mature __66__ about the age of two. But the most popular theory __67__ that, since adults do not think like children, they cannot __68__ childhood memories. Adults think in words, and their life memories are like stories or __69__ —one event follows __70__ as in a novel or film. But when they search through their mental __71__ for early childhood memories to add to this verbal life story, they don't find anything. As fits the __72__, it's like trying to find a Chinese word in an English dictionary.

Now psychologist Annette Simmons of the New York State University offers a new __73__ for childhood amnesia. She argues that there simply __74__ any early childhood memories to recall. According to Dr. Simmons, children need to learn to use __75__ spoken description of their personal experiences in order to turn their own short-term, quickly __76__ impressions of them into long-term memories. In other __77__ children have to talk about their experiences and hear others talk about __78__ Mother talking about the afternoon __79__ looking for seashells at the beach or Dad asking them about their day at Ocean Park. Without this __80__ reinforcement, says Dr. Simmons, children cannot form __81__ memories of their personal experiences.

62. A. listened B) heard C) touched D) felt
63. A. recall B) interpret C) involve D) resolve
64. A. largely B) really C) merely D) rarely
65. A. proposed B) witnessed C) canceled D) figured
66. A. after B) once C) until D) since
67. A. magnifies B) maintains C) contains D) intervenes
68. A. access B) attain C) reflect D) refer
69. A. regulations B) forecasts C) narratives D) descriptions
70. A. the rest B) others C) the other D) another
71. A. outputs B) files C) flashes D) detains
72. A. frame B) landscape C) footstep D) pattern
73. A. explanation B) arrangement C) emphasis D) factor
74. A. isn't B) weren't C) aren't D) wasn't
75. A. anyone else B) someone else's C) someone else D) anyone else's
76. A. forgetting B) remembered C) forgotten D) remembering
77. A. words B) cases C) senses D) means

78. A. him B) them C) it D) theirs
79. A. used B) spent C) taken D) chosen
80. A. habitual B) mutual C) pretty D) verbal
81. A. subordinate B) conscious C) permanent D) spiritual

Part Ⅵ Translation (5 minutes)

Directions:(略)

82. ________________________________(随后发生的那些事再次证实了我的猜疑是对的). The fire was a set rather than an accident.

83. ________________________________(我们相信他所说的是因为他受过良好的教育,出生于受人尊敬的家庭), and what's more, he is reliable.

84. We have to accept the fact that ________________________________(在一个多元化的社会里,见解不同是不可避免的).

85. From his own experience, he told us that ________________________________(那些面试未来雇员并具有决定权的人喜欢有充分准备的人).

86. ________________________________(对于一个国家而言,没有比未能教育好孩子更危险的事了). That's why we should carry out the Hope Project.

参考答案(8)

Part Ⅰ Sample Writing

According to the bar chart, there are many dramatic changes in the use of transport from 1950 to 1990.

The use of cars increased significantly from 1950 to 1990. In 1950, only a few people drove to work. But, in 1970, about one quarter of the people owned a car. By 1990, the number of people who went to work by car jumped to over 30%.

During the same period, there were gradual decline in the use of bicycle and on foot. In 1950, more than half of the people were cycling or walking to work. In 1970, the use of bicycle and on foot still occupied over 40%. But in 1990, the number of these people decreased to less than 20%.

The use of bus went up from 1950 to 1970 (approximately 20% and 30% respectively) and went down from 1970 to 1990 (under 20%).

The bar chart shows that automobiles have become the most popular means of transportation by 1990.

Part Ⅱ Reading Comprehension (Skimming and Scanning)

1. D 2. A 3. B 4. C 5. A 6. A 7. D

8. processes of thinking and discernment
9. (merely) objects that can be destroyed
10. an image

Part Ⅲ Listening Comprehension

Section A

11—15 BCDDC 16—20 BCBDB 21—25 ACBAD

Section B

26—30 CDABA 31—35 CBDAC

Section C

36. challenge 37. conference 38. Laboratory 39. aimed
40. useful 41. frustrated 42. 6km/h 43. demonstrated
44. which have a vocabulary of about 100 words, could be "trained" for practical office and factory use in as little as five to six years
45. have tried to beat each other with what the robots can do at various technology events
46. The three designs, each built by a different research group are not commercially available, as a way of showing off computing power and engineering expertise

Part Ⅳ Reading Comprehension (Reading in Depth)

Section A

47. impact/effect
48. They are flexible and convenient. /They easily surpass trains or buses as a flexible and convenient mode of personal transport.
49. choice
50. Redesigning cities and neighborhoods so that car journeys are not necessary.
51. likely/practical

Section B

52—56 CDCBA 57—61 CDABB

Part Ⅴ Cloze

62—66 BADAC 67—71 BCCDB
72—76 DACBC 77—81 ABBDC

Part Ⅵ Translation

82. The subsequent events confirmed my suspicions once again
83. We believe what he said on the ground that he is well-educated, from a respectable family
84. in this pluralistic society, there are inevitably different opinions
85. the decision makers who interview prospective employees like people who are well prepared
86. Nothing is more dangerous than the failure to properly educate its children

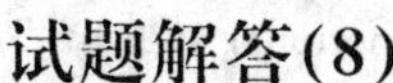

试题解答(8)

Part Ⅱ Reading Comprehension (Skimming and Scanning)

1. [D] 文章第二段指出孩子们最容易受电视的影响,他们成年之后对生活的现实缺乏心理防御。根据原文"No wonder, then, that when they grow up they are not prepared for the frontline of life; they simply have no mental defenses to confront the reality of the world."可知本题正确答案为D项。
2. [A] "The Truth About TV"部分第二段指出电视对语言的影响:"The mechanics of the English language have been tortured to pieces by TV. Visual, moving images can't be held in the net of careful language. They want to break out. They really have nothing to do with language. So language, grammar and rhetoric have become fractured."。作者认为电视把英语语言结构都分解成了碎片。语言、语法和修辞都支离破碎。因此,电视破坏了英语语言。故本题正确答案为A项。
3. [B] 由"The Truth About TV"部分第五段第一句"Even more importantly, the growing influence of television has changed people's habits and values and affected their assumptions about the world."可知电视改变人们的习惯和价值观,影响人们对世界的看法。由"TV: Eating Out Our Substance"部分第一段第三句"It eats positive character traits."可知电视对人的性格是有影响的,而且有的只是负面影响。故本题正确答案为B项。
4. [C] 由"The Truth About TV"部分第一段"One of the most disturbing truths about TV is that it eats books. Once out of school, nearly 60% of all adult Americans have never read a single book, and most of the rest read only one book a year. Alvin Kernan, author of The Death of Literature, says that reading books 'is ceasing to be the primary way of knowing something in our society.'"可知电视的出现使读书不再是获取信息、了解事物的主要方法了。故本题正确答案为C项。
5. [A] 由"The Truth About TV"部分第四段第一句"Passive as it is, television has invaded our culture so completely that you see its effects in every quarter, even in the literary world."可知尽管电视是一种被动的娱乐,它彻底地侵入了我们的文化,甚至影响了文学界。可见本题正确答案为A项。
6. [A] 由"The Cyclops"部分第三段"What I find particularly appropriate about this myth as it applies today is that first, the Cyclops imprisons these men in darkness, and that, second, he beats their brains out before he devours them. It doesn't take much imagination to apply this to the effects of TV on us and our children."可知作者认为只要稍具想象力我们就可以看出电视和独眼巨人在这方面的相似之处。言下之意,电视也是先让我们失丧失思考能力,再彻底毁灭我们。故本题正确答案为A项。
7. [D] "TV: Eating Out Our Substance"部分最后一段中Muggeridge对电视做了总结:"There is a danger in translating life into an image, and that is what television is doing. In doing it, it is falsifying life. Far from the camera's being an accurate recorder of what is going on, it is the exact opposite. It cannot convey reality, nor does it even want to."可见在把生活转换成图像的过程中,电视窜改了生活,并非真实地记录了生活。故本题正确答案为D项。

8. 由“TV's Effect on Learning”部分第一句“... when we watch television our usual processes of thinking and discernment are semi-functional at best.”可知人们看电视的时候,他们的思维能力和识别能力最多起一半作用。故此题答案为“processes of thinking and discernment”。
9. 由“Shadows on the Screen”部分第二句“Unfortunately, the tendency is to start thinking of them in the way children think when they see too many cartoons: that people are merely objects that can be destroyed.”可见孩子们看多了卡通片会把人看作可以随意毁灭的物体。故此题答案为“(merely) objects that can be destroyed”。
10. 由文章最后一部分“TV: Eating Out Our Substance”中第四段第一句“Muggeridge concluded: ‘There is a danger in translating life into an image, and that is what television is doing. In doing it, it is falsifying life.’”可知正确答案为“an image”。

Part Ⅲ Listening Comprehension(听力原文在光盘中)

Part Ⅳ Reading Comprehension (Reading in Depth)

Section A

47. 第三段第一、二句讲到欧洲为适应汽车交通必须增添环城公路、单行系统和停车场。而美国在汽车运输方面耗费的土地比住宅还多(In Europe most cities are still designed for the old modes of transport. Adaptation to the motor car has involved adding ring roads, one-way systems and parking lots. In the United Sates, more land is assigned to car use than to housing.)。由此可见汽车交通的出现对城市的发展有很大的影响。因此,答案需要填可以和 have... on 搭配的词,表示“有影响”的词。故正确答案为“impact/ effect”。
48. 由第四段倒数第二句“Yet cars easily surpass trains or buses as a flexible and convenient mode of personal transport.”可知,正确答案为“They are flexible and convenient.”或者“They easily surpass trains or buses as a flexible and convenient mode of personal transport.”。
49. 由第五段第二句“But fuel consumption and exhaust emissions depend on which cars are preferred by customers and how they are driven.”可见燃料的消耗和污染排放取决于顾客选择什么样的车和怎么开车。所以单单靠技术是无法解决污染和能源耗竭的问题的。因此,此题要填的词意思应是“选择”,因此正确答案为“choice”。
50. 由文章最后一段的第一句话“One solution that has been put forward is the long-term solution of designing cities and neighborhoods so that car journeys are not necessary—all essential services being located within walking distance or easily accessible by public transport.”可知,正确答案是“Redesigning cities and neighborhoods so that car journeys are not necessary.”。
51. 由文章最后一句“A more likely scenario seems to be a combination of mass transit systems for travel into and around cities, with small low emission cars for urban use and larger hybrid or lean burn cars for use elsewhere.”可见,这样的方法和前面提到的“通过技术解决问题”和“重新规划城市的长远方法”相比是更为适当、更为可能、更为实际的。因此,我们可以回答为“likely”、“practical”或者其他含义相近的词。

Section B

52. [C] 因果推断题。第二段开篇就描述了铁路合并支持者们认为合并有助于减少成本以及更好地合作服务,不用担心垄断,因为还有来自卡车等运输方式的强烈竞争,即“... these

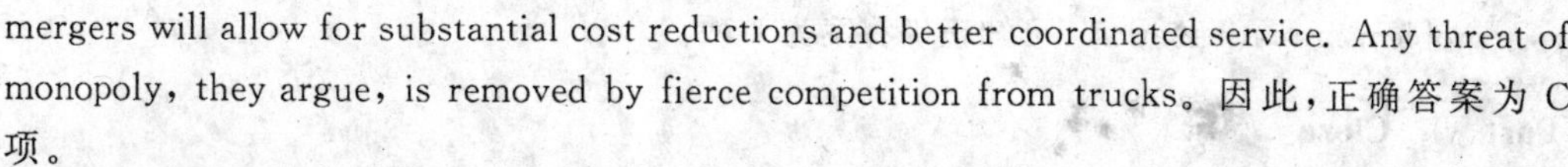

mergers will allow for substantial cost reductions and better coordinated service. Any threat of monopoly, they argue, is removed by fierce competition from trucks。因此,正确答案为C项。

53. [D] 态度揣摩题。关于 captive shipper 文中提及很多次,多次表达了他们对铁路合并的态度,如"i) many shippers complain that for heavy bulk commodities traveling long distances, trucking is too costly; ii) Shippers who feel that they are being overcharged... iii) Many captive shippers also worry they will soon be hit with a round of huge rate increases; iv) Many captive shippers fear that they will, as Norfolk Southern and CSX increase their grip on the market.",总体而言,captive shippers 是不满、抱怨、担忧和担心的态度,因此正确答案为D项。

54. [C] 推断题。由第三段"... consolidation... means that most shippers are served by only one rail company... Shippers who feel that they are being overcharged have the right to appeal to the federal government... but the process is expensive, time consuming..."可见合并将会导致绝大部分 shippers 由一家 rail company 垄断(但不是所有的),挨宰的人有权申诉但这一过程会耗费大量时间和金钱,所以他们一般不会诉诸法律,因此正确答案为C项

55. [B] 词义推断题。由"arbiters"所在句 Do we really want railroads to be the arbiters of who wins and who loses in the marketplace. 可以猜测出 arbiters 的意思,因为他/她可以决定谁赢谁输,懂体育的人就很容易猜出大概是"裁判"的意思。

56. [A] 因果推断题。文章最后一段提到 shippers 担心会有新一轮 rate 增加,因为铁路运输尽管赚钱,但还不足以挽回所有合并成本以及投资成本来满足运输需求的大幅度增长。他们仍在不断借钱去合并,业务收入是运营成本的一半不到。这中间的赤字谁来买单呢? shippers。是什么原因导致 rate 增加呢?追根究底,还是合并惹的祸,故正确答案为A项。

57. [C] 主旨题。通读本篇文章,第一段中提到日常生活中很多物品被科学所影响,然而也有很多被 nonscientific thinking 所影响;第二段中提到 nonscientific thinking 在生活中处处可见,并举例说明;第三段中提到设计课程本来是纯科学的,但也应该引进 nonscientific thinking;最后一段用一个反面例子论证如果设计不引入 nonscientific thinking in engineering 后果,因此正确答案为C项。

58. [D] 细节查找题。从第一、二段中找出在论述 nonverbal thinking 时"未提及的例证",阅读并比对发现作者提及了 pyramids,cathedrals, rockets 和 diesel engine,因而此正确答案为D项。

59. [A] 推断题。由最后一段第一句"If courses in design... are not provided, we can expect to encounter silly but costly errors occurring in advanced engineering system."可见设计是一门强分析的工程科目,能提供解决实际问题所需的背景知识。如果工程学里不引入设计课,则大的工程系统很可能面临愚蠢、巨大的错误。由此可以推断作者认为工程学是一门科学,工程学里必须有设计科目,设计科目必须有 nonscientific thinking。引入了 nonscientific thinking 的设计课将会更好,引入了设计科目的工程学将会更强,因此正确答案为A项。

60. [B] 因果推断题。第二段中引用柴油发动机例子是为了说明,由"supplied by experience, by physical requirement, by limitations of available space, and not in the least by a sense of form"可知其构造主要由经验、物理条件、有限空间和对形态把握的感觉决定。因此正确答案为B项。

61. [B] 理解判断题。由文章最后一句"Absurd random failures that plague automatic control systems are a reflection of the chaos that results when design is assumed to be primarily a

problem in mathematics."可知正确答案为B项。

Part Ⅴ Cloze

62. 本题考查词汇的逻辑搭配。thunder"雷声"是本句的宾语,因此B项heard是最佳的谓语动词。
63. 本题考查考生利用上下文选择判断的能力。文章第一行有remember一词出现,有所暗示。而且全文主题是"儿童失忆症"。A项recall表示"回忆",符合句意。
64. 本题考查上下文的连贯理解能力。前半句中出现了seldom一词,just as在这里提示后半句也应该是表示否定意义,且横线后的any一词也起到了暗示作用。可见,D项rarely为正确答案。
65. 本题考查词汇的搭配。和explanations搭配,A项propose为最佳选择。B项witness意为"目睹,作证",C项cancel意为"取消",D项figure搭配介词to意为"估计,推测"。
66. 本题考查结构知识。根据句意"……直到一两岁才能成熟"的意思,所以应该使用not...until结构。因此,C项为正确答案。
67. 本题考查考生的词汇结构。B项maintain后接从句,意为"坚持认为某事正确",故B项为正确答案。
68. 本题考查上下文的连贯理解能力。第二题的recall events对本题有提示作用。C项reflect意为"反映,反省",带入句中符合题意,与上文呼应,因此C项为正确答案。
69. 本题考查结构知识。句中出现or连接的并列结构,故此处所选的词应与or前面的story为近义词。C项narratives意为"叙述,故事",故正确答案为C项。
70. 本题考查固定搭配。与前面one搭配的应该是another,因此D项为正确答案。
71. 本题考查词汇知识。本句句意为"在心智档案中寻找对儿时的记忆……",B项files意为"文件,答案",为最佳答案。
72. 本题考查词汇知识。A项frame意为"框架",B项landscape意为"风景线",C项footstep意为"脚印",D项pattern意为"模式"。可见,D项为正确答案。
73. 本题考查词汇知识。文章第二段第四行"a variety of explanations"有提示作用,表示对儿童失忆症有很多解释。这里是另一位心理学家提出的新的解释。因此,选项A为正确答案。
74. 本题考查语法知识。There be句型单复数需要和后面的名词保持一致,故用复数形式。时态为一般现在时。可见,选项C为正确答案。
75. 本题考查一般词汇知识。本句句意为"儿童们需要学会用别人对自己经验的口头描述来把短期记忆转化成长期记忆"。B项someone else's意为"别人的",因此正确答案为B项。
76. 本题考查词汇知识。根据句意,short-term memories会quickly forgotten,即短期记忆会很快被忘却,因此,选项C为正确答案。
77. 本题考查固定搭配。in other words意为"换句话说"。可见,选项A为正确答案。
78. 本题考查代词知识。指代others的应该是them。可见选项B为正确答案。
79. 本题考查词汇的固定搭配。spend time doing... 为固定搭配,因此,选项B为正确答案。
80. 本题考查词汇知识。根据前句的talk about可得到提示,此处应该是D项verbal,意为"文字的,口头的"。
81. 本题考查上下文的理解能力。根据句意,此处"儿童要形成的"应该是前文提到的"长期记忆"。四个选项中C项permanent意为"永久的",符合句意,为正确答案。

Part Ⅵ Translation

82. [答案]:The subsequent events confirmed my suspicions once again

[注释]:本句虽短但翻译的难点分别为"随后的"、"证实"、"猜疑",分别译作 subsequent、confirm、suspicion。

83. [答案]:We believe what he said on the ground that he is well-educated, from a respectable family

[注释]:本句是个并列句,翻译中要注意 on the ground 的使用。当然,也可以使用其他相近的表达法如 because。

84. [答案]:in this pluralistic society, there are inevitably different opinions

[注释]:本句考查"多元化"和"不可避免"的翻译,即 pluralistic 和 inevitably 两词。

85. [答案]:the decision makers who interview prospective employees like people who are well prepared

[注释]:本句翻译难点之一为"具有决定权的人",即 decision maker;另一个难点是"未来的"的翻译,准确的译法为 prospective。

86. [答案]:To a country, nothing is more dangerous than the failure to properly educate its children

[注释]:本句首先考查 nothing more 的使用;另一个难点就是 failure 一词在本句中使用,表示"未能"。

College English Practice Test 9 (Band Ⅵ)

Part Ⅰ Writing (30 minutes)

Directions: *For this part, you are allowed 30 minutes to write a short essay entitled* ***My View on Automobiles****. You should write at least 150 words following the outline given below.*

1. 汽车给人类带来的益处;
2. 汽车给人类带来的副作用;
3. 我的观点。

Part Ⅱ Reading Comprehension (Skimming and Scanning) (15 minutes)

Directions:(略)

You don't have to be 18: Going to college as an adult

Every so often, especially when I'm feeling down, I take out my old college notes, textbooks and diplomas, and take a little stroll down memory lane. I remember the fun I had in college, the people I met, the professors who taught me and the experiences that changed my life. And I'm glad I made the sacrifices.

After graduating high school, I thought college wasn't for me. I served a four-year stint in the U. S. Marine Corps, and then took a job with the postal service. In my na vet , I thought that moving up within the agency would be fairly easy. I was bright, knowledgeable, eager to learn new things and willing to put in the time needed to develop myself. But I ran into a brick wall. It seemed there was an inside track, and I was definitely not on it. After about a year and a half, I realized that my chances of advancement were nil, and it was time to do something about it.

I floated the idea of attending college to my coworkers and superiors and the response was mostly negative. But there were a few people who thought it was a good idea, and I did a lot of thinking. I saw two choices: 1. Stay where I was, miserable in a low-level job. 2. Take a chance and give college a try. Since my job was leading me nowhere, I decided to start college.

Overcoming the initial obstacles

When I started, I encountered a lot of resistance from people at work. The phrase "career student" was bandied about at me, as if I was learning nothing practical and basically trying to avoid growing up. Actually it was the other way around. I saw staying in my job as a way to avoid facing responsibilities, and college as a more real world—and an island of sanity in my life.

While it made little difference to me if my coworkers or bosses supported my decision to attend college, I did want my family behind me. The support was there—I didn't need any financial help, but I got a lot of moral support from my parents, as well as from friends and relatives.

Probably the biggest obstacle I faced, since I was plagued by doubts about my own intelligence and abilities, was just getting started. I decided to start close to home and do my first two years of college at Palm Beach Community College, which was on the way to work, and then transfer to Florida Atlantic University, which was more out of the way.

I had driven past the campus of Palm Beach Community College several times. In the spring of 1987, I finally worked up the nerve to go into the admissions office. For many people that first step is a big one, and it's easy to believe that one is stepping into an abyss, but PBCC was flexible enough for me. I had to take the American College Test and, after scoring well on that, was able to register for classes. My first class was introduction to the Social Sciences, and from the moment the professor began to lecture, I knew I had found a place where I could learn and grow.

Culture Shock

You might expect to experience culture shock in college after your day-to-day experiences. I found, instead, that most of the culture shock happens when you leave class and go back to work. For while your coworkers and bosses are not changing, you are.

You may find yourself colliding with the people at work. They may find that your new habits, like studying during breaks and lunch, and not going to the local bar to drink and gripe about work, are disturbing the *status quo*(当前的状况).

You may even be tempted to give up. Please don't. It may be difficult, you may be exhausted and you may have to tune out criticism, but I can tell you from experience that it's all worth it on the day you put on the cap and gown and receive your diploma.

College life for adults

So you've gone and done it. You have been accepted for *matriculation*(注册入学) at a community college or university, and have been given a date and time to register.

Your biggest worry may be about what things are like in the classroom. Does the professor take attendance? Some do, some don't, though all encourage perfect attendance and class participation. Is there a break? If the class is three hours long, there probably is. When you report to your first class, try to be there a little early. Get a good seat, preferably in the front of the classroom so you can see and hear the professor better.

Have all the required books for the class, and a notebook and pen. When class starts, the professor will hand out a syllabus, discuss it, talk about term papers and may then begin teaching.

You may be worried about how the professor will react to you. You needn't be that concerned. At the community college and university I attended, professors welcomed older students. We tended to be more focused on getting an education, had a lot to contribute to the class discussion because of our experience in the world and were less likely to argue over a grade.

As you get to know your classmates in the class, you may find yourself gravitating toward

other students your age. There's nothing wrong with this, but if there's a group project, the professor will probably want the generations to work together. This is a good opportunity to broaden your horizons.

That doesn't mean you should just show up, take classes and take off. There may be a club or activity for your major on campus that can help you in your job search later on. You may even find that the company of other scholars will help you expand your intellectual horizons. And taking in a college sports event once in a while can be a fun way to meet other people.

The Big Time

Graduation from Palm Beach Community College was a milestone in my life. Against the odds, I had achieved something. I was "walking on sunshine," as the song goes, and had learned to let all the negativity go in one ear and out the other. I had made friends with the professors, and the students I had worked with were wonderful. In truth, I was addicted to the challenges that college provided.

I graduated from community college in December 1990, then started at Florida Atlantic University the following month. Florida Atlantic University was a whole new world awaiting discovery. My first time there, I had been scared. It was so big and seemingly impersonal. Sure, there would be some people from the community college on the same track as I was on, but still there were lots of strangers.

In April 1994, I had accumulated enough credits to graduate from FAU. It was a bittersweet occasion. I loved education and learning, but wanted to make my career change sooner rather than later. Two months after graduation I left the post office, diploma in hand, and embarked on a new career. It hasn't always been easy and it hasn't always been that much fun, but I've never regretted reinventing my life.

I am now a copy editor for a newspaper, with a few years of experience under my belt, and have also earned a computer networking certification along the way. Even now, I have grand plans that involve law school someday, and maybe an MBA.

A college degree opens doors. It might not be possible to see the doors when you are just starting out, but they are there if you have the patience and drive to pursue your dreams. Good luck in your future endeavors.

1. The writer decided to attend college because ________.

A) he could see no hope of moving up the ladder in the postal agency

B) he was eager to learn new things all his life

C) his relatives and friends urged him to receive further education

D) without a diploma he could not get promotion in his organization

2. How did the writer's colleagues react when they got to know his decision?

A) They offered him a lot of moral support.

B) They thought it was a good idea.

C) They refused to give him any financial help.

D) Their responses were mostly negative.

3. According to the writer, most of the culture shock happens when he ________.
   A) went into the classroom after work
   B) left class and went back to work
   C) participated in a group project
   D) took in a college sports event
4. In the writer's opinion, unlike what other people thought, ________ is a way to avoid facing responsibilities.
   A) staying in his job　　B) being a "career student"
   C) quitting jobs　　D) going back to college
5. For the writer, the biggest obstacle during the whole process of attending college was ________.
   A) just getting started　　B) resistance from people at work
   C) to pass the American College Test　　D) culture shock experienced in college
6. Career students usually contribute more to the class discussion because of their ________.
   A) intelligence and abilities　　B) willingness to participate
   C) agreeable personality　　D) experience in the world
7. The writer thought that one of the achievements he had was that ________.
   A) he began to love learning
   B) he was promoted in the postal office after getting the diploma
   C) he had learned to ignore negative comments
   D) he had no difficulty when he embarked on a new career
8. One of the advantages of campus life was that one may ________ in the company of other scholars.
9. By saying ________ the author meant that with a college degree, one can expect more chances of employment and success.
10. Looking back on his decision to go to college, the writer ________.

Part Ⅲ　Listening Comprehension　(35 minutes)

Section A

Directions:(略)

11. A) It always snows during the winter here.
    B) The woman likes the cold weather but not the snow.
    C) The man doesn't like snow.
    D) The man agrees with the woman.
12. A) Prof. Green's class is awful.
    B) She loves Prof. Green's class but hates walking around the bush.
    C) She's not satisfied because Prof. Green doesn't stick to the point.
    D) She has no idea about Prof. Green's class.

13. A) The man thinks the decoration of the house is terrible.
    B) The man is looking forward to moving into the house.
    C) The man has no taste for the house's decoration.
    D) The decoration of the house is to the woman's taste.
14. A) The man thinks car racing is too exciting to miss.
    B) The man prefers dog racing to horse or car racing.
    C) The woman prefers horse racing to dog or car racing.
    D) The woman dislikes dogs and cars.
15. A) Mark wants to travel by air. B) Mark likes the CEO very much.
    C) Mark is greatly interested in power. D) Mark can seize opportunities in time.
16. A) The government should help those youngsters.
    B) The government should take the place of those youngsters.
    C) The government should encourage those youngsters.
    D) The government should place restrictions on those youngsters.
17. A) She likes riding horses. B) She has been promoted once a year.
    C) She won the second place in a contest. D) She is very excited.
18. A) He got the camera at a very low price. B) The camera is very expensive.
    C) The camera is worth nothing. D) He does not like the camera.

Questions 19 to 22 are based on the conversation you have just heard.

19. A) Richard hosts the program. B) Jill has many hobbies.
    C) Richard is a sportsman. D) Jill is brave.
20. A) Camping outside. B) Skating on real ice.
    C) Watching girls. D) Surfing the web.
21. A) Boating. B) Sailing.
    C) Hiking. D) Horsing.
22. A) Richard is not as brave as Jill. B) Richard also has many hobbies.
    C) Jill is kind of risky. D) Jill likes staying at home.

Questions 23 to 25 are based on the conversation you have just heard.

23. A) She probably works together with Jim in a business company.
    B) She probably works in an airport.
    C) She probably is an operator working in a telephone company.
    D) She probably works in Hong Kong.
24. A) Four days. B) A week.
    C) Six to nine days. D) He hasn't decided yet.
25. A) Because he thinks it is still too expensive.
    B) Because it is not a direct flight.
    C) Because it has a half-hour stop over in Tokyo.
    D) Because he has to arrive in Hong Kong on February the sixth.

Section B

Directions:(略)

Passage One

Questions 26 to 28 are based on the passage you have just heard.

26. A) Nothing. B) A lot.
    C) Hardly anything. D) A little.
27. A) They were able to fly it in the air.
    B) They were able to stay up in the air for half an hour and more in the machine.
    C) They were able to carry travelers.
    D) They were able to fly in around Dayton.
28. A) The newspapermen didn't believe what people told them about the flights.
    B) The Government didn't give the Rights any money.
    C) The Government didn't know the Rights had already built up an airplane.
    D) At the time it seemed no one could understand them.

Passage Two

Questions 29 to 31 are based on the passage you have just heard.

29. A) Helplessness. B) Anger.
    C) Fear. D) Sorrow.
30. A) Children under 11. B) Teenagers.
    C) Adults. D) Old people.
31. A) They may fail to feel secure later in the life.
    B) They may become bad-tempered.
    C) They may develop mental problems.
    D) They may lose trust in the society.

Passage Three

Questions 32 to 35 are based on the passage you have just heard.

32. A) In 1809. B) In 1863.
    C) In 1865. D) In 1860.
33. A) Because they didn't like Lincoln being their president.
    B) Because they wanted to set up their own government.
    C) Because they disagreed with Lincoln about the abolishment of slavery.
    D) Because they wanted to stage a war against Lincoln's government.
34. A) Four years. B) Five years.
    C) Three years. D) Six years.
35. A) The break-down of the United States.
    B) The withdrawal of some southern states from the Union.
    C) The creation of the Confederate States of America.
    D) The defeat of the Confederate States of America and the reunion of the United States.

Section C

Directions:(略)

The sea is the largest unknown part of our world. It covers (36) ________ percent of the earth. There is still much to be discovered about this (37) ________ blanket of water.

Some scientists are studying ways of bringing the ocean's huge (38) ________ of water to the deserts of the world. Others hope to control the weather by learning more about the (39) ________ of heat and moisture between the ocean and the air. Others are studying the ways in which sound travels and is (40) ________ by water and heat. What happens when seawater touches different elements is another (41) ________ of study.

(42) ________ the ocean floor is an important work among so many interesting studies. (43) ________, only a very small part of the ocean has been mapped. Now underwater photography is used in mapping parts of the ocean floor. (44) ____.

If the waters of the ocean could be moved away, the sea floor with its wide valleys, uneven mountains would be an unbelievable sight. Around the edges of the continents the ocean floor is flat and the water is not much deeper than about thirty miles. (45) ____. But where there are high young mountains along the coast, this flat part may be much less than thirty miles. (46) ____.

Part Ⅳ Reading Comprehension(Reading in Depth) (25 minutes)

Section A

Directions:(略)

Questions 47 to 51 are based on the following passage.

It has been called the Holy Grail of modern biology. Costing more than £2 billion, it is the most ambitious scientific project since the Apollo program that landed a man on the moon. And it will take longer to accomplish than the lunar missions, for it will not be complete until next century. Even before it is finished, according to those involved, this project should open up new understanding of, and new treatment for, many of the ailments that afflict humanity.

The objective of the Human Genome Project is simple to state but audacious in scope: to map and analyze every single gene within the double helix of humanity's DNA. The project will reveal a new human anatomy—not the bones, muscles and sinews, but the complete genetic blueprint for a human being. Those working on the Human Genome Project claim that the new genetic anatomy will transform medicine and reduce human suffering in the 21st century. But others see the future through a darker glass and fear that the project may open the door to a world peopled by Frankenstein's monsters and disfigured by a new *eugenics*(优生学).

The genetic inheritance a baby receives from its parents at the moment of conception fixes much of its later development. The human genome is the compendium of all these inherited genetic instructions. Witten out along the double helix of DNA are the chemical letters of the genetic text, for the human genome contains more than 3 billion letters. On the printed page it would fill about 7,000 volumes. Yet within little more than a decade, the position of every letter and its relation to its neighbors will have been tracked down, analyzed and recorded.

If properly applied, the new knowledge generated by the Human Genome Project may free humanity from the terrible scourge of diverse diseases. But if the new knowledge is not used wisely, it also holds the threat of creating new forms of discrimination and new methods of oppression. Once before in this century, the relentless curiosity of scientific researchers brought to light forces of nature in the power of the atom, the mastery of which has shaped the destiny of nations and overshadowed all our lives. The Human Genome Project holds the promise that, ultimately, we may be able to alter our genetic inheritance if we so choose. But there is the central moral problem: how can we ensure that when we choose, we choose correctly? That such a potential is a promise and not a threat? We need only look at the past to understand the danger.

47. The passage compares the Human Genome Project in scale to the ________.
48. Some people fear that genetic ________ may be created by such a project.
49. To write out the human genome on paper would require ________ books.
50. What benefits can we expect to get from the Human Genome Project?
51. Why does the writer mention the discovery of the atomic power in the last paragraph?

Section B

Directions:(略)

Passage One

Questions 52 to 56 are based on the following passage.

Unlike the scientist, the engineer is not free to select the problem which interests him; he must solve the problems as they arise, and his solutions must satisfy conflicting requirements. Typically, the engineering solution to most problems must take into account many factors.

To the engineer, efficiency means output divided by input. His job is to secure a maximum output for a given input or to secure a given output with a minimum input. The **ratio** may be expressed in terms of energy, materials, money, time, or man. Most commonly the *denominator* (分母) is money; in fact, most engineering problems are answered ultimately in dollars and cents.

The emphasis on efficiency leads to the large, complex operations which are characteristic of engineering. The processing of the new antibiotic and vaccines in the test-tube stage belongs in the field of biochemistry, but when great quantities must be produced at low cost, it becomes an engineering problem. It is the desire for efficiency and economy that distinguishes ceramic engineering from the work of the potter, textile engineering from weaving, and agricultural engineering from farming.

Since output equals input minus losses, the engineer must keep losses and waste to a

minimum. One way is to develop uses for products which otherwise would be waste. The work of the chemical engineer in utilizing successively greater fractions of raw materials such as crude oil is well known. Losses due to friction occur in every machine and in every organization. Efficient functioning depends on good design, careful attention to operating difficulties, and lubrication of rough spots, whether they are mechanical or personal.

The raw materials with which engineers work are seldom found in useful forms. Engineering of the highest type is required to conceive, design, and achieve the conversion of the energy of a turbulent mountain stream into the powerful *torque*(转矩) of an electric motor a hundred miles away. Similarly many engineering operations are required to change the sands of the seashore into the precise lenses which permit us to observe the minute bacteria in a drop of water and study a giant mass of stars in outer space.

52. What might be inferred about the scientist from the sentences at the beginning of the text?
    A) He must choose the long-term solution to a problem.
    B) He may study the problem he has an interest in.
    C) He can avoid the conflict between work and pleasure.
    D) He should be familiar with some engineering problems.
53. In the second paragraph, the word "ratio" refers to ________.
    A) minimum input divided by maximum output
    B) given input divided by maximum output
    C) output divided by input
    D) money divided by output
54. According to the passage, the processing of the new antibiotic and vaccines becomes an engineering problem when ________.
    A) it involves the low-cost production of large quantities
    B) these items originate in the work of biochemistry
    C) people are engaged in safe operations in the test-tube stage
    D) business agents use efficient methods to market these items
55. Which of the following can be best answered by the information about the reduction of losses and waste in engineering?
    A) When do losses and waste soar in a machine?
    B) Why is the work of the chemical engineer important to oil refining?
    C) How does the engineer achieve the good design of a product?
    D) What are essential for the efficient functioning of a machine?
56. The organization of the last paragraph can be best described as ________.
    A) following the time order B) from specific to general
    C) cause and effect D) statement and examples

Passage Two

Questions 57 to 61 are based on the following passage.

Being a man has always been dangerous. There are about 105 males born for every 100 females, but this ratio drops to near balance at the age of maturity, and among 70-year-olds there are twice as many women as men. But the great universal of male mortality is being changed. Now boy babies survive almost as well as girls do. This means that, for the first time, there will be an excess of boys in those crucial years when they are searching for a mate. More important, another chance for natural selection has been removed. Fifty years ago, the chance of a baby (particularly a boy baby) surviving depended on its weight. A kilogram too light or too heavy meant almost certain death. Today it makes almost no difference. Since much of the variation is due to genes, one more agent of evolution has gone.

There is another way to commit evolutionary suicide: stay alive, but have fewer children. Few people are as fertile as in the past. Except in some religious communities, very few women have 15 children. Nowadays the number of births, like the age of death, has become average. Most of us have roughly the same number of offspring. Again, differences between people and the opportunity for natural selection to take advantage of it have diminished. India shows what is happening. The country offers wealth for a few in the great cites and poverty for the remaining tribal peoples. The grand mediocrity of today everyone being the same in survival and number of offspring—means that natural selection has lost 80% of its power in upper-middle-class Indian compared with other tribes.

For us, this means that evolution is over; the biological Utopia has arrived. Strangely, it has involved little physical change. No other species fills so many places in nature. But in the past 100,000 years—even the past 100 years—our lives have been transformed but our bodies have not. We did not evolve, because machines and society did it for us. Darwin had a phrase to describe those ignorant of evolution: they "look at an organic being as a savage looks at a ship, as at something wholly beyond his comprehension". No doubt we will remember a 20th century way of life beyond comprehension for its ugliness. But however amazed our descendants may be at how far from Utopia we were, they will look just like us.

57. What used to be the danger of a man according to the first paragraph?
    A) Lake of mates.
    B) A defective gene.
    C) A fierce competition.
    D) A lower survival rate.
58. The word "diminished" (Para. 2) probably means "________".
    A) decreased
    B) increased
    C) changed
    D) gone away
59. What does the example of India illustrate?
    A) Wealth people tend to have fewer children than poor people.
    B) The upper class population is 80% smaller than that of the tribes.
    C) Natural selection hardly works among the rich and the poor.
    D) India is one of the countries with a very high birth rate.
60. The author argues that our bodies have stopped evolving because ________.
    A) life has been improved by technological advance
    B) the number of female babies has been declining
    C) the difference between wealth and poverty is disappearing
    D) our species has reached the highest stage of evolution

61. Which of the following is most probably the best title for the passage?

A) Human Evolution Going Nowhere.

B) Sex Ratio Changes in Human Evolution.

C) Ways of Continuing Man's Evolution.

D) The Evolutionary Future of Nature.

Part Ⅴ Error Correction (15 minutes)

Directions:（略）

Surfing is a thrilling and dangerous activity in which a person
balances on a board and rides the surface of a big, crash ocean wave. 62. ________
Channel surfing is a bit different. In this activity a person sits on a couch
and pushes the button of a television remote-control devices many times a
minute check and recheck all the channels. In the United States, channel 63. ________
surfing is by far the more popular sport. When television first replaced
radio, in the 1950s, channel surfing was known. Back then, there were 64. ________
only a few stations. Viewers had their favorite shows and watched it 65. ________
devotedly all the way through. In fact, studies showed that when a family
sat down to watch a favorite program at 7 p. m. , they stayed with the
same channel rest of the evening. With the coming of the cable television, 66. ________
dozens of channels now offer a great variety of featured films, situation 67. ________
comedies, news, weather, talk, science shows, documentaries, and
advertising. Facing with so many choices, viewers often become quiet and 68. ________
feel a need to check in all the other stations. 69. ________
Some studies show that men in a unique U. S. household usually want 70. ________
to hold the remote control and surf the channel; women usually like to
choose one program and watch through. 71. ________

Part Ⅵ Translation (5 minutes)

Directions:（略）

72. The cause of work holism is the perception that ________________________
________________（通过长时间地工作,完成更多项目,我们便能提高自身价值）.

73. Many women today feel the same stress to produce and get ahead, and ________________
________________________（同时又要养育子女,承担起各种家庭责任）.

74. ____
________（通过使用卫星辅助的全球定位系统,汽车里的计算机能给汽车精确定位）; and with the application of sensors, smart cars can eliminate most car accidents.

75. In folk tales, ____
________________（全家年龄最小的总是最善良、最有成就）.

76. The parents realize that ________________________________

______________________(他们不能任由孩子们再那样浪费钱).

参考答案(9)

Part Ⅰ Sample Writing

My View on Automobiles

Automobiles, as the product of modern civilization, have been playing a vital part in the daily activities of human society. First of all, cars offer convenience and mobility. We can now drive to work, go shopping, visit friends, and even travel across the country. Fast and labor saving, automobiles have become so essential and indispensable to us that it is no exaggeration to say that our modern society is moving on four wheels.

But automobiles have also given rise to a series of problems. Pollution, traffic accidents, and energy consumption, to name just a few, are following in the work of automobiles. However, these problems are offset by the advantages derived from auto development.

Obviously, automobiles, like anything else, have more than one face. While taking advantage of automobiles, we must try to find ways to reduce their disadvantages to a minimum so as to let them serve our purposes better. With the number of cars in our country, the era of the automobile, like any other technological age, will come.

Part Ⅱ Reading Comprehension (Skimming and Scanning)

1. A 2. D 3. B 4. A 5. A 6. D 7. C

8. expand his intellectual horizons

9. "A college degree opens door."

10. had never regretted reinventing his life/ was glad he had made the sacrifices

Part Ⅲ Listening Comprehension

Section A

11—15 CCBCC 16—20 CDABD 21—25 DCBAD

Section B

26—30 CBBDA

31—35 CDCAD

Section C

36. seventy-one 37. vast 38. supply 39. exchange

40. affected 41. subject 42. Mapping 43. Currently

44. With the newly developed methods, cameras can take pictures of the underwater valleys, even in color

45. Where rivers flow into the sea, the flat area may extend for hundreds of miles

46. The region near the continents, where the water is not so deep, is the place where the ocean's greatest riches in marine life are found

Part Ⅳ Reading Comprehension (Reading in Depth)

Section A

47. Apollo program
48. monsters
49. 7,000
50. It may free humanity from the terrible scourge of diverse diseases. /It may reduce people's suffering from some terrible diseases.
51. He wants to show that from past experience humans may not use the new knowledge wisely.

Section B

52—56 BCADD 57—61 DACAA

Part Ⅴ Error Correction

62. crash → crashing
63. check → to check
64. known → unknown
65. it → them
66. rest → the rest
67. featured → feature
68. facing → faced
69. quiet → restless
70. unique → typical
71. watch ∧ through → watch it through

Part Ⅵ Translation

72. by working longer hours and completing more projects, we will enhance our value
73. at the same time, to nurture their offspring and shoulder a variety of family responsibilities
74. By using the satellite-aided GPS, a computer in the automobile can locate the vehicle's precise position
75. the youngest of the family is always the nicest and the most successful
76. they can not have their children wasting the money that way

试题解答(9)

Part Ⅱ Reading Comprehension (Skimming and Scanning)

1. [A] 全文第二段作者提到他原来以为自己聪明好学、知识渊博,升迁应该是件容易的事。可后来他才感觉到其中有些内幕他是不明白的。一年半后,他意识到升迁的机会等于零,故而决定有所改变,即"After about a year and a half, I realized that my chances of advancement were nil, and it was time to do something about it."。故本题的正确答案为A项。

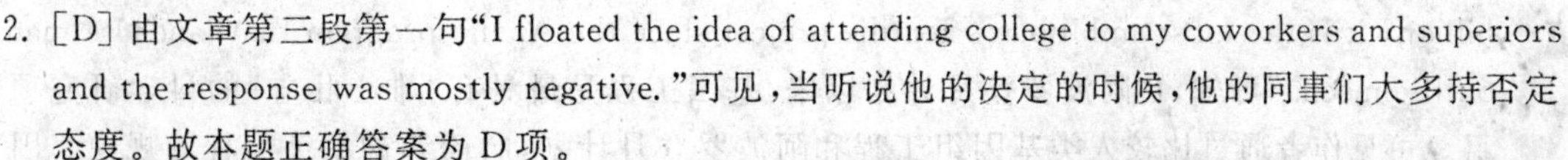

2. [D] 由文章第三段第一句"I floated the idea of attending college to my coworkers and superiors and the response was mostly negative."可见,当听说他的决定的时候,他的同事们大多持否定态度。故本题正确答案为D项。
3. [B] 由"Culture Shock"部分第一段最后两句 "I found, instead, that most of the culture shock happens when you leave class and go back to work. For while your coworkers and bosses are not changing, you are."可见,大多数的"文化休克"发生在作者从学校重新回到工作单位的时候。故本题正确答案为B项。
4. [A] 由"Overcoming the initial obstacles"部分第一段第三、第四句 "Actually it was the other way around. I saw staying in my job as a way to avoid facing responsibilities, and college as a more real world-and an island of sanity in my life."可见,作者认为继续原来的工作才是逃避责任的做法。故正确答案为A项。
5. [A] 由"Overcoming the initial obstacles"第三段第一句 "Probably the biggest obstacle I faced, since I was plagued by doubts about my own intelligence and abilities, was just getting started."可知本题正确答案是A项。
6. [D] 由"College life for adults"部分第四段第三句 "We tended to be more focused on getting an education, had a lot to contribute to the class discussion because of our experience in the world and were less likely to argue over a grade."可知本题正确答案为D项。
7. [C] 在 "The Big Time"部分第一段中作者指出"Against the odds, I had achieved something... had learned to let all the negativity go in one ear and out the other.",故本题正确答案为C项。
8. 由"College life for adults"部分最后一段第三句"You may even find that the company of other scholars will help you expand your intellectual horizons"可见,此题正确答案为"expand his intellectual horizons"。
9. 由"The Big Time"部分的最后一段"A college degree opens doors. It might not be possible to see the doors when you are just starting out, but they are there if you have the patience and drive to pursue your dreams."可见,作者认为大学文凭打开了大门。刚开始的时候也许看不到这些大门(机会)。只要有耐心有精力去追寻梦想,机会就会出现。因而可以看出,作者说"A college degree opens door."是指获得大学文凭可以让人们有更多的成功机会。
10. 文章开头和结尾部分,作者都提到了他对上大学这个决定的看法。由第一段的第二、三两句"I remember the fun I had in college, the people I met, the professors who taught me and the experiences that changed my life. And I'm glad I made the sacrifices."可见,作者很高兴他当初做出了牺牲,下定决心去读书。可见本题答案可以是"was glad he had made the sacrifices"。由"The Big Time"部分第三段最后一句"It hasn't always been easy and it hasn't always been that much fun, but I've never regretted reinventing my life."可见,作者从不后悔重新塑造自己的生活。故本题答案也可以是"had never regretted reinventing his life"。

Part Ⅲ Listening Comprehension(听力原文在光盘中)

Part Ⅳ Reading Comprehension (Reading in Depth)

Section A

47. 文章一开始就讲到了人类基因工程规模浩大。从第二段第二句"Costing more than £2

billion, it is the most ambitious scientific project since the Apollo program that landed a man on the moon."可知,自阿波罗登月计划以来,基因工程是最具有"雄心壮志"的科学研究项目。可见作者通过比较人类基因组工程和阿波罗登月计划,向读者揭示该工程的规模。因此,正确答案为"Apollo program"。

48. 第二段最后一句"But others see the future through a darker glass and fear that the project may open the door to a world peopled by Frankenstein's monsters and disfigured by a new eugenics."中的弗朗肯斯坦的怪物出自19世纪英国著名小说家玛丽·雪莱的科幻小说《弗朗肯斯坦》,其中讲述生物学家弗朗肯斯坦创造了一个面目可憎、奇丑无比的怪物,最终被其杀死的故事。可见有人担心基因组工程一旦解开人类基因的全部秘密,最终毁灭缔造者的基因怪兽可能会由此产生。因此,本题正确答案为"monsters"。

49. 第三段第三、四句"Witten out along the double helix of DNA are the chemical letters of the genetic text, for the human genome contains more than 3 billion letters. On the printed page it would fill about 7,000 volumes."中的 volume 指"一册书、一卷书"。由此可知正确答案是"7,000"。

50. 第二段第三句"Those working on the Human Genome Project claim that the new genetic anatomy will transform medicine and reduce human suffering in the 21st century."和第四段第一句"If properly applied, the new knowledge generated by the Human Genome Project may free humanity from the terrible scourge of diverse diseases."都提到如果合理应用该工程的研究结果,人类可以免受很多可怕的疾病的折磨。由此可见,本题可以回答为"It may free humanity from the terrible scourge of diverse diseases. / It may reduce people's suffering from some terrible diseases. "。

51. 最后一段第二句作者提到如果不能明智地运用基因组工程带来的新知识,就有产生新的歧视和新的压迫的危险(But if the new knowledge is not used wisely, it also holds the threat of creating new forms of discrimination and new methods of oppression.)。随后作者提到了原子能的发现,并说明掌握原子能改变了国家的命运,也给我们的生活蒙上了阴影。作者由此表达了自己的担心,即基因组工程如果不能被人类明智使用,也会给人类带来无尽的威胁。因此,本题答案可以归纳为"He wants to show that from past experience humans may not use the new knowledge wisely. "。

Section B

52. [B] 推断题。第一段第一句话"Unlike the scientist, the engineer is not free to select the problem which interests him"反过来说就是:"Unlike the engineer, the scientist is free to select the problem which interests him."。故正确答案为B项。

53. [C] 词义推断题。由上下文"... efficiency means output divided by input... The **ratio** may be expressed in terms of..."可以看出 ratio(比率)即"投入和产出比",故正确答案为C项。

54. [A] 细节选择题。由第三段第二句"The processing of the new antibiotic and vaccines in the test-tube stage belongs in the field of biochemistry, but when great quantities must be produced at low cost, it becomes an engineering problem"可知正确答案为A项。

55. [D] 意义理解题。由第四段第一句"Since output equals input minus losses..."可知控制 loss 和 waste,则 output 增加,则 ratio=output/input 值增大,效率提高。第四段后半部分也提到"Efficient functioning depends on good design, careful attention to operating difficulties, and

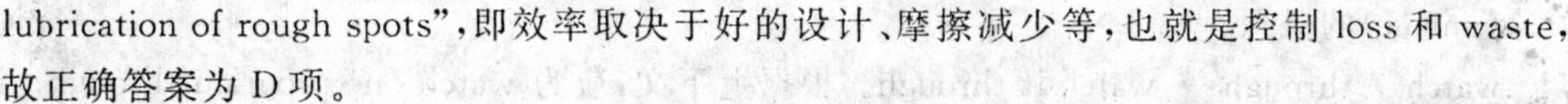
lubrication of rough spots",即效率取决于好的设计、摩擦减少等,也就是控制 loss 和 waste,故正确答案为 D 项。

56. [D] 由最后一段"The raw materials with which engineers work are seldom found in useful forms. Engineering of the highest type is required to conceive, design, and achieve the conversion of the energy of ... into ... Similarly ... change the sands into..."可知,工程就是把看似无用的原材料转变为对人类有用的东西。然后举例说明,比如让山间急流转动百里外的发电机,把海滩沙砾变成望远镜观察太空等。
57. [D] 细节题。文章第一段第二句话指出每 100 个女婴出生就会有 105 个男婴出生,但男女比例在成年后就接近平衡,而 70 岁的老年人中女性的人数是男性的两倍。这说明男性曾面临低成活率的问题,故正确答案为 D 项
58. [A] 词义判断题。文章第二段指出,对人类进化不利的另一个因素是现在出生的人口比以前少,而且人们拥有的后代人数几乎相等,因此人与人之间的差异缩小了,大自然利用这种差异进行优胜劣汰的机会都减少了。所以 diminished 是"减少"的意思,故正确答案为 A 项。
59. [C] 细节推断题。文章第二段以印度人为例说明到现在印度人的存活率和后代人数都基本上没有差异,这使自然选择无法分辨好坏,从而很难在有钱人和穷人之间进行物竞天择。因此,正确答案为 C 项。
60. [A] 细节推断题。文章第三段第四和第五句提到近一百年来我们的生活发生了巨大的变化,而我们的身体没有任何变化,因为机器和社会替我们做了进化该做的事。因此可以推断人类停止进化的原因是技术进步改善了人类的生活并帮助人类不断适应环境的变化,故正确答案为 A 项。
61. [A] 主旨题。文章的第一段中作者指出婴儿成活率的提高妨碍了优胜劣汰。文章第二段中作者明确提出人类新生人口的减少和拥有相同数量后代的趋势进一步使自然选择失去了效力。第三段开始作者就提出进化对我们来说已经结束了。技术和社会的发展使人类的进化失去了必要性。纵观全文,作者认为"人类进化已经无路可走"的观点十分清楚。故正确答案为 A 项。

Part Ⅴ Error Correction

62. crash → crashing。用现在分词 crashing 与 big 一同修饰 ocean wave。
63. check → to check。用动词不定式作目的状语,修饰谓语动词 pushes。
64. known → unknown。根据上下文的语义,应该是"人们并不知道搜索频道"。
65. it → them。根据上下文应该是电视观众"收看他们喜欢的节目",即"watch their favorite shows"。
66. rest → the rest。rest 作名词,意为"其余之物,其余的人,余下的",常常需要在其前加定冠词 the。
67. featured → feature。feature film 为"故事片,情节片,长片"。例如:There are two feature films and three cartoons in the program(节目单上有两部故事片和三部卡通片)。
68. facing → faced。此处应有过去分词短语用作状语,修饰谓语,以说明下文的动作发生的背景。
69. quiet → restless。根据上文"由于有太多的选择而使电视观看者显得手足无措",所以应该用 restless,而不是 quiet。
70. unique → typical。根据上下文,此处应该表达"典型的"(typical)意义,而不是"独一无二"

(unique)的概念。

71. watch ∧ through → watch it through。根据上下文,应为 watch one program through。it 替代 one program,作 watch 的宾语,through 为副词。

Part Ⅵ Translation

72. [答案]:by working longer hours and completing more projects, we will enhance our value

[注释]:本句是个并列句,没有过难的语言点。

73. [答案]: at the same time, to nurture their offspring and shoulder a variety of family responsibilities

[注释]:本句翻译重点之一是"养育"一词,nurture 是最佳答案;其次,是"承担"的翻译,除了 shoulder 之外,还有其他表示相近含义的词,如 take。

74. [答案]:By using the satellite-aided GPS, a computer in the automobile can locate the vehicle's precise position

[注释]:本句的难点是"定位"的翻译,也就是 locate 的使用。

75. [答案]:the youngest of the family is always the nicest and the most successful

[注释]:本句考查最高级的使用。

76. [答案]:they can not have their children wasting the money that way

[注释]:本句考查"任由"的翻译,也就是 have sb. doing sth. 的使用。

College English Practice Test 10 (Band Ⅵ)

Part Ⅰ Writing (30 minutes)

Directions: *For this part, you are allowed 30 minutes to write a short essay entitled* **Nature or Nurture**. *You should write at least* **150** *words following the outline given below.*

1. 有些人认为遗传因素起决定作用;
2. 也有人认为环境影响作用更大;
3. 你的观点。

Part Ⅱ Reading Comprehension (Skimming and Scanning) (15 minutes)

Directions: (略)

Suggestions for Improving Reading Speed

Improvement of Reading Rate

It is safe to say that almost anyone can double his or her speed of reading while maintaining equal or even better comprehension. In other words, you can improve the speed with which you get what you want from your reading.

The average college student reads between 250 and 350 words per minute on fiction and non-technical materials. A "good" reading speed is around 500 to 700 words per minute, but some people can read 1,000 words per minute or more on these materials.

What makes the difference? There are three main factors involved in improving reading speed: (1) the desire to improve, (2) the willingness to try new techniques and (3) the motivation to practice.

Learning to read rapidly and well presupposes that you have the necessary vocabulary and comprehension skills. When you have advanced on the reading comprehension materials to a level at which you can understand college-level materials, you will be ready to practice speed reading in earnest.

The Role of Speed in the Reading Process

Understanding the role of speed in the reading process is essential. Research shows a close relation between speed and understanding—although it is the opposite of what you might expect! Among thousands of individuals taking reading training, in most cases an increase in rate was

accompanied by an increase in comprehension and a decrease in rate brought decreased comprehension with it. It appears that plodding or word-by-word analysis inhibits rather than increases understanding.

Most adults are able to increase their reading rate considerably and rather quickly without lowering their comprehension. These same individuals usually show a decrease in comprehension when they reduce their rate. Such results, of course, are heavily dependent upon the method used to gain the increased rate. Simply reading more rapidly without actual improvement in basic reading habits usually results in lowered comprehension.

Factors that Reduce Reading Rate

Some of the factors which reduce reading rate:

1. Limited perceptual span (word-by-word reading);
2. Slow perceptual reaction time (slow recognition and response to the material);
3. Vocalization (reading aloud);
4. Faulty eye movements (including inaccuracy in placement of the page, in return sweep, in rhythm and regularity of movement, etc.);
5. Regression (needless or unconscious re-reading);
6. Faulty habits of attention and concentration (including simple inattention during the reading act and faulty processes of retention);
7. Lack of practice in reading—use it or lose it!
8. Fear of losing comprehension, causing the person to deliberately read more slowly;
9. Habitual slow reading, in which the person cannot read faster because he or she has always read slowly;
10. Poor evaluation of which aspects are important and which are unimportant;
11. The effort to remember everything rather than to remember selectively.

Since these conditions also tend to reduce comprehension, increasing the reading rate by eliminating them is likely to produce increased comprehension, too. This is entirely different from simply speeding up the rate of reading—which may actually make the real reading problem more severe. In addition, forced acceleration may destroy confidence in one's ability to read. The obvious solution, then, is to increase rate as a part of a total improvement of the whole reading process, as special training programs in reading do.

Basic Conditions for Increasing Reading Rate

A well-planned program prepares for maximum increase in rate by establishing the necessary conditions. Four basic conditions include:

1. Have your eyes checked. Often, very slow reading is related to uncorrected eye defects. Before embarking on a speed reading program, make sure that any correctable eye defects you may have are taken care of.
2. Eliminate the habit of pronouncing words as you read. If you sound out words in your throat or whisper them, your reading rate is slowed considerably. You should be able to read most materials at least two or three times faster silently than orally, because you can

get meaning from phrases without reading each word individually. If you are aware of sounding or "hearing" words as you read, try to concentrate on key words and meaningful ideas as you force yourself to read faster.

3. Avoid regressing (rereading). The average student reading at 250 words per minute regresses or rereads about 20 times per page. Rereading words and phrases is a habit which will slow your reading speed down to a snail's pace. Usually, it is unnecessary to reread words, for the ideas you want are explained and elaborated more fully later. Furthermore, the slowest reader usually regresses most frequently. Because he reads slowly, his mind has time to wander and his rereading reflects both his inability to concentrate and his lack of confidence in his comprehension skills.
4. Develop a wider eye-span. This will help you read more than one word at a glance. Since written material is less meaningful if read word by word, this will help you learn to read by phrases or thought units.

Rate Adjustment

Poor results are inevitable if the reader attempts to use the same rate for all types of material and for all reading purposes. He must learn to adjust his rate to his purpose in reading and to the difficulty of the material. The fastest rate works on easy, familiar, interesting material or in reading to gather information on a particular point. A slower rate is better for material which is unfamiliar in content and language structure or which must be thoroughly digested. The effective reader adjusts his rate; the ineffective reader always uses the same.

Rate may be adjusted overall for an entire article, or internally for parts of an article. As an analogy, imagine that you plan to take a 100-mile mountain trip. Since this trip will include hills, curves, and a mountain pass, you estimate it will take three hours for the total trip, averaging about 35 miles an hour. This is your overall rate adjustment. In actual driving, however, you may slow down to no more than 15 miles per hour on some curves and hills, while speeding up to 50 miles per hour or more on relatively straight and level sections. This is your internal rate adjustment. Similarly, there is no set rate which the good reader follows inflexibly in reading a particular selection, even though he has set himself an overall rate for the total job.

Reading rate should vary according to your reading purpose. To understand information, for example, skim or scan at a rapid rate. To determine the value of material or to read for enjoyment, read rapidly or slowly according to your feeling. To read analytically, read at a moderate pace to permit you to interrelated ideas.

The nature and difficulty of the material also calls for adjustments in rate. Obviously, level of difficulty depends greatly on the particular reader's knowledge. While Einstein's theories may be extremely difficult for most laymen, they would be very simple and clear to a professor of physics. Hence, the layman and the physics professor will read the same material at different rates. Generally, difficult material will entail a slower rate; simpler material will permit a faster rate.

In general, decrease speed when you find the following:

1. Unfamiliar terminology. Try to understand it in context at that point; otherwise, read on

and return to it later.

2. Difficult sentence and paragraph structure. Slow down enough to enable you to untangle them and get accurate context for the passage.
3. Unfamiliar or abstract concepts. Look for applications or examples of your own as well as studying those of the writer. Take enough time to get them clearly in mind.
4. Detailed, technical material. This includes complicated directions, statements of difficult principles, and materials on which you have scant background.
5. Material on which you want detailed retention.

In general, increase speed when you meet the following:

1. Simple material with few ideas which are new to you. Move rapidly over the familiar ones; spend most of your time on the unfamiliar ideas.
2. Unnecessary examples and illustrations. Since these are included to clarify ideas, move over them rapidly when they are not needed.
3. Detailed explanation and idea elaboration which you do not need.
4. Broad, generalized ideas and ideas which are restatements of previous ones. These can be readily grasped, even with scan techniques.

1. A person with a good reading speed usually reads between 250 and 350 words per minute on fiction and non-technical materials.
2. If one attempts to remember everything rather than to remember selectively during reading, he/she may have a comparatively slow reading rate.
3. The writer proposes to use the same rate for all types of material and for all reading purposes.
4. Knowledgeable people read faster.
5. If one has the desire to improve his reading speed, the motivation to practice and ________, he may improve his reading speed.
6. A precondition for a reader to learn to read rapidly and well is that he must have the necessary ________.
7. Different from what most people expect, the research shows that an increase in reading rate may lead to ________.
8. To avoid destroying confidence in one's ability to read, one should speed up the rate of reading as a part of ________.
9. Rereading of a slow reader reflects both his ________ and his lack of confidence in his comprehension skills.
10. An effective reader usually adjusts his rate to his purpose in reading and to the difficulty of the material while an ineffective reader always ________.

Part Ⅲ Listening Comprehension (35 minutes)

Section A

Directions:(略)

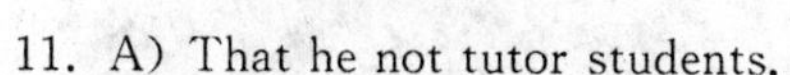

11. A) That he not tutor students.
    B) That he work on improving his languages skills.
    C) That he work as a tutor to pay his tuition.
    D) That he try to find a job in Italy.
12. A) To act as an interpreter.
    B) To check the patient as a doctor.
    C) To work as nurse in the hospital.
    D) To chat with the patient.
13. A) He thinks the woman is right.
    B) He thinks it better to post the card earlier.
    C) He is sure the card will be delayed.
    D) He thinks a delay is impossible.
14. A) In a cafeteria.
    B) At a zoo.
    C) At an art museum.
    D) On a college campus.
15. A) The woman is afraid of thunderstorms.
    B) The man works for a good roofing company.
    C) The roof of the woman's house needs repairing.
    D) The man's roof is leaking and he asks the woman to help him.
16. A) He thinks that the salesman was realistic.
    B) He thinks that the salesman exaggerated his part.
    C) He thinks that the salesman was not dramatic enough.
    D) He thinks that the salesman played his part well.
17. A) March 3rd.
    B) March 29th.
    C) March 12th.
    D) March 30th.
18. A) He should sit in the smoking section.
    B) He should ask the stewardess for help.
    C) He should move to another part of the plane.
    D) He should extinguish his cigarette at once.

Questions 19 to 22 are based on the conversation you have just heard.

19. A) More than 20 minutes.
    B) More than 18 minutes.
    C) Less than 6 minutes.
    D) Less than 12 minutes.
20. A) She is an artist.
    B) She is a tourist.
    C) She is a staff of the Museum.
    D) She is the owner of a restaurant.
21. A) For its cheap price.
    B) For its authentic decoration.
    C) For its quiet environment.
    D) For its tasty food.
22. A) By taxi.
    B) By bus.
    C) By subway.
    D) By bicycle.

Questions 23 to 25 are based on the conversation you have just heard.

23. A) Teacher and student.
    B) Mother and son.
    C) Classmates.
    D) Brother and sister
24. A) Warm-hearted, self-disciplined, patient.
    B) Hot-tempered, diligent, kind.

C) Easy-going, warm-hearted, stubborn.

D) Self-centered, hard-working, considerate.

25. A) He spends much school time playing computer games.

B) He often dozes off in class.

C) He doesn't take the assignments seriously.

D) He plays computer games because the textbooks are dull and lectures are boring.

Section B

Directions: (略)

Passage One

Questions 26 to 28 are based on the passage you have just heard.

26. A) Red. B) Yellow. C) White. D) Blue.

27. A) The 2000 Olympic Games.

B) The Euro 2004 international soccer contest.

C) The 2004 Olympic Games.

D) Both B) and C).

28. A) Aggression. B) Ambition. C) Danger. D) Vigor.

Passage Two

Questions 29 to 31 are based on the passage you have just heard.

29. A) Campus facilities for international students.

B) Optional courses for international students.

C) Activities on and off campus for international students.

D) Accommodation choices for international students.

30. A) Keeping their dormitory clean. B) Their behavior in the dormitory.

C) The furniture in the dormitory. D) The public facilities in the dormitory.

31. A) Traveling in a car to the campus.

B) No housework to do.

C) Some freedom of choosing a roommate.

D) Arrange the furniture at will.

Passage Three

Questions 32 to 35 are based on the passage you have just heard.

32. A) The population of elderly people. B) Nuclear weapon.

C) Violence in crime. D) Living standards.

33. A) Growth of violence on TV.

B) Destructive threat from nuclear explosives.

C) Decreasing of moral standards.

D) All of the above.

34. A) People are more destructive.
B) People are more selfish.
C) People do what they preach now.
D) People do not have moral principles to follow now.

35. A) Indifferent. B) Surprised. C) Worried. D) Confident.

Section C

Directions:(略)

Stress is the "wear and tear" our bodies experience as we (36) ________ to our changing environment. As a (37) ________ influence, stress can help us take action. As a (38) ________ influence, it can lead to health problems such as (39) ________, insomnia, ulcers, high blood pressure and heart disease.

Our goal is not to eliminate stress but to learn how to (40) ________ it and how to use it to help us. (41) ________ stress may make us feel bored; on the other hand, (42) ________ stress may make us feel tied up in knots. What we need to do is to find the optimal level of stress which will (43) ________ but not overwhelm us.

There is no single level of stress that is optimal for all people. (44) ________________________________. Moreover, our personal stress requirements and the amount which we can tolerate changes with our ages.

It has been revealed that most illness is related to unrelieved stress. (45) ________________________________. There are many sources of stress, and there are many possibilities for its management. Here are three principles as to how to manage stress:

1. ________________________________.
2. Recognize what you can change.
3. Reduce the intensity of your emotional reactions to stress.

Part Ⅳ Reading Comprehension(Reading in Depth) (25 minutes)

Section A

Directions:(略)

Questions 47 to 51 are based on the following passage.

The first time anybody knew about Dutchman Frank Siegmund and his family was when workmen tramping through a field found a narrow steel chimney protruding through the grass. Closer inspection revealed a chink of sky-light window among the thistles and when amazed investigators moved down the side of the hill they came across a pine door and a brass knocker set into an underground building. The Siegmunds had managed to live undetected for six years outside the border town of Breda, in Holland. They are the latest in a clutch of individualistic homemakers who have burrowed underground in search of tranquility.

Most, falling foul of strict building regulations, have been forced to dismantle their

individualistic homes and return to more conventional lifestyles. But subterranean suburbia Dutch-style, is about to become respectable and chic. Seven luxury homes cosseted away inside a high earth-covered noise embankment next to the main Tilburg city road recently went on the market for $ 296,500 each. The foundations had yet to be dug, but customers queued up to buy the unusual part-submerged houses.

Building big commercial buildings underground can be a way to avoid disfiguring or threatening a beautiful or environmentally sensitive landscape. Indeed many of the buildings which consume most land—such as cinemas, supermarkets, theatres, warehouses or libraries—have no need to be on the surface since they do not need windows. There are big advantages, too, when it comes to private homes. A development of 194 houses which would take up 14 hectares of land above ground would occupy 2.7 hectares below it, while the number of roads would be halved. Under several meters of earth, noise is minimal and insulation is excellent.

In Europe, the obstacle has been conservative local authorities and developers who prefer to ensure quick sales with conventional mass-produced housing. But the Dutch development was greeted with undisguised relief by South Limburg planners because of Holland's chronic shortage of land. In the US, where energy-efficient homes became popular after the oil crisis of 1973, 10,000 underground houses have been built. A terrace of five homes, Britain's first subterranean development, is under way in Nottinghamshire. Italy's outstanding example of subterranean architecture is the Olivetti residential centre in Ivreg.

Not everyone adapts so well, and in Japan scientists at the Shimizu Corporation have developed "space creation" system which mix light, sound, breezes and scents to simulate people who spend long periods below ground. Underground offices in Japan are being equipped with virtual windows and mirrors, while underground departments in the University of Minnesota have periscopes to reflect views and light.

Frank Siegmund and his family love their hobbit lifestyle. Their home evolved when he dug a cool room for his bakery business in a hill he had created. During a heat-wave they took to sleeping there. "We felt at peace and so close to nature," he says, "Gradually I began adding to the rooms. It sounds strange but we are so close to the earth we draw strength from its vibrations."

47. Why have some underground houses been pulled down?
48. What are the advantages of constructing private homes underground?
49. Many developer prefer mass-produced houses because they ________.
50. Japanese scientists are helping people ________ underground life.
51. Frank Siegmund's first underground room was used for ________.

Section B

Directions: (略)

Passage One

Questions 52 to 56 are based on the following passage.

Before, whenever we had wealth, we started discussing poverty. Why not now? Why is the current politics of wealth and poverty seemingly about wealth alone? Eight years ago, when Bill Clinton first ran for president, the Dow Jones average was under 3,500, yearly federal budget deficits were projected at hundreds of billions of dollars forever and beyond, and no one talked about the "permanent boom" or the "new economy." Yet in that more **straitened** time, Clinton made much of the importance of "not leaving a single person behind." It is possible that similar "compassionate" rhetoric might yet play a role in the general election.

But it is striking how much less talk there is about the poor than there was eight years ago, when the country was economically uncertain, or in previous eras, when the country felt flush. Even last summer, when Clinton spent several days on a remarkable, Bobby Kennedy-like pilgrimage through impoverished areas from Indian reservations in South Dakota to ghetto neighborhoods in East St. Louis, the administration decided to refer to the effort not as a poverty tour but as a "new markets initiative."

What is happening is partly a logical, policy-driven reaction. Poverty really is lower than it has been in decades, especially for minority groups. The most attractive solution to it—a growing economy—is being applied. The people who have been totally left out of this boom often have medical, mental or other problems for which no one has an immediate solution. "The economy has sucked in anyone who has any preparation, any ability to cope with modern life," says Franklin D. Raines, the former director of the Office of Management and Budget who is now head of Fannie Mae. When he and other people who specialize in the issue talk about solutions, they talk analytically and long-term: education, development of work skills, shifts in the labor market, adjustments in welfare reform.

But I think there is another force that has made this a rich era with barely visible poor people. It is the unusual social and imaginative separation between prosperous America and those still left out. It's simple invisibility, because of increasing geographic, occupational, and social barriers that block one group from the other's view.

52. In the first paragraph of this passage, the word "straitened" probably means "________".
   A) difficult　　B) past　　C) wealthy　　D) distant

53. The main idea of the passage is that ________.
   A) the country is enjoying economic growth
   B) the poor are benefiting from today's good economy
   C) in the past we were more aware of the poor than we are today
   D) in the past there were many more poor people than there are today

54. After reading this passage, you can conclude that ________.
   A) the relationship between the rich and the poor has changed
   B) the good economy will soon end
   C) poverty will be obliterated as a result of increased wealth
   D) all people benefit from good economic conditions

55. The author states that one important reason that we do not talk much about poverty is that ________.

A) no one knows what to do about it

B) poverty really is lower than in the past

C) no one has been left out of the current boom

D) the president is not concerned about the poor

56. What is the author's purpose in writing this passage?

A) To entertain. B) To tell a story.

C) To describe. D) To persuade.

Passage Two

Questions 57 to 61 are based on the following passage.

My writing was to develop topics and themes from my Native American background. The experience in my village of Deetziyamah and Acoma Pueblo was readily accessible. My mother was a potter of the well-known Acoma clayware. My father carved figures from wood and did beadwork. This was not unusual, as Native American people know; there was always some kind of artistic endeavor that people set themselves to, although they did not necessarily articulate it as "Art" in the sense of Western civilization. One lived and expressed an artful life, whether it was in ceremonial singing and dancing, architecture, painting, speaking or in the way one's social-cultural life was structured. I did so because this was my identity, the substance of who I was, and I wanted to write about what that meant. My desire was to write about the integrity of a Native American identity.

To a great extent my writing has a natural political-cultural bent simply because I was nurtured intellectually and emotionally with an atmosphere of Native American resistance. The Acoma Pueblo, despite losing much of their land and surrounded by a foreign civilization, have not lost sight of their native heritage. This is the factual case with most other Native American peoples, and the clear explanation for this has been the fight-back we have found necessary to wage. At times, in the past, it was outright-armed struggle; currently, it is often in the legal arena, and it is in the field of literature. In 1981, when I was invited to the White House for an event celebrating American poets and poetry, I did not immediately accept the invitation. I questioned myself about the possibility that I was merely being exploited as an Indian, and I hedged against accepting. But then I recalled the elders going among our people in the poor days of the 1950s, asking for donations—a dollar here and there, a sheep, perhaps a piece of pottery—in order to finance a trip to the nation's capital, to demand justice, to reclaim lost land even though there was only **spare** hope they would be successful. I went to the White House realizing that I was to do no less than they and those who had fought n the Pueblo Revolt of 1680, and I read my poems and sang songs that were later described as **"guttural"** by a newspaper. I suppose it is more or less understandable why such a view of Native American literature is held by many, and it is also clear why there should be a political stand taken in my writing and those of my sister and brother Native American writers.

The 1960s and afterward have been a invigorating and liberating period for Native American people. It has been only a little more than twenty years since Native American writers began to write and publish extensively, but we are writing and publishing more and more; we can only go forward. We come from an ageless, continuing oral tradition that informs us of our values, concepts, and notions as native people, and it is amazing how much of this tradition is ingrained so deeply in our contemporary writing, considering the brutal efforts of cultural repression that was not long ago outright U. S. policy. We were not to speak our languages, practice our spiritual beliefs, or accept the values of our past generations; and we were discouraged from pressing for our natural rights as Native American human beings. In spite of the fact that there is to some extent the same repression today, we persist and insist on living, believing, hoping, loving, speaking and writing as Native Americans.

57. The central idea conveyed in the passage is that ________.
   A) the author remembers his childhood, especially his parents and the elders in his community, in a very positive way
   B) a desire to cling to traditional Native American values led the author to write about Native American issues
   C) art is an important part of Native American life and should be a part of everyone's existence
   D) the artful nature of Native American life compels the author to explore and worship that heritage
58. The author the quoted word "guttural" (Para. 2) to ________.
   A) communicate the newspaper's lack of understanding and respect for the author's presentation
   B) describe most accurately how the author felt about his White House reading of his poems
   C) emphasize the dramatic effect on the White House audience of the author's reading of his poems and performance of traditional Pueblo songs
   D) convey the sound of the Acoma Pueblo language to readers who are unfamiliar with it
59. Why did the author change his mind to accept the invitation to the White House?
   A) He was eager to read his poetry to an audience of other poets and literary critics.
   B) He wanted his writing and the writing of other Native American men and women to take on a more political tone.
   C) He remembered the sacrifices that his ancestors had made for the privilege of going there, even if only to be ignored.
   D) He realized that he had not been invited to the event as a representative of Native Americans.
60. The author's main view in this passage was most influenced by the following assumption that ________.
   A) the artistic traditions of Native American peoples are similar to those of European cultures
   B) all writings produced by Native Americans express, either directly or indirectly, a political position
   C) the major responsibility of Native American writers is to celebrate and preserve the cultural traditions of their people
   D) literature can be a powerful tool fro asserting the cultural values and political rights of ethnic groups

61. The word "spare" (Para. 2) is close in meaning to "________".

A) free　　B) extra　　C) frugal　　D) meager

Part Ⅴ　Error Correction　(15 minutes)

Directions:（略）

The role of the farmer has always been an important one. Two hundred
years ago, 95% of American workers were farmers. Agriculture is 62. ________
America's biggest industry. Today, less than 3% of American workers are
farmers. Yet agriculture still is America's biggest industry. It employs more
workers than any other industry, and it produces more food than Americans
can consume enough to make the United States the world's largest importer 63. ________
of agricultural goods. American farmers used to grow only enough food to
feed their families and animals. Now each farmer grows enough to feed 78
other people. American farmers produce more today because they have to
use modern farm and business methods. This means they have to know more 64. ________
than ever before. They still learn about soil, the weather, harmless insects, 65. ________
and plant and animal diseases, but they also must learn about economics,
international trade, and even computers. It has said that farming in America 66. ________
today is three fourths paper work and one fourth physical labor. Because of
this, American farmers now are able to work for more years. In the past,
most were old and tired of by the time they were about 40. Today, 67. ________
however, the average age of the American farmer is 48—five years older
than the average age of other American workers. Almost all new farmers in
the United states have completed at most 12 years of schooling, and many 68. ________
young Americans study agriculture at a state university. The federal
government provided with the establishment of these schools in a law signed 69. ________
by President Abraham Lincoln in 1862. Today there is a so-called land-grant
university in each state. The land-grant law also created the cooperative
extension service. This is a series of local offices around the country that
informs farmers about the latest developments in agriculture. American 70. ________
farmers also get information from the many agricultural publications in the
United States. Farmers also join organizations which they and their families 71. ________
can exchange information.

Part Ⅵ　Translation　(5 minutes)

Directions:（略）

72. It's common sense that ______________________（商务信函应以正式文体书写而不是以私人风格书写）.

73. ______________________（他因证据不足而被判决无罪）, which made his

mother so relaxed.

74. People here still keep their lifestyle today ______________________(殊不知他们的习惯对他们自己和后代都有害).

75. ______________________(只有积极投身于社会实践) can you accumulate enough working experience.

76. It's quite strange that ______________________(无论他说什么、做什么都被认为是错的).

参考答案(10)

Part Ⅰ Sample Writing

Nature or Nurture?

Today the way we consider human psychology and mental development is heavily determined by the genetic sciences. We now understand the importance of inherited characteristics more than ever before. Yet we are still unable to decide whether an individual's personality and development are more influenced by genetic factors (nature) or by the environment (nurture).

Research, relating to identical twins, has highlighted how significant inherited characteristics can be for an individual's life. But whether these characteristics are able to develop within the personality of an individual surely depends on whether the circumstances allow such a development. It seems that the experiences we have in life are so unpredictable and so powerful, that they can boost or over-ride other influences, and there seems to be plenty of research findings to confirm this.

My own view is that there is no one major influence in a person's life. Instead, the traits we inherit from our parents and the situation and experiences that we encounter in life are constantly interacting. It is the interaction of the two that shapes a person's personality and dictates how that personality develops. If this were not true, we would be able to predict the behavior and character of a person from the moment they were born. In conclusion, I do not think that either nature or nurture is the major influence on a person, but that both have powerful effects.

Part Ⅱ Reading Comprehension (Skimming and Scanning)

1. N 2. Y 3. N 4. NG
5. the willingness to try new techniques
6. vocabulary and comprehension skills
7. an increase in comprehension
8. a total improvement of the whole reading process
9. inability to concentrate
10. uses the same reading rate

Part Ⅲ Listening Comprehension

Section A

11—15　CABBC　16—20　BCCDB　21—25　BCCAD

Section B

26—30　ADBDB　31—35　CCDBC

Section C

36. adjust　37. positive　38. negative　39. headaches
40. manage　41. Insufficient　42. excessive　43. motivate

44. What is distressing to one may be a joy to another.

45. Being aware of stress and its effect on our lives can help reduce its harmful effects.

46. Become aware of your stressors and your emotional and physical reactions

Part Ⅳ　Reading Comprehension (Reading in Depth)

Section A

47. Because they fell foul of strict building regulations. /Because they violated strict building regulations.

48. Taking up less land, minimal noise and excellent insulation. /Saving land, saving energy and tranquility.

49. ensure quick sales/are sold quickly

50. adapt to

51. his bakery business

Section B

52—56　ACABD　57—61　BACDD

Part Ⅴ　Error Correction

62. is → was
63. importer → exporter
64. farm → farming
65. harmless → harmful
66. 在 has 和 said 之间 ∧ been
67. 删除 tired 之后的 of
68. most → least
69. with → for
70. informs → inform
71. which → where

Part Ⅵ　Translation

72. a business letter should be written in a formal style rather than in a personal style
73. He was found not guilty for insufficient evidence
74. without knowing that their habits are doing bad to themselves and their offspring
75. Only by actively involving yourself in social practice
76. whatever he says and whatever he does are always considered to be wrong

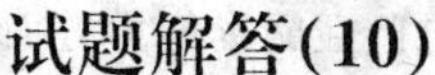

试题解答(10)

Part Ⅱ Reading Comprehension (Skimming and Scanning)

1. [N] 由"Improvement of Reading Rate"部分第二段"The average college student reads between 250 and 350 words per minute on fiction and non-technical materials. A "good" reading speed is around 500 to 700 words per minute, but some people can read 1000 words per minute or more on these materials."可见阅读速度快的人,每分钟可阅读500到700词。故此句判断为NO。
2. [Y] 由"Factors that Reduce Reading Rate"部分第11点"The effort to remember everything rather than to remember selectively."可见阅读过程中试图记住所有阅读内容会影响阅读的速度。故此句判断为YES。
3. [N] 由"Rate Adjustment"部分第一句"Poor results are inevitable if the reader attempts to use the same rate for all types of material and for all reading purposes."可知如果无视阅读材料的类型和不同的阅读目的而用同一种速度来阅读,结果肯定是不理想的。因此,作者显然不会建议用同一种阅读速度来阅读不同类型的材料,应对不同的阅读目的。故此句判断NO。
4. [NG] 文章只在"Rate Adjustment"部分提到阅读者的知识问题。由这部分第四段的第一、二句:"The nature and difficulty of the material also calls for adjustments in rate. Obviously, level of difficulty depends greatly on the particular reader's knowledge."可知阅读材料的难易影响阅读速度的调节。而材料的难易往往取决于阅读者的知识水平。因此,阅读者的知识影响他对材料的阅读。但是否一定"有知识的人阅读速度快",作者并没有明确指出。故此句判断为NOT GIVEN。
5. 由"Improvement of Reading Rate"部分第三段中的"There are three main factors involved in improving reading speed: (1) the desire to improve, (2) the willingness to try new techniques and (3) the motivation to practice."可知要提高阅读速度,阅读者必须有提高阅读的愿望,愿意尝试新的技巧并且有进行训练的动机。故本题的正确答案为"the willingness to try new techniques"。
6. 由"Improvement of Reading Rate"部分第四段第一句"Learning to read rapidly and well presupposes that you have the necessary vocabulary and comprehension skills."可知要提高阅读速度和质量的前提是你必须有必要的词汇量和阅读技巧。故此题答案为"vocabulary and comprehension skills"。
7. 由"The Role of Speed in the Reading Process"部分第一段"Research shows a close relation between speed and understanding—although it is the opposite of what you might expect! Among thousands of individuals taking reading training, in most cases an increase in rate was accompanied by an increase in comprehension and a decrease in rate brought decreased comprehension with it."可知研究表明,和人们预计的不一样,阅读速度的增加并不以牺牲理解为代价。相反,提高速度也会提高理解。故本题正确答案为"an increase in comprehension"。
8. 由"Factors that Reduce Reading Rate"部分最后一段"This is entirely different from simply speeding up the rate of reading—which may actually make the real reading problem more severe. In addition, forced acceleration may destroy confidence in one's ability to read. The obvious solution, then, is to increase rate as a part of a total improvement of the whole reading

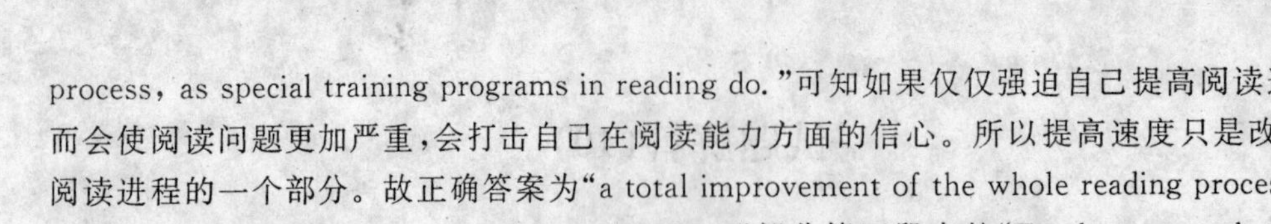

process, as special training programs in reading do."可知如果仅仅强迫自己提高阅读速度,反而会使阅读问题更加严重,会打击自己在阅读能力方面的信心。所以提高速度只是改善整个阅读进程的一个部分。故正确答案为"a total improvement of the whole reading process"。

9. 由"Basic Conditions for Increasing Reading Rate"部分第四段中的"Furthermore, the slowest reader usually regresses most frequently. Because he reads slowly, his mind has time to wander and his rereading reflects both his inability to concentrate and his lack of confidence in his comprehension skills."可见阅读速度最慢的读者,回读的频率也最高。由于读得慢,他也容易开小差。而回读也反映出他缺乏集中注意力的能力并对自己的阅读技巧缺乏信心。故此题正确答案为"inability to concentrate"。

10. 由"Rate Adjustment"部分第一段"Poor results are inevitable if the reader attempts to use the same rate for all types of material and for all reading purposes. He must learn to adjust his rate to his purpose in reading and to the difficulty of the material... The effective reader adjusts his rate; the ineffective reader always uses the same."可见效率高的阅读者会根据阅读的目的和阅读材料的难易调整阅读速度。而效率低的阅读者往往用同样的速度应对所有的阅读目的和阅读材料。故此题正确答案是"uses the same reading rate"。

Part Ⅲ Listening Comprehension(听力原文在光盘中)

Part Ⅳ Reading Comprehension (Reading in Depth)

Section A

47. 第一段最后一句说明 Siegmund 一家是为了寻求宁静而到地下建住所。由文章第二段第一句"Most, falling foul of strict building regulations, have been forced to dismantle their individualistic homes and return to more conventional lifestyles."可知地下住所被拆除的原因是违背了严格的建筑法规。因此答案为"Because they fell foul of strict building regulations."或者"Because they violated strict building regulations."。

48. 第三段作者说"There are big advantages, too, when it comes to private homes. A development of 194 houses which would take up 14 hectares of land above ground would occupy 2.7 hectares below it, while the number of roads would be halved. Under several meters of earth, noise is minimal and insulation is excellent.",由此可见,如果在地下建居室,可以节省土地,比较安静,绝缘(insulation)好,省能源。所以答案可用句中原词:"Taking up less land, minimal noise and excellent insulation."或者概括为"Saving land, energy and tranquility."。

49. 由第四段第一句"In Europe, the obstacle has been conservative local authorities and developers who prefer to ensure quick sales with conventional mass-produced housing."可知在欧洲,在地下建住房的障碍主要来自保守的地方政府和开发商。他们更喜欢建造大批量传统的房子来保证快速销售。可见,正确答案为"ensure quick sales"或"are sold quickly"。

50. 第五段第一句作者说"Not everyone adapts so well...",接着讲到日本的科学家如何在地下加入声、光、气味等等来模拟地上的自然环境,帮助长时间待在地下的人适应环境。可见题目中要填的词是"适应"。adapt 为不及物动词,所以正确答案为"adapt to"。

51. 文章最后一段呼应全文开头,讲述了 Siegmund 一家是如何想到建造地下住所的。第二句"Their home evolved when he dug a cool room for his bakery business in a hill he had

created."说明他们最初是为自己的烘烤生意挖了个冷却室,后来在天气热的时候,睡到里面,发现了住在地下的好处。然后开始增加房间,建成了一个家。因此,正确答案是"his bakery business"。

Section B

52. [A] 词义推断题。第一段开始作者提出话题:过去当我们拥有财富的时候,我们就开始讨论贫穷的问题。为什么现在的政治只涉及财富这一方面呢?紧接着,作者提到八年前,当克林顿初次竞选总统的时候,道琼斯指数低于 3 500 点,而每年联邦政府的财政赤字则高达数千亿美元。但是在那样一个时期,克林顿却强调"不让一个人掉队(穷困)"的重要性。可见,那个时期是经济比较困难的时期。因此,正确答案为 A 项。

53. [C] 主旨题。第一段作者提出话题,第二段作者进一步指出无论是和八年前经济不稳定的时候相比,还是和更早的时候相比,人们今天对穷人的关注都少了很多。文章最后两段则分析了导致这一现象的原因。因此,全文的主旨应该是现在对穷人的关注比过去少。故正确答案为 C 项。

54. [A] 推断题。选项 B 和 C 的内容作者在文章中并未提到。文章第三段指出和过去相比,贫困状况确实有所改善,尤其是对占人口比重少数的群体而言。但作者接着指出:"The people who have been totally left out of this boom often have medical, mental or other problems for which no one has an immediate solution.",可见还是有人没有从经济繁荣中获益。所以选项 D 也可以被排除。故正确答案为 A 项。

55. [B] 细节题。作者从第三段开始分析原因。第三段的第二和第三句话提到经济的整体增长使贫困问题有所缓解。这是人们对贫困问题关注减少的原因之一。故正确答案为 B 项,其他三个选项文中均未有明确陈述。

56. [D] 写作目的题。作者从文章一开始就围绕"贫困"话题提出观点,继而展开分析和论述。因此是一篇议论文,选项 B 和 C 都可以排除。对于"贫穷受到忽视"这一现状,作者是忧虑的,态度严肃,不可能是为娱乐读者而写。因此,正确答案是 D 项。

57. [B] 主旨题。作者在文章第一段就指出自己的写作是基于美洲土著人的背景。他写作的目的是为了描绘美洲土著人的尊严和他们身份的完整性。作者接着分析了他抱有这样的写作立场的原因以及美洲土著人和他们的作家为了争取平等、争取民族权利和保持自己的文化传统所进行的漫长而艰难的斗争。由此可见正确答案为 B 项。

58. [A] 推断题。文章通篇讲述美洲土著人及其作家为保持自己的文化传统所做的不屈斗争,由此可见,土著人和主流社会之间存在价值观、文化观乃至政治立场的冲突。第二段最后两句又说明:许多人对土著文学持有诸如前文所提到的报纸上的观点以及土著作家的作品总带有政治立场的原因都是可以理解的。由此可知,"guttural"很有可能表示报纸对土著文学的蔑视。故正确答案为 A 项。

59. [C] 细节题。第二段提到作者本想拒绝去白宫朗诵诗歌的邀请,但当他想到先辈们为了能到首都去争取平等权利所做出的努力,就接受了邀请。故正确答案为 C 项。

60. [D] 主旨题。作者指出自己的写作宗旨就是为了捍卫美洲土著人的尊严,争取他们的平等权利并解释了他这样做的原因。第二段第四句指出美洲土著人过去进行武装斗争,而现在则更多地在法律和文学领域进行斗争。因此,最佳答案为 D 项。

61. [D] 词义推断题。由第二段中的"... in order to finance a trip to the nation's capital, to demand justice, to reclaim lost land even though there was only **spare** hope they would be

successful."可知,土著人不屈不挠地斗争,尽管希望渺茫。D项 meager 意思是"贫乏,不足",最合题意,故正确答案为D项。

Part Ⅴ Error Correction

62. is → was。通过上下文可以看出文章是在对此200年前的美国和今日美国,此处意在说明"200年前农业是美国最大的产业",因此此处时态应为对应的过去时。
63. importer → exporter。上文指出美国的农业生产的食品量远大于美国人所需的消费量,文章进而提出美国的农产品量足以使美国成为世界上最大的农产品出口国。
64. farm → farming。farming 与 business 一并作定语修饰 methods,即"农耕和经营方式"。
65. harmless → harmful。根据常理,如果昆虫是无害的,那就不需要特别进行学习和研究,而此处谈到的是成为农场经营者必须要学习的农业基础知识,显然对害虫的学习更有必要。
66. 在 has 和 said 之间加入 been。此处为句型 It has been said,意为"据说",其中 it 为形式主语,真正主语是 that farming in America today is three fourths paper work and one fourth physical labor。
67. 删除 tired 之后的 of,根据 American farmers now are able to work for more years 和 by the time they were about 40 判断,tired 是"退休"之意,而不是"疲劳"之意,不能跟介词 of 搭配,而且 of 之后也没有宾语。
68. most → least。美国现行的是12年义务教育制,并且高等教育已经大众化,所以一般情况下,美国公民至少接受12年的义务教育。
69. with → for。provide 的搭配有两种,provide sb. with sth.,如"Sheep provides us with wool";或者是 provide for,为多义词组,如 provide food for the family,意为"提供"。而在例句"The rule provided for the adoption of collective measure"则意为"规定"。在此题中,也为"规定"之意。
70. informs → inform。主语为 local offices,为复数。
71. which → where。先行词为 organization,而且 where 在定语从句中作地点状语。

Part Ⅵ Translation

72. [答案]:a business letter should be written in a formal style rather than in a personal style
    [注释]:此句的翻译主要在于"是A而不是B"句型的使用,应注意使用"rather than"的句型。此外,就是"正式"与"非正式"这一对反义词应严格使用 formal 与 informal。
73. [答案]:He was found not guilty for insufficient evidence
    [注释]:此句的翻译有两个难点。在"判决"一词的翻译上,考生容易惯性地翻译为 be sentenced,但实际上常用的表达却是 be found。sentence 只有在宣判具体的刑期或刑罚时使用;宣布有罪无罪应使用 be found...。另一个难点是"证据不足"中"不足"的翻译。
74. [答案]:without knowing that their habits are doing bad to themselves and their offspring
    [注释]:此句的翻译就是考查 without 复杂介词结构作为原因状语的使用。
75. [答案]:Only by actively involving yourself in social practice
    [注释]:此句的翻译第一考查 Only 在句首作唯一性条件状语从句的使用。其次,是"投身于"的翻译,应该是 involve...in...,退一步可以翻译为 take part in 或 participate in。
76. [答案]:whatever he says and whatever he does are always considered to be wrong
    [注释]:此句的翻译重点在于 whatever 句型的使用。

College English Test (Band Ⅵ)(Dec. 2006)

Part Ⅰ Writing (30 minutes)

Directions: *For this part, you are allowed 30 minutes to write a short essay entitled* ***The Importance of Reading Classics****. You should write at least* ***150*** *words following the outline given below.*

1. 阅读经典著作对人的成长至关重要
2. 现在人们越来越少阅读经典著作,原因是……
3. 作为大学生,你应该怎么做

Part Ⅱ Reading Comprehension (Skimming and Scanning) (15 minutes)

Directions:(略)

Space Tourism

Make your reservations now. The space tourism industry is officially open for business, and tickets are going for a mere $ 20 million for a one-week stay in space. Despite reluctance from National Air and Space Administration (NASA), Russia made American businessman Dennis Tito the world's first space tourist. Tito flew into space aboard a Russian Soyuz rocket that arrived at the International Space Station (ISS) on April 30, 2001. The second space tourist, South African businessman Mark Shuttleworth, took off aboard the Russian Soyuz on April 25, 2002, also bound for the ISS.

Lance Bass of N Sync was supposed to be the third to make the $ 20 million trip, but he did not join the three-man crew as they blasted off on October 30, 2002, due to lack of payment. Probably the most incredible aspect of this proposed space tour was that NASA approved of it.

These trips are the beginning of what could be a profitable 21st century industry. There are already several space tourism companies planning to build suborbital vehicles and orbital cities within the next two decades. These companies have invested millions, believing that the space tourism industry is on the verge of taking off.

In 1997, NASA published a report concluding that selling trips into space to private citizens could be worth billions of dollars. A Japanese report supports these findings, and projects that space tourism could be a $ 10 billion per year industry within the next two decades. The only obstacles to opening up space to tourists are the space agencies, who are concerned with safety and the development of a reliable, reusable launch vehicle.

Space Accommodations

Russia's Mir space station was supposed to be the first destination for space tourists. But in March 2001, the Russian Aerospace Agency brought Mir down into the Pacific Ocean. As it turned out, bringing down Mir only temporarily delayed the first tourist trip into space.

The Mir crash did cancel plans for a new reality-based game show from NBC, which was going to be called Destination Mir. The *Survivor*-like TV show was scheduled to air in fall 2001. Participants on the show were to go through training at Russia's *cosmonaut* (宇航员) training center, Star City. Each week, one of the participants would be eliminated from the show, with the winner receiving a trip to the Mir space station. The Mir crash has ruled out NBC's space plans for now. NASA is against beginning space tourism until the International Space Station is completed in 2006.

Russia is not alone in its interest in space tourism. There are several projects underway to commercialize space travel. Here are a few of the groups that might take tourists to space:

- Space Island Group is going to build a ring-shaped, rotating "commercial space *infrastructure* (基础结构)" that will resemble the Discovery spacecraft in the movie "2001: A Space Odyssey." Space Island says it will build its space city out of empty NASA space-shuttle fuel tanks (to start, it should take around 12 or so), and place it about 400 miles above Earth. The space city will rotate once per minute to create a gravitational pull one third as strong as Earth's.
- According to their vision statement, Space Adventures plans to "fly tens of thousands of people in space over the next 10—15 years and beyond, around the moon, and back, from spaceports both on Earth and in space, to and from private space stations, and abroad dozens of different vehicles."
- Even Hilton Hotels has shown interest in the space tourism industry and the possibility of building or co-funding a space hotel. However, the company did say that it believes such a space hotel is 15 to 20 years away.

Initially, space tourism will offer simple accommodations at best. For instance, if the International Space Station is used as a tourist attraction, guests won't find the luxurious surroundings of a hotel room on Earth. It has been designed for conducting research, not entertainment. However, the first generation of space hotels should offer tourists a much more comfortable experience.

In regard to a concept for a space hotel initially planned by Space Island, such a hotel could offer guests every convenience they might find at a hotel on Earth, and some they might not. The small gravitational pull created by rotating space city would allow space-tourists and residents to walk around and function normally within the structure. Everything from running water to a recycling plant to medical facilities would be possible. Additionally, space tourists would even be able to take space walks.

Many of these companies believe that they have to offer an extremely enjoyable experience in order for passengers to pay thousands, if not millions, of dollars to ride into space. So will space create another separation between the haves and have-nots?

The Most Expensive Vacation

Will space be an exotic retreat reserved for only the wealthy? Or will middle-class folks have a chance to take their families to space? Make no mistake about it, going to space will be the most expensive vacation you ever take. Prices right now are in the tens of millions of dollars. Currently, the only vehicles that can take you into space are the space shuttle and the Russian Soyuz, both of which are terribly inefficient. Each spacecraft requires millions of pounds of fuel to take off into space, which makes them expensive to launch. One pound of *payload*（有效载重）costs about $ 10,000 to put into Earth's orbit.

NASA and Lockheed Martin are currently developing a single-stage-to-orbit launch space plane, called the VentureStar, that could be launched for about a tenth of what the space shuttle costs to launch. If the VentureStar takes off, the number of people who could afford to take a trip into space would move into the millions.

In 1998, a joint project from NASA and the Space Transportation Association stated that improvements in technology could push fares to space as low as $ 55,000, and possibly down to $ 20,000 or $ 10,000 a decade later. The report concluded that at a ticket price of 50,000, there could be 500,000 passengers flying into space each year. While still leaving out many people, these prices would open up space to a tremendous amount of traffic.

Since the beginning of the space race, the general public has said, "Isn't that great—when do I get to go?" Well, our chance might be closer than ever. Within the next 20 years, space planes could be taking off for the Moon at the same frequency as airplanes flying between New York and Los Angeles.

1. Lance Bass wasn't able to go on a tour of space because of health problems.
2. Several tourism companies believe space travel is going to be a new profitable industry.
3. The space agencies are reluctant to open up space to tourists.
4. Two Australian billionaires have been placed on the waiting list for entering space as private passengers.
5. The prize for the winner in the fall 2001 NBC TV game show would have been ________.
6. Hilton Hotels believes it won't be long before it is possible to build a ________.
7. In order for space tourists to walk around and function normally, it is necessary for the space city to create a ________.
8. What makes going to space the most expensive vacation is the enormous cost involved in ________.
9. Each year 500,000 space tourists could be flying into space if ticket prices could be lowered to ________.
10. Within the next two decades, ________ could be as common as intercity air travel.

Part Ⅲ Listening Comprehension (35 minutes)

Section A

Directions:(略)

11. A) Dr. Smith's waiting room isn't tidy.
    B) Dr. Smith enjoys reading magazines.
    C) Dr. Smith has left a good impression on her.
    D) Dr. Smith may not be a good choice.
12. A) The man will rent the apartment when it is available.
    B) The man made a bargain with the landlady over the rent.
    C) The man insists on having a look at the apartment first.
    D) The man is not fully satisfied with the apartment.
13. A) Packing up to go abroad.
    B) Brushing up on her English.
    C) Drawing up a plan for her English course.
    D) Applying for a visa to the United States.
14. A) He is anxious to find a cure for his high blood pressure.
    B) He doesn't think high blood pressure is a problem for him.
    C) He was not aware of his illness until diagnosed with it.
    D) He did not take the symptoms of his illness seriously.
15. A) To investigate the causes of AIDS.
    B) To raise money for AIDS patients.
    C) To rally support for AIDS victims in Africa.
    D) To draw attention to the spread of AIDS in Asia.
16. A) It has a very long history.
    B) It is a private institution.
    C) It was founded by Thomas Jefferson.
    D) It stresses the comprehensive study of nature.
17. A) They can't fit into the machine.
    B) They have not been delivered yet.
    C) They were sent to the wrong address.
    D) They were found to be of the wrong type.
18. A) The food served in the cafeteria usually lacks variety.
    B) The cafeteria sometimes provides rare food for the students.
    C) The students find the service in the cafeteria satisfactory.
    D) The cafeteria tries hard to cater to the students' needs.

Questions 19 to 22 are based on the conversation you have just heard.

19. A) He picked up some apples in his yard.
    B) He cut some branches off the apple tree.

C) He quarreled with his neighbor over the fence.

D) He cleaned up all the garbage in the woman's yard.

20. A) Trim the apple trees in her yard.

B) Pick up the apples that fell in her yard.

C) Take the garbage to the curb for her.

D) Remove the branches from her yard.

21. A) File a lawsuit against the man. B) Ask the man for compensation.

C) Have the man's apple tree cut down. D) Throw garbage into the man's yard.

22. A) He was ready to make a concession. B) He was not prepared to go to court.

C) He was not intimidated. D) He was a bit concerned.

Questions 23 to 25 are based on the conversation you have just heard.

23. A) Bad weather. B) Human error.

C) Breakdown of the engines. D) Failure of the communications system.

24. A) Two thousand feet. B) Twelve thousand feet.

C) Twenty thousand feet. D) Twenty-two thousand feet.

25. A) Accurate communication is of utmost importance.

B) Pilots should be able to speak several foreign languages.

C) Air controllers should keep a close watch on the weather.

D) Cooperation between pilots and air controllers is essential.

Section B

Directions:(略)

Passage One

Questions 26 to 29 are based on the passage you have just heard.

26. A) His father caught a serious disease.

B) His mother passed away.

C) His mother left him to marry a rich businessman.

D) His father took to drinking.

27. A) He disliked being disciplined. B) He was expelled by the university.

C) He couldn't pay his gambling debts. D) He enjoyed working for a magazine.

28. A) His poems are heavily influenced by French writers.

B) His stories are mainly set in the State of Virginia.

C) His work is difficult to read.

D) His language is not refined.

29. A) He grieved to death over the loss of his wife.

B) He committed suicide for unknown reasons.

C) He was shot dead at the age of 40.

D) He died of heavy drinking.

Passage Two

Questions 30 to 32 are based on the passage you have just heard.

30. A) Women. B) Prisoners.
    C) Manual workers. D) School age children.

31. A) He taught his students how to pronounce the letters first.
    B) He matched the letters with the sounds familiar to the learners.
    C) He showed the learners how to combine the letters into simple words.
    D) He divided the letters into groups according to the way they are written.

32. A) It can help people to become literate within a short time.
    B) It was originally designed for teaching the English language.
    C) It enables the learners to master a language within three months.
    D) It is effective in teaching any alphabetical language to Brazilians.

Passage Three

Questions 33 to 35 are based on the passage you have just heard.

33. A) The crop's blooming period is delayed.
    B) The roots of crops are cut off.
    C) The top soil is seriously damaged.
    D) The growth of weeds is accelerated.

34. A) It's a new way of applying chemical fertilizer.
    B) It's an improved method of harvesting crops.
    C) It's a creative technique for saving labor.
    D) It's a farming process limiting the use of ploughs.

35. A) In areas with few weeds and unwanted plants.
    B) In areas with a severe shortage of water.
    C) In areas lacking in chemical fertilizer.
    D) In areas dependent on imported food.

Section C

Directions:(略)

Adults are getting smarter about how smart babies are. Not long ago, researchers learned that 4-day-olds could understand (36) ______ and subtraction. Now, British research (37) ______ Graham Schafer has discovered that infants can learn words or uncommon things long before they can speak. He found that 9-month-old infants could be taught, through repeated show-and-tell, to (38) ______ the names of objects that were foreign to them, a result that (39) ______ in some ways, the received (40) ______ that apart from learning to (41) ______ things common to their daily lives, children don't begin to build vocabulary until well into their second year. "It's no (42) ______ that children learn words, but the words they tend to know are linked to (43) ______ situations in the home," explains Schafer. (44) ______

____________ with an unfamiliar voice giving instructions in an unfamiliar setting.

"Figuring out how humans acquire language may shed light on why some children learn to read and write later than others," Schafer says, "and could lead to better treatments for developed mental problems." (45) ____. "Language is a test case for human cognitive development," says Schafer, "but parents eager to teach their infants should take note: (46) ____." "This is not about advancing development," he says, "its' just about what children can do at an earlier age than what educators have often thought."

Part Ⅳ Reading Comprehension(Reading in Depth) (25 minutes)

Section A

Directions:(略)

Questions 47 to 51 are based on the following passage.

I've heard from and talked to many people who described how Mother Nature simplified their lives for them. They'd lost their home and many or all of their possessions through fires, floods, earthquakes, or some other disaster. Losing everything you own under such circumstances can be distressing, but the people I've heard from all saw their loss, ultimately, as a blessing.

"The fire saved us the agony of deciding what to keep and what to get rid of," one woman wrote. And once all those things were no longer there, she and her husband saw how they had weighed them down and complicated their lives.

"There was so much stuff we never used and that was just taking up space. We vowed when we started over, we'd replace only what we needed, and this time we'd do it right. We've kept our promise: we don't have much now, but what we have is exactly what we want."

Though we've never had a catastrophic loss such as that, Gibbs and I did have a close call shortly before we decided to simplify. At that time we lived in a fire zone. One night a firestorm raged through and destroyed over six hundred homes in our community. That tragedy gave us the opportunity to look objectively at the goods we'd accumulated.

We saw that there was so much we could get rid of and not only never miss, but be better off without. Having almost lost it all, we found it much easier to let go of the things we knew we'd never use again.

Obviously, there's a tremendous difference between getting rid of possessions and losing them through a natural disaster without having a say in the matter. And this is not to minimize the tragedy and pain such a loss can generate.

But you might think about how you would approach the acquisition process if you had it to do all over again. Look around your home and make a list of what you would replace.

Make another list of things you wouldn't acquire again no matter what, and in fact would be happy to be rid of.

When you're ready to start unloading some of your stuff, that list will be a good place to

start.

47. Many people whose possessions were destroyed in natural disasters eventually considered their loss ________.
48. Now that all their possessions were lost in the fire, the woman and her husband felt that their lives had been ________.
49. What do we know about the author's house from the sentence "Gibbs and I did have a close call..."(Lines 1-2, Para. 4)?
50. According to the author, getting rid of possessions and losing them through a natural disaster are vastly ________.
51. What does the author suggest people do with unnecessary things?

Section B

Directions:(略)

Passage One

Questions 52 to 56 are based on the following passage.

In a purely biological sense, fear begins with the body's system for reacting to things that can harm us—the so-called fight-or-flight response. "An animal that can't detect danger can't stay alive, says Joseph LeDoux. Like animals, humans evolved with an elaborate mechanism for processing information about potential threats. At its core is a cluster of *neurons*(神经元) deep in the brain known as the *amygdala*(扁桃核).

LeDoux studies the way animals and humans respond to threats to understand how we form memories of significant events in our lives. The amygdala receives input from many parts of the brain, including regions responsible for retrieving memories. Using this information, the amygdala appraises a situation—*I think this charging dog wants to bite me*—and triggers a response by radiating nerve signals throughout the body. These signals produce the familiar signs of distress: trembling, perspiration and fast-moving feet, just to name three.

This fear mechanism is critical to the survival of all animals, but no one can say for sure whether beasts other than humans know they're afraid. That is, as LeDoux says, "if you put that system into a brain that has consciousness, then you get the feeling of fear."

Humans, says Edward M. Hallowell, have the ability to call up images of bad things that happened in the past and to anticipate future events. Combine these higher thought processes with our hardwired danger-detection systems, and you get a near-universal human phenomenon: worry.

That's not necessarily a bad thing, says Hallowell. "When used properly, worry is an incredible device," he says. After all, a little healthy worrying is okay if it leads to constructive action—like having a doctor look at that weird spot on your back.

Hallowell insists, though, that there's right way to worry. "Never do it alone, get the facts and then make a plan," he says. Most of us have survived a recession, so we're familiar with the belt-tightening strategies needed to survive a slump.

Unfortunately, few of us have much experience dealing with the threat of terrorism, so it's been difficult to get facts about how we should respond. That's why Hallowell believes it was okay for people to indulge some extreme worries last fall by asking doctors for *Cipro*(抗炭疽菌的药物) and buying gas masks.

52. The "so-called fight-or-flight response" (Line 2, Para. 1) refers to "________".
   A) the biological process in which human beings sense of self-defense evolves
   B) the instinctive fear human beings feel when faced with potential danger
   C) the act of evaluating a dangerous situation and making a quick decision
   D) the elaborate mechanism in the human brain for retrieving information
53. From the studies conducted by LeDoux we learn that ________.
   A) reactions of humans and animals to dangerous situations are often unpredictable
   B) memories of significant events enable people to control fear and distress
   C) people's unpleasant memories are derived from their feelings of fear
   D) the amygdala plays a vital part in human and animal responses to potential danger
54. From the passage we know that ________.
   A) a little worry will do us good if handled properly
   B) a little worry will enable us to survive a recession
   C) fear strengthens the human desire to survive danger
   D) fear helps people to anticipate certain future events
55. Which of the following is the best way to deal with your worries according to Hallowell?
   A) Ask for help from the people around you.
   B) Use the belt-tightening strategies for survival.
   C) Seek professional advice and take action.
   D) Understand the situation and be fully prepared.
56. In Hallowell's view, people's reaction to the terrorist threat last fall was ________.
   A) ridiculous B) understandable
   C) over-cautious D) sensible

Passage Two

Questions 57 to 61 are based on the following passage.

Amitai Etzioni is not surprised by the latest headings about scheming corporate *crooks*(骗子). As a visiting professor at the Harvard Business School in 1989, he ended his work there disgusted with his students' overwhelming lust for money. "They're taught that profit is all that matters," he says. Many schools don't even offer *ethics*(伦理学) courses at all.

Etzioni expressed his frustration about the interests of his graduate students. "By and large, I clearly had not found a way to help classes full of MBAs see that there is more to life than money, power, fame and self-interest," he wrote at the time. Today he still takes the blame for not educating these business-leaders-to-be. "I really feel like I failed them," he says. "If I was a better teacher maybe I could have reached them."

Etzioni was a respected ethics expert when he arrived at Harvard. He hoped his work at the

university would give him insight into how questions of morality could be applied to places where self-interest flourished. What he found wasn't encouraging. Those would-be executives had, says Etzioni, little interest in concepts of ethics and morality in the boardroom—and their professor was met with blank stares when he urged his students to see business in new and different ways.

Etzioni sees the experience at Harvard as an eye-opening one and says there's much about business schools that he'd like to change. "A lot of the faculty teaching businesses are bad news themselves," Etzioni says. From offering classes that teach students how to legally manipulate contracts, to reinforcing the notion of profit over community interests, Etzioni has seen a lot that's left him shaking his head. And because of what he's seen taught in business schools, he's not surprised by the latest rash of corporate scandals. "In many ways things have got a lot worse at business schools, I suspect," says Etzioni.

Etzioni is still teaching the sociology of right and wrong and still calling for ethical business leadership. "People with poor motives will always exist," he says. "Sometimes environments constrain those people and sometimes environments give those people opportunity." Etzioni says the booming economy of the last decade enabled those individuals with poor motives to get rich before getting in trouble. His hope now: that the cries for reform will provide more fertile soil for his long-standing messages about business ethics.

57. What impressed Amitai Etzioni most about Harvard MBA students?
   A) Their keen interest in business courses.
   B) Their intense desire for money.
   C) Their tactics for making profits.
   D) Their potential to become business leaders.
58. Why did Amitai Etzioni say "I really feel like I failed them" (Line 4, Para. 2)?
   A) He was unable to alert his students to corporate malpractice.
   B) He didn't teach his students to see business in new and different ways.
   C) He could not get his students to understand the importance of ethics in business.
   D) He didn't offer courses that would meet the expectations of the business-leaders-to-be.
59. Most would-be executives at the Harvard Business School believed that ________.
   A) questions of morality were of utmost importance in business affairs
   B) self-interest should not be the top priority in business dealings
   C) new and different principles should be taught at business schools
   D) there was no place for ethics and morality in business dealings
60. In Etzioni's view, the latest rash of corporate scandals could be attributed to ________.
   A) the tendency in business schools to stress self-interest over business ethics
   B) the executives lack of knowledge in legally manipulating contracts
   C) the increasingly fierce competition in the modern business world
   D) the moral corruption of business school graduates
61. We learn from the last paragraph that ________.
   A) the calls for reform will help promote business ethics
   B) businessmen with poor motives will gain the upper hand

C) business ethics courses should be taught in all business schools

D) reform in business management contributes to economic growth

Part Ⅴ Error Correction (15 minutes)

Directions:(略)

The National Endowment for the Arts recently released the results of its "Reading at Risk" survey, which described the movement of the American public away from books and literature and toward television and electronic media. According to the survey, "reading is on the decline on every region, within every ethnic group, and at every educational level". 62. ______

The day the NEA report released, the U. S. House, in a tie Vote, upheld the government's right to obtain bookstore and library records under a provision of the USA Patriot Act. The House proposal would have barred the federal government from demand library records, reading lists, book customer lists and other material in terrorism and intelligence investigations. 63. ______ 64. ______

These two events are completely unrelated to, yet they echo each other in the message they send about the place of books and reading in American culture. At the heart of the NEA survey is the belief in our democratic system depends on the leaders who can think critically, analyze texts and writing clearly. All of these are skills promoted by reading and discussing books and literature. At the same time, through a provision of the Patriot Act, the leaders of our country are unconsciously sending the message that reading may be connected to desirable activities that might undermine our system of government rather than helping democracy flourish. 65. ______ 66. ______ 67. ______ 68. ______

Our culture's decline in reading begin well before the existence of the Patriot Act. During the 1980s' culture wars, school systems across the country pulled some books from library shelves because its content was deemed by parents and teachers to be inappropriate. Now what started in schools across the country is playing itself on a nation stage and is possibly having an impact on the reading habits of the American public. 69. ______ 70. ______ 71. ______

Part Ⅵ Translation (5 minutes)

Directions:(略)

72. If you had ______________________(听从了我的忠告,你就不会陷入麻烦).

73. With tears on her face, the lady ______________________ ______(看着她受伤的儿子被送进手术室).

74. After the terrorist attack, tourists ______________________ ______(被劝告暂时不要去该国旅游).

75. I prefer to communicate with my customers ______________________

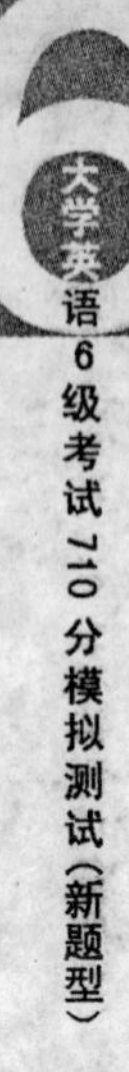

(通过写电子邮件而不是打电话).

76. ____________________(直到截止日他才寄出) his application form.

参考答案(Dec. 2006)

Part Ⅰ Sample Writing

The Importance of Reading Classics

Now some people, especially the elderly, are of the view that classics play a significant role in the life. English learners, for example, can benefit a lot from the famous readings, or classical books. Besides, they maintain that their childhood is exposed to these great minds.

However, young men in growing numbers seldom enjoy reading these articles or books. In other words, they find few interests in reading so-called classics. A lot of reasons are responsible for this. To begin with, they are in the shadow of practical minds. These classics may not meet the needs. What's more, online reading is a good way for people to get information easily and efficiently. Moreover, the young people are too busy to read them.

From what has been discussed above, we may safely draw the conclusion that effective actions should be taken to prevent the situation. First, we can enjoy these minds in our free time. Second, these articles or novels will be arranged for further reading in our retirement. Certainly, it is high time that we placed great emphasis on the issue.

Part Ⅱ eading Comprehension (Skimming and Scanning)

1. N 2. Y 3. Y 4. NG
5. The prize for the winner in the fall 2001 NBC TV game show would have been a trip to the Mir space station.
6. Hilton Hotels believes it won't be long before it is possible to build a space hotel.
7. In order for space tourists to walk around and function normally, it is necessary for the space city to create a small gravitational pull.
8. What makes going to space the most expensive vacation is the enormous cost involved in launching the spacecraft.
9. Each year 500,000 space tourists could be flying into space if ticket prices could be lowered to $50,000.
10. Within the next two decades, space travel could be as common as intercity air travel.

Part Ⅲ Listening Comprehension

Section A

11—15 DCBCD 16—20 ABABD 21—25 ACBAA

Section B

26—30 BCCDA 31—35 DACDB

Section C

36. addition 37. psychologist 38. recognize 39. challenges

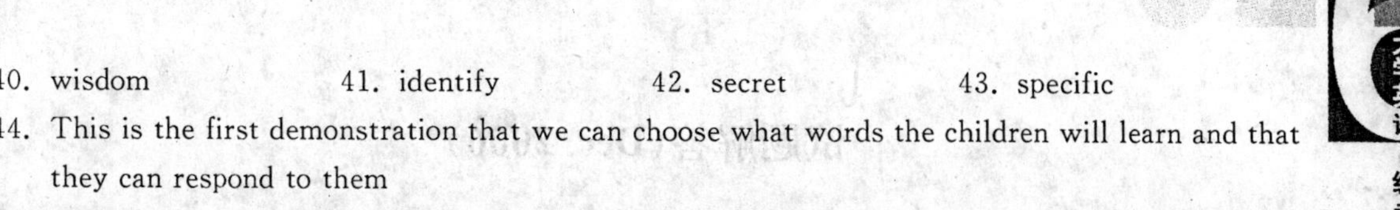

40. wisdom　　41. identify　　42. secret　　43. specific

44. This is the first demonstration that we can choose what words the children will learn and that they can respond to them

45. What's more, the study of language acquisition offers direct insight into how humans learn

46. even without being taught new words a control group caught up with the other infants within a few months

Part Ⅳ　Reading Comprehension (Reading in Depth)

Section A

47. as a blessing

48. simplified

49. Their house narrowly escaped the fire.

50. different

51. Make a list to get rid of them.

Section B

52—56　BDADB　57—61　BCDAA

Part Ⅴ　Error Correction

62. on → in

63. report ∧ released → was

64. demand → demanding

65. to → /

66. in → that

67. writing → write

68. desirable → undesirable

69. begin → began

70. its → theirs

71. nation → national

Part Ⅵ　Translation

72. followed my advice, you would not have got into trouble

73. watched her injured son taken to the operating room

74. were advised not to visit the country for the time being

75. via/by email instead of by phone through writing email rather than/instead of talking over the phone

76. It was not until the deadline that he sent/Not until the deadline did he send

试题解答(Dec. 2006)

Part Ⅱ Reading Comprehension (Skimming and Scanning)

1. [N] 由文章第二段第一句" Lance Bass of N Sync was supposed to be the third to make the $20 million trip, but he did not join the three-man crew as they blasted off on October 30, 2002, due to lack of payment. "可见他未能旅行的原因是资金问题而非健康问题。故本题判断为 NO。
2. [Y] 由文章第三段第一、三句"These trips are the beginning of what could be a profitable 21st century industry... These companies have invested millions, believing that the space tourism industry is on the verge of taking off. "可见太空旅行被认为是最有利可赚的行业，并有很多公司投资。故本题判断为 YES。
3. [Y] 由文章第四段最后一句"The only obstacles to opening up space to tourists are the space agencies, who are concerned with safety and the development of a reliable, reusable launch vehicle. "可知，对游客开放太空旅行的唯一障碍是一些宇航机构，他们担忧的是安全问题以及怎样研发可靠的、可再用的飞行器。因此，宇航机构对向游客开放太空旅行这一想法是犹豫的。此句判断为 YES。
4. [NG] 文章只提到美国商人 Tito、南非商人 Shuttleworth 和 Lance Bass 等尝试太空飞行的游客，并未提到"two Australian billionaires" 。故此题判断为 NOT GIVEN。
5. 由"Space Accommodations"部分第二段第四句"Each week, one of the participants would be eliminated from the show, with the winner receiving a trip to the Mir space station. "可知答案是"a trip to the Mir space station"。
6. 由"Space Accommodations"部分第三段最后两句"Even Hilton Hotels has shown interest in the space tourism industry and the possibility of building or co-funding a space hotel. However, the company did say that it believes such a space hotel is 15 to 20 years away. "可见希尔顿酒店相信不久的将来是有可能建造太空酒店的。故正确答案为"space hotel"。
7. 由"Space Accommodations"部分倒数第二段第二句"The small gravitational pull created by rotating space city would allow space-tourists and residents to walk around and function normally within the structure. "可知，要让太空旅游者正常生活，太空城市必须创造出重力才行。故本题答案为"small gravitational pull"。
8. 由"The Most Expensive Vacation"部分第一段倒数第二句"Each spacecraft requires millions of pounds of fuel to take off into space, which makes them expensive to launch. "可知昂贵的燃料使发射太空飞船价格不菲。故本题答案可以是"launching the spacecraft"或者是"the fuel of spacecraft"。
9. 由"The Most Expensive Vacation"部分第三段第二句"The report concluded that at a ticket price of 50,000, there could be 500,000 passengers flying into space each year. "可知答案为"$50,000"。
10. 由全文最后一句"Within the next 20 years, space planes could be taking off for the Moon at the same frequency as airplanes flying between New York and Los Angeles. "可知未来的二十年里，星际飞行器的起飞可能和现在的城际飞机一样频繁。也就意味着太空旅行和现在的

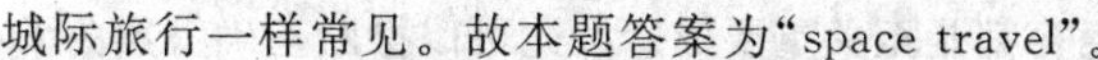

城际旅行一样常见。故本题答案为“space travel”。

Part Ⅲ Listening Comprehension(听力原文在光盘中)

Part Ⅳ Reading Comprehension (Reading in Depth)

Section A

47. 由文章第一段最后一句“Losing everything you own under such circumstances can be distressing, but the people I've heard from all saw their loss, ultimately, as a blessing.”可知在自然灾难中失去所拥有的一切可能令人沮丧,但也有人最终都将他们的损失看作是一种福分。故本题答案为“as a blessing”。
48. 文章第一段第一句指出许多人都曾描绘过大自然是如何帮助他们简化生活(simplify their lives). 第二段举一对夫妇为例,最后一句“And once all those things were no longer there, she and her husband saw how they had weighed them down and complicated their lives.”中提到当所有的财物都化为灰烬的时候,她和丈夫才意识到它们是累赘,曾经使他们的生活复杂。可见这对夫妇认为火灾帮助他们简化了生活。故答案为“simplified”。
49. 本题考查对“have a close call”的理解。文章第四段讲到作者夫妇两人所在的街区曾遭遇过一次火灾,六百多户人家的房屋财产被毁。那次悲剧使他们得以客观地看待自己多年囤积的那些财物。因此,本段第一句“Though we've never had a catastrophic loss such as that, Gibbs and I did have a close call shortly before we decided to simplify.”可以理解为:他们没有遭受灾难性的损失,他们的房屋侥幸逃脱了火灾。故答案是“Their house narrowly escaped the fire.”。
50. 由文章第六段第一句“Obviously, there's a tremendous difference between getting rid of possessions and losing them through a natural disaster without having a say in the matter.”可知作者认为主动抛弃财物与在自然灾难中无助地失去财物之间存在极大的差异。故答案为“different”。
51. 由文章最后两段“Make another list of things you wouldn't acquire again no matter what, and in fact would be happy to be rid of. When you're ready to start unloading some of your stuff, that list will be a good place to start.”可知对于没有用的财物,最好的办法就是列个清单,然后把它们扔掉。故本题答案为“Make a list to get rid of them.”。

Section B

52. [B] 细节题。由文章第一段第一句“In a purely biological sense, fear begins with the body's system for reacting to things that can harm us—the so-called fight-or-flight response.”可知从纯粹的生物学意义上说,恐惧始于人体对可能伤害我们的东西作出的反应,即所谓的“斗争或脱险”反应。因此,所谓的“斗争或脱险”反应也就是面对潜在危险时人的本能的恐惧感。故正确答案为B项。
53. [D] 细节综合推断题。第一段最后和第二段讲到LeDoux关于恐惧机制的研究。“Like animals, humans evolved with an elaborate mechanism for processing information about potential threats. At its core is a cluster of *neurons* deep in the brain known as the *amygdala*.”一句中指出该机制的核心是一组位于大脑深处被称为“扁桃核”的神经元。第三段第一句作者又提到“This fear mechanism is critical to the survival of all animals...”,说明

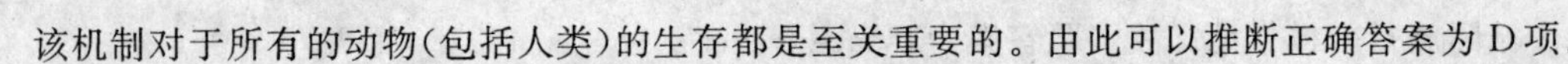

该机制对于所有的动物(包括人类)的生存都是至关重要的。由此可以推断正确答案为D项。

54. [A] 细节题。由第五段第一句"That's not necessarily a bad thing, says Hallowell. "When used properly, worry is an incredible device," he says."可知"担忧"不一定是坏事,若运用得当,它有极好的效果。由此可见正确答案为A项。

55. [D] 细节题。由第六段第一、二句"Hallowell insists, though, that there's right way to worry. "Never do it alone, get the facts and then make a plan," he says."可知Hollowell坚持认为要以合理的方式对待担忧。永远不要独自忧虑,弄清问题真相,做出相应计划。因此,正确答案为D项。

56. [B] 细节推断题。文章最后一段作者指出不幸的是我们中很少有人对恐怖主义的威胁有应对经验,所以很难了解我们该如何反应。因此,Hallowell认为,去年秋天人们不断向医生索要抗炭疽药物、购买防毒面具的极端恐惧行为并不离谱。可见,他认为由于缺乏应对经验,人们的过激反应是可以理解的。故正确答案为B项。

57. [B] 细节题。由第一段第二句"As a visiting professor at the Harvard Business School in 1989, he ended his work there disgusted with his students' overwhelming lust for money."可见Etzioni作为客座教授到哈佛商校讲学时,学生对金钱的强烈欲望令他十分反感。因此,哈佛大学MBA学员给Etzioni留下的最深印象是他们对金钱的强烈欲望。故正确答案为B项。

58. [C] 细节题。由第二段第二句"'By and large, I clearly had not found a way to help classes full of MBAs see that there is more to life than money, power, fame and self-interest,' he wrote at the time."可知Etzioni是教授伦理学的。当他没有找到很好的办法去帮助那些MBA学员看清生活不仅仅是金钱、权力、名望与个人利益的时候,他觉得自己有负于他们。他没能使学生明白商业伦理的重要性。故本题答案为C项。

59. [D] 细节推断题。由第三段最后一句"Those would-be executives had, says Etzioni, little interest in concepts of ethics and morality in the boardroom—and their professor was met with blank stares when he urged his students to see business in new and different ways."。可见那些未来的管理者对董事会议室里的伦理与道德概念没有什么兴趣。对他们来说,伦理道德在商业交易中没有一席之地。故正确答案为D项。

60. [A] 细节推断题。由第四段的第三、四句"From offering classes that teach students how to legally manipulate contracts, to reinforcing the notion of profit over community interests, Etzioni has seen a lot that's left him shaking his head. And because of what he's seen taught in business schools, he's not surprised by the latest rash of corporate scandals."可知Etzioni目睹了商业学校教学生如何合法利用合同,强调利润高于社区利益,所以他并不奇怪为什么最近公司丑闻不断。这些丑闻可以归咎于商业学校的教学倾向于强调个人利益而忽视商业伦理。故正确答案为A项。

61. [A] 细节题。由全文最后一句"His hope now: that the cries for reform will provide more fertile soil for his long-standing messages about business ethics."可知Etzioni希望对改革的呼吁将为他所长期传播的关于商业伦理重要性的思想提供肥沃的土壤。也就是说对改革的呼吁将促进商业伦理的传播,被人们广泛接受。故正确答案为A项。

Part Ⅴ Error Correction

62. on every region → in every region。表示"在每个地区"应用介词in,介词搭配错误。

63. the NEA report ∧ released → the NEA report was released NEA。表示"在报告被公布的那

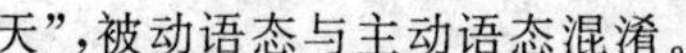

天”，被动语态与主动语态混淆。

64. demand → demanding。非谓语动词错误。句中“demand library records...”是作介词 from 的宾语，所以应该使用动名词 demanding。

65. to → /。此处为多余赘述。此处 unrelated 后无其他名词或代词，无需使用介词 to。

66. our democratic system ∧ depends → our democratic system that depends。同位语从句关系代词遗漏。此句并非考查“believe in something”这一搭配，believe 后应为同位语从句，引导该从句的是连接代词 that。

67. writing → write。本句考查一致问题。“... the leaders who can think critically, analyze texts and writing clearly.”一句中 think, analyze, write 为三个并列谓语动词，均置于情态动词 can 之后，应使用动词原形。

68. desirable → undesirable。逻辑语义相悖。从该句 that 引导的定语从句中的“activities that might undermine our system of government”意为“削弱政府体制的不良活动”，可以看出这些 activities 应该是 undesirable，是“不受欢迎的”，而并非“受欢迎的”。

69. begin → began。时态错误。从句中的“well before the existence of the Patriot Act”可知应用一般过去时。

70. its → their。代词指代错误。本句中的 content 指代前文提到的 some books 的内容，故应该使用复数代词。

71. nation → national。词性错误。on the national stage 意为“在全国的范围内”。

Part Ⅵ Translation

72. [答案]: followed my advice, you would not have got into trouble

[注释]: 本句考点：①“听从……劝告”：follow sb.'s advice；②“陷入麻烦”：be in trouble, get into trouble；③虚拟语气。与过去事实相反的虚拟条件句，条件从句用过去完成时，主句用过去将来完成时，即句型“if... had done..., ... would have done”。

73. [答案]: watched her injured son taken to the operating room

[注释]: 本句考点：①感官动词 watch 通常用于 watch sb. do sth. 或 watch sb. doing sth. 句型中，本句中 her injured son 是 watch 的宾语，后接表被动的过去分词短语作宾补；②“手术室”：operation room。

74. [答案]: were advised not to visit the country for the time being

[注释]: 本句考点：① advise sb. to do sth. 句型的被动语态和不定式的否定形式，即 be advised not to do sth.；②“暂时”：for the time being。

75. [答案]: via/by email instead of by phone 或 through writing email rather than/instead of talking over the phone

[注释]: 本句考点：①“通过”：via 或 through；②“而不是”的两种翻译方法：instead of 或“... rather than...”句型。

76. [答案]: It was not until the deadline that he sent/Not until the deadline did he send

[注释]: 本句考点：①“截止日”：deadline；②“直到……才……”：not until...；③强调或倒装句：由于 his application from 放在句末，因此应该使用强调或倒装句。

College English Test（Band Ⅵ）（June 2007）

Part Ⅰ Writing （30minutes）

Directions：*For this part，you are allowed 30 minutes to write a short essay entitled* ***Should One Expect a Reward When Doing a Good Deed***? *You should write at least* **150** *words following the outline given below.*

1. 有人做好事期望得到回报；
2. 有人认为应该像雷锋那样做好事不图回报；
3. 我的观点。

Part Ⅱ Reading Comprehension（Skimming and Scanning） （15 minutes）

Directions：（略）

Seven Steps to a More Fulfilling Job

Many people today find themselves in unfulfilling work situations. In fact，one in four workers is dissatisfied with their current job，according to the recent “Plans for 2004” survey. Their career path may be financially rewarding，but it doesn’t meet their emotional，social or creative needs. They’re stuck，unhappy，and have no idea what to do about it，except move to another job.

Mary Lyn Miller，veteran career consultant and founder of the Life and Career Clinic，says that when most people are unhappy about their work，their first thought is to get a different job. Instead，Miller suggests looking at the possibility of a different life. Through her book，8 Myths of Making a Living，as well as workshops，seminars and personal coaching and consulting，she has helped thousands of dissatisfied workers reassess life and work.

Like the way of Zen，which includes understanding of oneself as one really is，Miller encourages job seekers and those dissatisfied with work or life to examine their beliefs about work and recognize that “in many cases your beliefs are what brought you to where you are today.” You may have been raised to think that women were best at nurturing and caring and，therefore，should be teachers and nurses. So that’s what you did. Or，perhaps you were brought up to believe that you should do what your father did，so you have taken over the family business，or become a dentist “just like dad.” If this sounds familiar，it’s probably time to look at the new possibilities for your future.

Miller developed a 7-step process to help potential job seekers assess their current situation and beliefs, identify their real passion, and start on a journey that allows them to pursue their passion through work.

Step 1: Willingness to do something different.

Breaking the cycle of doing what you have always done is one of the most difficult tasks for job seekers. Many find it difficult to steer away from a career path or make a change, even if it doesn't feel right. Miller urges job seekers to open their minds to other possibilities beyond what they are currently doing.

Step 2: Commitment to being who you are, not who or what someone wants you to be.

Look at the gifts and talents you have and make a commitment to pursue those things that you love most. If you love the social aspects of your job, but are stuck inside an office or "chained to your desk" most of the time, vow to follow your instinct and investigate alternative careers and work that allow you more time to interact with others. Dawn worked as a manager for a large retail clothing store for several years. Though she had advanced within the company, she felt frustrated and longed to be involved with nature and the outdoors. She decided to go to school nights and weekends to pursue her true passion by earning her master's degree in forestry. She now works in the biotech forestry division of a major paper company.

Step 3: Self-definition.

Miller suggests that once job seekers know who they are, they need to know how to sell themselves. "In the job market, you are a product. And just like a product, you must know the features and benefits that you have to offer a potential client, or employer." Examine the skills and knowledge that you have and identify how they can apply to your desired occupation. Your qualities will exhibit to employers why they should hire you over other candidates.

Step 4: Attain a level of self-honoring.

Self-honoring or self-love may seem like an odd step for job hunters, but being able to accept yourself, without judgment, helps eliminate insecurities and will make you more self-assured. By accepting who you are—all your emotions, hopes and dreams, your personality, and your unique way of being—you'll project more confidence when networking and talking with potential employers. The power of self-honoring can help to break all the falsehoods you were programmed to believe—those that made you feel that you were not good enough, or strong enough, or intelligent enough to do what you truly desire.

Step 5: Vision.

Miller suggests that job seekers develop a vision that embraces the answer to "What do I really want to do?" One should create a solid statement in a dozen or so sentences that describe in detail how they see their life related to work. For instance, the secretary who longs to be an actress describes a life that allows her to express her love of Shakespeare on stage. A real estate agent, attracted to his current job because her loves fixing up old homes, describes buying

properties that need a little tender loving care to make them more saleable.

Step 6: Appropriate risk.

Some philosophers believe that the way to enlightenment comes through facing obstacles and difficulties. Once people discover their passion, many are too scared to do anything about it. Instead, they do nothing. With this step, job seekers should assess what they are willing to give up, or risk, in pursuit of their dream. For one working mom, that meant taking night classes to learn new computer-aided design skills, while still earning a salary and keeping her day job. For someone else, it may mean quitting his or her job, taking out loan and going back to school full time. You'll move one step closer to your ideal work life if you identify how much risk you are willing to take and the sacrifices you are willing to make.

Step 7: Action.

Some teachers of philosophy describe action in this way, "If one wants to get to the top of a mountain, just sitting at the foot thinking about it will not bring one there. It is by making the effort of climbing up the mountain, step by step, that eventually the summit is reached." All too often, it is the lack of action that ultimately holds people back from attaining their ideals. Creating a plan and taking it one step at a time can lead to new and different job opportunities. Job-hunting tasks gain added meaning as you sense their importance in your quest for a more meaningful work life. The plan can include researching industries and occupations, talking to people who are in your desired area of work, taking classes, or accepting volunteer work in your targeted field.

Each of these steps will lead you on a journey to a happier and more rewarding work life. After all, it is the journey, not the destination, that is most important.

1. According to the recent "Plans for 2004" survey, most people are unhappy with their current jobs.
2. Mary Lyn Miller's job is to advise people on their life and career.
3. Mary Lyn Miller herself was once quite dissatisfied with her own work.
4. Many people find it difficult to make up their minds whether to change their career path.
5. According to Mary Lyn Miller, people considering changing their careers should commit themselves to the pursuit of ________.
6. In the job market, job seekers need to know how to sell themselves like ________.
7. During an interview with potential employers, self-honoring or self-love may help a job seeker to show ________.
8. Mary Lyn Miller suggests that a job seeker develop a vision that answers the question "________"
9. Many people are too scared to pursue their dreams because they are unwilling to ________.
10. What ultimately holds people back from attaining their ideals is ________.

Part Ⅲ Listening Comprehension (35 minutes)

Section A

Directions：(略)

11. A) Surfing the net. B) Watching a talk show.
    C) Packing a birthday gift. D) Shopping at a jewelry store.
12. A) He enjoys finding fault with exams.
    B) He is sure of his success in the exam.
    C) He doesn't know if he can do well in the exam.
    D) He used to get straight A's in the exams he took.
13. A) The man is generous with his good comments on people.
    B) The woman is unsure if there will be peace in the world.
    C) The woman is doubtful about newspaper stories.
    D) The man is quite optimistic about human nature.
14. A) Study for some profession. B) Attend a medical school.
    C) Stay in business. D) Sell his shop.
15. A) More money. B) Fair treatment.
    C) A college education. D) Shorter work hours.
16. A) She was exhausted from her trip. B) She missed the comforts of home.
    C) She was impressed by Mexican food. D) She will not go to Mexico again.
17. A) Cheer herself up a bit. B) Find a more suitable job.
    C) Seek professional advice. D) Take a psychology course.
18. A) He dresses more formally now.
    B) What he wears does not match his position.
    C) He has ignored his friends since graduation.
    D) He failed to do well at college.

Questions 19 to 22 are based on the conversation you have just heard.

19. A) To go sightseeing. B) To have meetings.
    C) To promote a new champagne. D) To join in a training program.
20. A) It can reduce the number of passenger complaints.
    B) It can make air travel more entertaining.
    C) It can cut down the expenses for air travel.
    D) It can lessen the discomfort caused by air travel.
21. A) Took balanced meals with champagne.
    B) Ate vegetables and fruit only.
    C) Refrained from fish or meat.
    D) Avoided eating rich food.

22. A) Many of them found it difficult to exercise on a plane.
    B) Many of them were concerned with their well-being.
    C) Not many of them chose to do what she did.
    D) Not many of them understood the program.

Questions 23 to 25 are based on the conversation you have just heard.

23. A) At a fair. B) At a cafeteria.
    C) In a computer lab. D) In a shopping mall.
24. A) The latest computer technology.
    B) The organizing of an exhibition.
    C) The purchasing of some equipment.
    D) The dramatic changes in the job market.
25. A) Data collection. B) Training consultancy.
    C) Corporate management. D) Information processing.

Section B

Directions:(略)

Passage One

Questions 26 to 28 are based on the passage you have just heard.

26. A) Improve themselves. B) Get rid of empty dreams.
    C) Follow the cultural tradition. D) Attempt something impossible.
27. A) By finding sufficient support for implementation.
    B) By taking into account their own ability to change.
    C) By constantly keeping in mind their ultimate goals.
    D) By making detailed plans and carrying them out.
28. A) To show people how to get their lives back to normal.
    B) To show how difficult it is for people to lose weight.
    C) To remind people to check the calories on food bags.
    D) To illustrate how easily people abandon their goals.

Passage Two

Questions 29 to 31 are based on the passage you have just heard.

29. A) Michael's parents got divorced.
    B) Karen was adopted by Ray Anderson.
    C) Karen's mother died in a car accident.
    D) A truck driver lost his life in a collision.
30. A) He ran a red light and collided with a truck.
    B) He sacrificed his life to save a baby girl.
    C) He was killed instantly in a burning car.
    D) He got married to Karen's mother.

31. A) The reported hero turned out to be his father.
    B) He did not understand his father till too late.
    C) Such misfortune should have fallen on him.
    D) It reminded him of his miserable childhood.

Passage Three

Questions 32 to 35 are based on the passage you have just heard.

32. A) Germany. B) Japan.
    C) The U. S. D) The U. K.
33. A) By doing odd jobs at weekends.
    B) By working long hours every day.
    C) By putting in more hours each week.
    D) By taking shorter vacations each year.
34. A) To combat competition and raise productivity.
    B) To provide them with more job opportunities.
    C) To help them maintain their living standard.
    D) To prevent them from holding a second job.
35. A) Change their jobs. B) Earn more money.
    C) Reduce their working hours. D) Strengthen the government's role.

Section C

Directions:(略)

Nursing, as a typically female profession, must deal constantly with the false impression that nurses are there to wait on the physician. As nurses, we are (36) ________ to provide nursing care only. We do not have any legal or moral (37) ________ to any physician. We provide health teaching, (38) ________ physical as well as emotional problems, (39) ________ patient-related services, and make all of our nursing decisions based upon what is best or suitable for the patient. If, in any (40) ________, we feel that a physician's order is (41) ________ or unsafe, we have a legal (42) ________ to question that order or refuse to carry it out.

Nursing is not a nine-to-five job with every weekend off. All nurses are aware of that before they enter the profession. The emotional and physical stress. However, that occurs due to odd working hours is a (43) ________ reason for a lot of the career dissatisfaction. (44) ____. That disturbs our personal lives, disrupts our sleeping and eating habits, and isolates us from everything except job-related friends and activities.

The quality of nursing care is being affected dramatically by these situations. (45) ____. Consumers of medically related services have evidently not been affected enough yet to demand changes in our medical system. But if trends continue as predicted, (46) ____

____.

Part Ⅳ Reading Comprehension(Reading in Depth) (25 minutes)

Section A

Directions:(略)

Questions 47 to 51 are based on the following passage.

Google is a world-famous company, with its headquarters in Mountain View, California. It was set up in a Silicon Valley garage in 1998, and *inflated*(膨胀) with the Internet bubble. Even when everything around it collapsed the company kept on inflating. Google's search engine is so widespread across the world that search became Google, and google became a verb. The world fell in love with the effective, fascinatingly fast technology.

Google owes much of its success to the brilliance of S. Brin and L. Page, but also to a series of fortunate events. It was Page who, at Stanford in 1996, initiated the academic project that eventually became Google's search engine. Brin, who had met Page at a student orientation a year earlier, joined the project early on. They were both Ph. D. candidates when they devised the search engine which was better than the rest and, without any marketing, spread by word of mouth from early adopters to, eventually, your grandmother.

Their breakthrough, simply put, was that when their search engine crawled the Web, it did more than just look for word matches, it also *tallied*(统计) and ranked a host of other critical factors like how websites link to one another. That delivered far better results than anything else. Brin and Page meant to name their creation Googol (the mathematical term for the number 1 followed by 100 zeroes), but someone misspelled the word so it stuck as Google. They raised money from *prescient*(有先见之明的) professors and venture capitalists, and moved off campus to turn Google into business. Perhaps their biggest stroke of luck came early on when they tried to sell their technology to other search engines, but no one met their price, and they built it up on their own.

The next breakthrough came in 2000, when Google figured out how to make money with its invention. It had lots of users, but almost no one was paying. The solution turned out to be advertising, and it's not an exaggeration to say that Google is now essentially an advertising company, given that that's the source of nearly all its revenue. Today it is a giant advertising company, worth $100 billion.

47. Apart from a series of fortunate events, what is it that has made Google so successful?
48. Google's search engine originated from ________ started by L. Page.
49. How did Google's search engine spread all over the world?
50. Brin and Page decided to set up their own business because no one would ________.
51. The revenue of the Google company is largely generated from ________.

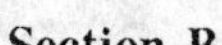

Section B

Directions:(略)

Passage One

Questions 52 to 56 are based on the following passage.

You hear the refrain all the time: the U. S. economy looks good statistically, but it doesn't feel good. Why doesn't ever-greater wealth promote ever-greater happiness? It is a question that dates at least to the appearance in 1958 of *The Affluent* (富裕的) *Society* by John Kenneth Galbraith, who died recently at 97.

The Affluent Society is a modern classic because it helped define a new moment in the human condition. For most of history, "hunger, sickness, and cold" threatened nearly everyone, Galbraith wrote. "Poverty was found everywhere in that world. Obviously it is not of ours." After World War Ⅱ, the dread of another Great Depression gave way to an economic boom. In the 1930s unemployment had averaged 18.2 percent; in the 1950s it was 4.5 percent.

To Galbraith, materialism had gone mad and would breed discontent. Through advertising, companies conditioned consumers to buy things they didn't really want or need. Because so much spending was artificial, it would be unfulfilling. Meanwhile, government spending that would make everyone better off was being cut down because people instinctively—and wrongly—labeled government only as "a necessary evil."

It's often said that only the rich are getting ahead; everyone else is standing still or falling behind. Well, there are many undeserving rich—overpaid chief executives, for instance. But over any meaningful period, most people's incomes are increasing. From 1995 to 2004, inflation-adjusted average family income rose 14.3 percent, to $43,200. People feel "squeezed" because their rising incomes often don't satisfy their rising wants—for bigger homes, more health care, more education, faster Internet connections.

The other great frustration is that it has not eliminated insecurity. People regard job stability as part of their standard of living. As corporate layoffs increased, that part has eroded. More workers fear they've become "the disposable American," as Louis Uchitelle puts it in his book by the same name.

Because so much previous suffering and social conflict stemmed from poverty, the arrival of widespread affluence suggested *utopian* (乌托邦式的) possibilities. Up to a point, affluence succeeds. There is much less physical misery than before. People are better off. Unfortunately, affluence also creates new complaints and contradictions.

Advanced societies need economic growth to satisfy the multiplying wants of their citizens. But the quest for growth lets loose new anxieties and economic conflicts that disturb the social order. Affluence liberates the individual, promising that everyone can choose a unique way to self-fulfillment. But the promise is so extravagant that it predestines many disappointments and sometimes inspires choices that have anti-social consequences, including family breakdown and *obesity* (肥胖症). Statistical indicators of happiness have not risen with incomes.

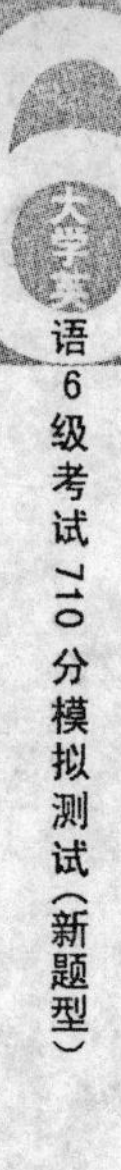

Should we be surprised? Not really. We've simply reaffirmed an old truth: the pursuit of affluence does not always end with happiness.

52. What question does John Kenneth Galbraith raise in his book *The Affluent Society*?
    A) Why statistics don't tell the truth about the economy.
    B) Why affluence doesn't guarantee happiness.
    C) How happiness can be promoted today.
    D) What lies behind an economic boom.
53. According to Galbraith, people feel discontented because ________.
    A) public spending hasn't been cut down as expected
    B) the government has proved to be a necessary evil
    C) they are in fear of another Great Depression
    D) materialism has run wild in modern society
54. Why do people feel squeezed when their average income rises considerably?
    A) Their material pursuits have gone far ahead of their earnings.
    B) Their purchasing power has dropped markedly with inflation.
    C) The distribution of wealth is uneven between the rich and the poor.
    D) Health care and educational cost have somehow gone out of control.
55. What does Louis Uchitelle mean by "the disposable American" (Line 3, Para. 5)?
    A) Those who see job stability as part of their living standard.
    B) People full of utopian ideas resulting from affluence.
    C) People who have little say in American politics.
    D) Workers who no longer have secure jobs.
56. What has affluence brought to American society?
    A) Renewed economic security.
    B) A sense of self-fulfillment.
    C) New conflicts and complaints.
    D) Misery and anti-social behavior.

Passage Two

Questions 57 to 61 are based on the following passage.

The use of *deferential* (恭敬的) language is symbolic of the Confucian ideal of the woman, which dominates conservative gender norms in Japan. This ideal presents a woman who withdraws quietly to the background, subordinating her life and needs to those of her family and its male head. She is a dutiful daughter, wife, and mother, master of the domestic arts. The typical refined Japanese woman excels in modesty and delicacy; she "*treads softly* (谨言慎行) in the world," elevating feminine beauty and grace to an art form.

Nowadays, it is commonly observed that young women are not conforming to the feminine *linguistic* (语言的) ideal. They are using fewer of the very deferential "women's" forms, and even using the few strong forms that are know as "men's." This, of course, attracts considerable attention and has led to an outcry in the Japanese media against the defeminization of women's language. Indeed, we didn't hear about "men's language" until people began to respond to girls' appropriation of forms normally reserved for boys and men. There is considerable sentiment about the "corruption" of women's language—which of course is viewed as part of the loss of feminine ideals and morality—and this sentiment is crystallized by nationwide opinion polls that are regularly carried out by the media.

Yoshiko Matsumoto has argued that young women probably never used as many of the highly deferential forms as older women. This highly polite style is no doubt something that young women have been expected to "grow into"—after all, it is a sign not simply of femininity, but of maturity and refinement, and its use could be taken to indicate a change in the nature of one's social relations as well. One might well imagine little girls using exceedingly polite forms when playing house or imitating older women—in a fashion analogous to little girls' use of a high-pitched voice to do "teacher talk" or "mother talk" in role play.

The fact that young Japanese women are using less deferential language is a sure sign of change-of social change and of linguistic change. But it is most certainly not a sign of the "masculization" of girls. In some instances, it may be a sign that girls are making the same claim to authority as boys and men, but that is very different from saying that they are trying to be "masculine." Katsue Reynolds has argued that girls nowadays are using more assertive language strategies in order to be able to compete with boys in schools and out. Social change also brings not simply different positions for women and girls, but different relations to life stages, and adolescent girls are participating in new subcultural forms. Thus what may, to an older speaker, seem like "masculine" speech may seem to an adolescent like "liberated" or "hip" speech.

57. The first paragraph describes in detail ________.

A) the standards set for contemporary Japanese women

B) the Confucian influence on gender norms in Japan

C) the stereotyped role of women in Japanese families

D) the norms for traditional Japanese women to follow

58. What change has been observed in today's young Japanese women?

A) They pay less attention to their linguistic behavior.

B) The use fewer of the deferential linguistic forms.

C) They confuse male and female forms of language.

D) They employ very strong linguistic expressions.

59. How do some people react to women's appropriation of men's language forms as reported in the Japanese media?

A) They call for a campaign to stop the defeminization.

B) The see it as an expression of women's sentiment.

C) They accept it as a modern trend.

D) They express strong disapproval.

60. According to Yoshiko Matsumoto, the linguistic behavior observed in today's young women ________.

A) may lead to changes in social relations

B) has been true of all past generations

C) is viewed as a sign of their maturity

D) is a result of rapid social progress

61. The author believes that the use of assertive language by young Japanese women is ________.

A) a sure sign of their defeminization and maturation

B) an indication of their defiance against social change

C) one of their strategies to compete in a male-dominated society

D) an inevitable trend of linguistic development in Japan today

Part Ⅴ Cloze (15 minutes)

Directions:（略）

Historically, humans get serious about avoiding disasters only after one has just struck them. __62__ that logic, 2006 should have been a breakthrough year for rational behavior. With the memory of 9 • 11 still __63__ in their minds, Americans watched hurricane Katrina, the most expensive disaster in U. S. history, on __64__ TV. Anyone who didn't know it before should have learned that bad things can happen. And they are made __65__ worse by our willful blindness to risk as much as our __66__ to work together before everything goes to hell.

Granted, some amount of *delusion*（错觉）is probably part of the __67__ condition. In A. D. 63, Pompeii was seriously damaged by an earthquake, and the locals immediately went to work __68__, in the same spot—until they were buried altogether by a volcano eruption 16 years later. But a __69__ of the past year in disaster history suggests that modern Americans are particularly bad at __70__ themselves from guaranteed threats. We know more than we __71__ did about the dangers we face. But it turns __72__ that in times of crisis, our greatest enemy is __73__ the storm, the quake or the __74__ itself. More often, it is ourselves.

So what has happened in the year that __75__ the disaster on the Gulf Coast? In New Orleans, the Army Corps of Engineers has worked day and night to rebuild the flood walls. They have got the walls to __76__ they were before Katrina, more or less. That's not __77__, we can now say with confidence. But it may be all __78__ can be expected from one year of *hustle*（忙碌）.

Meanwhile, New Orleans officials have crafted a plan to use buses and trains to __79__ the sick and the disabled. The city estimates that 15,000 people will need a __80__ out. However, state officials have not yet determined where these people will be taken. The __81__ with neighboring communities are ongoing and difficult.

62. A) To B) By C) On D) For
63. A) fresh B) obvious C) apparent D) evident
64. A) visual B) vivid C) live D) lively
65. A) little B) less C) more D) much
66. A) reluctance B) rejection C) denial D) decline
67. A) natural B) world C) social D) human
68. A) revising B) refining C) rebuilding D) retrieving
69. A) review B) reminder C) concept D) prospect

70. A) preparing B) protesting C) protecting D) prevailing
71. A) never B) ever C) then D) before
72. A) up B) down C) over D) out
73. A) merely B) rarely C) incidentally D) accidentally
74. A) surge B) spur C) surf D) splash
75. A) ensued B) traced C) followed D) occurred
76. A) which B) where C) what D) when
77. A) enough B) certain C) conclusive D) final
78. A) but B) as C) that D) those
79. A) exile B) evacuate C) dismiss D) displace
80. A) ride B) trail C) path D) track
81. A) conventions B) notifications C) communications D) negotiations

Part Ⅵ Translation

Directions:(略)

82. The auto manufacturers found themselves ____________(正在同外国公司竞争市场的份额).
83. Only in the small town ____________(他才感到安全和放松).
84. It is absolutely unfair that these children ____________(被剥夺了受教育的权利).
85. Our years of hard work are all in vain, ____________(更别提我们花费的大量金钱了).
86. The problems of blacks and women ____________(最近几十年受到公众相当大的关注).

参考答案(June 2007)

Part Ⅰ Sample Writing

Should One Expect a Reward When Doing a Good Deed?

A great many people presume upon a reward when conducting a good deed. First and foremost, there is a natural tendency to equate doing good deeds with a certain amount of pecuniary reward, and reward with a certain sum of money. What is more, they maintain that since the basis of contemporary society is money, one of the major means of earning money is getting reward by conducting good deeds.

Conversely, the vast majority of people assume that doing a good deed should be based on people's individual consciousness of responsibility. Hence, conducting a good deed is fulfilling itself and little significance should be attached to monetary reward. Numerous illustrations can be given, but this will suffice. Mr. Leifeng lived an austere life dedicated to doing good deeds without expecting any reward and succoring people from all walks of life, yet he was remembered as one of

the most successful idol of our time.

Generally speaking, it is imperative for us to conduct good deeds without expecting any rewards. For one thing, we should appeal to the authorities to legislate strict laws and regulations to encourage people to do good deeds. For another, we should cultivate people's awareness that conducting good deeds is extremely crucial to us. It is universally acknowledged that we do this for enjoyment, self-fulfillment and spiritual enhancement, not for the purpose of pecuniary reward.

Part Ⅱ Reading Comprehension (Skimming and Scanning)

1. N 2. Y 3. NG 4. Y

5. According to Mary Lyn Miller, people considering changing their careers should commit themselves to the pursuit of those things that they love most.
6. In the job market, job seekers need to know how to sell themselves like products.
7. During an interview with potential employers, self-honoring or self-love may help a job seeker to show more confidence.
8. Mary Lyn Miller suggests that a job seeker develop a vision that answers the question "What do I really want to do?"
9. Many people are too scared to pursue their dreams because they are unwilling to give up/ risk.
10. What ultimately holds people back from attaining their ideals is the lack of action.

Part Ⅲ Listening Comprehension

Section A

11—15 ABDCA 16—20 BCABD 21—25 DCACB

Section B

26—30 ADDCB 31—35 ABDAC

Section C

36. licensed 37. obligation 38. assess 39. coordinate
40. circumstance 41. inappropriate 42. responsibility 43. prime
44. It is sometimes required that we work overtime, and that we change shifts four or five times a month
45. Most hospitals are now staffed by new graduates as experienced nurses finally give up trying to change the system
46. they will find that most critical hospital care will be provided by new, inexperienced, and sometimes inadequately trained nurses

Part Ⅳ Reading Comprehension (Reading in Depth)

Section A

47. The brilliance of S. Brin and L. Page.
48. the academic project
49. By word of mouth.
50. meet their price
51. advertising

Section B

52—56 BDADC 57—61 BBDAC

Part Ⅴ Cloze

62—66 BACDA 67—71 DCACB 72—76 DBACB 77—81 ACBAD

Part Ⅵ Translation

82. competing with foreign firms for market share
83. does he feel secure and relaxed
84. are deprived of the rights to receive education
85. not to mention/let alone the large amount of money we have spent
86. have gained/caused considerable public concern in recent decades

试题解答(June 2007)

Part Ⅱ Reading Comprehension (Skimming and Scanning)

1. [N] 由文章第一段第二句"In fact, one in four workers is dissatisfied with their current job, according to the recent "Plans for 2004" survey."可见四分之一的人而非大多数人对目前的工作不满意。故本题判断为 NO。
2. [Y] 第二段开头即提到 Mary Lyn Miller 是资深的职业顾问,紧接着该段最后一句提到"Through her book, 8 Myths of Making a Living, as well as workshops, seminars and personal coaching and consulting, she has helped thousands of dissatisfied workers reassess life and work.",由此可知她帮助数以万计不满意的人重新评价他们的工作和生活。可见她的工作是向人们提供有关工作和生活的建议。故本题判断为 YES。
3. [NG] 文章没有提到 Mary Lyn Miller 本人是否对自己的工作满意。故本题判断为 NOT GIVEN。
4. [Y] 由"Step 1: Willingness to do something different."部分第二句"Many find it difficult to steer away from a career path or make a change, even if it doesn't feel right."可知很多人发现很难驶离原来的职业道路或者进行改变。换言之,做出改换职业的决定是困难的。故本题判断为 YES。
5. "Step 2: Commitment to being who you are, not who or what someone wants you to be."部分第一句"Look at the gifts and talents you have and make a commitment to pursue those things that you love most."中的"make a commitment to pursue"是题干中"commit themselves to the pursuit of"的同义表达。故正确答案为"those things that they love most"。
6. 由"Step 3: Self-definition"部分第一、二句"Miller suggests that once job seekers know who they are, they need to know how to sell themselves. 'In the job market, you are a product. And just like a product, you must know the features and benefits that you have to offer a potential client, or employer.'"可见求职者要像推销产品一样推销自己才行。故正确答案为"product"。

7. 由“Step 4：Attain a level of self-honoring.”部分第二句“By accepting who you are—all your emotions，hopes and dreams，your personality，and your unique way of being—you'll project more confidence when networking and talking with potential employers.”可知原文中的“project”和题干中的“show”意思相近。故正确答案为“more confidence”。
8. 由“Step 5：Vision.”部分第一句“Miller suggests that job seekers develop a vision that embraces the answer to ‘What do I really want to do?’”可知 Miller 建议求职者对未来进行展望，而展望能为“我到底想要做什么?”这样的问题提供答案。故正确答案为：“What do I really want to do?”。
9. 由“Step 6：Appropriate risk.”部分中的“Once people discover their passion，many are too scared to do anything about it. Instead，they do nothing. With this step，job seekers should assess what they are willing to give up，or risk，in pursuit of their dream.”可见求职者应该确定为追寻梦想他们愿意放弃什么或者冒怎样的险。若非如此，他们只能无所作为。故正确答案为“give up/risk”。
10. 由“Step 7：Action.”部分第三句“All too often，it is the lack of action that ultimately holds people back from attaining their ideals.”可知缺乏行动是妨碍人们实现理想的最终原因。故正确答案是“the lack of action”。

Part Ⅲ　Listening Comprehension(听力原文在光盘中)

Part Ⅳ　Reading Comprehension (Reading in Depth)

Section A

47. 由文章第二段第一句“Google owes much of its success to the brilliance of S. Brin and L. Page，but also to a series of fortunate events.”可知谷歌公司的成功归因于 S. Brin 和 L. Page 的智慧以及一系列的幸运事件。故正确答案为“The brilliance of S. Brin and L. Page.”。
48. 由第二段的第二句“It was Page who，at Stanford in 1996，initiated the academic project that eventually became Google's search engine.”可知 Page 于 1996 年在斯坦福发起了一个学术项目。它最终成为了谷歌的搜索引擎。换言之，谷歌的搜索引擎始于 L. Page 发起的学术项目。故正确答案为“the academic project”。
49. 由第二段的最后一句“They were both Ph. D. candidates when they devised the search engine which was better than the rest and，without any marketing，spread by word of mouth from early adopters to，eventually，your grandmother.”可见谷歌的搜索引擎最初没有进行市场推销，是凭借其优势，靠口口相传使其家喻户晓的。故正确答案为“By word of mouth.”。
50. 由第三段最后一句“Perhaps their biggest stroke of luck came early on when they tried to sell their technology to other search engines，but no one met their price，and they built it up on their own.”可知他们自己创建公司的原因是当时没人出得起价购买他们的技术。原文的“built it up on their own”即是题干中“set up their own business”的同义表达。故正确答案为“meet their price”。
51. 由最后一段的第三句“The solution turned out to be advertising，and it's not an exaggeration to say that Google is now essentially an advertising company，given that that's the source of nearly all its revenue”，可知谷歌公司的收入主要来源于广告。题干中的“largely generated

from"对应了原文的"the source of nearly all",故正确答案为"advertising"。

Section B

52. [B] 细节题。由第一段的最后两句"Why doesn't ever-greater wealth promote ever-greater happiness? It is a question that dates at least to the appearance in 1958 of *The Affluent Society* by John Kenneth Galbraith, who died recently at 97."可知,为什么越来越多的财富不能促进幸福的增长这一问题至少可以追溯到1958年,出现在《富裕社会》一书中。其作者是最近刚刚去世终年97岁的John Kenneth Galbraith。因此,选项B(为什么财富不能保证幸福?)就是John Kenneth Galbraith在《富裕社会》一书中提出的问题。故正确答案为B项。

53. [D] 细节题。由第三段第一句:"To Galbraith, materialism had gone mad and would breed discontent."可见Galbraith认为,人们感觉到不满是因为现代社会中的物质主义已经变得疯狂。选项D中的"run wild"和原文中的"had gone mad"是同义表达。故正确答案为D项。

54. [A] 细节题。由第四段最后一句"People feel 'squeezed' because their rising incomes often don't satisfy their rising wants—for bigger homes, more health care, more education, faster Internet connections."可知人们感到"手头紧"是因为日渐丰厚的收入常常不能满足他们增长的需求——更大的住房、更多的健康保障、更好的教育以及更快的互联网连接速度。故正确答案为A项。

55. [D] 词义推断题。由第五段第二到第四句"People regard job stability as part of their standard of living. As corporate layoffs increased, that part has eroded. More workers fear they've become 'the disposable American,' as Louis Uchitelle puts it in his book by the same name."可以看出人们把工作稳定看作生活水平的一部分。随着公司失业人数的增多,这部分水平下降了。因此,最后一句中更多的人担心自己失去工作,成为"the disposable American",故该表达根据上下文可以理解为失去工作或者没有稳定工作的人。所以正确答案为D项。

56. [C] 细节推断题。由第六段最后四句"Up to a point, affluence succeeds. There is much less physical misery than before. People are better off. Unfortunately, affluence also creates new complaints and contradictions."可知在某种程度上,实现了乌托邦式的可能。比起过去,人们身体上遭受的痛苦少多了。人们过得更好了。但不幸的是,富裕也制造了新的抱怨和矛盾。据此可以推断,富裕带给美国社会的是新的矛盾和抱怨。故正确答案为C项。

57. [B] 细节题。第一段首句为本段主题句。其他各句是对该主题句的进一步解释和支撑。由段首句"The use of deferential language is symbolic of the Confucian ideal of the woman, which dominates conservative gender norms in Japan."可知使用敬语是儒家理想女性的象征。它在日本保守的性别规范中占主导地位。故第一段主要描述了儒家思想影响下的日本女性的性别规范。因此,正确答案为B项。

58. [B] 细节题。由第二段第一、二句"Nowadays, it is commonly observed that young women are not conforming to the feminine linguistic ideal. They are using fewer of the very deferential 'women's' forms, and even using the few strong forms that are know as 'men's.'"可知日本年轻女性使用敬语越来越少了,甚至开始使用强烈的"男性化"的语言。故本题答案为B项。

59. [D] 细节推断题。由第二段最后两句"Indeed, we didn't hear about 'men's language' until people began to respond to girls' appropriation of forms normally reserved for boys and men. There is considerable sentiment about the 'corruption' of women's language—which of course

is viewed as part of the loss of feminine ideals and morality—and this sentiment is crystallized by nationwide opinion polls that are regularly carried out by the media."可知当人们开始对女孩使用男孩或者男人专用的语言形式这一现象做出反应的时候,我们才听到"男性语言"的说法。女性语言的颓败被看作是女性理想和道德沦丧的一部分。人们对此有很大的意见。而这种情绪在媒体定期进行的民意调查中表现得很清楚。据此可以推断,在日本,人们对女性使用男性语言是强烈不满的。故正确答案为D项。

60. [A] 细节推断题。由最后一段第一、五句"The fact that young Japanese women are using less deferential language is a sure sign of change—of social change and of linguistic change... Social change also brings not simply different positions for women and girls, but different relations to life stages, and adolescent girls are participating in new subcultural forms."。可以看出作者认为日本年轻女性减少使用敬语不仅是语言变化的表现,也是社会变化的表现。第五句中作者继续讲到,这种社会变化给女性带来的不但是地位的变化,而且是不同生活阶段社会关系的变化。由此可以推断,这种语言行为的变化可能引起社会关系的变化。故正确答案为A项。

61. [C] 细节推断题。文章最后一段作者试图探讨日本年轻女性减少使用敬语的原因。在本段第四句,他引用了 Katsue Reynolds 的观点:"Katsue Reynolds has argued that girls nowadays are using more assertive language strategies in order to be able to compete with boys in schools and out.",认为女孩使用更为坚定自信的语言策略是为了能够在校内校外和男孩竞争。由此可以推断,正确答案为B项。

Part Ⅴ Cloze

62. 本题考查介词辨义。根据上下文,本句表示"依此逻辑",因此要选择B项 by,表示"按照,根据"。

63. 本题考查上下文辨义及形容词辨义。根据上下文,本句意为"人们对于9·11事件依然记忆犹新",A项 fresh 意为"新的,(记忆)清晰的",可与 memory 搭配,意为"记忆犹新"。

64. 本题考查上下文辨义及形容词辨义。根据上下文,本句意为"电视现场直播",因此只有C项 live,作定语,可以表示"广播或电视的现场直播的,实况转播的"。

65. 本题考查副词用法。在修饰形容词或副词的比较级时,可用副词 much 表示程度,文中的意思是,灾害本来就造成了巨大损失,再加上人为的忽视,损失就更加惨重了,因此要选择D项 much 来修饰 worse。

66. 本题考查上下文辨义。根据上下文可知,作者要表示人们通常要到事情变得最糟糕的时候才愿意齐心努力,因此,A项 reluctance 表示"不情愿,勉强",符合句意。

67. 本题考查上下文理解。根据语境,下文开始回顾人类历史上对灾难事件缺乏警惕的其他案例。因此这个空格需填一个词,表示"与人类有关的",因此D项 human 是最佳选项。

68. 本题考查上下文理解。文中提到庞贝古城在经受第一次地震后,人们马上又在同一地点重建,直到16年后被火山喷发彻底掩埋。因此应该选C项 rebuilding。

69. 本题考查上下文理解。由后文中的"the past year in disaster history"可知应该是对过去一年发生的灾难的回顾。因此,应该选择A项 review。

70. 本题考查动词辨义。由后文中的"... from..."，可知需要选择一个和 from 搭配并符合上下文句义的动词。因此,C项 protecting 是正确选项。

71. 本题考查副词辨义。根据文章,作者要表达的是在面对危险时,美国人比以往任何时候了解

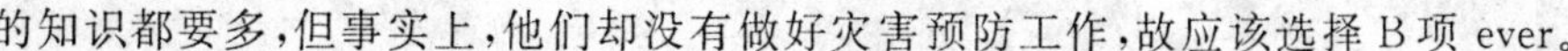

的知识都要多,但事实上,他们却没有做好灾害预防工作,故应该选择B项 ever。

72. 本题考查固定搭配。"It turns out that..."是固定句型,意为"原来是……,事实上是……"。
73. 本题考查副词辨义。根据句义判断,作者表示在危急关头,美国人的最大的威胁不是来自灾害,而是来自自身,因此需要一个副词与 more often 相对,B项 rarely 是正确答案。
74. 本题考查名词辨义。通过文章中提到的"暴风雨"、"地震"可知,此处也应该填入与灾难有关的词,因此A项 surge,意为"海啸",是正确答案。
75. 本题考查动词辨义。文中指的是在墨西哥湾灾难后接下来的一年中所发生的事,因此C项 followed 是正确答案。
76. 本题考查语义衔接。根据文章可知,Katrina 飓风到来前已有防洪墙存在,但被飓风摧毁了,而在飓风过后美国陆军工兵部队又进行了重建工作,现在已经建到原来防洪墙所在的位置了,因此B项 where 是正确选项。
77. 本题考查语义衔接。根据上文可知,重建到原来的位置是不够的。因此,A项 enough 是正确答案。
78. 本题考查结构衔接。从句子结构上看应是一个定语从句,缺少的部分正是关系代词,先行词是不定代词 all,因此C项 that 是正确答案,表示"这是一年的忙碌所能期待的一切"。
79. 本题考查动词辨义。从后文可知,宾语是病人和残疾人,表示新奥尔良政府打算疏散病人和残疾人,exile 和 dismiss 暗示以高压手段驱散,不合上下文语境,因此B项 evacuate 是正确答案,意为"疏散,撤离"。
80. 本题考查名词辨义。根据上句可知新奥尔良政府已经制定了用巴士和火车疏散病人和残疾人的计划,估计约有15 000人要搭乘,因此A项 ride 是正确答案。
81. 本题考查上下文理解。根据文章可知,州政府尚未决定这些人要被迁到哪里,因此D项 negotiation 是正确答案。

Part Ⅵ Translation

82. [答案]:competing with foreign firms for market share

    [注释]:本句考点:① find oneself doing 结构,oneself 是动词 find 的宾语,doing 是宾语补足语,表示"发觉自己在做某事";②compete with sb. for sth. 结构,表示"为……和某人竞争";③market share 表示"市场份额"。

83. [答案]:does he feel secure and relaxed

    [注释]:本句考点:①倒装结构,only 位于句首修饰后面的状语时,该句主谓要部分倒装;②secure 表示"安全的,有保障的",relaxed 表示"轻松的,放松的"。

84. [答案]:are deprived of the rights to receive education

    [注释]:本句考点:①deprive sb./sth. of sth. 结构,表示"剥夺";②the right to do sth.,表示"做某事的权力"。

85. [答案]:not to mention / let alone the large amount of money we have spent

    [注释]:本句考点:①"更别提,更不用说",用 not to mention 或 let alone 表示;②"大量",用 a large amount of。

86. [答案]:have gained / caused considerable public concern in recent decades

    [注释]:本句考点:①"受到……的关注",用 gain/cause... concern 表示;②"最近几十年",用 in recent decades 表示,decade 表示"十年"。

College English Test (Band Ⅵ) (Dec. 2007)

Part Ⅰ Writing (30 minutes)

Directions: *For this part, you are allowed 30 minutes to write a short essay entitled* **The Digital Age**. *You should write at least* **150** *words following the outline given below.*

1. 如今,数字化产品越来越多,如……
2. 使用数字化产品对于人们学习工作和生活的影响。

Part Ⅱ Reading Comprehension (Skimming and Scanning) (15 minutes)

Directions: *In this part, you will have 15 minutes to go over the passage quickly and answer the questions on the Answer Sheet. For questions 1－7, choose the best answer from the four choices marked A), B), C) and D). For questions 8－10, complete the sentences with the information given in the passage.*

Seven Ways to Save the World

Forget the old idea that conserving energy is a form of self-denial—riding bicycles, dimming the lights, and taking fewer showers. These days conservation is all about efficiency: getting the same—or better—results from just a fraction of the energy. When a slump in business travel forced Ulrich Romer to cut costs at his family-owned hotel in Germany, he replaced hundreds of the hotel's wasteful light bulbs, getting the same light for 80 percent less power. He bought a new water boiler with a digitally controlled pump, and wrapped insulation around the pipes. Spending about €100,000 on these and other improvements, he slashed his €90,000 fuel and power bill by €60,000. As a bonus, the hotel's lower energy needs have reduced its annual carbon emissions by more than 200 metric tons. "For us, saving energy has been very, very profitable," he says. "And most importantly, we're not giving up a single comfort for our guests."

Efficiency is also a great way to lower carbon emissions and help slow global warming. But the best argument for efficiency is its cost—or, more precisely, its profitability. That's because quickly growing energy demand requires immense investment in new supply, not to mention the drain of rising energy prices.

No wonder efficiency has moved to the top of the political agenda. On Jan. 10, the European Union unveiled a plan to cut energy use across the continent by 20 percent by 2020. Last March, China imposed a 20 percent increase in energy efficiency by 2020. Even George W. Bush, the

Texas oilman, is expected to talk about energy conservation in his State of the Union speech this week.

The good news is that the world is full of proven, cheap ways to save energy. Here are the seven that could have the biggest impact:

Insulate

Space heating and cooling eats up 36 percent of all the world's energy. There's virtually no limit to how much of that can be saved, as prototype "zero-energy homes" in Switzerland and Germany have shown. There's been a surge in new ways of keeping heat in and cold out (or vice versa). The most advanced insulation follows the law of increasing returns: if you add enough, you can scale down or even eliminate heating and air-conditioning equipment, lowering costs even before you start saving on utility bills. Studies have shown that green workplaces (ones that don't constantly need to have the heat or air-conditioner running) have higher worker productivity and lower sick rates.

Change Bulbs

Lighting eats up 20 percent of the world's electricity, or the equivalent of roughly 600,000 tons of coal a day. Forty percent of that powers old-fashioned incandescent light bulbs—a 19th-century technology that wastes most of the power it consumes on unwanted heat.

Compact fluorescent lamps, or CFLs, not only use 75 to 80 percent less electricity than incandescent bulbs to generate the same amount of light, but they also last 10 times longer. Phasing old bulbs out by 2030 would save the output of 650 power plants and avoid the release of 700 million tons of carbon into the atmosphere each year.

Comfort Zone

Water boilers, space heaters and air conditioners have been notoriously inefficient. The heat pump has altered that equation. It removes heat from the air outside or the ground below and uses it to supply heat to a building or its water supply. In the summer, the system can be reversed to cool buildings as well.

Most new residential buildings in Sweden are already heated with ground-source heat pumps. Such systems consume almost no conventional fuel at all. Several countries have used subsidies to jump-start the market, including Japan, where almost 1 million heat pumps have been installed in the past two years to heat water for showers and hot tubs.

Remake Factories

From steel mills to paper factories, industry eats up about a third of the world's energy. The opportunities to save are vast. In Ludwigshafen, German chemicals giant BASF runs an interconnected complex of more than 200 chemical factories, where heat produced by one chemical process is used to power the next. At the Ludwigshafen site alone, such recycling of heat and energy saves the company 200 million a year and almost halt its CO_2 emissions. Now BASF is doing the same for new plants in China. "*Optimizing*(优化) energy efficiency is a decisive

competitive advantage," says BASF CEO Jurgen Hambrecht.

Green Driving

A quarter of the world's energy—including two thirds of the annual production of oil—is used for transportation. Some savings come free of charge: you can boost fuel efficiency by 6 percent simply by keeping your car's tires properly *inflated*(充气). Gasoline-electric *hybrid*(混合型的) models like the Toyota Prius improve mileage by a further 20 percent over conventional models.

A Better Fridge

More than half of all residential power goes into running household appliances, producing a fifth of the world's carbon emissions. And that's true even though manufacturers have already hiked the efficiency of refrigerators and other white goods by as much as 70 percent since the 1980s. According to an International Energy Agency study, if consumers chose those models that would save them the most money over the life of the appliance, they'd cut global residential power consumption (and their utility bills) by 43 percent.

Flexible Payment

Who says you have to pay for all your conservation investments? "Energy service contractors" will pay for *retrofitting*(翻新改造)in return for a share of the client's annual utility-bill savings. In Beijing, Shenwu Thermal Energy Technology Co. specializes in retrofitting China's steel furnaces. Shenwu puts up the initial investment to install a heat exchanger that preheats the air going into the furnace, slashing the client's fuel costs. Shenwu pockets a cut of those savings, so both Shenwu and the client profit.

If saving energy is so easy and profitable, why isn't everyone doing it? It has to do with psychology and a lack of information. Most of us tend to look at today's price tag more than tomorrow's potential savings. That holds double for the landlord or developer, who won't actually see a penny of the savings his investment in better insulation or a better heating system might generate. In many people's minds, conservation is still associated with self-denial. Many environmentalists still push that view.

Smart governments can help push the market in the right direction. The EU's 1994 law on labeling was such a success that it extended the same idea to entire buildings last year. To boost the market value of efficiency, all new buildings are required to have an "energy pass" detailing power and heating consumption. Countries like Japan and Germany have successively tightened building codes, requiring an increase in insulation levels but leaving it up to builders to decide how to meet them.

The most powerful incentives, of course, will come from the market itself. Over the past year, sky-high fuel prices have focused minds on efficiency like never before. Ever-increasing pressure to cut costs has finally forced more companies to do some math on their energy use.

Will it be enough? With global demand and emissions rising so fast, we may not have any choice but to try. Efficient technology is here now, proven and cheap. Compared with all other options, it's the biggest, easiest and most profitable bang for the buck.

1. What is said to be the best way to conserve energy nowadays?
A) Raising efficiency. B) Cutting unnecessary costs.
C) Finding alternative resources. D) Sacrificing some personal comforts.
2. What does the European Union plan to do?
A) Diversify energy supply. B) Cut energy consumption.
C) Reduce carbon emissions. D) Raise production efficiency.
3. If you add enough insulation to your house, you may be able to ________.
A) improve your work environment B) cut your utility bills by half
C) get rid of air-conditioners D) enjoy much better health
4. How much of the power consumed by incandescent bulbs is converted into light?
A) A small portion. B) Some 40 percent.
C) Almost half. D) 75 to 80 percent.
5. Some countries have tried to jump-start the market of heat pumps by ________.
A) upgrading the equipment B) encouraging investments
C) implementing high-tech D) providing subsidies
6. German chemicals giant BASF saves 200 million a year by ________.
A) recycling heat and energy B) setting up factories in China
C) using the newest technology D) reducing the CO_2 emissions of its plants
7. Global residential power consumption can be cut by 43 percent if ________.
A) we increase the insulation of walls and water pipes
B) we choose simpler models of electrical appliances
C) we cut down on the use of refrigerators and other white goods
D) we choose the most efficient models of refrigerators and other white goods
8. Energy service contractors profit by taking a part of clients' ________.
9. Many environmentalist maintain the view that conservation has much to do with ________.
10. The strongest incentives for energy conservation will derive from ________.

Part Ⅲ Listening Comprehension (35 minutes)

Section A

Directions:(略)

11. A) Proceed in his own way. B) Stick to the original plan.
C) Compromise with his colleague. D) Try to change his colleague's mind.
12. A) Mary has a keen eye for style.
B) Nancy regrets buying the dress.
C) Nancy and Mary went shopping together in Rome.
D) Nancy and Mary like to follow the latest fashion.
13. A) Wash the dishes. B) Go to the theatre.
C) Pick up George and Martha. D) Take her daughter to hospital.

14. A) She enjoys making up stories about other people.
    B) She can never keep anything to herself for long.
    C) She is eager to share news with the woman.
    D) She is the best informed woman in town.
15. A) A car dealer. B) A mechanic.
    C) A driving examiner. D) A technical consultant.
16. A) The shopping mall has been deserted recently.
    B) Shoppers can only find good stores in the mall.
    C) Lots of people moved out of the downtown area.
    D) There isn't much business downtown nowadays.
17. A) He will help the woman with her reading.
    B) The lounge is not a place for him to study in.
    C) He feels sleepy whenever he tries to study.
    D) A cozy place is rather hard to find on campus.
18. A) To protect her from getting scratches. B) To help relieve her of the pain.
    C) To prevent mosquito bites. D) To avoid getting sunburnt.

Questions 19 to 22 are based on the conversation you have just heard.

19. A) In a studio. B) In a clothing store.
    C) At a beach resort. D) At a fashion show.
20. A) To live there permanently.
    B) To stay there for half a year.
    C) To find a better job to support herself.
    D) To sell leather goods for a British company.
21. A) Designing fashion items for several companies.
    B) Modeling for a world-famous Italian company.
    C) Working as an employee for Ferragamo.
    D) Serving as a sales agent for Burberrys.
22. A) It has seen a steady decline in its profits.
    B) It has become much more competitive.
    C) It has lost many customers to foreign companies.
    D) It has attracted a lot more designers from abroad.

Questions 23 to 25 are based on the conversation you have just heard.

23. A) It helps her to attract more public attention.
    B) It improves her chance of getting promoted.
    C) It strengthens her relationship with students.
    D) It enables her to understand people better.
24. A) Passively. B) Positively. C) Skeptically. D) Sensitively.
25. A) It keeps haunting her day and night.
    B) Her teaching was somewhat affected by it.
    C) It vanishes the moment she steps into her role.
    D) Her mind goes blank once she gets on the stage.

Section B

Directions:（略）

Passage One

Questions 26 to 29 are based on the passage you have just heard.

26. A) To win over the majority of passengers from airlines in twenty years.
    B) To reform railroad management in western European countries.
    C) To electrify the railway lines between major European cities.
    D) To set up an express train network throughout Europe.
27. A) Major European airlines will go bankrupt.
    B) Europeans will pay much less for traveling.
    C) Traveling time by train between major European cities will be cut by half.
    D) Trains will become the safest and most efficient means of travel in Europe.
28. A) Train travel will prove much more comfortable than air travel.
    B) Passengers will feel much safer on board a train than on a plane.
    C) Rail transport will be environmentally friendlier than air transport.
    D) Traveling by train may be as quick as, or even quicker than, by air.
29. A) In 1981. B) In 1989. C) In 1990. D) In 2000.

Passage Two

Questions 30 to 32 are based on the passage you have just heard.

30. A) There can be no speedy recovery for mental patients.
    B) Approaches to healing patients are essentially the same.
    C) The mind and body should be taken as an integral whole.
    D) There is no clear division of labor in the medical profession.
31. A) A doctor's fame strengthens the patients' faith in them.
    B) Abuse of medicines is widespread in many urban hospitals.
    C) One third of the patients depend on harmless substances for cure.
    D) A patient's expectations of a drug have an effect on their recovery.
32. A) Expensive drugs may not prove the most effective.
    B) The workings of the mind may help patients recover.
    C) Doctors often exaggerate the effect of their remedies.
    D) Most illnesses can be cured without medication.

Passage Three

Questions 33 to 35 are based on the passage you have just heard.

33. A) Enjoying strong feelings and emotions.
    B) Defying all dangers when they have to.
    C) Being fond of making sensational news.

D) Dreaming of becoming famous one day.

34. A) Working in an emergency room. B) Watching horror movies.
C) Listening to rock music. D) Doing daily routines.

35. A) A rock climber. B) A psychologist.
C) A resident doctor. D) A career consultant.

Section C

Directions:(略)

If you are like most people, you've indulged in fake listening many times. You go to history class, sit in the 3rd row, and look (36) ________ at the instructor as she speaks. But your mind is far away, (37) ________ in the clouds of pleasant daydreams. (38) ________ you come back to earth. The instructor writes an important term on the chalkboard, and you (39) ________ copy it in your notebook. Every once in a while the instructor makes a (40) ________ remark, causing others in the class to laugh. You smile politely, pretending that you've heard the remark and found it mildly (41) ________. You have a vague sense of (42) ________ that you aren't paying close attention. But you tell yourself that any (43) ________ you miss can be picked up from a friend's notes. Besides, (44) ________________________. So back you go into your private little world, only later do you realize you've missed important information for a test.

Fake listening may be easily exposed, since many speakers are sensitive to facial cues and can tell if you're merely pretending to listen. (45) ________________________.

Even if you are not exposed there's another reason to avoid fakery. It's easy for this behavior to become a habit. For some people, the habit is so deeply rooted that (46) ________________________.

As a result, they miss lots of valuable information.

Part Ⅳ Reading Comprehension(Reading in Depth) (25 minutes)

Section A

Directions:(略)

Questions 47 to 51 are based on the following passage.

Men, these days, are embracing fatherhood with the round-the-clock involvement their partners have always dreamed of—handling night feedings, packing lunches and bandaging knees. But unlike women, many find they're negotiating their new roles with little support or information. "Men in my generation (aged 25-40) have a fear of becoming dads because we have no role models," says Jon Smith, a writer. They often find themselves excluded from mothers' support networks, and are eyed *warily* (警觉地) on the playground.

The challenge is particularly evident in the work-place. There, men are still expected to be breadwinners climbing the corporate ladder; traditionally-minded bosses are often unsympathetic to family needs. In Denmark most new fathers only take two weeks of *paternity leave*(父亲的陪产假)—even though they are allowed 34 days. As much as if not more so than women, fathers struggle to be taken seriously when they request flexible arrangements.

Though Wilfried-Fritz Maring, 54, a data-bank and Internet specialist with German firm FIZ Karlsruhe, feels that the time he spends with his daughter outweighs any disadvantages, he admits, "With my decision to work from home I dismissed any opportunity for promotion."

Mind-sets(思维定式)are changing gradually. When Maring had a daughter, the company equipped him with a home office and allowed him to choose a job that could be performed from there. Danish telecom company TDC initiated an internal campaign last year to encourage dads to take paternity leave: 97 percent now do. "When an employee goes on paternity leave and is with his kids, he gets a new kind of training: in how to keep cool under stress," says spokesperson Christine Elberg Holm. For a new generation of dads, kids may come before the company—but it's a shift that benefits both.

47. Unlike women, men often get little support or information from ________.
48. Besides supporting the family, men were also expected to ________.
49. Like women, men hope that their desire for a flexible schedule will be ________.
50. When Maring was on paternity leave, he was allowed by his company to work ________.
51. Christine Holm believes paternity leave provides a new kind of training for men in that it can help them cope with ________.

Section B

Directions:(略)

Passage One

Questions 52 to 56 are based on the following passage.

Like most people, I've long understood that I will be judged by my occupation, that my profession is a gauge people use to see how smart or talented I am. Recently, however, I was disappointed to see that it also decides how I'm treated as a person.

Last year I left a professional position as a small-town reporter and took a job waiting tables. As someone paid to serve food to people, I had customers say and do things to me I suspect they'd never say or do to their most casual acquaintances. One night a man talking on his cell phone waved me away, then *beckoned*(示意)me back with his finger a minute later, complaining he was ready to order and asking where I'd been.

I had waited tables during summers in college and was treated like a *peon*(勤杂工) by plenty of people. But at 19 years old, I believed I deserved inferior treatment from professional adults. Besides, people responded to me differently after I told them I was in college. Customers would joke that one day I'd be sitting at their table, waiting to be served.

Once I graduated I took a job at a community newspaper. From my first day, I heard a respectful tone from everyone who called me. I assumed this was the way the professional world

worked—cordially.

I soon found out differently. I sat several feet away from an advertising sales representative with a similar name. Our calls would often get mixed up and someone asking for Kristen would be transferred to Christie. The mistake was immediately evident. Perhaps it was because money was involved, but people used a tone with Kristen that they never used with me.

My job title made people treat me with courtesy. So it was a shock to return to the restaurant industry.

It's no secret that there's a lot to put up with when waiting tables, and fortunately, much of it can be easily forgotten when you pocket the tips. The service industry, by definition, exists to cater to other's needs. Still, it seemed that many of my customers didn't get the difference between *server* and *servant*.

I'm now applying to graduate school, which means someday I'll return to a profession where people need to be nice to me in order to get what they want. I think I'll take them to dinner first, and see how they treat someone whose only job is to serve them.

52. The author was disappointed to find that ________.
   A) one's position is used as a gauge to measure one's intelligence
   B) talented people like her should fail to get a respectable job
   C) one's occupation affects the way one is treated as a person
   D) professionals tend to look down upon manual workers
53. What does the author intend to say by the example in the second paragraph?
   A) Some customers simply show no respect to those who serve them.
   B) People absorbed in a phone conversation tend to be absent-minded.
   C) Waitresses are often treated by customers as casual acquaintances.
   D) Some customers like to make loud complaints for no reason at all.
54. How did the author feel when waiting tables at the age of 19?
   A) She felt it unfair to be treated as a mere servant by professionals.
   B) She felt badly hurt when her customers regarded her as a peon.
   C) She was embarrassed each time her customers joked with her.
   D) She found it natural for professionals to treat her as inferior.
55. What does the author imply by saying "... many of my customers didn't get the difference between *server* and *servant*" (Lines 3-4, Para. 7)?
   A) Those who cater to others' needs are destined to be looked down upon.
   B) Those working in the service industry shouldn't be treated as servants.
   C) Those serving others have to put up with rough treatment to earn a living.
   D) The majority of customers tend to look on a servant as a server nowadays.
56. The author says she'll one day take her clients to dinner in order to ________.
   A) see what kind of person they are
   B) experience the feeling of being served
   C) show her generosity towards people inferior to her
   D) arouse their sympathy for people living a humble life

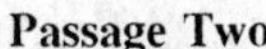

Passage Two

Questions 57 to 61 are based on the following passage.

What's hot for 2007 among the very rich? A $7.3 million diamond ring. A trip to Tanzania to hunt wild animals. Oh, and income inequality.

Sure, some leftish billionaires like George Soros have been railing against income inequality for years. But increasingly, centrist and right-wing billionaires are starting to worry about income inequality and the fate of the middle class.

In December, Mortimer Zuckerman wrote a column in *U. S. News & World Report*, which he owns. "Our nation's core bargain with the middle class is disintegrating," *lamented*(哀叹) the 117th-richest man in America. "Most of our economic gains have gone to people at the very top of the income ladder. Average income for a household of people of working age, by contrast, has fallen five years in a row." He noted that "tens of millions of Americans live in fear that a major health problem can reduce them to bankruptcy."

Wilbur Ross Jr. has echoed Zuckerman's anger over the bitter struggles faced by middle-class Americans. "It's an outrage that any American's life expectancy should be shortened simply because the company they worked for went bankrupt and ended health-care coverage," said the former chairman of the International Steel Group.

What's happening? The very rich are just as trendy as you and I, and can be so when it comes to politics and policy. Given the recent change of control in Congress, the popularity of measures like increasing the minimum wage, and efforts by California's governor to offer universal health care, these guys don't need their own personal weathermen to know which way the wind blows.

It's possible that *plutocrats*(有钱有势的人) are expressing solidarity with the struggling middle class as part of an effort to insulate themselves from *confiscatory*(没收性的) tax policies. But the prospect that income inequality will lead to higher taxes on the wealthy doesn't keep plutocrats up at night. They can live with that.

No, what they fear was that the political challenges of sustaining support for global economic integration will be more difficult in the United States because of what has happened to the distribution of income and economic insecurity.

In other words, if middle-class Americans continue to struggle financially as the ultrawealthy grow ever wealthier, it will be increasingly difficult to maintain political support for the free flow of goods, services, and capital across borders. And when the United States places obstacles in the way of foreign investors and foreign goods, it's likely to encourage reciprocal action abroad. For people who buy and sell companies, or who allocate capital to markets all around the world, that's the real nightmare.

57. What is the current topic of common interest among the very rich in America?
    A) The fate of the ultrawealthy people.
    B) The disintegration of the middle class.
    C) The inequality in the distribution of wealth.
    D) The conflict between the left and the right wing.

58. What do we learn from Mortimer Zuckerman's lamentation?
   A) Many middle-income families have failed to make a bargain for better welfare.
   B) The American economic system has caused many companies to go bankrupt.
   C) The American nation is becoming more and more divided despite its wealth.
   D) The majority of Americans benefit little from the nation's growing wealth.
59. From the fifth paragraph we can learn that ________.
   A) the very rich are fashion-conscious
   B) the very rich are politically sensitive
   C) universal health care is to be implemented throughout America
   D) Congress has gained popularity by increasing the minimum wage
60. What is the real reason for plutocrats to express solidarity with the middle class?
   A) They want to protect themselves from confiscatory taxation.
   B) They know that the middle class contributes most to society.
   C) They want to gain support for global economic integration.
   D) They feel increasingly threatened by economic insecurity.
61. What may happen if the United States places obstacles in the way of foreign investors and foreign goods?
   A) The prices of imported goods will inevitably soar beyond control.
   B) The investors will have to make great efforts to re-allocate capital.
   C) The wealthy will attempt to buy foreign companies across borders.
   D) Foreign countries will place the same economic barriers in return.

Part Ⅴ Cloze (15 minutes)

Directions:(略)

In 1915 Einstein made a trip to Göttingen to give some lectures at the invitation of the mathematical physicist David Hilbert. He was particularly eager—too eager, it would turn __62__—to explain all the intricacies of relativity to him. The visit was a triumph, and he said to a friend excitedly, "I was able to __63__ Hilbert of the general theory of relativity."

__64__ all of Einstein's personal *turmoil*(焦躁)at that time, a new scientific anxiety was about to __65__. He was struggling to find the right equations that would __66__ his new concept of gravity, __67__ that would define how objects move __68__ space and how space is curved by objects. By the end of the summer, he __69__ the mathematical approach he had been __70__ for almost three years was flawed. And now there was a __71__ pressure. Einstein discovered to his __72__ that Hilbert had taken what he had learned from Einstein's lectures and was racing to come up __73__ the correct equations first.

It was an enormously complex task. Although Einstein was the better physicist, Hilbert was the better mathematician. So in October 1915 Einstein __74__ himself into a month-long frantic endeavor in __75__ he returned to an earlier mathematical strategy and wrestled with equations, proofs, corrections and updates that he __76__ to give as lectures to Berlin's Prussian Academy of Sciences on four __77__ Thursdays.

His first lecture was delivered on Nov. 4, 1915, and it explained his new approach, __78__ he admitted he did not ye have the precise mathematical formulation of it. Einstein also took time off from __79__ revising his equations to engage in an awkward *fandango* (方丹戈双人舞) with his competitor Hilbert. Worried __80__ being scooped, he sent Hilbert a copy of his Nov. 4 lecture. "I am __81__ to know whether you will take kindly to this new solution," Einstein noted with a touch of defensiveness.

62. A) up	B) over	C) out	D) off
63. A) convince	B) counsel	C) persuade	D) preach
64. A) Above	B) Around	C) Amid	D) Along
65. A) emit	B) emerge	C) submit	D) submerge
66. A) imitate	B) ignite	C) describe	D) ascribe
67. A) ones	B) those	C) all	D) none
68. A) into	B) beyond	C) among	D) through
69. A) resolved	B) realized	C) accepted	D) assured
70. A) pursuing	B) protecting	C) contesting	D) contending
71. A) complex	B) compatible	C) comparative	D) competitive
72. A) humor	B) horror	C) excitement	D) extinction
73. A) to	B) for	C) with	D) against
74. A) threw	B) thrust	C) huddled	D) hopped
75. A) how	B) that	C) what	D) which
76. A) dashed	B) darted	C) rushed	D) reeled
77. A) successive	B) progressive	C) extensive	D) repetitive
78. A) so	B) since	C) though	D) because
79. A) casually	B) coarsely	C) violently	D) furiously
80. A) after	B) about	C) on	D) in
81. A) curious	B) conscious	C) ambitious	D) ambiguous

Part Ⅵ Translation

Directions:(略)

82. But for mobile phones, ______________ (我们的通信就不可能如此迅速和方便).
83. In handling an embarrassing situation, ______________ (没有什么比幽默感更有帮助的了).
84. The Foreign Minister said he was resigning, ______________ (但他拒绝进一步解释这样做的原因).
85. Human behavior is mostly a product of learning ______________ (而动物的行为主要依靠本能).
86. The witness was told that under no circumstances ______________ ______________ (他都不应该对法庭说谎).

参考答案(Dec. 2007)

Part Ⅰ Sample Writing

The Digital Age

Living in the digital age, we are unavoidably exposed to all kinds of digital products, such as digital camera, digital computer, digital television, and so on, and they grow in an increasing categories and quantities. Believe it or not, look around ourself and we can easily find one or two of these stuffs.

Here is a question, what kind of influence do the digital products bring to people's life? Admittedly, these modern digital products offer us a more convenient life than before. For example, the digital camera makes it possible to delete or correct the "unsuccessful" photo of ours, which was impossible with the traditional camera. Nevertheless, these fashionable digital items have cultivated a generation more isolated from the real life. For example, if a man is accustomed to the digital on-line chatting, he is usually incapable of the practical communication with others. Furthermore, too dependent on the digital things, people seem to be more indifferent to the real world.

Thus, as the generation assailed by all kinds of digital miracles, we might as well initiatively avoid some of them despite efficiency and comfort they can supply. Don't forget those old days when you were going to visit an old school friend though there would be a long train journey, which, in today's digital era, has been thoroughly replaced by the digital on-line chatting.

Part Ⅱ Reading Comprehension (Skimming and Scanning)

1. A 2. B 3. C 4. A 5. D 6. A 7. D

8. Energy service contractors profit by taking a part of clients' annual utility-bill savings.

9. Many environmentalist maintain the view that conservation has much to do with self-denial.

10. The strongest incentives for energy conservation will derive from the market itself.

Part Ⅲ Listening Comprehension

Section A

11—15 CBACB 16—20 DBCAB 21—25 ABDBC

Section B

26—30 DCDAC 31—35 DBADB

Section C

36. squarely 37. floating 38. Occasionally 39. dutifully

40. witty 41. humorous 42. guilt 43. material

44. the instructor's talking about road construction in ancient Rome, and nothing could be more boring

45. Your blank expression, and the faraway look in your eyes are the cues that betray you inattentiveness.

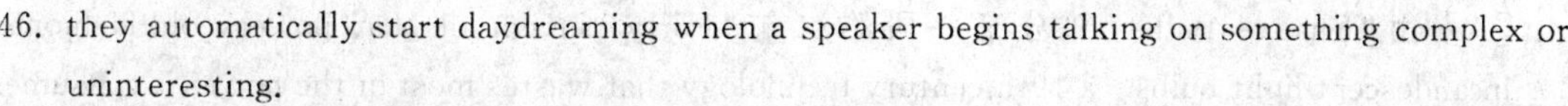

46. they automatically start daydreaming when a speaker begins talking on something complex or uninteresting.

Part Ⅳ Reading Comprehension (Reading in Depth)

Section A

47. mother's support network
48. climb the corporate ladder
49. taken seriously
50. at home / in a home office
51. stress

Section B

52—56 CADBA 57—61 CDBCD

Part Ⅴ Cloze

62—66 CACBC 67—71 ADBAD 72—76 BCADC 77—81 ACDBA

Part Ⅵ Translation

82. our communication would not have been so rapid and convenient
83. nothing is more helpful than a sense of humor
84. but (he) refused to make further explanation (for doing so)/but (he) refused to further explain why
85. while animal behavior depends mainly upon/ on their instincts
86. should he lie to the court

试题解答(Dec. 2007)

Part Ⅱ Reading Comprehension (Skimming and Scanning)

1. [A] 由文章开头的第一、二句"Forget the old idea that conserving energy is a form of self-denial—riding bicycles, dimming the lights, and taking fewer showers. These days conservation is all about efficiency: getting the same—or better—results from just a fraction of the energy."可见今天节能和提高能源使用效率有关。使用少量能源，达到同样或者更好效果才是节能的方法。故本题正确答案为A项。
2. [B] 由第三段第二句"On Jan. 10, the European Union unveiled a plan to cut energy use across the continent by 20 percent by 2020."可知欧盟计划到2020年时全欧洲能源消耗减少20%。故欧盟的计划是削减能源消耗。正确答案为B项。
3. [C] 由"Insulate"部分第四句"The most advanced insulation follows the law of increasing returns: if you add enough, you can scale down or even eliminate heating and air-conditioning equipment, lowering costs even before you start saving on utility bills."可见如果房屋的绝缘性能达到一定的标准，可以减少使用或甚至不用供暖或者空调设施。故本题答案是C项。

4. [A] 由"Change Bulbs"部分第一段第二句"Forty percent of that powers old-fashioned incandescent light bulbs—a 19th-century technology that wastes most of the power it consumes on unwanted heat."可知照明消耗了全世界电能总量的20%,而这些电能的40%又用在了老式的白炽灯照明上。这项19世纪的技术把其消耗的大部分电能用于产生没必要的热能。由此可见,白炽灯只把很少的一部分电能转化成光能,其余的大部分都转化成热能了。故本题答案为A项。

5. [D] 由"Comfort Zone"部分第二段最后一句"Several countries have used subsidies to jump-start the market, including Japan, where almost 1 million heat pumps have been installed in the past two years to heat water for showers and hot tubs."可知很多国家以提供资助的形式来推动热泵市场的发展。故本题答案为D项。

6. [A] 由"Remake Factories"部分第四句"At the Ludwigshafen site alone, such recycling of heat and energy saves the company 200 million a year and almost halt its CO_2 emissions."可知通过循环利用热能和能源,公司一年可以节省两亿欧元。故本题正确答案为A项。

7. [D] 由"A Better Fridge"部分最后一句"According to an International Energy Agency study, if consumers chose those models that would save them the most money over the life of the appliance, they'd cut global residential power consumption (and their utility bills) by 43 percent."可知其中"those models"指的是提高能耗效率的家用电器。故本题正确答案为D项。

8. 由"Flexible Payment"部分第一段第二句"'Energy service contractors' will pay for retrofitting in return for a share of the client's annual utility-bill savings."可见能源服务承造者从客户每年节省的能源费用中分一部分作为自己的收益。故本题答案为"annual utility-bill savings"。

9. 由"Flexible Payment"部分第二段最后两句"In many people's minds, conservation is still associated with self-denial. Many environmentalists still push that view."可知很多环境保护主义者仍然认为保护能源和自我克制有关。题干中的"has much to do with"对应了原文中的"is still associated with"。故本题答案为"self-denial"。

10. 由全文倒数第二段第一句"The most powerful incentives, of course, will come from the market itself."可见最强烈的动机来自于市场本身。故本题答案为"the market itself"。

Part Ⅲ Listening Comprehension(听力原文在光盘中)

Part Ⅳ Reading Comprehension (Reading in Depth)

Section A

47. 由文章第一段第一、四句"But unlike women, many find they're negotiating their new roles with little support or information... They often find themselves excluded from mothers' support networks, and are eyed warily on the playground."可见,和女性不同,男性在为人父时没有一个支持和协助的网络来向他们提供信息和帮助。他们没有角色模型可以效仿。故本题答案为"mother's support network"。

48. 由第二段第一、二句"The challenge is particularly evident in the work-place. There, men are still expected to be breadwinners climbing the corporate ladder; traditionally-minded bosses are often unsympathetic to family needs."可知在工作单位,人们不仅期待男性挣钱养家,还希望他们能不断晋升职位。原文中的"be breadwinners"就是题干中的"supporting the

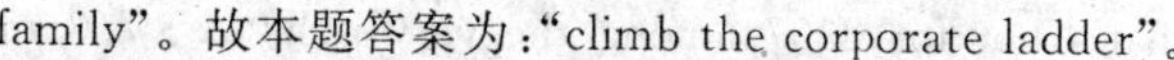
family"。故本题答案为:"climb the corporate ladder"。

49. 由第二段最后一句"As much as if not more so than women, fathers struggle to be taken seriously when they request flexible arrangements."可知当男性为了刚出生的孩子申请灵活的工作安排时,他们希望自己的要求能得到管理者的慎重考虑。故本题答案为"taken seriously"。

50. 由第四段第二句"When Maring had a daughter, the company equipped him with a home office and allowed him to choose a job that could be performed from there."可见公司为 Maring 配备了家庭办公室并允许他选择在家可以完成的工作。换言之,当 Maring 休陪产假的时候,公司允许他在家(在家庭办公室)工作。故本题正确答案为"at home/in a home office"。

51. 由第四段第四句"'When an employee goes on paternity leave and is with his kids, he gets a new kind of training: in how to keep cool under stress,' says spokesperson Christine Elberg Holm."可知 Holm 认为雇员休陪产假去照顾孩子的时候,他得到了一种新的培训,即如何面对压力保持冷静。换言之,休陪产假可以帮助男性学会应对压力。故本题正确答案为"stress"。

Section B

52. [C] 细节题。由第一段最后一句"Recently, however, I was disappointed to see that it also decides how I'm treated as a person."可以看出对于职业决定一个人得到怎样的对待,作者感到失望。"it"指前一句所提到的"职业"。故本题答案为 C 项。

53. [A] 细节推断题。本题考查作者举例的原因。通过找到上下文中的相关细节,对其进行推断,就可以找到答案。由第二段第二句"As someone paid to serve food to people, I had customers say and do things to me I suspect they'd never say or do to their most casual acquaintances."可知作为向他人提供就餐服务而获得报酬的工作人员,作者遇到过一些言行粗鄙的顾客,并猜想哪怕对和他们关系最为疏远的熟人,他们也不会如此。紧接着作者就举了例子。结合例子,可以推断作者认为这些顾客对服务人员不够尊重。故本题正确答案为 A 项。

54. [D] 细节题。由第三段第一、二句"I had waited tables during summers in college and was treated like a peon by plenty of people. But at 19 years old, I believed I deserved inferior treatment from professional adults."可见,当时,她认为受到职业领域的成年人低人一等的对待是正常的。故本题答案为 D 项。

55. [B] 推断题。由第七段最后两句"The service industry, by definition, exists to cater to other's needs. Still, it seemed that many of my customers didn't get the difference between *server* and *servant*."可知作者认为服务业是为满足他人的需求而存在的,但很多顾客仍然不明白"服务提供者"和"仆人"的差别。由此可以推断,作者认为从事服务业的人是"服务提供者"而非"仆人"。他们不应该受到低人一等的对待。服务业是应市场需求而产生的。故本题答案为 B 项。

56. [A] 细节推断题。由全文最后一句"I think I'll take them to dinner first, and see how they treat someone whose only job is to serve them."可知作者带客户去就餐的目的是想看看客户如何对待餐馆的服务人员。结合前文可以推断,作者认为餐馆的服务人员并非仆人,他们应该得到尊重,得到与其他职业的就业人员一样的平等对待。而就餐者对服务人员的态度恰恰可以反映他们对人的态度,反映出他们自己是哪一类型的人。故本题答案为 A 项。

57. [C] 细节题。由文章第一段“What's hot for 2007 among the very rich? A $7.3 million diamond ring. A trip to Tanzania to hunt wild animals. Oh, and income inequality.”可知作者是在提出全文的话题。借助设问,作者指出目前最最富有的人所关注的话题是收入的不平等,或者说是财富分配的不平等。故本题正确答案是C项。

58. [D] 细节推断题。由第三段第一、二句“...‘Our nation's core bargain with the middle class is disintegrating,’ lamented the 117th-richest man in America. ‘Most of our economic gains have gone to people at the very top of the income ladder. Average income for a household of people of working age, by contrast, has fallen five years in a row.’”可知 Mortimer Zuckerman 哀叹之后解释说经济收入的大部分都到了少数最富有的人手中。而普通工作者的人均家庭收入则连续五年下滑。可见他所哀叹的是经济收入的不平等。也可以看出,尽管经济增长,普通工作者的收入反而下滑。他们从整个国家的经济增长中受益微小。故本题答案为D项。

59. [B] 细节题。由第五段第一句“The very rich are just as trendy as you and I, and can be so when it comes to politics and policy.”可知作者认为那些非常富有的人是和普通人一样的时尚人士,尤其是在政治和政策方面。紧接着作者举例,指出通过观察国会最近的政策变化,如提高最低工资、提供普遍的健康保障,这些富人完全明白政策导向。可见富人们在政治方面是十分敏感的。故正确答案为B项。

60. [C] 归纳推断题。从第六段起,作者开始探讨富豪们声援中产阶级的原因。他首先提出一种可能性:富豪们这样做是为了使自己免受没收性税收政策的影响。但他马上对此进行了否定。到第七段,作者提出了富豪们声援中产阶级的真正原因,即收入的不平等可能会导致政府难以持续支持全球性经济融合,即“No, what they fear was that the political challenges of sustaining support for global economic integration will be more difficult in the United States because of what has happened to the distribution of income and economic insecurity.”,到第八段,作者又对此做了详细解释。故本题正确答案为C项。

61. [D] 细节题。由最后一段第二句“And when the United States places obstacles in the way of foreign investors and foreign goods, it's likely to encourage reciprocal action abroad.”可知,一旦美国政府对外国投资者和商品设置障碍,很可能会引起国外相应的行为。也就是说,外国政府会同样对美国投资者和商品设置经济障碍。这是美国的富豪们最最害怕的。故本题答案为D项。

Part Ⅴ Cloze

62. 本题考查固定搭配。根据上下文,此处为句型 it turns out that...,意为“结果,证明为”,所以C项 out 为正确答案,表示“事实证明他过于渴望向他解释有关相对论的复杂内容”,后文中也提到 Hilbert 接受了这一理论,并成为 Einstein 的竞争者。

63. 本题考查上下文语义辨析。根据上文可知此次讲学是一大成功,因此他很兴奋地告诉自己的朋友这一消息,而后文也说到 Hilbert 接受了这一理论,并研究其数学公式。因此,A项 convince 意为“使确信,使信服”,是正确答案。

64. 本题考查介词辨义。后文中有“all of”的提示,所以C项 Amid“在……中”,是正确答案。

65. 本题考查动词辨义。根据上下文可知,Einstein 将要面临新的问题,因此B项 emerge,意为“出现”,是正确答案。

66. 本题考查动词辨义。根据前文可知,Einstein 苦于要找到能描述他的重力的新概念的正确公

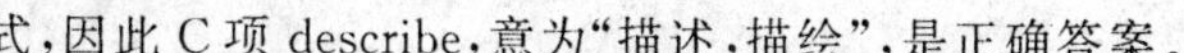

式，因此C项describe，意为“描述，描绘”，是正确答案。

67. 本题考查结构衔接。从句子结构上看应是并列的定语从句，指的是“能够描述他的重力新概念，并能够定义物体如何在空间中移动和空间如何因物体的运动而弯曲的正确公式”，所以这里缺的是定语从句的先行词，也就是指上文的“equations”，所以A项ones是正确答案。

68. 本题考查介词辨义。根据本句句意，这里指的是物体在空间中运动，因此动词move搭配的介词应该是D项through，意为“穿过”。

69. 本题考查动词辨义。根据下文，夏末时，Einstein发现自己近三年来所采纳的数学方程式是有瑕疵的，因此B项realized，意为“发现，明白”，是正确答案。

70. 本题考查动词辨义。根据下文可知此处的动词所搭配的宾语是“approach”，即“研究方法”，能与之搭配并吻合上下文语义的只有A项pursuing，意为“执行”。

71. 本题考查上下文语义辨析。根据下文可知，Hilbert接受了Einstein的相对论之后，也在争先寻求它的数学方程式，下文中“racing”这个词提醒我们本题只有D项competitive，是正确答案，与pressure搭配，意为“竞争压力”。

72. 本题考查上下文语义辨析。根据下文可知Einstein很担心Hilbert会捷足先登，得出相对论的数学方程式，因此他应该是很害怕的，所以B项horror是正确答案，意为“恐惧，担忧”。

73. 本题考查固定搭配。词组come up with意为“提出，得出”，与宾语the correct equations正好搭配。

74. 本题考查动词辨义。根据后文可知，Einstein忘我地工作了一个月之久，能体现出这种状态的只有A项threw，意为“投身于”。B项thrust意为“强行推进”，C项huddled意为“挤作一团”，而D项hopped意为“单脚跳跃”，都不符合句意。

75. 本题考查结构衔接。从句子结构上看应是一个定语从句，说明Einstein在一个月内的努力工作，在这个位置所缺的是“介词＋关系代词”结构中的关系代词，而能够当担介词后的关系代词只有D项which。

76. 本题考查动词辨义。从上下文可知Einstein希望抢在Hilbert之前提出相对论的数学公式，确立自己的地位，因此能够表明他的这种焦急的心态的只有C项rushed，意为“匆忙”。A项dash意为“猛掷或使破灭”，B项dart意为“飞奔”，D项reel意为“蹒跚，退缩”，均不符合句意。

77. 本题考查形容词辨义。从上下文可知本题寻求能够表达“连续”含义的形容词，因此只有A项successive意为“连续的”，是正确答案。

78. 本题考查结构衔接。从句子结构上看，前文说明Einstein解释了他的新方法，后文却说他尚未得出准确的数学方程式，因此此部分是个表转折关系的从句，所以只有C项though是正确答案。

79. 本题考查上下文副词辨析。从前后文可知Einstein一面加紧修改公式与对手Hilbert竞争，一面不忘休息一下，给对手制造一些难题。所以，能够修饰revising来表现Einstein紧张的工作状态的只有D项furiously，意为“激烈地”。A项casually意为“不经意地”，B项coarsely意为“粗糙地”，C项violently意为“暴力地，极端地”，都不符合上下文语义。

80. 本题考查介词辨义。词组be worried about sth.，意为“担心，担忧”，是固定搭配。

81. 本题考查上下文形容词语义辨析。根据前文可知，Einstein意图拖慢Hilbert的步伐，所以就给他寄去了自己的最新的讲稿。那么信中的内容就是要试探对方对自己新的解决方案的态度如何。因此，A项curious是正确答案，意为“好奇”。

Part Ⅵ Translation

82. [答案]:our communication would not have been so rapid and convenient

[注释]:本句考点:①虚拟语气,"but for"是虚拟语气的标志,所以从句表示与现在事实相反的情况,主句则要使用 would have done 表示虚拟;②"通信"应该使用 communication 一词。

83. [答案]:nothing is more helpful than a sense of humor

[注释]:本句考点:①句型"没有什么比……更……"的翻译应为 nothing be more... than...;②"幽默感"的翻译应该是 sense of humor。

84. [答案]:but (he) refused to make further explanation (for doing so)

或 but (he) refused to further explain why

[注释]:本句考点:①"进一步"的翻译常常使用 further 来表示;②表示原因时既可以使用介词结构 for sth.,也可以使用原因状语从句 why+从句。

85. [答案]:while animal behavior depends mainly upon/on their instincts

[注释]:本句考点:①表示相对的比较状语从句既可以使用 while 也可以使用 whereas 来引导从句;②"依靠"应翻译为词组 depend on;③"本能"应翻译为 instinct。

86. [答案]:should he lie to the court

[注释]:本句考点:①从句中有 under no circumstance 这一词组,因此应使用 should 来表虚拟语气,同时由于否定副词提前,主谓的部分要倒装;②"对法庭撒谎"应翻译为 lie to court。

College English Test (Band Ⅵ) (June 2008)

Part Ⅰ Writing (30 minutes)

Directions: *For this part, you are allowed 30 minutes to write a short essay entitled* ***Will e-books replace traditional books****? You should write at least* ***150*** *words following the outline given below.*

电子书是否能够取代传统的书?

1. 随着信息技术的发展,电子图书越来越多
2. 有人认为电子图书会取代传统图书,理由是……
3. 我的看法

Part Ⅱ Reading Comprehension (Skimming and Scanning) (15minutes)

Directions: (略)

What will the world be like in fifty years?

This week some top scientists, including Nobel Prize winners, gave their vision of how the world will look in 2056, from gas-powered cars to extraordinary health advances, John Ingham reports on what the world's finest minds believe our futures will be.

For those of us lucky enough to live that long, 2056 will be a world of almost perpetual youth, where obesity is a remote memory and robots become our companions.

We will be rubbing shoulders with aliens and colonising outer space. Better still, our descendants might at last live in a world at peace with itself.

The prediction is that we will have found a source of inexhaustible, safe, green energy, and that science will have killed off religion. If they are right we will have removed two of the main causes of war—our dependence on oil and religious prejudice.

Will we really, as today's scientists claim, be able to live for ever or at least cheat the ageing process so that the average person lives to 150?

Of course, all these predictions come with a scientific health warning. Harvard professor Steven Pinker says: "This is an invitation to look foolish, as with the predictions of domed cities and nuclear-powered vacuum cleaners that were made 50 year ago."

Living longer

Anthony Atala, director of the Wake Forest Institute in North Carolina, believes failing organs will be repaired by injecting cells into the body. They will naturally go straight to the injury

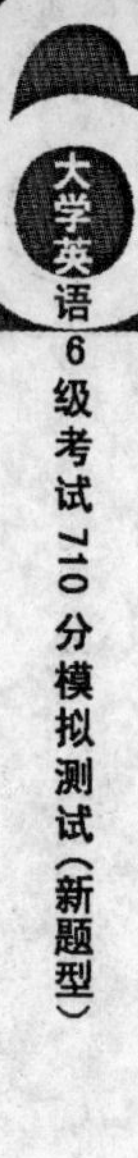

and help heal it. A system of injections without needles could also slow the ageing process by using the same process to "tune" cells.

Bruce Lahn, professor of human genetics at the University of Chicago, anticipates the ability to produce "unlimited supplies" of transplantable human organs without the need for human donors. These organs would be grown in animas such as pigs. When a patient needed a new organ, such as kidney, the surgeon would contact a commercial organ producer, give him the patient's immuno-logical profile and would then be sent a kidney with the correct tissue type.

These organs would be entirely composed of human cells, grown by introducing them into animal hosts, and allowing them to develop into an organ in place of the animal's own. But Prof. Lahn believes that farmed brains would be "off limits". He says: "very few people would want to have their brains replaced by someone else's and we probably don't want to put a human brain in an animal body."

Richard Miller, a professor at the University of Michigan, thinks scientist could develop "authentic anti-ageing drugs" by working out how cells in larger animals such as whales and human resist many forms of injuries. He says: "It's is now routine, in laboratory mammals, to extend lifespan by about 40%. Turning on the same protective systems in people should, by 2056, create the first class of 100-year-olds who are as vigorous and productive as today's people in their 60s."

Aliens

Conlin Pillinger, professor of planetary sciences at the Open University, says: "I fancy that at least we will be able to show that life did start to evolve on Mars as well as Earth." Within 50 years he hopes scientists will prove that alien life came here in Martian *meteorites*(陨石).

Chris McKay, a planetary scientist at NASA's Ames Research Center believes that in 50 years we may find evidence of alien life in ancient permanent frost of Mars or on other planets.

He adds: "There is even a chance we will find alien life forms here on Earth. It might be as different as English is to Chinese."

Princeton professor Freeman Dyson thinks it "likely" that life from outer space will be discovered before 2056 because the tools for finding it, such as optical and radio detection and data processing are improving.

He says: "As soon as the first evidence is found, we will know what to look for and additional discoveries are likely to follow quickly. Such discoveries are likely to have revolutionary consequences for biology, astronomy and philosophy. They may change the way we look at ourselves and our place in the universe."

Colonies in space

Richard Gott, professor of astrophysics at Princeton, hopes man will set up a self-sufficient colony on Mars, which would be a "life insurance policy against whatever catastrophes, natural or otherwise, might occur on Earth."

"The real space race is whether we will colonise off Earth on to other worlds before money for the space programme runs out."

Spinal injuries

Ellen Heber-Katz, a professor at the Wistar Institute in Philadelphia, foresees cures for injuries causing paralysis such as the one that afflicted Superman star Christopher Reeve.

She says: "I believe that the day is not far off when we will be able to prescribe drugs that cause *severed*(断裂的) spinal cords to heal, hearts to regenerate and lost limbs to regrow."

"People will come to expect that injured or diseased organs are meant to be repaired from within, in much the same way that we fix an appliance or automobile: by replacing the damaged part with a manufacturer-certified new part." She predicts that within 5 to 10 years fingers and toes will be regrown and limbs will start to be regrown a few years later. Repairs to the nervous system will start with optic nerves and, in time, the spinal cord. "Within 50 years whole body replacement will be routine," Prof. Heber-Katz adds.

Obesity

Sydney Brenner, senior distinguished fellow of the Crick-Jacobs Center in California, won the 2002 Nobel Prize for Medicine and says that if there is a global disaster some humans will survive—and evolution will favor small people with bodies large enough to support the required amount of brain power. "Obesity," he says, "will have been solved."

Robots

Rodney Brooks, professor of robotics at MIT, says the problems of developing artificial intelligence for robots will be at least partly overcome. As a result, "the possibilities for robots working with people will open up immensely".

Energy

Bill Joy, green technology expert in California, says: "The most significant breakthrough would be to have an inexhaustible source of safe, green energy that is substantially cheaper than any existing energy source."

Ideally, such a source would be safe in that it could not be made into weapons and would not make hazardous or toxic waste or carbon dioxide, the main greenhouse gas blamed for global warming.

Society

Geoffrey Miller, evolutionary psychologist at the University of New Mexico, says: "The US will follow the UK in realizing that religion is not a *prerequisite*(前提) for ordinary human decency."

"Thus, science will kill religion — not by reason challenging faith but by offering a more practical, universal and rewarding moral framework for human interaction."

He also predicts that "absurdly wasteful" displays of wealth will become unfashionable while the importance of close-knit communities and families will become clearer.

These three changes, he says, will help make us all "brighter, wiser, happier and kinder."

1. What is John Ingham's report about?
   A) A solution to the global energy crisis.
   B) Extraordinary advances in technology.
   C) The latest developments of medical science.
   D) Scientists' vision of the world in half a century.
2. According to Harvard professor Steven Pinker, predictions about the future ________.
   A) may invite trouble
   B) may not come true
   C) will fool the public
   D) do more harm than good
3. Professor Bruce Lahn of the University of Chicago predicts that ________.
   A) humans won't have to donate organs for transplantation
   B) more people will donate their organs for transplantation
   C) animal organs could be transplanted into human bodies
   D) organ transplantation won't be as scary as it is today
4. According to professor Richard Miller of the University of Michigan, people will ________.
   A) live for as long as they wish
   B) be relieved from all sufferings
   C) live to 100 and more with vitality
   D) be able to live longer than whales
5. Princeton professor Freeman Dyson thinks that ________.
   A) scientists will find alien life similar to ours
   B) humans will be able to settle on Mars
   C) alien life will likely be discovered
   D) life will start to evolve on Mars
6. According to Princeton professor Richard Gott, by setting up a self-sufficient colony on Mars, humans ________.
   A) might survive all catastrophes on earth
   B) might acquire ample natural resources
   C) will be able to travel to Mars freely
   D) will move there to live a better life
7. Ellen Heber-Katz, professor at the Wistar Institute in Philadelphia, predicts that ________.
   A) human organs can be manufactured like appliances
   B) people will be as strong and dynamic as supermen
   C) human nerves can be replaced by optic fibers
   D) lost fingers and limbs will be able to regrow
8. Rodney Brooks says that it will be possible for robots to work with humans as a result of the development of ________.
9. The most significant breakthrough predicted by Bill Joy will be an inexhaustible green energy source that can't be used to make ________.

10. According to Geoffrey Miller, science will offer a more practical, universal and rewarding moral framework in place of ________.

Part Ⅲ Listening Comprehension (35 minutes)

Section A

Directions:（略）

11. A) The man might be able to play in the World Cup.
    B) The man's football career seems to be at an end.
    C) The man was operated on a few weeks ago.
    D) The man is a fan of world-famous football players.
12. A) Work out a plan to tighten his budget.
    B) Find out the opening hours of the cafeteria.
    C) Apply for a senior position in the restaurant.
    D) Solve his problem by doing a part-time job.
13. A) A financial burden. B) A good companion.
    C) A real nuisance. D) A well-trained pet.
14. A) The errors will be corrected soon.
    B) The woman was mistaken herself.
    C) The computing system is too complex.
    D) He has called the woman several times.
15. A) He needs help to retrieve his files.
    B) He has to type his paper once more.
    C) He needs some time to polish his paper.
    D) He will be away for a two-week conference.
16. A) They might have to change their plan.
    B) He has got everything set for their trip.
    C) He has a heavier workload than the woman.
    D) They could stay in the mountains until June 8.
17. A) They have wait a month to apply for a student loan.
    B) They can find the application forms in the brochure.
    C) They are not eligible for a student loan.
    D) They are not late for a loan application.
18. A) New laws are yet to be made to reduce pollutant release.
    B) Pollution has attracted little attention from the public.
    C) The quality of air will surely change for the better.
    D) It'll take years to bring air pollution under control.

Questions 19 to 22 are based on the conversation you have just heard.

19. A) Enormous size of its stores. B) Numerous varieties of food.

C) Its appealing surroundings.　　D) Its rich and colorful history.

20. A) An ancient building.　　B) A world of antiques.
    C) An Egyptian museum.　　D) An Egyptian Memorial.

21. A) Its power bill reaches $9 million a year.
    B) It sells thousands of light bulbs a day.
    C) It supplies power to a nearby town.
    D) It generates 70% of the electricity it uses.

22. A) 11,500　　B) 30,000　　C) 250,000　　D) 300,000

Questions 23 to 25 are based on the conversation you have just heard.

23. A) Transferring to another department.
    B) Studying accounting at a university.
    C) Thinking about doing a different job.
    D) Making preparation for her wedding.

24. A) She has finally got a promotion and a pay raise.
    B) She has got a satisfactory job in another company.
    C) She could at last leave the accounting department.
    D) She managed to keep her position in the company.

25. A) He and Andrea have proved to be a perfect match.
    B) He changed his mind about marriage unexpectedly.
    C) He declared that he would remain single all his life.
    D) He would marry Andrea even without meeting her.

Section B

Directions:(略)

Passage One

Questions 26 to 29 are based on the passage you have just heard.

26. A) They are motorcycles designated for water sports.
    B) They are speedy boats restricted in narrow waterways.
    C) They are becoming an efficient form of water transportation.
    D) They are getting more popular as a means or water recreation.

27. A) Water scooter operators' lack of experience.
    B) Vacationers' disregard of water safety rules.
    C) Overloading of small boats and other craft.
    D) Carelessness of people boating along the shore.

28. A) They scare whales to death.
    B) They produce too much noise.
    C) They discharge toxic emissions.
    D) They endanger lots of water life.

29. A) Expand operating areas.

B) Restrict operating hours.

C) Limit the use of water scooters.

D) Enforce necessary regulations.

Passage Two

Questions 30 to 32 are based on the passage you have just heard.

30. A) They are stable. B) They are close.

C) They are strained. D) They are changing.

31. A) They are fully occupied with their own business.

B) Not many of them stay in the same place for long.

C) Not many of them can win trust from their neighbors.

D) They attach less importance to interpersonal relations.

32. A) Count on each other for help.

B) Give each other a cold shoulder.

C) Keep a friendly distance.

D) Build a fence between them.

Passage Three

Questions 33 to 35 are based on the passage you have just heard.

33. A) It may produce an increasing number of idle youngsters.

B) It may affect the quality of higher education in America.

C) It may cause many schools to go out of operation.

D) It may lead to a lack of properly educated workers.

34. A) It is less serious in cities than in rural areas.

B) It affects both junior and senior high schools.

C) It results from a worsening economic climate.

D) It is a new challenge facing American educators.

35. A) Allowing them to choose their favorite teachers.

B) Creating a more relaxed learning environment.

C) Rewarding excellent academic performance.

D) Helping them to develop better study habits.

Section C

Directions:(略)

I'm interested in the criminal justice system of our country. It seems to me that something has to be done if we are to (36) ________ as a country. I certainly don't know what the answers to our problems are. Things certainly get (37) ________ in a hurry when you get into them. But I wonder if something couldn't be done to deal with some of these problems.

One thing I'm concerned about is our practice of putting (38) ________ in jail who haven't harmed anyone. Why not work out some system (39) ________ they can pay back the debts they

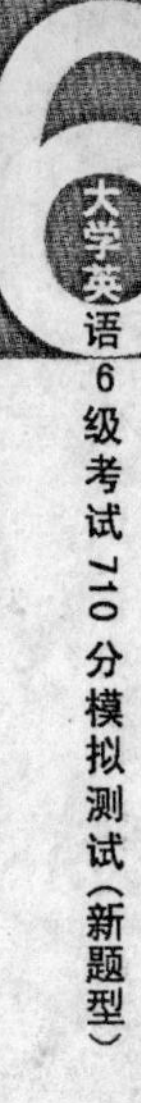

owe society instead of (40) ________ another debt by going to prison, and of course, coming under the (41) ________ of hardened criminals? I'm also concerned about the short prison sentences people are (42) ________ for serious crimes. Of course, one alternative to this is to (43) ________ capital punishment, but I'm not sure I would be for that. I'm not sure it's right to take an eye for eye.

(44) ____.

I also think we must do something about the insanity plea. In my opinion, anyone who takes another person's life intentionally is insane. However, (45) ____.

It's sad, of course, that a person may have to spend the rest of his life, or (46) ____.

Part Ⅳ Reading Comprehension (Reading in Depth) (25 minutes)

Section A

Directions:(略)

Questions 47 to 51 are based on the following passage.

If movie *trailers* (预告片) are supposed to cause a reaction, the preview for "United 93" more than succeeds. Featuring no famous actors, it begins with images of a beautiful morning and passengers boarding an airplane. It takes you a minute to realize what the movie's even about. That's when a plane hits the World Trade Center. The effect is *visceral* (震撼心灵的). When the trailer played before "Inside Man" last week at a Hollywood Theater, audience members began calling out, "Too soon!" In New York City, the response was even more dramatic. The Loews Theater in Manhattan took the rare step of pulling the trailer from its screens after several complaints.

"United 93" is the first feature film to deal explicitly with the events of September 11, 2001, and is certain to ignite an emotional debate. Is it too soon? Should the film have been made at all? More to the point, will anyone want to see it? Other 9/11 projects are on the way as the fifth anniversary of the attacks approaches, most notably Oliver Stone's "World Trade Center." But as the forerunner, "United 93" will take most of the heat, whether it deserves it or not.

The real United 93 crashed in a Pennsylvania field after 40 passengers and crew fought back against the terrorists. Writer-director Paul Greengrass has gone to great lengths to be respectful in his depiction of what occurred, proceeding with the film only after securing the approval of every victim's family. "Was I surprised at the agreement? Yes. Very. Usually there're one or two families who're more reluctant," Greengrass writes in an e-mail. "I was surprised at the extraordinary way the United 93 families have welcomed us into their lives and shared their experiences with us." Carole O'Hare, a family member, says, "They were very open and honest with us, and they made us a part of this whole project." *Universal*, which is releasing the film, plans to donate 10% of its opening weekend gross to the Flight 93 National Memorial Fund. That hasn't stopped criticism that the studio is exploiting a national tragedy. O'Hare thinks that's unfair. "This story has to be told to honor the passengers and crew for what they did," she says. "But more than that, it raises awareness. Our ports aren't secure. Our borders aren't secure. Our airlines still aren't secure, and this is what happens when you're not secure. That's the message I want people to hear."

47. The trailer for "United 93" succeeded in ________ when it played in the theaters in Hollywood and New York City.
48. The movie "United 93" is sure to give rise to ________.
49. What did writer-director Paul Greengrass obtain before he proceeded with the movie?
50. *Universal*, which is releasing "United 93", has been criticized for ________.
51. Carole O'Hare thinks that besides honoring the passengers and crew for what they did, the purpose of telling the story is ________ about security.

Section B

Directions:(略)

Passage One

Questions 52 to 56 are based on the following passage.

Imagine waking up and finding the value of your assets has been halved. No, you're not an investor in one of those hedge funds that failed completely. With the dollar slumping to a 26-year low against the pound, already-expensive London has become quite unaffordable. A coffee at Starbucks, just as unavoidable in England as it is in the United States, runs about $8.

The once all-powerful dollar isn't doing a Titanic against just the pound. It is sitting at a record low against the euro and at a 30-year low against the Canadian dollar. Even the Argentine peso and Brazilian real are thriving against the dollar.

The weak dollar is a source of humiliation, for a nation's self-esteem rests in part on the strength of its currency. It's also a potential economic problem, since a declining dollar makes imported food more expensive and exerts upward pressure on interest rates. And yet there are substantial sectors of the vast U. S. economy—from giant companies like Coca-Cola to mom-and-pop restaurant operators in Miami—for which the weak dollar is most excellent news.

Many Europeans may view the U. S. as an arrogant superpower that has become hostile to foreigners. But nothing makes people think more warmly of the U. S. than a weak dollar. Through April, the total number of visitors from abroad was up 6. 8 percent from last year. Should the trend continue, the number of tourists this year will finally top the 2000 peak. Many Europeans now apparently view the U. S. the way many Americans view Mexico—as a cheap place to vacation, shop and party, all while ignoring the fact that the poorer locals can't afford to join the merrymaking.

The money tourists spend helps decrease our chronic trade deficit. So do exports, which

thanks in part to the weak dollar, soared 11 percent between May 2006 and May 2007. For first five months of 2007, the trade deficit actually fell 7 percent from 2006.

If you own shares in large American corporations, you're a winner in the weak-dollar gamble. Last week Coca-Cola's stock bubbled to a five-year high after it reported a fantastic quarter. Foreign sales accounted for 65 percent of Coke's *beverage*(饮料) business. Other American companies profiting from this trend include McDonald's and IBM.

American tourists, however, shouldn't expect any relief soon. The dollar lost strength the way many marriages break up—slowly, and then all at once. And currencies don't turn on a dime. So if you want to avoid the pain inflicted by the increasingly pathetic dollar, cancel that summer vacation to England and look to New England. There, the dollar is still treated with a little respect.

52. Why do Americans feel humiliated?
    A) Their economy is plunging.
    B) They can't afford trips to Europe.
    C) Their currency has slumped.
    D) They have lost half of their assets.
53. How does the current dollar affect the life of ordinary Americans?
    A) They have to cancel their vacations in New England.
    B) They find it unaffordable to dine in mom-and-pop restaurants.
    C) They have to spend more money when buying imported goods.
    D) They might lose their jobs due to potential economic problems.
54. How do many Europeans feel about the U. S with the devalued dollar?
    A) They feel contemptuous of it.
    B) They are sympathetic with it.
    C) They regard it as a superpower on the decline.
    D) They think of it as a good tourist destination.
55. What is the author's advice to Americans?
    A) They treat the dollar with a little respect.
    B) They try to win in the weak-dollar gamble.
    C) They vacation at home rather than abroad.
    D) They treasure their marriages all the more.
56. What does the author imply by saying "currencies don't turn on a dime" (Line 2, Para. 7)?
    A) The dollar's value will not increase in the short term.
    B) The value of a dollar will not be reduced to a dime.
    C) The dollar's value will drop, but within a small margin.
    D) Few Americans will change dollars into other currencies.

Passage Two

Questions 57 to 61 are based on the following passage.

In the college-admissions wars, we parents are the true fighters. We are pushing our kids to

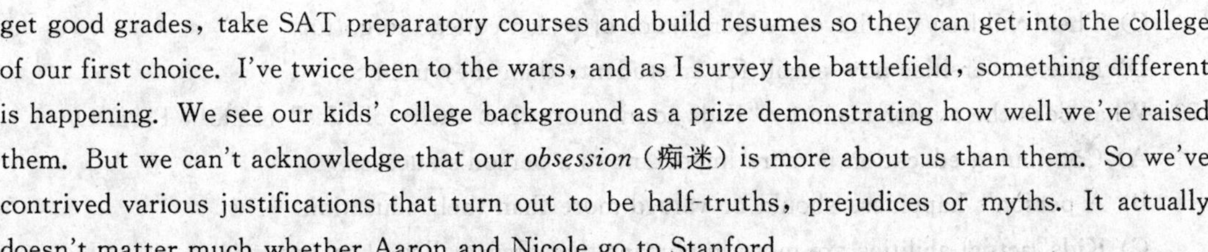

get good grades, take SAT preparatory courses and build resumes so they can get into the college of our first choice. I've twice been to the wars, and as I survey the battlefield, something different is happening. We see our kids' college background as a prize demonstrating how well we've raised them. But we can't acknowledge that our *obsession* (痴迷) is more about us than them. So we've contrived various justifications that turn out to be half-truths, prejudices or myths. It actually doesn't matter much whether Aaron and Nicole go to Stanford.

We have a full-blown prestige panic; we worry that there won't be enough prizes to go around. Fearful parents urge their children to apply to more schools than ever. Underlying the *hysteria* (歇斯底里) is the belief that scarce elite degrees must be highly valuable. Their graduates must enjoy more success because they get a better education and develop better contacts. All that is plausible—and mostly wrong. We haven't found any convincing evidence that selectivity or prestige matters. Selective schools don't systematically employ better instructional approaches than less selective schools. On two measures—professors' feedback and the number of essay exams—selective schools do slightly worse.

By some studies, selective schools do enhance their graduates' lifetime earnings. The gain is reckoned at 2-4% for every 100-point increase in a school's average SAT scores. But even this advantage is probably a statistical *fluke* (偶然). A well-known study examined students who got into highly selective schools and then went elsewhere. They earned just as much as graduates from higher-status schools.

Kids count more than their colleges. Getting into Yale may signify intelligence, talent and ambition. But it's not the only indicator and, paradoxically, its significance is declining. The reason: so many similar people go elsewhere. Getting into college is not life's only competition. In the next competition-the job market and graduate school-the results may change. Old-boy networks are breaking down. Princeton economist Alan Krueger studied admissions to one top Ph. D. program. High scores on the GRE helped explain who got in; degrees of prestigious universities didn't.

So, parents, lighten up. The stakes have been vastly exaggerated. Up to a point, we can rationalize our pushiness. America is a competitive society; our kids need to adjust to that. But too much pushiness can be destructive. The very ambition we impose on our children may get some into Harvard but may also set them up for disappointment. One study found that, other things being equal, graduates of highly selective schools experienced more job dissatisfaction. They may have been so conditioned to being on top that anything less disappoints.

57. Why does the author say that parents are the true fighters in the college-admission wars?

A) They have the final say in which university their children are to attend.

B) They know best which universities are most suitable for their children.

C) They have to carry out intensive surveys of colleges before children make an application.

D) They care more about which college their children go to than the children themselves.

58. Why do parents urge their children to apply to more schools than ever?

A) They want to increase their children chances of entering a prestigious college.

B) They hope their children can enter a university that offers attractive scholarships.

C) Their children will have a wider choice of which college to go to.

D) Elite universities now enroll fewer students than they used to.

59. What does the author mean by "Kids count more than their colleges" (Line1, Para. 4)?

A) Continuing education is more important to a person's success.

B) A person's happiness should be valued more than their education.

C) Kids' actual abilities are more important than their college backgrounds.

D) What kids learn at college cannot keep up with job market requirements.

60. What does Krueger's study tell us?

A) Getting into Ph. D. programs may be more competitive than getting into college.

B) Degrees of prestigious universities do not guarantee entry to graduate programs.

C) Graduates from prestigious universities do not care much about their GRE scores.

D) Connections built in prestigious universities may be sustained long after graduation.

61. One possible result of pushing children into elite universities is that ________.

A) they earn less than their peers from other institutions

B) they turn out to be less competitive in the job market

C) they experience more job dissatisfaction after graduation

D) they overemphasize their qualifications in job applications

Part Ⅴ Cloze (15 minutes)

Directions: (略)

Seven years ago, when I was visiting Germany, I met with an official who explained to me that the country had a perfect solution to its economic problems. Watching the U. S. economy __62__ during the '90s, the Germans had decided that they, too, needed to go the high-technology __63__. But how? In the late '90s, the answer schemed obvious. Indians. __64__ all, Indian entrepreneurs accounted for one of every three Silicon Valley start-ups. So the German government decided that it would __65__ Indians to Germany just as America does by __66__ green cards. Officials created something called the German Green Card and __67__ that they would issue 20,000 in the first year. __68__, the Germans expected that tens of thousands more Indians would soon be begging to come, and perhaps the __69__ would have to be increased. But the program was a failure. A year later __70__ half of the 20,000 cards had been issued. After a few extensions, the program was __71__.

I told the German official at the time that I was sure the __72__ would fail. It's not that I had any particular expertise in immigration policy, __73__ I understood something about green cards, because I had one (the American __74__). The German Green Card was misnamed, I argued, __75__ it never, under any circumstances, translated into German citizenship. The U. S. green card, by contrast, is an almost __76__ path to becoming American (after five years and a clean record). The official __77__ my objection, saying that there was no way Germany was going to offer these people citizenship. "we need young tech workers," he said. "That's what this program is all __78__." So Germany was asking bright young __79__ to leave their country, culture and families, move thousands of miles away, learn a new language and work in a strange land—but without any ___80___ of ever being part of their new home. Germany was sending a signal, one that was ___81___ received in India and other countries, and also by Germany's own immigrant community.

62. A) soar B) hover C) amplify D) intensify
63. A) circuit B) strategy C) trait D) route
64. A) Of B) After C) In D) At
65. A) import B) kidnap C) convey D) lure
66. A) offering B) installing C) evacuating D) formulating
67. A) conferred B) inferred C) announced D) verified
68. A) Specially B) Naturally C) Particularly D) Consistently
69. A) quotas B) digits C) measures D) scales
70. A) invariably B) literally C) barely D) solely
71. A) repelled B) deleted C) combated D) abolished
72. A) adventure B) response C) initiative D) impulse
73. A) and B) but C) so D) or
74. A) heritage B) revision C) notion D) version
75. A) because B) unless C) if D) while
76. A) aggressive B) automatic C) vulnerable D) voluntary
77. A) overtook B) fascinated C) submitted D) dismissed
78. A) towards B) round C) about D) over
79. A) dwellers B) citizens C) professionals D) amateurs
80. A) prospect B) suspicion C) outcome D) destination
81. A) partially B) clearly C) brightly D) vividly

Part Ⅵ Translation (5 minutes)

Directions:（略）

82. We can say a lot of things about those ________________（毕生致力于诗歌的人）: they are passionate, impulsive, and unique.
83. Mary couldn't have received my letter, ________________（否则她上周就该回信了）.
84. Nancy is supposed to ________________（做完化学实验）at least two weeks ago.
85. Never once ________________（老两口互相争吵）since they were married 40 years ago.
86. ________________（一个国家未来的繁荣在很大程度上有赖于）the quality of education of its people.

参考答案(June 2008)

Part Ⅰ Sample Writing

Will e-books replace traditional books?

With the development of the information technology, electric books (e-books) have attracted the attention from all our society. Wherever we go, we can see them, such as in the libraries, in the classroom as well as on the Internet. Just as some experts predicted in a recent TV interview, e-books would possibly dominate the reading in the next few decades.

Some people claim that the e-books will substitute the traditional ones. For one thing, the e-books can not only bring them great amount of convenience, but also free them from going to the bookstores to select traditional books. For another, e-books save them lots of space as well as money. They can just put them in computers and take them while traveling. In contrast, traditional books are too heavy and bulk for them to carry.

From my perspective, I firmly believe the e-books can not totally take the traditional books' place. They will unquestionably co-exist for a long period. Although the e-books offer us lots of favorable consequences, the traditional books can provide us opportunities to take notes on them and are easy for collection. Therefore, the e-books and the traditional books are preferable to different people, and both of them can bring us benefits.

Part Ⅱ Reading Comprehension (Skimming and Scanning)

1\. D 2. B 3. A 4. C 5. C 6. D 7. D

8. Rodney Brooks says that it will be possible for robots to work with humans as a result of the development of artificial intelligence.
9. The most significant breakthrough predicted by Bill Joy will be an inexhaustible green energy source that can't be used to make weapons/pollution.
10. According to Geoffrey Miller, science will offer a more practical, universal and rewarding moral framework in place of religion.

Part Ⅲ Listening Comprehension

Section A

11—15 ADCAB 16—20 ADCBA 21—25 DBCAB

Section B

26—30 DABDD 31—35 BCDBC

Section C

36\. survive 37. complicated 38. offenders 39. whereby

40\. incurring 41. influence 42. serving 43. restore

44. The alternative to capital punishment is longer sentences, but they would certainly cost the tax-payers much money
45. that does not mean that the person isn't guilty of the crime, or that he shouldn't pay society

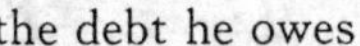
the debt he owes

46. a large part of it, in prison for acts that he committed while not in full control of his mind

Part Ⅳ Reading Comprehension (Reading in Depth)

Section A

47. causing a reaction
48. an emotional debate
49. the approval of every victim's family
50. exploiting a national tragedy
51. to raise the awareness

Section B

52—56 CCDCA 57—61 DACBC

Part Ⅴ Cloze

62—66 ADADA 67—71 CBACD

72—76 CBDAB 77—81 DCCAB

Part Ⅵ Translation

82. who have spent their whole lives on poems
83. or she should have replied to me last week
84. have finished her chemistry experiments
85. has the old couple quarreled with each other
86. The prosperity of a nation is largely dependent upon

试题解答(June 2008)

Part Ⅱ Reading Comprehension (Skimming and Scanning)

1. [D] 由文章第一段第一句"This week some top scientists, including Nobel Prize winners, gave their vision of how the world will look in 2056, from gas-powered cars to extraordinary health advances, John Ingham reports on what the world's finest minds believe our futures will be."可见,他的报道是关于科学家们对于50年后(即2056年)的预测。故正确答案为D项。
2. [B]由文章第六段的第二句"Harvard professor Steven Pinker says: 'This is an invitation to look foolish, as with the predictions of domed cities and nuclear-powered vacuum cleaners that were made 50 year ago.'"可见,在哈佛教授Steven Pinker看来,这种预测会招致嘲笑,就像50年前人们预测建造带顶的城市和制造核动力的吸尘器一样可笑。换言之,这种预测不太可能实现。故本题正确答案为B项。
3. [A] 由"Living longer"部分的第二段第一句"Bruce Lahn, professor of human genetics at the University of Chicago, anticipates the ability to produce "unlimited supplies" of transplantable human organs without the need for human donors."可见,芝加哥大学的这位人类基因学教授预测人类可能会不需要任何捐赠者,无限制地拥有可移植的人类器官。换言之,未来人们不

需要有人捐赠就可以获得移植所需要的器官。故本题正确答案为A项。

4. [C] 由"Living longer"部分的第四段最后一句:"Turning on the same protective systems in people should, by 2056, create the first class of 100-year-olds who are as vigorous and productive as today's people in their 60s."可见,密歇根大学的 Richard Miller 教授预测到2056年,抗衰老系统可以使100岁的老人像今天60多岁的老人一样充满活力和创造力。故正确答案是C项。

5. [C] 由"Aliens"部分第四段"Princeton professor Freeman Dyson thinks it "likely" that life from outer space will be discovered before 2056 because the tools for finding it, such as optical and radio detection and data processing are improving."可见,普林斯顿大学的 Freeman Dyson 教授认为由于探测和数据分析技术的不断更新,在2056年之前,人类很可能将会发现来自外太空的生命。故本题正确答案为C项。

6. [A] 由"Colonies in space"部分第一段"Richard Gott, professor of astrophysics at Princeton, hopes man will set up a self-sufficient colony on Mars, which would be a 'life insurance policy against whatever catastrophes, natural or otherwise, might occur on Earth.'"可知,普林斯顿的天体物理学教授 Richard Gott 希望人类能在火星上建立一个自给自足的殖民区。这可以成为地球上发生无论是自然灾难还是人为灾难时拯救生命的方法。因此,本题的正确答案为A项。

7. [D] 由"Spinal injuries"部分第二段"... I believe that the day is not far off when we will be able to prescribe drugs that cause severed spinal cords to heal, hearts to regenerate and lost limbs to regrow."可知,Ellen Heber-Katz 教授认为不久的将来人类就能够开出让断裂的脊髓愈合、让心脏重新跳动、让失去的肢体再长出来的药物。故本题正确答案为D项。

8. 由"Robots"部分"Rodney Brooks, professor of robotics at MIT, says the problems of developing artificial intelligence for robots will be at least partly overcome. As a result, 'the possibilities for robots working with people will open up immensely'."可见,克服了人工智能问题,人类就有了和机器人一起工作的可能性。故本题的正确答案为"artificial intelligence"。

9. "Energy"部分第二段"Ideally, such a source would be safe in that it could not be made into weapons and would not make hazardous or toxic waste or carbon dioxide, the main greenhouse gas blamed for global warming."可见,该能源是安全的,因为它不会被用于制造武器。故本题正确答案为:"weapons/pollution"。

10. 由"Society"部分的第二段"Thus, science will kill religion—not by reason challenging faith but by offering a more practical, universal and rewarding moral framework for human interaction."可见,这样的道德体系是用来替代宗教的。故本题的正确答案为"religion"。

Part Ⅲ Listening Comprehension (听力原文在光盘中)

Part Ⅳ Reading Comprehension (Reading in Depth)

Section A

47. 由文章第一句"If movie trailers are supposed to cause a reaction, the preview for "United 93" more than succeeds."可知该片在引发人们的反响方面取得了巨大成功。故正确答案为"causing a reaction"。

48. 文章第二段第一句"'United 93' is the first feature film to deal explicitly with the events of

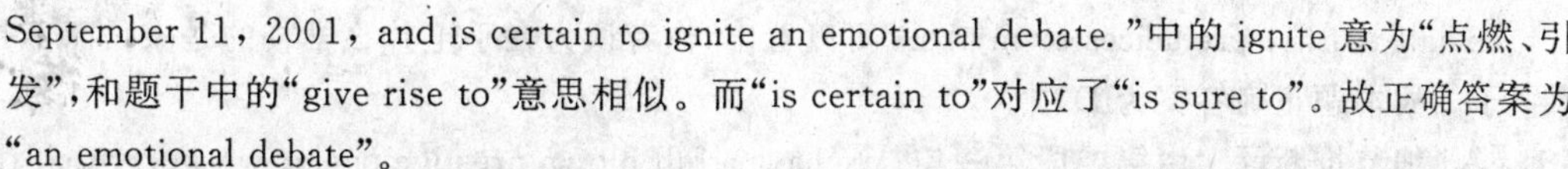

September 11, 2001, and is certain to ignite an emotional debate."中的 ignite 意为"点燃、引发",和题干中的"give rise to"意思相似。而"is certain to"对应了"is sure to"。故正确答案为"an emotional debate"。

49. 由文章第三段第二句"Writer-director Paul Greengrass has gone to great lengths to be respectful in his depiction of what occurred, proceeding with the film only after securing the approval of every victim's family."可知,导演在得到每一个受害者家人的同意之后才继续拍摄该电影。故正确答案为:"the approval of every victim's family"。

50. 由文章的倒数第八句"That hasn't stopped criticism that the studio is exploiting a national tragedy."可知,尽管环球电影公司决定把公映第一周收入的10%捐给93航班国家纪念基金,但它仍遭到批评,认为其是在发国难财。故正确答案为:"exploiting a national tragedy"。

51. 由文章的最后七句"O'Hare thinks that's unfair. "This story has to be told to honor the passengers and crew for what they did," she says. "But more than that, it raises awareness. ... That's the message I want people to hear."可见,O'Hare 认为拍摄该电影除了纪念遇难的乘客和航班工作人员,更重要的是提高人们的意识。让人们意识到我们的港口、边境、飞机等等都是不安全的。也可以理解为用电影叙述这样的一个故事是为了提高人们的安全意识。故本题答案为"to raise the awareness"。

Section B

52. [C] 细节综合题。由文章第一段第二句"With the dollar slumping to a 26-year low against the pound, already-expensive London has become quite unaffordable."可见文章的话题是美国遭遇到的货币贬值问题。再由第三段第一句"The weak dollar is a source of humiliation, for a nation's self-esteem rests in part on the strength of its currency."可以看出美元疲软使美国人感到羞辱。故本题正确答案是C项。

53. [C] 由第三段第二句"It's also a potential economic problem, since a declining dollar makes imported food more expensive and exerts upward pressure on interest rates."可见,美元贬值会使进口食物的价格昂贵,从而影响到美国大众的生活。故本题正确答案为C项。

54. [D] 细节题。由第四段最后一句"Many Europeans now apparently view the U.S. the way many Americans view Mexico—as a cheap place to vacation, shop and party, all while ignoring the fact that the poorer locals can't afford to join the merrymaking."可知,很多欧洲人显然把美国当成了度假、购物和狂欢的地方。因此,正确答案为D项。

55. [C] 细节题。由文章最后两句话"So if you want to avoid the pain inflicted by the increasingly pathetic dollar, cancel that summer vacation to England and look to New England. There, the dollar is still treated with a little respect."可知,作者在文章最后建议美国人如果想避免不断贬值的货币带来的痛苦,就要取消去英国度假的计划,而改到本国的新英格兰去消磨夏日假期。因此正确答案C项。

56. [A] 语义推断题。由第七段第一句话:"American tourists, however, shouldn't expect any relief soon."可知,货币贬值的情况在短期内并不会改善。短语"turn on a dime"意为"向好的方向发展变化"。故本题答案为A项。

57. [D] 细节综合题。由文章第一段的第四句到第六句"We see our kids' college background as a prize demonstrating how well we've raised them. But we can't acknowledge that our *obsession* (痴迷) is more about us than them. So we've contrived various justifications that turn out to

be half-truths, prejudices or myths."可以看出,作者认为在乎上什么学校的是家长而不是孩子。故本题正确答案为D项。

58. [A] 细节推断题。由第二段第一句"We have a full-blown prestige panic; we worry that there won't be enough prizes to go around."和第二句"Fearful parents urge their children to apply to more schools than ever."可知,忧虑的家长迫使孩子们申请更多的学校,以增加被录取的机会。故本题答案为A项。
59. [C] 句义推断题。由第四段第二句和第三句"Getting into Yale may signify intelligence, talent and ambition. But it's not the only indicator and, paradoxically, its significance is declining."以及最后一句"High scores on the GRE helped explain who got in; degrees of prestigious universities didn't."可见,名校的背景已经不再能决定一切了,孩子本身的能力更为重要。故本题正确答案为C项。
60. [B] 细节推断题。由第四段中的最后两句"Princeton economist Alan Krueger studied admissions to one top Ph. D. program. High scores on the GRE helped explain who got in; degrees of prestigious universities didn't."可知,GRE分数的高低而非名校的背景决定申请者能否被录取攻读博士。因此,正确答案为B项。
61. [C] 细节题。由文章的最后两句"One study found that, other things being equal, graduates of highly selective schools experienced more job dissatisfaction. They may have been so conditioned to being on top that anything less disappoints."可知,在其他条件等同的情况下,名校的毕业生在工作中遭受更多的不满意。他们可能已经习惯了名类前茅,也因此更容易有受挫感。因此,本题正确答案为C项。

Part Ⅴ Cloze

62. 语意干扰题,考查实义词。A项 soar 意为"高涨,骤升",B项 hover 意为"翱翔,盘旋",C项 amplifier 意为"扩大,放大",D项 intensify 意为"使强烈,加强"。根据句意,正确答案为A项。
63. 固定搭配题。根据句意,"走高科技的路线",go the route 为固定搭配,故正确答案为D项。
64. 语意干扰题,考查形近的短语。本句的意思是"在所有的硅谷企业中,印度人的企业占到三分之一"。故正确答案为A项 of all。
65. 本题为语意干扰题。A项 import 意为"进口",B项 kidnap 意为"绑架",C项 convey 意为"传达",D项 lure,意为"诱惑;引诱"。根据句意正确答案为D项。
66. 词汇辨析题。此处所填单词在第77题和78题之间有提示。故正确答案为A项 offer。
67. 本题考查形近词。A项 confer 意为"授予,商讨",B项 infer 意为"推论,推断"。C项 announce 意为"正式宣布,宣告",D项 verify 意为"证实,查证"。因此,根据上下文意思,正确答案是C项。
68. 本题为语意干扰题。A项 Specially 意为"特别地,特殊地",B项 Naturally 意为"自然地,必然地",C项 Particularly 意为"异常地;显著地",D项 Consistently 意为"一贯地,一向,始终如一地"。根据上下文语境,正确答案是B项。
69. 语意干扰题,考查实义词。A项 quotas 表示"配额",B项 digits 表示"数字",C项 measures 表示"尺寸,尺度",D项 scales 表示"尺度,刻度"。根据语境,正确答案为A项。
70. 同义词词义辨析题。选项词 barely 和 solely 为同义词,不过侧重点不同,前者表达"仅仅,勉强地",而后者意为"唯一地,单独地,仅仅"。根据上下文句意,正确答案为C项 barely。

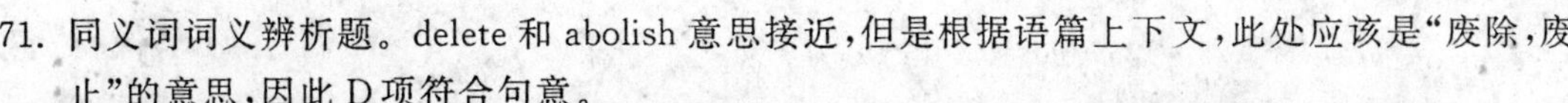

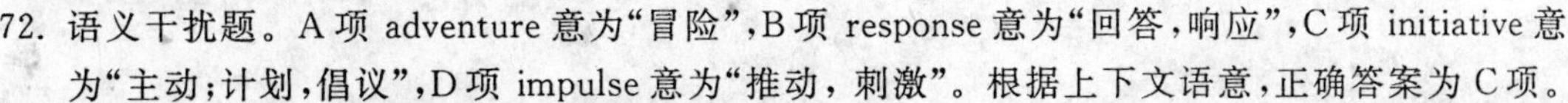

71. 同义词词义辨析题。delete 和 abolish 意思接近,但是根据语篇上下文,此处应该是“废除,废止”的意思,因此 D 项符合句意。

72. 语义干扰题。A 项 adventure 意为“冒险”,B 项 response 意为“回答,响应”,C 项 initiative 意为“主动;计划,倡议”,D 项 impulse 意为“推动,刺激”。根据上下文语意,正确答案为 C 项。

73. 逻辑关系词。根据句意,此处须填表示转折关系的连词,而分句中的 not 和 but 构成“不是……而是……”的用法。

74. 本题考查实义词。根据句意,D 项 version 表示“版本”,符合句意。

75. 逻辑关系词。根据句意,此空格处需要表示因果关系的连词。因此正确答案为 A 项。

76. 词汇辨析题。A 项 aggressive 表示“侵略的,攻击的,挑衅的”,B 项 automatic 表示“自动的”,C 项 vulnerable 表示“脆弱的,敏感的”,D 项 voluntary 表示“自愿的,自发的”,因此,根据句意,正确答案为 B 项。

77. 语义干扰题。A 项 overtook 意为“赶上,追上”,B 项 fascinated 意为“迷住,使神魂颠倒,吸引”,C 项 submitted 意为“提交,委托”,D 项 dismissed 意为“不考虑,摒弃”。故正确答案为 D 项。

78. 固定搭配题。all 与 C 项 about 构成固定用法,意为“关于…… 的一切”。

79. 词汇辨析题。A 项 dwellers 意为“居住者,居民”,B 项 citizens 意为“公民,国民”,C 项 professionals 意为“专业人员”,D 项 amateurs 意为“业余活动者”。根据语境,正确答案为 C 项。

80. 语篇理解题。利用逻辑推理和常识判断能力,根据上下文语境,A 项 prospect 表示“前景、展望”,符合句意。

81. 词汇辨析题。根据句意,B 项 clearly 为正确答案。